DORN OF THE MOUNTAINS

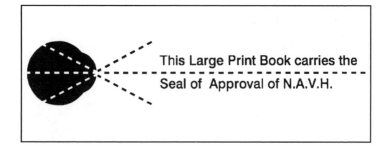

DORN OF THE MOUNTAINS

A WESTERN STORY

ZANE GREY®

THORNDIKE PRESS
A part of Gale, Cengage Learning

GALE
CENGAGE Learning™

Detroit • New York • San Francisco • New Haven, Conn • Waterville, Maine • London

GALE
CENGAGE Learning™

LIBRARY OF CONGRESS CATALOGING-IN-PUBLICATION DATA

Grey, Zane, 1872–1939.
    Dorn of the mountains : a western story / by Zane Grey.
        p. cm. — (Thorndike Press large print western.)
    An earlier version of Dorn of the mountains first appeared
as a fifteen-part serial titled 'Man of the Forest' in The
Country Gentleman (10/20/17–1/26/18)—T.p. verso.
    ISBN-13: 978-1-4104-0512-8 (hardcover : alk. paper)
    ISBN-10: 1-4104-0512-5 (hardcover : alk. paper)
    1. Arizona — Fiction. 2. Large type books. I. Title.
PS3513.R6545D66 2008b
813'.52—dc22   2007046712

Published in 2008 by arrangement with Golden West Literary Agency.

Printed in the United States of America
1 2 3 4 5 6 7 12 11 10 09 08

FOREWORD

JON TUSKA

It is unfortunate that a truly comprehensive and accurate biography of Zane Grey™ is not likely ever to be written. Over the years since Grey's death on October 23, 1939, most of the essential documents in one way or another have been dispersed, or destroyed as in the case of most of his diaries written in a private code he had devised. Correspondence has been scattered to the winds, sold at auction, or acquired by private collectors. Those who have attempted biographical portraits have singularly neglected to read the books Zane Grey wrote, and, when a plot description is attempted, it is usually wrong. Stephen J. May in *Zane Grey: Romancing the West* (Ohio University Press, 1997) wrote: "*Man of the Forest* has a simple, even trivial plot with influences from Grey's beloved Robinson Crusoe. It tells the story of Milt Dale, an uncouth misfit living in the White Mountains of Arizona, who loathes people and bonds to animals instead. Psychologically 'marooned,' Dale finds a woman in the village who is in *real* trouble. Removing Helen Rayner to his remote cabin in the mountains, he soon falls in love with her and through their relationship begins a slow connection to humanity." This summary does not remotely resemble the novel Harper & Brothers published in 1920 as *Man of the Forest,* but in the second film version, *Man of the Forest* (Paramount, 1933), Randolph Scott as Brett Dale does live in a remote cabin to which he brings Alice Gayner who he kidnaps on her journey from the East to her uncle's ranch in order to prevent her being kidnapped by Clint Beasley. In both Grey's original holographic manuscript of *Dorn of the Mountains* and in the book version published in 1920, Helen Rayner and her sister Bo are rescued before being taken captive by Beasley. Stephen J. May left Bo out altogether. In *Man of the Forest* (Paramount, 1921) the villain is named Lem Beasley and is a bootlegger. In the 1933 film version, Clint Beasley is a landowner who covets water rights to a lake owned by the girl's uncle. In Zane Grey's story Beasley is not given a first name.

Grey's original name for his protagonist

was Milt Dorn. Dorn means "thorn" in German. The story first appeared serially in fifteen installments in *The Country Gentleman* from October 1917 through January 1918, during the time when the United States was at war with Germany. Anti-German sentiment was widespread, and doubtless for this reason the name was changed to Milt Dale in the magazine version, and Grey left it that way for the subsequent book version. Helen Rayner in this story was based on Lillian Wilhelm and Bo was modeled on Lillian's younger sister Claire, both cousins of Dolly Grey, Zane's wife, and both — to use Dolly Grey's word for them — among Zane Grey's "inamoratas." Beasley calls Bo a "cat-eyed slut" in Grey's holographic manuscript, and from what is known of Grey's relationship with Claire, it was tempestuous.

Zen Ervin is a member of Zane Grey's West Society and a contributor to *The Zane Grey Review*. Based on his research, Paradise Park in this story is a real place in the White Mountains. Ervin has physically traced the route taken by the characters from Magdalena, New Mexico across the mountains and into Paradise Park, commenting that while "it is impossible to know for certain what trails they followed, I used Grey's descriptions and compared them to landmarks in the mountains, paid close attention to travel time, etc." According to Ervin's research, Milt Dorn was based on a real person, Jack Funk, who Grey most probably met in the White Mountains in 1916 when Grey hired John Butler of Greer, Arizona to guide his party into the White Mountains for hunting and fishing. To make that trip, Butler hired as wranglers two of the four Hall brothers, Roy and John, and Roy Hall later recalled Zane Grey and Zane's brother Romer on that journey in which the party crossed the White River. Ervin believes that Roy and John Hall served as models for the Beeman brothers in this story.

It is relatively easy by a process of comparison to see what Ripley Hitchcock, Zane Grey's editor at Harper & Brothers, removed from the original story. It is far more difficult to determine who added passages to the novel as published in what became Chapters X, XI, and XII of the Harper edition. The only thing that can be stated with certainty is that it wasn't Zane Grey. Helen Rayner for that brief period becomes a wholly different character than she is in Zane Grey's manuscript before and after this section. I know Ripley Hitchcock rewrote the second half of The Lone Star

Ranger, a bogus Zane Grey novel made up of the first half of Zane Grey's *Last of the Duanes* and the last half of his serial, *Rangers of the Lone Star.* Hitchcock may have done the same thing here. Or it might be we will never know, as we do not know absolutely who rewrote Zane Grey's *Open Range* (Five Star, 2002) to form the book, *Valley of Wild Horses* (Harper, 1947). Romer Grey, the author's elder son and long president of Zane Grey, Inc., told me in 1972 that he simply did not know, but he was willing to take the credit for it. I suspected it was veteran author Tom Curry who ghost-wrote all the Buck Duane stories as Romer Zane Grey, and Tom Curry admitted as much to me long before his son Stephen Curry became a Golden West client for his father's literary estate. What I can say with total certitude is that *Dorn of the Mountains* appears now for the first time as Zane Grey wrote it ninety years ago. The title alone has been changed so that there can be no confusion between the two books. Clipped to the original holographic manuscript donated to the Library of Congress by Dolly Grey was a note in Zane Grey's handwriting that reads: "Original Man of the Forest." Here it is.

9

CHAPTER ONE

At sunset hour the forest was still, lonely, sweet with tang of fir and spruce, blazing in gold and red and green, and the man who glided stealthily on under the great trees seemed to blend with the colors and, disappearing, to have become a part of the wild woodland.

Old Baldy, highest of the White Mountains, stood up round and bare and bold, rimmed bright gold in the last glow of the setting sun. Then as the fire dropped behind the domed peak a change, a cold and darkening blight, passed down the black spear-pointed slopes over all that mountain world.

It was a vast wild richly timbered and abundantly watered region of dark forest and grassy parks, 10,000 feet above sea level, isolated on all sides by the southern Arizona desert — the virgin home of elk and deer, of bear and lion, of wolf and fox, and the birthplace as well as the hiding place of the fierce Apache.

September in that latitude was marked by the sudden cool night breeze following shortly after sundown. Twilight appeared to come on its wings, as did faint sounds, not distinguishable before in the stillness.

Milt Dorn, man of the forest, halted at the edge of a timbered ridge, to listen and to watch. Beneath him lay a narrow valley, open and grassy, from which rose a faint low murmur of running water. Its music was pierced and marred by the wild staccato yelp of a hunting coyote. From overhead in a giant fir came a twittering and rustling of grouse settling for the night, and from across the valley drifted the last low calls of wild turkeys going to roost.

To Dorn's keen ear these sounds were all they should have been, betokening an unchanged serenity of forestland. He was glad, for he had expected to hear the *clip-clop* of white men's horses — which to hear, up in those fastnesses, was hateful to him. He and the Indian were friends. That fierce foe had no enmity toward the lone hunter. But there hid somewhere in the forest a gang of bad men, sheep thieves, who Dorn did not want to meet.

As he started out upon the slope, a sudden flaring of the afterglow of sunset flooded down from Old Baldy, filling the valley with lights and shadows, yellow and blue, like the radiance of the sky. The pools in the curves of the brook shone darkly bright. Dorn's gaze swept up and down the valley, and then tried to pierce the black shadow across the brook where the wall of spruce stood up, its speared and spiked crest against the pale clouds. The wind began to moan in the trees and there was a feeling of rain in the air. Dorn, striking a trail, turned his back to the fading afterglow and strode down the valley.

With night at hand and a rainstorm brewing, he did not head for his own camp, some miles distant, but directed his steps toward an old log cabin. When he reached it, darkness had almost set in. He approached with caution. This cabin, like the few others scattered in the valleys, might harbor Indians or a bear or a panther. Nothing, however, appeared to be there. Then Dorn studied the clouds driving across the sky and he felt the cool dampness of a fine misty rain on his face. It would rain off and on during the night. Whereupon he entered the cabin.

And the next moment he heard quick hoof beats of trotting horses. Peering out, he saw dim moving forms in the darkness, quite

13

close at hand. They had approached against the wind so that sound had been deadened. Five horses with riders Dorn made out — saw them loom up close. Then he heard rough voices. Quickly he turned to feel in the dark for a ladder he knew led to a loft, and, finding it, he quickly mounted, taking care not to make a noise with his rifle, and lay down upon the floor of brush and poles. Scarcely had he done so when heavy steps, with accompaniment of *clinking* spurs, passed through the door below into the cabin.

"Wal, Beasley, are you here?" queried a loud voice.

There was no reply. The man below growled under his breath, and again the spurs *jingled.*

"Fellars, Beasley ain't here yet!" he called. "Put the hosses under the shed. We'll wait."

"Wait, huh!" came a harsh reply. "Mebbe all night . . . an' we got nuthin' to eat."

"Shut up, Moze. Reckon you're no good fer anythin' but eatin'. Put them hosses away an' some of you rustle firewood in here."

Low muttered curses then mingled with dull *thuds* of hoofs and strain of leather and heaves of tired horses.

Another shuffling *clinking* footstep entered

14

the cabin.

"Snake, it'd been sense to fetch a pack along," drawled this newcomer.

"Reckon so, Jim. But we didn't an' what's the use hollerin'. Beasley won't keep us waitin' long."

Dorn, lying still and prone, felt a slow start in all his blood — a thrilling wave. That deep-voiced man below was Snake Anson, the worst and most dangerous character of the region, and the others, undoubtedly, composed his gang, long notorious in that sparsely settled country. And the Beasley mentioned — he was one of the two biggest ranchers and sheep raisers of the White Mountain ranges. What was the meaning of a rendezvous between Snake Anson and Beasley? Milt Dorn answered that question to Beasley's discredit, and many strange matters pertaining to sheep and herders, always a mystery to the little village of Pine, now became as clear as daylight.

Other men entered the cabin.

"It ain't a-goin' to rain much," said one. Then came a *crash* of wood thrown to the ground.

"Jim, hyar's a chunk of pine log, dry as punk," said another.

Rustlings and slow footsteps, and then heavy *thuds* attested to the probability that

15

Jim was knocking the end of a log upon the ground to split off a corner, whereby a handful of dry splinters could be procured.

"Snake, lemme your pipe an' I'll hev a fire in a jiffy."

"Wal, I want my terbacco an' I ain't carin' about no fire," replied Snake.

"Reckon you're the meanest cuss in these woods," drawled Jim.

Sharp *click* of steel on flint — many times — and then a sound of hard blowing and sputtering told of Jim's efforts to start a fire. Presently the pitchy blackness of the cabin changed; there came a little *crackling* of wood and the rustle of flame, and then a steady growing roar.

As it chanced, Dorn lay face down upon the floor of the loft and right near his eyes were cracks between the boughs. When the fire blazed up, he was fairly well able to see the men below. The only one who he had ever seen was Jim Wilson, who had been well known at Pine before Snake Anson had ever been heard of. Jim was the best of a bad lot and he had friends among honest people. It was rumored that he and Snake did not pull well together.

"Fire feels good," said the burly Moze, who appeared as broad as he was black-visaged. "Fall's sure a-comin'. . . . Now if

16

we only had some grub!"

"Moze, there's a hunk of deer meat in my saddlebag, an', if you git it, you can have half," spoke up another voice.

Moze shuffled out with alacrity.

In the firelight Snake Anson's face looked lean and serpent-like, his eyes glittered, and his long neck, and all of his long length, carried out the analogy of his name.

"Snake, what's this here deal with Beasley?" inquired Jim.

"Reckon you'll larn when I do," replied the leader. He appeared tired and thoughtful.

"Ain't we done away with enough of them poor greaser sheepherders . . . fer nuthin'?" queried the youngest of the gang, a boy in years, whose hard bitter lips and hungry eyes somehow set him apart from his comrades.

"You're dead right, Burt . . . an' thet's my stand," replied the man who had sent Moze out.

"Snake, snow'll be flyin' around these woods before long," said Jim Wilson. "Are we goin' to winter down in the Tonto Basin or over on the Gila?"

"Reckon we'll do some tall ridin' before we strike south," replied Snake gruffly.

At this juncture Moze returned. "Boss, I

17

heerd a hoss comin' up the trail," he said.

Snake rose and stood at the door, listening. Outside, the wind moaned fitfully and scattering raindrops pattered upon the cabin.

"Ahuh!" exclaimed Snake in relief.

Silence ensued then for a moment, at the end of which interval Dorn heard a rapid *clip-clop* on the rocky trail outside. The men below shuffled uneasily, but none of them spoke. The fire cracked cheerily. Snake Anson stepped back from before the door with an action that expressed both doubt and caution.

The trotting horse had halted out there somewhere.

"Ho there inside!" called a voice from the darkness.

"Ho yourself!" replied Anson.

"That you, Snake?" quickly followed the query.

"Reckon so," returned Anson, showing himself. "Come on in."

A newcomer entered. He was a large man, wearing a heavy slicker that shone wet in the firelight. His sombrero, pulled well down, shadowed his face so that the upper half of his features might as well have been masked. He had a black drooping mustache and a chin like a rock. A potential force, matured and powerful, seemed to be wrapped in his movements.

"Hullo Snake. Hullo Wilson," he said. "My boss backed out on the deal. Sent me on another little matter . . . particular private." Here he indicated with a significant gesture that Snake's men were to leave the cabin.

"Ahuh!" ejaculated Anson dubiously. Then he turned abruptly. "Moze, you an' Shady an' Burt go wait outside. Reckon this ain't the deal I expected. . . . An' you can saddle the hosses."

The three members of the gang filed out, all glancing keenly at the stranger who had moved back in the shadow.

"All right now, Beasley," said Anson, low-voiced. "What's your game? Jim here is in on my deals."

Then Beasley came forward to the fire, stretching his hands to the blaze.

"Nothin' to do with sheep," he replied.

"Wal, I reckoned not," assented the other. "An' say . . . whatever your game is, I ain't likin' the way you kept me waitin' an' ridin' around. We waited near all day at Big Spring. Then thet greaser rode up an' sent us here. We're a long way from camp with no grub . . . an' no blankets."

"I won't keep you long," said Beasley.

19

"But even if I did, you'd not mind . . . when I tell you this deal concerns Al Auchincloss . . . the man who made an outlaw of you."

Anson's sudden action then seemed a leap of his whole frame. Wilson, likewise, bent forward eagerly. Beasley glanced at the door — then began to whisper.

"Old Auchincloss is on his last legs. He's goin' to croak. He sent back to Missouri for a niece . . . a young girl . . . an' he means to leave his ranches an' sheep . . . all his stock to her. Seems he has no one else. . . . Them ranches . . . an' all them sheep an' hosses! You know me an' Al were pardners in the sheep raisin' for years. He swore I cheated him an' he threw me out. An' all these years I've been swearin' he did me dirt . . . owed me sheep an' money. I've got as many friends in Pine . . . an' all the way down the trail . . . as Auchincloss has. . . . An', Snake, see here. . . ."

He paused to draw a deep breath and the big hands trembled over the blaze. Anson leaned forward like a serpent ready to strike, and Jim Wilson was as tense with his divination of the plot at hand.

"See here . . . ," panted Beasley. "The girl's due to arrive at Magdalena on the Sixteenth. That's a week from tomorrow.

20

She'll take the stage to Snowdrop, where some of Auchincloss's men will meet her with a team."

"Ahuh," grunted Anson as Beasley halted again. "An' what of all thet?"

"She mustn't never get as far as Snowdrop!"

"You want me to hold up the stage . . . an' get the girl?"

"Exactly."

"Wal . . . an' what then?"

"Make way with her! She disappears. That's your affair. . . . I'll press my claims on Auchincloss . . . hound him, an' be ready when he croaks to take over his property. . . . You an' Wilson fix up the deal between you. If you have to let the gang in on it, don't give them any hunch as to who an' what. This'll make you a rich stake. An' providin' when it's paid, you strike for new territory."

"Thet might be wise," muttered Snake Anson. "Beasley, the weak point in your game is the uncertainty of life. Old Al is tough. He may fool you."

"Auchincloss is a dyin' man," declared Beasley with such positiveness that it could not be doubted.

"Wal, he sure wasn't plumb hearty when I last seen him. . . . Beasley, in case I play your game . . . how'm I to know thet girl?"

21

"Her name's Helen Rayner," replied Beasley eagerly. "She's twenty years old. All of them Auchinclosses was handsome an' they say she's the handsomest."

"Ahuh! Beasley, that's sure a bigger deal . . . an' one I ain't fancyin'. . . . But I never doubted your word. . . . Come on . . . an' talk out. What's in it for me . . . me to take care of Jim, or anyone I need?"

"Don't let anyone in on this. You two can hold up the stage. Why, it never was held up. . . . But you want to mask. . . . How about ten thousand sheep . . . or what they bring at Phoenix in gold?"

Jim Wilson whistled low.

"An' leave for new territory?" repeated Snake Anson under his breath.

"You've said it."

"Wal, I ain't fancyin' the girl end of this deal, but you can count on me. . . . September Sixteenth at Magdalena . . . an' her name's Helen . . . an' she's handsome?"

"Yes. . . . My herders will begin drivin' south in about two weeks. Later, if the weather holds good, send me word by one of them an' I'll meet you."

Beasley spread his hands once more over the blaze, pulled on his gloves and pulled down his sombrero, and with abrupt word of parting strode out into the night.

"Jim, what do you make of him?" queried Snake Anson.

"Pard, he's got us beat two ways for Sunday," replied Wilson.

"Ahuh! Wal, let's get back to camp." And he led the way out.

Low voices drifted into the cabin, then came snorts of horses and striking hoofs, and after that a steady trot, gradually ceasing. Once more the moan of wind and soft patter of rain filled the forest stillness.

CHAPTER TWO

Milt Dorn quietly sat up to gaze with thoughtful eyes at the flickering fire.

He was thirty years old. As a boy of fourteen he had run off from his school and home in Iowa, and, joining a wagon train of pioneers, he was one of the first to see log cabins built on the slopes of the White Mountains. But he had not taken kindly to farming or sheep raising or monotonous visits to Pine and Slow Down and Snowdrop. This wandering forest life of his was not that he did not care for the villagers, for he did care, and he was welcome everywhere, but that he loved wild life and solitude and beauty with the primitive instinctive force of a savage.

And upon this night he had stumbled upon a dark plot against the only one of all the honest white people in that region who he could not call a friend.

"That man Beasley," he soliloquized.

"Beasley . . . preacher at Pine . . . in cahoots with Snake Anson! Well, he was right. Al Auchincloss is on his last legs. . . . Poor old man. . . . When I tell him . . . he'll never believe *me,* that's sure."

Discovery of the plot meant to Dorn that he must hurry down to Pine, and, of all seasons, the autumn was the one he loved best in the mountains. He reflected, however, that he need not lose more than several days on the journey. It seemed that he took for granted a necessity of befriending Auchincloss, even though that hard old stockman had wronged him.

"A girl . . . Helen Rayner . . . twenty years old," he mused. "Beasley wants her made way with. . . . That means . . . killed."

Dorn accepted facts of life with that equanimity and fatality acquired by one long versed in the cruel annals of forest lore. Bad men worked their evil just as savage wolves relayed a deer. He had shot wolves for that trick. With men, good or bad, he had not clashed. Old women and children appealed to him, but he had never had any interest in girls. The image then of this Helen Rayner came strangely to Dorn, and he suddenly realized that he meant somehow to circumvent Beasley, not to befriend old Al Auchincloss, but for the sake of the girl. Probably she was already on her way West, alone, eager, hopeful of a future home. How little people guessed what awaited them at a journey's end. Many trails ended abruptly in the forest — and only trained woodsmen could read the tragedy.

"Strange how I cut across country today from Spruce Swamp," went on Dorn reflectively. Circumstances, movements usually were not strange to him. His methods and habits were seldom changed by chance. The matter, then, of his turning off a course, out of his way, for no apparent reason, and of his having overheard a plot singularly involving a young girl, was indeed an adventure to provoke thought. It provoked more, for Dorn grew conscious of an unfamiliar smoldering heat along his veins. He, who had little to do with the strife of men, and nothing to do with anger, felt his blood grow hot at the cowardly trap laid for an innocent girl.

"Old Al won't listen to me," pondered Dorn. "An' even if he did . . . he wouldn't believe me. Maybe nobody will. . . . All the same Snake Anson won't get that girl."

With these last words Dorn satisfied himself of his own position, and his pondering ceased. Taking his rifle, he descended from the loft and peered out of the door.

The night had grown darker, windier, cooler; broken clouds were scudding across the sky; only a few stars showed; fine rain was blowing from the northwest; the forest seemed full of a low dull roar.

"Reckon I'd better hang up here," he said, and turned to the fire. The coals were red now. From the depths of his hunting coat he procured a little bag of salt and some strips of dried meat. These strips he laid for a moment on the hot embers, until they began to sizzle and curl, then with a sharpened stick he removed them and ate like a hungry hunter grateful for little.

He sat on a block of wood with his palms spread to the dying warmth of the fire and his eyes fixed upon the changing glowing golden embers. Outside, the wind continued to rise and the moan of the forest increased to a roar. Dorn felt the comfortable warmth stealing over him, drowsily lulling; he heard the storm wind in the trees, now like a waterfall, and anon like a retreating army, and again low and sad, and he saw pictures in the glowing embers, strange as dreams.

Presently he rose, and, climbing to the loft, he stretched himself out upon the boughs, and soon fell asleep.

When the gray dawn broke, he was on his

way, cross-country, to the village of Pine.

During the night the wind had shifted and the rain had ceased. A suspicion of frost shone in the grass in open places. All was gray — the parks — the glades — and deeper darker gray were the aisles of the forest. Shadows lurked under the trees and the silence seemed consistent with spectral forms. Then the east kindled, the gray lightened, the dreaming woodland awoke to the far-reaching rays of a bursting red sun.

This was always the happiest moment of Dorn's lonely days, as sunset was his saddest. He responded, and there was something in his blood that answered the whistle of a stag from a nearby ridge. His strides were long, noiseless, and they left dark trace where his feet brushed the dew-laden grass.

Dorn pursued a zigzag course over the ridges, to escape the hardest climbing, but the *parques,* those park-like meadows so named by Mexican sheepherders, were as round and level as if they had been made by man to show beautiful contrast to the dark-green, rough, and rugged ridges. Both open *parque* and dense wooded ridges showed to his quick eye an abundance of game. The *cracking* of twigs and disappearing flash of gray among the spruces, a round black lumbering object, a *twittering* in the

28

brush, and stealthy steps — were all easy signs for Dorn to read. Once, as he noiselessly emerged into a little glade, he espied a red fox stalking some quarry, which, as he advanced, proved to be a flock of partridges. They whirred up, brushing the branches, and the fox trotted away. In every *parque* Dorn encountered wild turkeys, feeding on the seeds of the high grass.

It had always been his custom, on his visits to Pine, to kill and pack fresh meat down to several old friends, who were glad to give him lodging. And hurried as he was now, he did not intend to make an exception of this trip.

At length he got down into the pine belt, where the great gnarled yellow trees soared aloft, stately and aloof from one another, and the ground was a brown odorous springy mat of pine needles, level as a floor. Squirrels watched him from all around, scurrying away at his near approach — tiny brown light-striped squirrels, and larger ones, russet colored, and the splendid dark grays, with their white bushy tails and plumed ears.

This belt of pine ended abruptly upon wide gray rolling open land, almost like a prairie, with foothills lifting near and far, and the red-gold blaze of aspen thickets, catching the morning sun. Here Dorn flushed a flock of wild turkeys, upwards of forty in number and their subdued color of gray flecked with white, and graceful sleek build, showed them to be hens. There was not a gobbler in the flock. They began to run pell-mell out into the grass, until only their heads appeared bobbing along, and finally disappeared. Dorn caught a glimpse of skulking coyotes that evidently had been stalking the turkeys, and, as they saw him and darted into the timber, he took a quick shot at the hindmost. His bullet struck low, as he had meant it to, but too low, and the coyote got only a dusting of earth and pine needles thrown up in his face. This frightened him so that he leaped aside blindly to butt into a tree, rolled over, gained his feet, and then the cover of the forest. Dorn was amused at this. His hand was against all the predatory beasts of the forest, although he had learned that lion and bear and wolf were all as necessary to the great scheme of Nature as were the gentle beautiful wild creatures upon which they preyed. But some he loved better than others, and so deplored the inexplicable cruelty.

He crossed the wide grassy plain, and struck another gradual descent where aspens and pines crowded a shallow ravine and warm sun-lighted glades bordered along a sparkling brook. Here he heard a turkey gobble, and that was a signal for him to change his course and make a crouching silent detour around a clump of aspens. In a sunny patch of grass a dozen or more big gobblers stood, all suspiciously facing in his direction, heads erect with that wild aspect peculiar to their species. Old wild turkey gobblers were the most difficult game to stalk. Dorn shot two of them. The others began to run like ostriches, *thudding* over the ground, spreading their wings, and with that running start launched their heavy bodies into whirring flight. They flew low, at about the height of a man from the grass, and vanished in the woods.

Dorn threw the two turkeys over his shoulder and went on his way. Soon he came to a break in the forest level, from which he gazed down a league-long slope of pine and cedar, out upon the bare glistening desert, stretching away, endlessly rolling out to the dim, dark horizon line.

The little hamlet of Pine lay on the last level of sparsely timbered forest. A road, running parallel with a dark-watered swift-flowing stream, divided the cluster of log cabins from which columns of blue smoke drifted lazily aloft. Fields of corn and fields of oats, yellow in the sunlight, surrounded the village, and green pastures, dotted with horses and cattle, reached away to the denser woodland. This site appeared to be a natural clearing, for there was no evidence of cut timber. The scene was rather too wild to be pastoral, but it was serene, tranquil, giving the impression of a remote community, prosperous and happy, drifting along the peaceful tenor of sequestered lives.

Dorn halted before a neat little log cabin and little patch of garden bordered with sunflowers. His call was answered by an old woman, gray and bent, but remarkably spry, who appeared at the door.

"Why, land's sakes, if it ain't Milt Dorn!" she exclaimed in welcome.

"Reckon it's me, Missus Cass," he replied. "An' I've brought you a turkey."

"Milt, you're that good boy who never forgits old Widow Cass. . . . What a gobbler! First one I've seen this fall. . . . My man Tom used to fetch home gobblers like that. . . . An' mebbe he'll come home again some time."

Her husband, Tom Cass, had gone into the forest years before and had never returned. But the old woman always looked for him and never gave up hope.

"Men have been lost in the forest an' yet

come back," replied Dorn as he had said to her many a time.

"Come right in. You air hungry, I know. . . . Now, son, when last did you eat a fresh egg or a flapjack?"

"You should remember," he answered, laughing as he followed her into a small clean kitchen.

"Lawsa' me! An' thet's months ago," she replied, shaking her gray head. "Milt, you should give up thet wild life . . . an' marry . . . an' have a home."

"You always tell me that."

"Yes, an' I'll see you do it yet. . . . Now you set there, an' pretty soon I'll give you thet to eat which'll make your mouth water."

"What's the news, auntie?" he asked.

"Nary news in this dead place. Why, nobody's been to Snowdrop in two weeks! Sary Jones died, poor old soul . . . she's better off . . . an' one of my cows run away. Milt, she's wild when she gits loose in the woods. An' you'll have to track her, 'cause nobody else can. An' John Dakker's heifer was killed by a lion, an' Lem Harden's fast hoss . . . you know his favorite . . . was stole by hoss thieves. Lem is jist crazy. . . . An' thet reminds me, Milt, where's your big bay Ranger . . . thet you'd never sell or lend?"

"My hosses are up in the woods, auntie,

safe, I reckon, from hoss thieves."

"Well, thet's a blessin'. We've had some stock stole this summer, Milt, an' no mistake."

Thus, while preparing a meal for Dorn, the old woman went on recounting all that had happened in the little village since his last visit. Dorn enjoyed her gossip and quaint philosophy, and it was exceedingly good to sit at her table. In his opinion nowhere else could there have been such butter and cream, such ham and eggs. Besides, she always had apple pie it seemed at any time he happened in, and apple pie was one of Dorn's few regrets while up in the lonely forest.

"How's old Al Auchincloss," presently inquired Dorn.

"Poorly . . . poorly." Mrs. Cass sighed. "But he tramps an' rides around same as ever. Al's not long for this world. . . . An', Milt, that reminds me . . . there's the biggest news you ever heard."

"You don't say so!" exclaimed Dorn to encourage the excited old woman.

"Al has sent back to Saint Joe fer his niece, Helen Rayner. She's to inherit all his property. We've heard much of her . . . a purty lass, they say. . . . Now, Milt Dorn, here's your chance. Stay out of the woods an' go to work. . . . You can marry that girl!"

"No chance for me, auntie," replied Dorn, smiling.

The old woman snorted. "Much you know! Any girl would have you, Milt Dorn, if you'd only throw a 'kerchief."

"Me! An' why, auntie?" he queried, half amused, half thoughtful. When he got back to civilization, he always had to adjust his thoughts to the ideas of people.

"Why? I declare, Milt, you live so in the woods you're like a boy of ten . . . an' then sometimes as old as the hills. There's no young man to compare with you hereabouts. An' this girl . . . she'll have all the spunk of the Auchinclosses."

"Then . . . maybe she'd not be such a catch after all," replied Dorn.

"Wal, you're no cause to love them . . . thet's sure. But, Milt, the Auchincloss women are always good wives."

"Dear auntie, you're dreamin'," said Dorn soberly. "I want no wife. I'm happy in the woods."

"Air you goin' to live like an Injun all your days, Milt Dorn?" she queried sharply.

"I hope and pray so."

"You ought to be ashamed. But some lass will change you, boy, an' mebbe it'll be this

Helen Auchincloss. *I* hope an' pray so, to that."

"Auntie, supposin' she did change me. She'd never change old Al. He hates me, you know."

"Wal, I ain't so sure, Milt. I met Al the other day. He inquired for you. An' said you was wild. But he reckoned men like you was good for pioneer settlements. Lord knows the good turns you've done this village! Milt, old Al doesn't approve of your wild life, but he never had any hard feelin's till that tame lion of yours killed so many of his sheep."

"Auntie, I don't believe Big Tom ever killed Al's sheep," declared Dorn positively.

"Wal, Al thinks so an' many other people," replied Mrs. Cass, shaking her gray head doubtfully. "You never swore he didn't. An' there was them two sheepherders who did swear they seen him."

"They only saw a cougar. An' they were so scared they ran."

"Who wouldn't? That big beast is enough to scare anyone. For land's sakes, don't ever fetch him down here again! I'll never fergit the time you did. All the folks an' children an' hosses in Pine broke an' run thet day."

"Yes, but Tom wasn't to blame. Auntie, he's the tamest of my pets. Didn't he try to

36

put his head on your lap an' lick your hand?"

"Wal, Milt, I ain't gainsayin' your cougar pet didn't act better'n a lot of people I know. Fer he did. But the looks of him an' what's been said was enough for me."

"An' what's all that, auntie?"

"They say he's wild when out of your sight. An' thet he'll trail an' kill anythin' you put him after."

"I trained him to be just that way."

"Wal, leave Big Tom to home . . . in the woods . . . when you visit us."

Dorn finished his hearty meal, and listened a while longer to the old woman's talk, then, taking up his rifle and the other turkey, he bade her good bye. She followed him out.

"Now, Milt, you'll come soon again, won't you . . . jest to see Al's niece . . . who'll be here in a week?"

"I reckon I'll drop in someday. . . . Auntie, have you seen my friends, the Mormon boys?"

"No, I ain't seen them an' don't want to," she retorted. "Milt Dorn, if anyone ever corrals you, it'll be Mormons."

"Don't worry, auntie. I like those boys. They often see me up in the woods, an' ask me to help them track a hoss or help kill some fresh meat."

"They're workin' for Beasley now."

"Is that so?" rejoined Dorn with sudden start. "An' what doin'?"

"Beasley is gettin' so rich, he's buildin' a fence, an' didn't have enough help. So I hear."

"Beasley gettin' rich?" repeated Dorn thoughtfully. "More sheep an' horses an' cattle than ever, I reckon?"

"Lawsa' me! Why, Milt, Beasley ain't any idee what he owns. Yes, he's the biggest man in these parts, since poor old Al's took to failin'. I reckon Al's health ain't none improved by Beasley's success. They've had some bitter quarrels lately . . . so I hear. Al ain't what he was."

Dorn bade good bye again to his old friend and strode away, thoughtful and serious. Beasley would not only be difficult to circumvent, but he would be dangerous to oppose. There did not appear much doubt of his driving his way roughshod to the dominance of affairs there in Pine. Dorn, passing down the road, began to meet acquaintances who had hearty welcome for his presence and interest in his doings, so that his pondering was interrupted for the time being. He carried the turkey to another old friend, and, when he left her house, he went on to the village store. This was a large log cabin, roughly covered with clapboards, with a wide plank platform in front and a hitching rail in the road. Several horses were standing there, and a group of lazy shirt-sleeved loungers.

"I'll be dog-goned if it ain't Milt Dorn!" exclaimed one.

"Howdy, Milt, old buckskin, right down glad to see you," greeted another.

"Hello, Dorn. You air shore good for sore eyes," drawled still another.

After a long period of absence, when Dorn met these acquaintances, he always experienced a singular warmth of feeling. It faded quickly when he got back to the intimacy of his woodland, and that was because the people of Pine with few exceptions, although they liked him and greatly admired his outdoor wisdom, regarded him as a sort of nonentity. Because he loved the wild and preferred it to village and range life, they had classed him as not one of them. Some believed him lazy, others believed him shift-less, others thought him an Indian in mind and habits, and there were many who called him slow-witted. Then there was another side to their regard for him, which always afforded him good-natured amusement. Two of this group asked him to bring in some turkey or venison; another wanted to hunt with him. Lem Harden came out of the store and appealed to Dorn to recover his stolen horse. Lem's brother wanted a wild-running mare tracked and brought home. Jesse Lyons wanted a colt broken, and broken with patience, not violence, as was the method of the hard-riding boys at Pine. So one and all, they besieged Dorn with their selfish needs, all unconscious of the flattering nature of these overtures. And on the moment there happened by two women whose remarks, as they entered the store, bore strong testimony to Dorn's personality.

"If there ain't Milt Dorn!" exclaimed the older of the two. "How lucky! My cow's sick, an' the men are no good doctorin'. I'll jest ask Milt over."

"No one like Milt!" responded the other woman heartily.

"Good day, there . . . you Milt Dorn!" called the first speaker. "When you git away from these lazy men, come over."

Dorn never refused a service, and that was why his infrequent visits to Pine were wont to be prolonged beyond his own pleasure.

Presently Beasley strode down the street, and, when about to enter the store, he espied Dorn.

"Hello there, Milt!" he called cordially as he came forward with extended hand. His greeting was sincere, but the lightning glance he shot over Dorn was not born of his pleasure. Seen in daylight Beasley was a big, bold, bluff man, with strong dark features. His aggressive presence suggested that he was a good friend and a bad enemy.

Dorn shook hands with him.

"How are you, Beasley?"

"Ain't complainin', Milt, though I got more work than I can rustle. . . . Reckon you wouldn't take a job bossin' my sheep-herders?"

"Reckon I wouldn't," replied Dorn. "Thanks all the same."

"What's goin' on up in the woods?"

"Plenty of turkey an' deer. Lots of bear, too. The Indians have worked back on the south side, early this fall. But I reckon winter will come late an' be mild."

"Good! An' where're you headin' from?"

"Cross-country from my camp," replied Dorn rather evasively.

"Your camp. Nobody ever found thet yet," declared Beasley gruffly.

"It's up there," said Dorn.

"Reckon you got thet cougar chained in your cabin door?" queried Beasley, and there was a barely distinguishable shudder

41

of his muscular frame. Also the pupils dilated in his hard brown eyes.

"Tom ain't chained. An' I haven't no cabin, Beasley."

"You mean to tell me that big brute stays in your camp without bein' hog-tied or corralled?" demanded Beasley.

"Sure he does."

"Beats me! But then I'm queer on cougars. Have had many a cougar trail me at night. Ain't sayin' I was scared. But I don't care for thet brand of varmint. . . . Milt, you goin' to stay down a while?"

"Yes, I'll hang around some."

"Come over to the ranch. Glad to see you anytime. Some old huntin' pards of yours are workin' for me."

"Thanks, Beasley. I reckon I'll come over."

Beasley turned away and took a step, and then, as if with an afterthought, he wheeled again. "Suppose you've heard about old Al Auchincloss bein' near petered out?" queried Beasley. A strong ponderous cast of thought seemed to emanate from his features. Dorn divined that Beasley's next step would be to further his advancement by some word or hint.

"Widow Cass was tellin' me all the news. Too bad about old Al," replied Dorn.

"Sure is. He's done for. An' I'm sorry . . .

though Al's never been square. . . ."

"Beasley," interrupted Dorn quickly. "You can't say that to me. . . . Al Auchincloss always was the whitest an' squarest man in this sheep country."

Beasley gave Dorn a fleeting dark glance.

"Dorn, what you think ain't goin' to influence feelin' on this range," returned Beasley deliberately. "You live in the woods, an'. . . ."

"Reckon livin' in the woods I might think . . . an' know a whole lot," interposed Dorn just as deliberately. The group of men exchanged surprised glances. This was Milt Dorn in different aspect. And Beasley did not conceal a puzzled surprise.

"About what . . . now?" he asked bluntly.

"Why, about what's goin' on in Pine," replied Dorn.

Some of the men laughed.

"Shore lots goin' on . . . an' no mistake," put in Lew Harden.

Probably the keen Beasley had never before considered Milt Dorn as a responsible person, certainly never one in any way to cross his trail. But on the instant perhaps some instinct was born or he divined an antagonism in Dorn that was both surprising and perplexing.

"Dorn, I've differences with Al Auchincloss . . . have had them for years," said Beasley. "Much of what he owns is mine. An' it's goin' to come to me. Now I reckon people will be takin' sides . . . some fer me an' some fer Al. Most are fer me. . . . Where do you stand? Al Auchincloss never had no use fer you, an', besides, he's a dyin' man. . . . Are you goin' on his side?"

"Yes, I reckon I am."

"Wal, I'm glad you've declared yourself," rejoined Beasley shortly, and he strode away with the ponderous gait of a man who would brush any obstacle from his path.

"Milt, thet's bad . . . makin' Beasley sore at you," said Lew Harden. "He's on the way to boss this outfit."

"He's sure goin' to step into Al's boots," said another.

"Thet was white of Milt to stick up for poor old Al," declared Lew's brother.

Dorn broke away from them and wended a thoughtful way down the road. The burden of what he knew about Beasley weighed less heavily upon him, and the close-lipped course he had decided upon appeared wisest. He needed to think before undertaking to call upon old Al Auchincloss, and to that end he sought an hour's seclusion under the pines.

CHAPTER THREE

In the afternoon Dorn, having accomplished some tasks imposed on him by his old friends at Pine, directed slow steps toward the Auchincloss Ranch.

The flat square stone and log cabin, of immense size, stood upon a little hill, half a mile out of the village. A home as well as fort, it had been the first structure erected in that region, and the process of building had more than once been interrupted by Indian attacks. The Apaches had for some time, however, confined their fierce raids to points south of the White Mountain range. Auchincloss's house looked down upon barns and sheds and corrals of all sizes and shapes, and hundreds of acres of well-cultivated soil. Fields of oats waved, gray and yellow, in the afternoon sun; an immense green pasture was divided by a willow-bordered brook, and there were droves of horses, and out on the rolling bare flats were straggling herds of cattle.

The whole ranch showed many years of toil, and the perseverance of man. The brook irrigated the verdant valley between the ranch and the village. Water for the house, however, came down from the high wooded slope of the mountain, and had been brought there by a simple expedient. Pine logs of uniform size had been laid end to end, with a deep trough cut in them, and they made a shining line down the slope, across the valley, and up the little hill to Auchincloss's home. Near the house the hollowed halves of logs had been bound together, making a crude pipe. Water really ran uphill in this case, one of the facts that had made the ranch famous, as it had always been a wonder and delight to the small boys of Pine. The two good women who managed Auchincloss's large household were often shocked by the strange things that floated into their clean kitchen with the ever-flowing stream of clear cold mountain water.

As it happened this day, Dorn encountered Al Auchincloss sitting in the shade of a porch, talking to some of his sheepherders and stock men. Auchincloss was a short man of extremely powerful build and enormous width of shoulders. He had no gray hairs and he did not look old, yet there was in his face a gray weariness, something that resembled sloping lines of distress, dim and pale, that told of age and the ebb tide of vitality. His features, cast in large mold, were clean-cut and comely, and he had frank blue eyes, somewhat sad, yet still full of spirit.

Dorn had no idea how his visit would be taken, and he certainly would not have been surprised to be ordered off the place. He had not set foot there for years. Therefore it was with surprise that he saw Auchincloss wave away the herders, and take his entrance without any particular expression. Someone had acquainted the old rancher with his presence in Pine and not improbably about how he had openly rebuked Beasley in Auchincloss's behalf.

"Howdy, Al. How are you?" greeted Dorn easily as he leaned his rifle against the log wall.

Auchincloss did not rise, but he offered his hand. "Wal, Milt Dorn, I reckon this is the first time I ever seen you thet I couldn't lay you flat on your back," replied the rancher. His tone was both testy and full of pathos.

"I take it you mean you ain't very well," replied Dorn. "I'm sorry, Al."

"No, it ain't thet. Never was sick in my life. I'm just played out, like a hoss thet had been strong an' willin', an' did too much. . . . Wal, you don't look a day older, Milt. Livin' in the woods rolls over a man's head."

"Yes, I'm feelin' fine, an' time never bothers me."

"Wal, mebbe you ain't such a fool after all. I've wondered lately . . . since I had time to think. . . . But, Milt, you don't git no richer."

"Al, I have all I want an' need."

"Wal, then you don't support anybody . . . you don't do any good in the world."

"We don't agree, Al," replied Dorn with his slow smile.

"Reckon we never did. . . . An' you jest come over to pay your respects to me, eh?"

"Not altogether," answered Dorn ponderingly. "First off, I'd like to say I'll pay back them sheep you always claimed my tame cougar killed."

"You will! An' how'd you go about thet?"

"Wasn't very many sheep, was there?"

"A matter of fifty head."

"So many? Al, do you still think old Tom killed them sheep?"

"*Humph!* Milt, I know damn' well he did."

"Al, now how could you know somethin'

48

I don't? Be reasonable now. Let's don't fall out about this again. I'll pay back the sheep. Work it out. . . ."

"Milt Dorn, you'll come down here an' work off that fifty head of sheep!" ejaculated the old rancher incredulously.

"Sure."

"Wal, I'll be damned!" He sat back and gazed with shrewd eyes at Dorn. "What's got into you, Milt? Hev you heerd about my niece thet's comin' an' think you'll shine up to her?"

"Yes, Al, her comin' has a good deal to do with my deal," replied Dorn soberly. "But I never thought to shine up to her, as you hint."

"*Haw! Haw!* You're jest like all the other colts hereabouts. Reckon it's a good sign, too. It'll take a woman to fetch you out of the woods. . . . But, boy, this niece of mine, Helen Rayner, will stand you on your head. I never seen her. They say she's jest like her mother. An' Nell Auchincloss . . . what a girl she was!"

"Honest, Al . . . ," he began.

"Son, don't lie to an old man."

"Lie! I wouldn't lie to anyone. Al, it's only men who live in towns an' are always makin' deals. *I* live in the forest where there's nothin' to make me lie."

"Wal, no offense meant, I'm sure," responded Auchincloss. "An' mebbe there's somethin' in what you say. . . . We was talkin' about them sheep your big cat killed. Wal, Milt, I can't prove it, thet's sure. And mebbe you'll think me doddery when I tell you my reason. It wasn't what them greaser herders said about seein' a cougar in the herd."

"What was it, then?" queried Dorn, much interested.

"Well, thet day, a year ago, I seen your pet. He was lyin' in front of the store an' you was inside tradin' fer supplies, I reckon. It was like meetin' an enemy face to face. . . . Because, damn me if I didn't know thet cougar was guilty when he looked in my eyes! There."

The old rancher expected to be laughed at. But Dorn was grave.

"Al, I know how you felt," he replied as if they were discussing an action of a human being. "Sure I'd hate to doubt old Tom. But he's a cougar. An' the ways of animals are strange. . . . Anyway, Al, I'll make the loss of your sheep good."

"No, you won't," rejoined Auchincloss quickly. "We'll call it off. I'm takin' it square of you to make the offer. So forget your worry about work, if you had any."

"There's somethin' else . . . Al . . . I wanted to say," began Dorn with hesitation. "An' it's about Beasley."

Auchincloss started violently and a flame of red shot to his face. Then he raised a big hand that shook. Dorn saw in a flash how the old man's nerves had gone.

"Don't mention . . . thet . . . thet greaser . . . to me!" burst out the rancher. "It makes me see . . . red. . . . Dorn, I ain't overlookin' thet you spoke up fer me to-day . . . stood for my side. Lem Harden told me. I was glad. An' thet's why . . . today . . . I forget our old quarrel. . . . But not a damn' word about thet sheep thief . . . or I'll drive you off the place!"

"But, Al . . . be reasonable," remonstrated Dorn. "It's necessary thet I speak of . . . of Beasley."

"It ain't. Not to me. I won't listen."

"Reckon you'll have to, Al," returned Dorn. "Beasley's after your property. He's made a deal. . . ."

"By heaven, I know thet!" shouted Auchincloss, tottering up, with his face now black-red. "Do you think thet's new to me? Shut up, Dorn! I can't stand it."

"But, Al . . . there's worse," went on Dorn hurriedly. "Worse! Your life's threatened . . . an' your niece Helen . . . she's to be. . . ."

51

"Shut up . . . an' clear out!" roared Auchincloss, waving his huge fists. He seemed on the verge of a collapse as, shaking all over, he backed into the door. A few seconds of rage had transformed him into a pitiful old man.

"But, Al . . . I'm your friend . . . ," began Dorn appealingly.

"Friend, hey?" returned the rancher with grim bitter passion. "Then you're the only one. . . . Milt Dorn, I'm rich an' I'm a dyin' man. I trust nobody. . . . But, you wild hunter . . . if you're my friend . . . prove it! Go kill thet greaser sheep thief! *Do somethin' . . . an' then come talk to me!*"

With that he lurched, half falling, into the house, and slammed the door.

Dorn stood there for a blank moment, and then, taking up his rifle, he strode away.

Toward sunset Dorn located the camp of his four Mormon friends, and reached it in time for supper.

John, Roy, Joe, and Hal Beeman were sons of a pioneer Mormon who had settled the little community of Snowdrop. They were young men in years, but hard labor and hard life in the open had made them look matured. Only a year's differences in age stood between John and Roy, and between

Roy and Joe, and likewise for Joe and Hal. When it came to appearance they were difficult to distinguish from one another. Horsemen, sheepherders, cattle raisers, hunters — they all possessed long wiry powerful frames, lean bronzed still faces, and the quiet keen eyes of men used to the open.

Their camp was situated beside a spring in a cove surrounded by aspens, some three miles from Pine, and, although working for Beasley near the village, they had ridden to and fro from camp, after the habit of seclusion peculiar to their kind.

Dorn and the brothers had much in common, from which a warm regard had sprung up. But their exchange of confidences had wholly concerned things pertaining to the forest. This, to be sure, was owing to the reticence of the close-lipped Mormons. Dorn ate supper with them, and talked as usually when he met them, without giving any hint of the purpose forming in his mind. After the meal he helped Joe round up the horses, hobble them for the night, and drive them into a grassy glade among the pines. Later, when the shadows stole through the forest on the cool wind and the campfire glowed comfortably, Dorn broached the subject that possessed him.

"An' so you're workin' for Beasley?" he queried, by way of starting conversation.

"We was," drawled John. "But today, bein' the end of our month, we got our pay an' quit. Beasley sure was sore."

"Why'd you knock off?"

John essayed no reply, and his brothers all had that quiet suppressed look of knowledge under restraint.

"Listen to what I come to tell you . . . then you'll talk," went on Dorn. And hurriedly he told of Beasley's plot to destroy Al Auchincloss's niece and claim the dying man's property, and of his failure to get the old rancher to hear his story.

When Dorn ended rather breathlessly, the Mormon boys sat without any show of surprise or feeling. John, the oldest, took up a stick and slowly poked the red embers of the fire, making the white sparks fly.

"Now, Milt . . . why'd you tell us thet?" he asked guardedly.

"You're the only friends I've got," replied Dorn. "It didn't seem safe for me to talk down in the village. I thought of you boys right off. I ain't goin' to let Snake Anson get that girl. An' I need help . . . so I come to you."

"Beasley's strong around Pine an' old Al's weakenin'. Beasley will git the property, girl

54

or no girl," said John.

"Things don't always turn out as they look. But no matter about that. The girl deal is what's riled me. . . . She's to arrive at Magdalena on the Sixteenth an' take the stage for Snowdrop. . . . Now what to do? If she travels in that stage, I'll be on it, you bet. But she oughtn't to be in it, at all. . . . Boys, somehow I'm goin' to save her. . . . Will you help me? I reckon I've been in some tight corners for you. . . . Sure, this's different. But are you my friends? You know now what Beasley is. An' you've all lost enough at the hand of Snake Anson's gang. You've got fast hosses, eyes for trackin', an' you can handle a rifle. You're the kind of fellars I'd want in a tight pinch with a bad gang. Will you stand by me or see me go alone?"

Then John Beeman, silently and with pale face, gave Dorn's hand a powerful grip, and one by one the other brothers rose to do likewise. Their eyes flashed with hard glint and a strange bitterness hovered around their thin lips.

"Milt, mebbe we know what Beasley is better'n you," said John at length. "He ruined my father. He's cheated other Mormons. We boys have proved to ourselves thet he gets the sheep Anson's gang steals. . . .

An' drives the herds to Phoenix! Our people won't let us accuse Beasley. So we've suffered in silence. My father always said let someone else say the first word against Beasley. . . . An' you've come to us!"

Roy Beeman put a hand on Dorn's shoulder. He, perhaps, was the keenest of the brothers, and the one to whom adventure and peril called most. He had been oftenest with Dorn, on many a long trail, and he was the hardest rider and the most relentless tracker in all that range country.

"An' we're goin' with you," he said in a strong and rolling voice.

They resumed their seats before the fire. John threw on more wood. And with a *crackling* and sparkling the blaze curled up, fanned by the wind. As twilight deepened into night, the moan in the pines increased to a roar. A pack of coyotes commenced to pierce the air in staccato cries.

The five young men conversed long and earnestly, considering, planning, rejecting ideas advanced by each. Dorn and Beeman suggested most of what became acceptable to all. Hunters of their type resembled explorers in slow and deliberate attention to details. What they had to deal with here was a situation of unlimited possibilities — the horses and outfit needed, a long detour to

56

reach Magdalena unobserved, the rescue of a strange girl who would no doubt be self-willed and determined to ride on the stage, the rescue, forcible if necessary, the fight and inevitable pursuit, the flight into the forest, and the safe delivery of the girl to Auchincloss.

"Then, Milt, will we go after Beasley?" queried Roy Beeman significantly.

Dorn was silent and thoughtful.

"Sufficient unto the day!" said John. "An' . . . fellars, let's go to bed."

They rolled out their tarpaulins, Dorn sharing Roy's blankets, and soon were asleep, while the red embers slowly faded, and the great roar of wind died down, and the forest stillness set in.

CHAPTER FOUR

Helen Rayner had been on the westbound overland train fully twenty-four hours before she made an alarming discovery.

Accompanied by her sister Bo, a precocious girl of sixteen, Helen had left St. Joseph with a heart saddened by farewells to loved ones at home, yet full of thrilling and vivid anticipations of new strange life in the far West. All her people had the pioneer spirit: love of change, action, adventure was in her blood. Then duty to a widowed mother with large and growing family had called to Helen to accept this rich uncle's offer. She had taught school and also her little brothers and sisters; she had helped along in other ways. And now, although the tearing up the roots of old loved ties was hard, this opportunity was irresistible in its call. The prayer of her dreams had been answered. To bring good fortune to her family, to take care of this beautiful wild little sister, to live on a wonderful ranch that was someday to be her own, to have fulfilled a deep instinctive and undeveloped love of horses, cattle, sheep, of desert and mountains, of trees and brooks and wildflowers — all this was the sum of her most passionate longings, now in some marvelous fairylike way to come true.

A check to her happy anticipations, a blank sickening dash of cold water upon her warm and intimate dreams had been the discovery that Harve Riggs was on the train. His presence could mean only one thing — that he had followed her. Riggs had been the worst of many sore trials back there in St. Joseph. He had possessed some claim or some undue influence upon her mother, who favored his offer of marriage to Helen; he was neither attractive, nor good, or industrious, or anything that interested her; he was the boastful strutting adventurer not genuinely Western, and he affected long hair and guns and notoriety. Helen had suspected the veracity of the many fights he claimed had been his, and also she suspected that he was not really big enough to be bad — as Western men were bad. But on the train, in the station at La Junta, one glimpse of him, manifestly spying upon her while trying to keep out of her sight, warned

59

Helen that she now might have to deal with a villain.

The recognition sobered her. All was not to be a road of roses to this new home in the West. Riggs would follow her, if he could not accompany her, and to gain his own ends he would stoop to anything. Helen felt the startling realization of being cast upon her own resources, and then a numbing discouragement and loneliness and helplessness. But these feelings did not long persist in the quick pride and flash of her temper. Opportunity knocked at her door and she meant to be at home to it. She would not have been Al Auchincloss's niece if she had faltered. And when temper succeeded to genuine anger, she could have laughed to scorn this Harve Riggs and his schemes, whatever they were. Once and for all she dismissed fear of him. When she left St. Joseph, she had faced the West with a beating heart and a high resolve to be worthy of that West. Homes had to be made out there in that far country, so Uncle Al had written, and women were needed to make homes. She meant to be one of these women and to make of her sister another. And with the thought that she would know definitely what to say to Riggs when he approached her sooner or later, Helen dismissed him from mind.

While the train was in motion, enabling Helen to watch the ever-changing scenery, and resting her from the strenuous task of keeping Bo well in hand at stations, she lapsed again into dreamy gaze at the pine forests and the red rocky gullies and the dim bold mountains.

She saw the sun set over distant ranges of New Mexico — a golden blaze of glory, as new to her as the strange fancies born in her, thrilling and fleeting by. Bo's raptures were not silent, and, the instant the sun sank and the color faded, she just as rapturously importuned Helen to get out the huge basket of food they had brought from home.

They had two seats, facing each other, at the end of the coach, and piled there, with the basket on top, was baggage that constituted all the girls owned in the world. Indeed it was very much more than they had ever owned before, because their mother, in her care for them and desire to have them look well in the eyes of this rich uncle, had spent money and pains to give them pretty and serviceable clothes.

The girls sat together, with the heavy basket upon their knees, and ate while they gazed out at the cool dark ridges. The train

61

clattered slowly on, apparently over a road that was all curves. And it was suppertime for everybody in that crowded coach. If Helen had not been so absorbed by the great wild mountain land, she would have had more interest in the passengers. As it was, she saw them and was amused and thoughtful at the men and women and a few children in the car, all middle-class people, poor and hopeful, traveling out there to the new West to find houses. It was splendid and beautiful, this fact, yet it inspired a brief and inexplicable sadness. From the train window that world of forest and crag, with its long bare reaches between, seemed so lonely, so wild, so unlivable. How endless the distance! For hours and miles upon miles no house, no hut, no Indian teepee! It was amazing the length and breadth of this beautiful land. And Helen, who loved brooks and running streams, saw no water at all.

The darkness settled down over this slow-moving panorama; a cool night wind blew in at the window; white stars began to blink out of the blue. The sisters, with hands clasped and heads nestled together, went to sleep under a heavy cloak.

Early the next morning, while the girls were

again delving into their apparently bottomless basket, the train stopped at Las Vegas.

"Look! Look!" cried Bo in thrilling voice. "*Cowboys!* Oh, Nell, look!"

Helen, laughing, looked first at her sister and thought how best of all she was good to look at. Bo was little, instinct with pulsating life, and she had chestnut hair and dark blue eyes. These eyes were flashing, roguish, and they drew like magnets.

Outside on the rude platform were railroad men, Mexicans, and a group of lounging cowboys. Long lean bowlegged fellows they were, with young frank faces and intent eyes. One of them seemed particularly attractive with his superb build, his red-bronze face and bright red scarf, his swinging gun, and the huge long curved spurs. Evidently he caught Bo's admiring gaze for, with a word to his companions, he sauntered toward the window where the girls sat. His gait was singular, almost awkward, as if he was not accustomed to walking. The long spurs *jingled* musically. He removed his sombrero and stood at ease, frank, cool, smiling. Helen liked him on sight, and, looking to see what effect he had on Bo, she found that young lady staring, frightened, stiff.

"Good mawnin'," drawled the cowboy

with slow good-humored smile. "Now where might you-all be travelin'?"

The sound of his voice, the clean-cut and droll geniality seemed new and delightful to Helen.

"We go to Magdalena . . . then take stage for the White Mountains," replied Helen.

The cowboy's still intent eyes showed surprise. "Apache country, miss," he said. "I reckon I'm sorry. Thet's shore no place for you-all. . . . Beggin' your pawdin . . . you ain't Mormons?"

"No. We're nieces of Al Auchincloss," rejoined Helen.

"Wal, you don't say! I've been down Magdalena way an' heerd of Al. . . . Reckon you're goin' a-visitin'?"

"It's to be home for us."

"Shore thet's fine! The West needs girls. . . . Yes, I've heered of Al. An old Arizona cattleman in a sheep country! Thet's bad. . . . Now I'm wonderin' . . . if I'd drift down there an' ask him for a job ridin' for him . . . would I get it?"

His lazy smile was infectious and his meaning was as clear as crystal water. The gaze he bent upon Bo somehow pleased Helen. The last year or two, since Bo had grown prettier all the time, she had been a magnet for admiring glances. This one of the cowboys inspired respect and liking, as well as amusement. It certainly was not lost upon Bo.

"My uncle once said in a letter that he never had enough men to run his ranch," replied Helen, smiling.

"Shore, I'll go. I reckon I'd jest naturally drift thet way . . . now."

He seemed so laconic, so easy, so nice that he could not be taken seriously, yet Helen's quick perceptions registered a daring, a something that was both sudden and inevitable in him. His last word was as clear as the soft look he fixed upon Bo.

Helen had a mischievous trait, which, subdue it as she would, occasionally cropped out, and Bo, who once in her willful life had been rendered speechless, offered such a temptation.

"Maybe my little sister will put in a good word for you . . . to Uncle Al," said Helen.

Just then the train jerked and started slowly. The cowboy took two long strides beside the car, his heated boyish face almost on a level with the window, his eyes, now shy and a little wistful, yet bold, fixed upon Bo.

"Good bye . . . *sweetheart!*" he called. He halted — was lost to view.

"Well!" ejaculated Helen contritely, half

sorry and half amused. "What a sudden young gentleman!"

Bo had blushed beautifully. "Nell, wasn't he glorious?" she burst out, with eyes shining.

"I'd hardly call him that, but he was . . . nice," replied Helen, much relieved that Bo had apparently not taken offense at her.

It appeared plain that Bo resisted a frantic desire to look out of the window and to wave her hand. But she only peeped out, manifestly to her disappointment.

"Do you think he . . . he'll come to Uncle Al's?" asked Bo.

"Child, he was only in fun."

"Nell, I'll bet you he comes. . . . Oh, it'd be great! I'm going to love cowboys. They don't look like that Harve Riggs who ran after you so."

Helen sighed, partly because of the reminder of her odious suitor, and partly because Bo's future already called mysteriously to the child. Helen had to be at once a mother and a protector to a girl of intense and willful spirit.

One of the train men directed the girls' attention to a green sloping mountain rising to bold blunt bluff of bare rock, and, calling it Starvation Peak, he told a story of how Indians had once driven Spaniards up there and starved them. Bo was intensely interested, and thereafter she watched more keenly than ever, and always had a question for a passing train man. The adobe houses of the Mexicans pleased her, and when the train got into Indian country, where pueblos appeared near the track and Indians with their bright colors and shaggy wild mustangs — then she was enraptured.

"But these Indians are peaceful!" she exclaimed once, regretfully.

"Gracious, child! You don't want to see hostile Indians, do you?" queried Helen.

"I do, you bet," was the frank rejoinder.

"Well, *I'll* bet that I'll be sorry I didn't leave you with Mother."

"Nell . . . you never will!"

They reached Albuquerque about noon, and this important station, where they had to change trains, had been the first dreaded anticipation of the journey. It certainly was a busy place — full of jabbering Mexicans, stalking red-faced wicked-looking cowboys, lolling Indians. In the confusion Helen would have been hard put to it to preserve calmness, with Bo to watch, and all that baggage to carry, and the other train to find, but the kindly train man who had been attentive to them now helped them off the train into the other — a service for which Helen was very grateful.

"Albuquerque's a hard place," confided the train man. "Better stay in the car . . . and don't hang out the windows. . . . Good luck to you!"

Only a few passengers were in the car and they were Mexicans at the forward end. This branch train consisted of the one passenger coach, with a baggage car, attached to a string of freight cars. Helen told herself, somewhat grimly, that soon she would know surely whether or not her suspicions of Harve Riggs had warrant. If he was going on to Magdalena on that day, he must go in this coach. Presently Bo, who was not obeying admonitions, drew her head out of the window. Her eyes were wide in amaze, her mouth open.

"Nell! I saw that man Riggs," she whispered. "He's going to get on this train."

"Bo, I saw him yesterday," replied Helen soberly.

"He's followed you . . . the . . . the. . . ."

"Now, Bo, don't get excited," remonstrated Helen. "We've left home now. We've got to take things as they come. Never mind if Riggs has followed me. I'll settle him."

"Oh! Then you won't speak . . . have anything to do with him?"

"I won't if I can help it."

Other passengers boarded the train, dusty uncouth rugged men, and some hard-featured, poorly clad women, marked by toil, and several more Mexicans. With bustle and loud talk they found their several seats.

Then Helen saw Harve Riggs enter, burdened with much luggage. He was a man of about medium height, of dark flashy appearance, cultivating long black mustache and hair. His apparel was striking, as it consisted of black frock coat, black trousers stuffed in high fancy tipped boots, an embroidered vest and flowing tie, and a black sombrero. His belt and gun were prominent. It was significant that he excited comment among the other passengers.

When he had deposited his pieces of luggage, he seemed to square himself and, turning abruptly, approached the seat occupied by the girls. When he reached it, he sat down upon the arm of the one opposite, took off his sombrero, and deliberately looked at Helen. His eyes were light, glinting with hard restless quiver, and his mouth was coarse and arrogant. Helen had never seen him detached from her home surroundings, and now the difference struck coldly upon her heart. Here was a character whose badness even she had underestimated.

"Hello, Nell," he said. "Surprised to see me?"

"No," she replied coldly.

"I'll gamble you are."

"Harve Riggs, I told you the day before I left home that nothing you could do or say mattered to me."

"Reckon that ain't so, Nell. Any woman I keep track of has reason to think. An' you know it."

"Then you followed me . . . out here?" demanded Helen, and her voice, despite her control, quivered with anger.

"I sure did," he replied, and there was as much thought of himself in the act as there was of her.

"Why? Why? It's useless . . . hopeless."

"I swore I'd have you or nobody else would," he replied, and here, in the passion of his voice, there sounded egotism, rather than hunger for a woman's love. "But, I reckon, I'd have struck West anyhow, sooner or later."

"You're not going to . . . all the way . . . to Pine?" faltered Helen, momentarily weakening.

"Nell, I'll camp on your trail from now on," he declared.

70

Then Bo sat bolt upright, with pale face and flashing eyes. "Harve Riggs, you leave Nell alone!" she burst out in a ringing brave young voice. "I'll tell you what . . . I'll bet . . . if you follow her and nag her any more . . . my Uncle Al or some cowboy will run you out of the country."

"Hello, Pepper," replied Riggs coolly. "I see your manners haven't improved an' you're still wild about cowboys."

"People don't have good manners with . . . with. . . ."

"Bo, hush!" admonished Helen. It was difficult to speak so to Bo just then, for that young lady had not the slightest fear of Riggs. Instead, she looked as if she could slap his face. And Helen realized that, however her intelligence had grasped the possibilities of leaving home for a wild country, and whatever her determination to be brave, the actual beginning of self-reliance had left her spirit weak. She would rise out of that. But just now this flashing-eyed little sister seemed a protector. Bo would readily adapt herself to the West, Helen thought, because she was so young, primitive, elemental.

Whereupon Bo turned her back to Riggs and looked out of the window. The man

71

laughed. Then he stood up and leaned over Helen.

"Nell, I'm goin' wherever you go," he said steadily. "You can take that friendly or not, just as it pleases you. But if you've got any sense, you'll not give these people out here a hunch against me. I might hurt somebody. . . . An' wouldn't it be better to act friends? For I'm goin' to look after you whether you like it or not."

Helen had considered this man an annoyance, and later a menace, and now she must declare open enmity with him. However disgusting the idea that he considered himself to be a factor in her new life, it was the truth. He existed, and he had control over his movements. She could not change that. She hated the need of thinking so much about him, and suddenly, she who had been only intolerant, with a hot bursting anger she hated the man.

"You'll not look after me. I'll take care of myself," she said, and she turned her back upon him. She heard him mutter under his breath and slowly move away down the car. Then Bo slipped a hand in hers.

"Never mind, Nell," she whispered. "You know what old Sheriff Haines said about Harve Riggs. 'A four-flush would-be gunfighter. If he ever strikes a real Western town, he'll get run out of it.' I just wish my red-faced cowboy had got on this train!"

Helen felt a rush of gladness that she had yielded to Bo's wild importunities to take her West. The spirit that had made Bo incorrigible at home probably would make her react happily to life out in this free country. Yet Helen with all her warmth and gratefulness had to laugh at her sister.

"Your red-faced cowboy! Why, Bo, you were scared stiff. And now you claim him."

"I certainly could love that fellow," replied Bo dreamily.

"Child, you've been saying that about fellows for a long time. And you've never looked twice at any of them yet."

"He was different. . . . Nell, I'll bet he comes to Pine."

"I hope he does. I wish he was in this train. I liked his looks, Bo."

"Well, Nell dear, he looked at *me* first and last . . . so don't get your hopes up. . . . Oh, the train's starting! Good bye Albu-ker. . . . What's that awful name? Nell, let's eat dinner. I'm starved."

Then Helen forgot her troubles and the uncertain future, and what with listening to Bo's chatter, and partaking again of the endless good things to eat in the huge basket, and watching the noble mountains, she drew once more into happy mood.

The valley of the Río Grande opened to view, wide, near at hand in a great gray-green gap between the bare black mountains, narrow in the distance, where the yellow river wound away, glistening under a hot sun. Bo squealed in glee at sight of naked little Mexican children that darted into the adobe huts as the train *clattered* by, and she exclaimed her pleasure in the Indians, and the mustangs, and particularly in a group of cowboys riding into town upon spirited horses. Helen saw all Bo pointed out, but it was to the wonderful rolling valley that her gaze clung longest, and to the dim purple distance that seemed to hold something from her. She had never before experienced any feeling like that; she had never seen a tenth so far. And the sight awoke something strange in her. The sun was burning hot, as she could tell when she put a hand outside the window, and a strong wind blew sheets of dry dust at the train. She gathered at once what tremendous factors in the Southwest were the sun and the dust and the wind. And her realization was to love them. It was there, the open, the wild, the beautiful, the lonely land, and she felt the poignant call of blood in her — to seek, to strive, to find, to live. One look down that yellow valley, endless between its dark iron ramparts, had given her understanding of her uncle. She must be like him in spirit as it was claimed she resembled him otherwise.

At length Bo grew tired of watching scenery that contained no life, and with her bright head upon the folded cloak she went to sleep. But Helen kept a steady far-seeing gaze out upon that land of rock and plain, and during the long hours, as she watched through clouds of dust and veils of heat, some strong and doubtful and restless sentiment seemed to change and then to fix. It was her physical acceptance — her eyes and her senses taking the West as she had already taken it in spirit.

A woman should love her home wherever fate placed her, Helen believed, and not so much from duty as from delight and romance and living. How could life ever be tedious or monotonous out here in this tremendous vastness of bare earth and open sky, where the need to achieve made thinking and pondering superficial?

It was with regret that she saw the last of the valley of the Río Grande, and then of its parallel mountain ranges. But the miles brought compensation in other valleys, other bold black upheavals of rock, and then again bare boundless yellow plains, and sparsely cedared ridges, and white dry washes, ghastly in the sunlight, and dazzling beds of alkali, and then a desert space where golden and blue flowers bloomed.

She noted, too, that the whites and yellows of earth and rock had begun to shade to red — and this she knew meant an approach to Arizona. Arizona, the wild, the lonely, the red desert, the green plateau — Arizona with its thundering rivers, its unknown spaces, its pasture lands, outlaws, wolves and lions and savages! As to a boy that name stirred and thrilled and sang to her of nameless, sweet, intangible things, mysterious, and all of adventure. But she, being a girl of twenty, who had accepted responsibilities, must conceal the depths of her heart and that which her mother had complained was her misfortune in not being born a boy.

Time passed while Helen watched and learned and dreamed. The train stopped at long intervals, at wayside stations where there seemed nothing but adobe sheds and lazy Mexicans, and dust and heat. Bo awoke and began to chatter, and to dig into the basket. She learned from the conductor that Magdalena was only two stations on. And she was full of conjectures as to whom would meet them, what would happen. So Helen was drawn back to sober realities in which there was considerable zest. Assuredly she did not know what was going to happen. Twice Riggs passed up and down the aisle, his dark face and light eyes and sardonic smile deliberately forced upon her sight. But again Helen fought a growing dread with contemptuous scorn. This fellow was not half a man. It was not conceivable what he could do, except annoy her, until she arrived at Pine. Her uncle was to meet her or send for her at Snowdrop, which place, Helen knew, was distant, a good long ride by stage from Magdalena. This stage ride was the climax and the dread of all the long journey in Helen's considerations.

"Oh, Nell!" cried Bo with delight. "We're nearly there! Next station, the conductor said."

"I wonder if the stage travels at night," said Helen thoughtfully.

"Sure it does," replied the irrepressible Bo.

The train, though it *clattered* along as usual, seemed to Helen to fly. There the sun was setting over bleak New Mexican bluffs, Magdalena was at hand, and night, and adventure. Helen's heart beat fast. She watched the yellow plains where the cattle grazed, and their presence, and irrigation ditches and cottonwood trees told her that the railroad part of the journey was nearly ended. Then, at Bo's little scream, she looked across the car and out of the window there to see a line of low flat red adobe houses. The train began to slow down. Helen saw children run, white children and Mexican together, and then more houses, and high upon a hill an immense adobe church, crude and glaring, yet somehow beautiful.

Helen told Bo to put on her bonnet, and, performing a like office for herself, she was ashamed of the trembling of her fingers. There were bustle and talk in the car.

The train stopped. Helen peered out to see a straggling crowd of Mexicans and Indians, all motionless and stolid, as if trains or nothing else mattered. Next Helen saw a white man and that was a relief. He stood out in front of the others. Tall and broad, somehow striking, he drew a second glance that showed him to be a hunter, clad in gray fringed buckskin, and carrying a rifle.

Chapter Five

Here there was no kindly brakeman to help the sisters with their luggage. Helen bade Bo take her share, and, thus burdened, they made an awkward and laborsome shift to get off the train.

Upon the platform of the car a strong hand seized Helen's heavy bag, with which she was straining, and a loud voice called out: "Girls, we're here . . . we're out in the wild an' woolly West!"

The speaker was Riggs and he had possessed himself of part of her baggage with action and speech meant more to impress the curious crowd than to be really kind. In the excitement of arriving Helen had forgotten him. The manner of sudden reminder — the insincerity of it made her temper flash. She almost fell, encumbered as she was, in her hurry to descend the steps. She saw the tall hunter in gray step forward close to her as she reached for the bag Riggs held.

"Mister Riggs, I'll carry my bag," she said.

"Let me lug this. You help Bo with hers," he replied familiarly.

"But I want it," she rejoined quietly, with sharp determination. No little force was needed to pull the bag away from Riggs.

"See here, Helen, you ain't goin' any further with that joke, are you?" he queried deprecatingly, and he still spoke quite loudly.

"It's no joke to me," replied Helen. "I told you I didn't want your attention."

"Sure. But that was temper. I'm your friend . . . from your home town. I ain't goin' to let a quarrel keep me from lookin' after you till you're safe at your uncle's."

Helen turned her back upon him. The tall hunter had just helped Bo off the car. Then Helen looked up into a smooth bronzed face and piercing gray eyes.

"Are you Helen Rayner?" he asked.

"Yes."

"My name's Dorn. I've come to meet you."

"*Ah!* My uncle sent you?" added Helen in quick relief.

"No. I can't say Al sent me," began the man, "but I reckon. . . ."

80

He was interrupted by Riggs, who, grasping Helen by the arm, pulled her back a step.

"Say, mister, did Auchincloss send you to meet my young friends here?" he demanded arrogantly.

Dorn's glance turned from Helen to Riggs. She could not read his quiet gray gaze, but it thrilled her.

"No. I come on my own hook," he answered.

"You'll understand then . . . they're in my charge," added Riggs.

This time the steady light-gray eyes met Helen's and, if there were not a smile in them or behind them, she was still further baffled.

"Helen, I reckon you said you didn't want this fellow's attention?"

"I certainly said that," replied Helen quickly. Just then Bo stepped close to her and gave her arm a little squeeze. Probably Bo's thought was like hers — here was a real Western man. That was her first impression and following swiftly upon it was a sensation of eased nerves.

Riggs swaggered closer to Dorn.

"Say, Buckskin, I hail from Texas. . . ."

"You're wastin' our time an' we've need to hurry," interrupted Dorn. His tone seemed friendly. "An' . . . if you ever lived long in Texas, you wouldn't pester a lady an' you sure wouldn't talk like you do."

"What!" shouted Riggs hotly. He dropped his right hand significantly to his hip.

"Don't throw your gun. It might go off," said Dorn.

Whatever Riggs's intention had been — and it was probably just what Dorn evidently had read it — he now flushed an angry red and jerked at his gun.

Dorn's hand flashed too swiftly for Helen's eye to follow it. But she heard the *thud* as it struck. The gun went flying to the platform and scattered a group of Indians and Mexicans.

"You'll hurt yourself someday," said Dorn.

Helen had never heard a slow cool voice like this hunter's. Without excitement or emotion or hurry, it yet seemed full and significant of things the words did not mean. Bo uttered a strange little exultant cry.

Riggs's arm had dropped limply. No doubt it was numb. He stared, and his predominating expression was surprise. As the shuffling crowd began to snicker and whisper, Riggs gave Dorn a malignant glance, shifted it to Helen, and then lurched away in the direction of his gun.

Dorn did not pay any more attention to him. Gathering up Helen's baggage, he said — "Come on." — and shouldered a lane through the gaping crowd. The girls followed closely at his heels.

"Nell . . . what'd I tell you?" whispered Bo. "Oh, you're all a-tremble."

Helen was aware of her unsteadiness; anger and fear and relief in quick succession had left her rather weak. Once through the motley crowd of loungers she saw an old gray stagecoach and four lean horses. A grizzled sunburned man sat in the driver's seat, whip and reins in hand. Beside him was a younger man with rifle across his knees. Another man, young, tall, lean, dark, stood holding the coach door open. He touched his sombrero to the girls. His eyes were sharp as he addressed Dorn.

"Milt, wasn't you held up?"

"No. But some long-haired galoot was tryin' to hold up the girls. Wanted to throw his gun at me. I was sure scared," replied Dorn as he deposited the luggage.

Bo laughed. Her eyes, resting upon Dorn, were warm and bright. The young man at the coach door took a second look at her, and then a smile changed the dark hardness of his face.

Dorn helped the girls up the high step into

the stage, and then, placing the lighter luggage in with them, he threw the heavier pieces up on top.

"Joe, climb up," he said.

"Wal, Milt," drawled the driver, "let's ooze along."

Dorn hesitated with his hand on the door. He glanced at the crowd, now edging close again, and then at Helen. "I reckon I ought to tell you," he said, and indecision appeared to concern him.

"What!" exclaimed Helen.

"Bad news. But talkin' takes time. An' we mustn't lose any."

"There's need of hurry?" queried Helen, sitting up sharply.

"I reckon."

"Is this the stage to Snowdrop?"

"No. That leaves in the mornin'. We rustled this old trap to get a start tonight."

"The sooner the better. But I . . . I don't understand," said Helen, bewildered.

"It'll not be safe for you to ride on the mornin' stage," returned Dorn.

"Safe! Oh, what do you mean?" exclaimed Helen. Apprehensively she gazed at him, and then back at Bo.

"Explainin' will take time. An' facts may change your mind. But if you can't trust me. . . ."

"Trust you?" interposed Helen blankly. "You mean to take us to Snowdrop?"

"I reckon we'd better go roundabout an' not hit Snowdrop," he replied shortly.

"Then to Pine . . . to my uncle . . . Al Auchincloss?"

"Yes, I'm goin' to try hard."

Helen caught her breath. She divined that some peril menaced her. She looked steadily, with all a woman's keenness, into this man's face. The moment was one of the fateful decisions she knew the West had in store for her. Her future and that of Bo's were now to be dependent upon her judgments. It was a hard moment, and, although she shivered inwardly, she welcomed the initial and inevitable step. This man Dorn, by his dress of buckskin, must be either scout or hunter. His size, his action, the tone of his voice had been reassuring. But Helen must decide from what she saw in his face whether or not to trust him. And that face was clear bronze, unlined, unshadowed, like a tranquil mask, clean-cut, strong jawed, with eyes of wonderful transparent gray.

"Yes, I'll trust you," she said. "Get in and let us hurry. Then you can explain."

"All ready, Bill. Send 'em along!" called Dorn.

He had to stoop to enter the stage, and,

once in, he appeared to fill that side upon which he sat. Then the driver cracked his whip; the stage lurched and began to roll; the motley crowd was left behind. Helen awakened to the reality, as she saw Bo staring with big eyes at the hunter, that a stranger adventure than she had ever dreamed of had begun with the rattling roll of that old stagecoach.

Dorn laid off his sombrero and leaned forward, holding his rifle between his knees. The light shone better upon his features now that he was bareheaded. Helen had never seen a face like that, which at first glance appeared darkly bronzed and hard, and then became clear, cold, aloof, still, intense. She wished she might see a smile upon it. And now that the die was cast she could not tell why she had trusted it. There was singular force in it, but she did not recognize what kind of force. One instant she thought it was stern, and the next that it was sweet, and again that it was neither.

"I'm glad you've got your sister," he said.

"How did you know she's my sister?"

"I reckon she looks like you."

"No one else ever thought so," replied Helen, trying to smile.

Bo had no difficulty in smiling as she said: "Wish I was half as pretty as Nell."

"Nell. Isn't your name Helen?" queried Dorn.

"Yes. But my . . . some few call me Nell."

"I like Nell better than Helen. An' what's yours?" went on Dorn, looking at Bo.

"Mine's Bo. Just plain B-o. Isn't it silly? But I wasn't asked when they gave it to me," she replied.

"Bo. It's nice an' short. Never heard it before. But I haven't met many people for years."

"Oh! We've left the town!" cried Bo. "Look, Nell! How bare! It's just like desert."

"It is desert. We've forty miles of that before we come to a hill or a tree."

Helen glanced out. A flat dull green expanse waved away from the road on and on to a bright dark horizon line where the sun was setting rayless on a clear sky. Open, desolate, and lonely, the scene gave her a cold thrill.

"Did your Uncle Al ever write anythin' about a man named Beasley?" asked Dorn.

"Indeed he did," replied Helen with a start of surprise. "Beasley! That name is familiar to us . . . and detestable. My uncle complained of this man for years. Then he grew bitter . . . accused Beasley. But the last year or so, not a word."

"Well, now," began the hunter earnestly.

"Let's get the bad news over. I'm sorry you must be worried. But you must learn to take the West as it is. There's good and bad, maybe more bad. That's because the country's young . . . so to come right out with it . . . this Beasley hired a gang of outlaws to meet the stage you was goin' in to Snowdrop . . . tomorrow . . . an' to make off with you."

"Make off with me?" ejaculated Helen, bewildered.

"Kidnap you! Which in that gang would be worse than killin' you," declared Dorn grimly, and he closed a huge fist on his knee.

Helen was utterly astounded. "How horrible!" she gasped out. "Make off with me! What in heaven's name for?"

Bo gave vent to a fierce little utterance.

"For reasons you ought to guess," replied Dorn, and he leaned forward again. Neither his voice nor face changed in the least, but yet there was a something about him that fascinated Helen. "I'm a hunter. I live in the woods. A few nights ago I happened to be caught out in a storm an' I took to an old log cabin. Soon as I got there, I heard horses. I hid up in the loft. Some men rode up an' come in. It was dark. They couldn't see me. An' they talked. It turned out they were Snake Anson an' his gang of sheep thieves. They expected to meet Beasley there. Pretty soon he came. He told Anson how old Al, your uncle, was on his last legs . . . how he had sent for you to have his property when he died. . . . Beasley swore he had claims on Al. An' he made a deal with Anson to get you out of the way. He named the day you were to reach Magdalena. With Al dead an' you not there, Beasley could get the property. An' then he wouldn't care if you did come to claim it. It'd be too late. . . . Well, they rode away that night. An' next day I rustled down to Pine. They're all my friends at Pine, except old Al. But they think I'm queer. I didn't want to confide in many people. Beasley is strong in Pine, an' for that matter I suspect Snake Anson has other friends there besides Beasley. . . . So I went to see your uncle. He never had any use for me because he thought I was lazy like an Indian. Old Al hates lazy men. Then we fell out . . . or he fell out . . . because he believed a tame lion of mine had killed some of his sheep. An' now I reckon that Tom might have done it. . . . I tried to lead up to this deal of Beasley's about you, but old Al wouldn't listen. He's cross . . . very cross. An' when I tried to tell him, why he went right out of his head. Sent me off the ranch.

"Now I reckon you begin to see what a pickle I was in. Finally I went to four friends I could trust. They're Mormon boys . . . brothers. That's Joe out on top with the driver. I told them all about Beasley's deal an' asked them to help me. So we planned to beat Anson an' his gang to Magdalena. It happens that Beasley is as strong in Magdalena as he is in Pine. An' we had to go careful. But the boys had a couple of friends here . . . Mormons, too, who agreed to help us. They had this old stage. . . . An' here you are."

Dorn spread out his big hands and looked gravely at Helen, and then at Bo.

"You're perfectly splendid!" cried Bo ringingly. She was white; her fingers were clenched; her eyes blazed.

Dorn appeared startled out of his gravity, and surprised, then pleased. A smile made his face like a boy's.

Helen felt her body all rigid, yet slightly trembling. Her hands were cold. The horror of this revelation held her speechless. But in her heart she echoed Bo's exclamation of admiration and gratitude.

"So far then," resumed Dorn, with a heavy breath of relief. "No wonder you're upset. I've a blunt way of talkin'. . . . Now we've thirty miles to ride on this Snowdrop road before we can turn off. Today, sometime, the rest of the boys . . . Roy, John, an' Hal were to leave Show Down, which is a town farther on from Snowdrop. They have my horses an' packs besides their own. Somewhere on the road we'll meet them . . . tonight maybe . . . or tomorrow. I hope not tonight because that'd mean Anson's gang was ridin' in to Magdalena."

Helen wrung her hands helplessly. "Oh, have I no courage," she whispered.

"Nell, I'm as scared as you are," said Bo consolingly, embracing her sister.

"I reckon that's natural," said Dorn, as if excusing them. "But scared or not you both brace up. It's a bad job. But I've done my best. An' you'll be safer with me an' the Beeman boys than you'd be in Magdalena, or anywhere else, except your uncle's."

"Mister . . . Mister Dorn," faltered Helen, with her tears falling. "Don't think me a coward . . . or . . . or ungrateful. I'm neither. It's only I'm so . . . so shocked. After all we hoped and expected . . . this . . . this is such a . . . a terrible surprise."

"Never mind, Nell dear. Let's take what comes," murmured Bo.

"That's the talk," said Dorn. "You see I've come right out with the worst. Maybe we'll get through easy. When we meet the boys,

91

we'll take to the horses an' the trails. Can you ride?"

"Bo has been used to hosses all her life and I ride fairly well," responded Helen. The idea of riding quickened her spirit.

"Good! We may have some hard ridin' before I get you up to Pine. . . . Hello, what's that?"

Above the *creaking, rattling,* rolling roar of the stage Helen heard a rapid beat of hoofs. A horse flashed by, galloping hard.

Dorn opened the door and peered out. The stage rolled to a halt. Dorn stepped down and peered ahead.

"Joe, who was that?" he queried.

"Nary me. An' Bill didn't know him, either," replied Joe. "I seen him 'way back. He was ridin' some. An' he slowed up goin' past us. Now he's runnin' again."

Dorn shook his head as if he did not like the circumstance.

"Milt, he'll never get by Roy on this road," said Joe.

"Maybe he'll get by before Roy strikes in on the road."

"It ain't likely."

Helen could not restrain her fears. "Mister Dorn, you think he was a messenger . . . going ahead to pass that . . . that Anson gang?"

"He might be," replied Dorn simply.

92

Then the young man called Joe leaned out from the seat above and called: "Miss Helen, don't you worry, thet fellar is more liable to stop lead than anythin' else!"

His words, meant to be kind and reasoning, were about as sinister to Helen as the menace to her own life. Long had she known how cheap life was held in the West, but she had only known it abstractly, and she had never let the fact remain before her consciousness. This cheerful young man spoke calmly of spilling blood on her behalf. The thought it roused was tragic . . . for bloodshed was insupportable to her . . . and then the thrills that followed now so new, strange, bold, and tingling that they were revolting. Helen grew conscious of unplumbed depths, of instincts at which she was amazed and ashamed.

"Joe, hand down that basket of grub . . . the small one with the canteen," said Dorn, reaching out a long arm. Presently he placed a cloth-covered basket inside the stage. "Girls, eat all you want an' then some."

"We have a basket half full yet," replied Helen.

"You'll need it all before we get to Pine. . . . Now I'll ride up on top with the boys an' eat my supper. It'll be dark presently, an' we'll stop often to listen. But don't be scared."

With that he took his rifle and, closing the door, clambered up to the driver's seat. Then the stage lurched again and began to roll along.

Not the least thing to wonder at of this eventful evening was the way Bo reached for the basket of food. Helen simply stared at her.

"Bo, you can't eat!" she exclaimed.

"I should smile I can," replied that practical young lady. "And you're going to if I have to stuff things in your mouth. Where's your wits, Nell? He said we must eat. That means our strength is going to have some pretty severe trials. . . . Gee, it's all great . . . just like a story! The unexpected . . . why, he looks like a prince turned hunter . . . long dark stage journey . . . held up . . . fight . . . escape . . . wild ride on horses . . . woods and camps and wild places . . . pursued . . . hidden in the forest . . . more hard rides . . . then safe at the ranch. And of course he falls madly in love with me . . . no you, for I'd be true to my Las Vegas lover. . . ."

"Hush, silly! Bo, tell me, aren't you *scared*?"

"Scared! I'm scared stiff. But if Western girls stand such things, we can. No Western girl is going to beat *me!*"

That brought Helen to a realization of the brave place she had given herself in dreams, and she was at once ashamed of herself, and wildly proud of this little sister.

"Bo, thank heaven I brought you with me!" exclaimed Helen fervently. "I'll eat if it chokes me."

Whereupon she found herself actually hungry, and, while she ate, she glanced out of the stage, first from one side, and then from the other. These windows had no glass and they let the cool night air blow in. The sun had long since sunk. Out to the west, where a long bold black horizon line swept away suddenly, the sky was clear gold shading to yellow and blue above. Stars were out, pale and wan, but growing brighter. The earth appeared bare and heaving, like a calm sea. The wind bore a fragrance new to Helen, acridly sweet and clean, and it was so cold it made her fingers numb.

"I heard some animal yelp," said Bo suddenly, and she listened with head poised.

But Helen heard nothing save the steady *clip-clop* of hoofs, the *clink* of chains, the *creak* and *rattle* of the old stage, and occasionally the low voices of the men above.

When the girls had satisfied hunger and thirst, night had settled down black. They pulled the cloaks up over them and, close together, leaned back in a corner of the seat and talked in whispers. Helen did not have much to say, but Bo was talkative.

"This beats me," she said once, after an interval. "Where are we, Nell? Those men up there are Mormons. Maybe they are abducting us."

"Mister Dorn isn't a Mormon," replied Helen.

"How do you know?"

"I could tell by the way he spoke of his friends."

"Well, I wish it wasn't so dark. I'm not afraid of men in daylight. . . . Nell, did you ever see such a wonderful-looking fellow? What'd they call him? Milt . . . Milt Dorn. He said he lived in the woods. If I hadn't fallen in love with that cowboy who called me . . . well, I'd be a goner now."

After an interval of silence Bo whispered startlingly: "Wonder if Harve Riggs is following us now?"

"Of course he is," replied Helen hopelessly.

"He'd better look out. Why, Nell, he never saw . . . he never . . . what did Uncle Al used to call it? . . . saw . . . savvied . . . that's it. Riggs never savvied that hunter. But I did, you bet."

"Savvied! What do you mean, Bo?"

"I mean that long-haired galoot never saw his real danger. But I felt it. Something went tight inside me. Dorn never took him seriously at all."

"Riggs will turn up at Uncle Al's sure as I'm born," said Helen.

"Let him turn," replied Bo contemptuously. "Nell, don't you ever bother your head again about him. I'll bet they're all men out here. And I wouldn't be in Harve Riggs's boots for a lot."

After that Bo talked of her uncle, and his fatal illness, and from that she drifted back to the loved ones at home, now seemingly at the other side of the world, and then she broke down and cried, after which she fell asleep on Helen's shoulder.

But Helen could not have fallen asleep if she had wanted to.

She had always, since she could remember, longed for a moving active life, and for want of a better ideal she had chosen to dream of Gypsies. And now it struck her grimly that, if these first few hours of her advent in the West were forecasts of the future, she was destined to have her longings fulfilled with a vengeance.

Presently the stage rolled slower and slower until it came to a halt. Then the horses heaved, the harnesses *clinked,* the men whispered. Otherwise, there was an intense quiet. She looked out, expecting to find it pitch dark. It was black, yet a transparent blackness. To her surprise she could see a long way. A shooting star electrified her. The men were listening. She listened, too, but, beyond the slight sounds about the stage, she heard nothing. Presently the driver clucked his horses, and travel was resumed.

For a while the stage rolled on rapidly, evidently downhill, swaying from side to side, and rolling as if about to fall to pieces. Then it slowed on a level, and again it halted for a few moments, and once more in motion it began a laborsome climb. Helen imagined miles had been covered. The desert appeared to heave into billows, growing rougher, and dark round bushes dimly stood out. The road grew uneven and rocky, and, when the stage began another descent, its violent rocking jolted Bo out of her sleep, and in fact almost out of Helen's arms.

"Where am I?" asked Bo dazedly.

"Bo, you're having your heart's desire, but I can't tell you where you are," replied Helen.

Bo awakened thoroughly, which fact was

now no wonder, considering the jostling of the old stage.

"Hold on to me, Nell! Is it a runaway?"

"We've come about a thousand miles like this, I think," replied Helen. "I've not a whole bone in my body."

Bo peered out of the window. "Oh, how dark and lonesome! But it'd be nice if it wasn't so cold. I'm freezing."

"I thought you loved cold air," taunted Helen.

"Say, Nell, you begin to talk like yourself," responded Bo.

It was difficult to hold on to the stage and each other and the cloak all at once, but they succeeded except on the roughest places, when from time to time they were bounced around. Bo sustained a sharp rap on the head.

"Ooooo!" she moaned. "Nell Rayner, I'll never forgive you for fetching me on this awful trip."

"Just think of your handsome Las Vegas cowboy," replied Helen.

Either this remark squelched Bo or the suggestion sufficed to reconcile her to the hardships of the ride.

Meanwhile, as they talked and maintained silence and tried to sleep, the driver of that stage kept at his task after the manner of

Western men who knew how to get the best out of horses and bad roads and distance.

By and by the stage halted again and remained at a standstill for so long, with the men whispering on top, that Helen and Bo were roused to apprehension.

Suddenly a sharp whistle came from the darkness ahead.

"Thet's Roy," said Joe Beeman in a low voice.

"I reckon. An' meetin' us so quick looks bad," replied Dorn. "Drive on, Bill."

"Mebbe it seems quick to you," muttered the driver. "But if we hain't come thirty miles, an' if thet ridge thar hasn't your turnin' off place, why I don't know nuthin'."

The stage rolled on a little farther while Helen and Bo sat clasping each other tightly, wondering with bated breath what was to be the next thing to happen.

Then once more they were at a standstill. Helen heard the *thud* of boots striking the ground and the snorts of horses.

"Nell, I see horses," whispered Bo excitedly. "There, to the side of the road . . . and here comes a man. . . . Oh! If he shouldn't be the one they're expecting!"

Helen peered out to see a tall dark form, moving silently, and beyond it a vague outline of horses, and then the pale gleam of what must have been pack loads.

Dorn loomed up and met the stranger in the road.

"Howdy, Milt. You got the girl sure or you wouldn't be here," said a low voice.

"Roy, I've got two girls . . . sisters," replied Dorn.

The man, Roy, whistled softly under his breath. Then another lean rangy form strode out of the darkness and was met by Dorn.

"Now boys . . . how about Anson's gang?" queried Dorn.

"At Snowdrop, drinkin' an' quarrelin'. Reckon they'll leave there about daybreak," replied Roy.

"How long have you been here?"

"Mebbe a couple of hours."

"Any horse go by?"

"No."

"Roy, a strange rider passed me last night before dark. He was hittin' the road. An' he's got by here before you came."

"I don't like thet news," replied Roy tersely. "Let's rustle. With girls on hossback, you'll need all the start you can get. Hey, John?"

"Snake Anson shore can foller hoss tracks," replied the third man.

"Milt, say the word," went on Roy as he looked up at the stars. "Daylight not far

101

away. Here's the forks of the road, an' your hosses, an' our outfit. You can be in the pines by sunup."

In the silence that ensued Helen heard the throb of her heart and the panting little breaths of her sister. They both peered out, hands clenched together, watching and listening in strained attention.

"It's possible that rider last night wasn't a messenger to Anson," said Dorn. "In that case Anson won't make anythin' of our wheel tracks or horse tracks. He'll go right on to meet the regular stage. Bill, can you go back an' meet the stage comin' before Anson does?"

"Wal, I reckon so . . . an' take it easy at thet," replied Bill.

"All right," continued Dorn instantly. "John, you an' Joe an' Hal ride back to meet the regular stage. An' when you meet it, get in an' be on it when Anson holds it up."

"Thet's shore agreeable to me," drawled John.

"I'd like to be on it, too," said Roy grimly.

"No, I'll need you till I'm safe in the woods. . . . Bill, hand down the bags. An' you, Roy, help me pack them. Did you get all the supplies I wanted?"

"Shore did. If the young ladies ain't powerful particular, you can feed them well for a couple of months."

Dorn wheeled, and, striding to the stage, he opened the door.

"Girls, you're not asleep? Come!" he called.

Bo stepped down first. "I was asleep till this . . . this vehicle fell off the road back a ways," she replied.

Roy Beeman's low laugh was significant. He took off his sombrero and stood silently. The old driver smothered a loud guffaw.

"Vee-hicle! Wal, I'll be dog-goned! Joe, did you hear thet? All the spunky gurls ain't born out West."

As Helen followed with cloak and bag, Roy assisted her, and she encountered keen eyes upon her face. He seemed both gentle and respectful, and she felt his solicitation. His heavy gun, swinging low, struck her as she stepped down.

Dorn reached in the stage and hauled out baskets and bags. Those he set down on the ground.

"Turn around, Bill, an' go along with you. John an' Hal will follow presently," ordered Dorn.

"Wal, gurls," said Bill, looking down upon them. "I was shore powerful glad to meet you-all. An' I'm ashamed of my country . . . offerin' two sich purty girls insults an' low-down tricks. But shore you'll go through safe now. You couldn't be in better company fer ridin' or huntin' or marryin' or gittin' religion. . . ."

"Shut up, you old grizzly," broke in Dorn sharply.

"*Haw! Haw!* Good bye, gurls, an' good luck," ended Bill as he began to whip the reins.

Bo said good bye quite distinctly, but Helen could only murmur hers. The old driver seemed a friend.

Then the horses wheeled and stamped, the stage careened and *creaked,* presently to roll out of sight in the gloom.

"You're shiverin'," said Dorn suddenly, looking down upon Helen. She felt his big hard hand clasp hers. "Cold as ice!"

"I am c-cold," replied Helen. "I guess we're not warmly dressed."

"Nell, we roasted all day and now we're freezing," declared Bo. "I didn't know it was winter at night out here."

"Miss, haven't you some warm gloves an' a coat?" asked Roy anxiously. "It ain't begun to get cold yet."

"Nell, we've heavy gloves, riding suits, and boots . . . all fine and new . . . in this black bag," said Bo, enthusiastically kicking a bag at her feet.

"Yes, so we have. But a lot of good they'll do us tonight," returned Helen.

"Miss, you'd do well to change right here," said Roy earnestly. "It'll save time in the long run an' a lot of sufferin' before sunup."

Helen stared at the young man, absolutely amazed with his simplicity. She was advised to change her traveling dress for a riding suit — out somewhere in a cold windy desert — in the middle of the night — among strange young men!

"Bo, which bag is it?" asked Dorn, as if she were his sister. And when she indicated the one, he picked it up. "Come off the road."

Bo followed him and Helen found herself mechanically at their heels. Dorn led them a few paces off the road behind some low bushes.

"Hurry an' change here," he said. "We'll make a pack of your outfit an' leave room for this bag." Then he stalked away and in few strides disappeared.

Bo sat down to begin unlacing her shoes. Helen could just see her pale pretty face and big gleaming eyes by the light of the stars. It struck her then that Bo was going to make eminently more of a success of Western life than she was.

"Nell, those fellows are n-nice," said Bo reflectively. "Aren't you c-cold? Say, he said hurry."

It was beyond Helen's comprehension how she ever began to disrobe out there in that open windy desert, but, after she had gotten launched on the task, she found that it required more fortitude than courage. The cold wind pierced right through her. Almost she could have laughed at the way Bo made things fly.

"G-g-g-gee!" chattered Bo. "I n-never w-was so c-c-cold in all my life. Nell Rayner . . . an' . . . may the g-good Lord forgive y-you!"

Helen was too intent on her new troubles to take breath to talk. She was a strong, healthy girl, swift and efficient with her hands, yet this, the hardest physical ordeal she had ever experienced, almost overcame her. Bo outdistanced her by moments, helped her with buttons, and laced one whole boot for her. Then with hands that stung, Helen packed the traveling suits in the bag.

"There! But what an awful mess!" exclaimed Helen. "Oh, Bo, our pretty traveling dresses!"

"We'll press them t-tomorrow . . . on a l-log," replied Bo, and she giggled.

They started for the road. Bo, strange to note, did not carry her share of the burden, and she seemed unsteady on her feet.

The men were waiting beside a group of horses, one of which carried a pack.

"Nothin' slow about you," said Dorn, relieving Helen of the grip. "Roy, put them up while I sling on this bag."

Roy led out two of the horses.

"Get up," he said, indicating Bo. "The stirrups are short on this saddle."

Bo was an adept at mounting, but she made so awkward and slow work of it in this instance that Helen could not believe her eyes.

"How're the stirrups?" asked Roy. "Stand in them. Guess they're about right. . . . Careful, now. Thet hoss is skitterish. Hold him in."

Bo was not living up to the reputation with which Helen had credited her.

"Now, miss, you get up," said Roy to Helen. And in another instant she found herself astride a black, spirited horse. Numb with cold as she was, she yet felt the coursing thrills along her veins.

Roy was at the stirrups, with swift hands.

"You're taller'n I guessed," he said. "Stay up, but lift your foot . . . shore now I'm glad you have them thick soft boots. Mebbe we'll ride all over the White Mountains."

"Bo, do you hear that?" called Helen.

But Bo did not answer. She was leaning rather unnaturally in her saddle. Helen became anxious. Just then Dorn strode back to them.

"All cinched up, Roy?"

"Jest ready," replied Roy.

Then Dorn stood beside Helen. How tall he was! His wide shoulders seemed on a level with the pommel of her saddle. He put an affectionate hand on the horse.

"His name's Ranger an' he's the fastest an' finest horse in this country."

"I reckon he shore is . . . along with my bay," corroborated Roy.

"Roy, if you rode Ranger, he'd beat your pet," said Dorn. "We can start now. Roy, you drive the pack horses." He took another look at Helen's saddle, and then moved to do likewise with Bo's.

"Are you . . . all right?" he asked quickly.

Bo reeled in her seat.

"I'm n-near froze," she replied in a faint voice. Her face shone white in the starlight. Helen recognized that Bo was more than cold.

"Oh, Bo!" she called in distress.

"Nell, don't you worry now."

"Let me carry you," suggested Dorn.

"No. I'll s-s-stick on this horse or d-die," fiercely retorted Bo.

The two men looked up at her white face, and then at each other. Then Roy walked away toward the dark bunch of horses off the road and Dorn swung astride the one horse left.

"Keep close to me," he said.

Bo fell in line and Helen brought up the rear.

Helen imagined she was near the end of a dream. Presently she would awaken with a start and see the pale walls of her little room at home, and hear the cherry branches brushing her windows and the old clarion-voiced cock proclaim the hour of dawn.

CHAPTER SIX

The horses trotted. And the exercise soon warmed Helen until she was fairly comfortable except in her fingers. In mind, however, she grew more miserable as she more fully realized her situation. The night now became so dark that, although the head of her horse was alongside the flank of Bo's, she could scarcely see Bo. From time to time Helen's anxious query brought from her sister the answer that she was all right.

Helen had not ridden a horse for more than a year, and for several years she had not ridden with any regularity. Despite her thrills upon mounting she had entertained misgivings. But she was agreeably surprised, for the horse, Ranger, had an easy gait and she found she had not forgotten how to ride. Bo, having been used to riding on a farm near home, might be expected to acquit herself admirably. It occurred to Helen what a job that would have been but for the thick comfortable riding outfits. The suits, like this unheard of adventure, had been ready for them.

Dark as the night was, Helen could dimly make out the road underneath. It was rocky, and apparently little used. When Dorn turned off the road into the low brush or sage of what seemed a level plain, the traveling was harder, rougher, and yet no slower. The horses kept to the gait of the leader. Helen, discovering it unnecessary, ceased attempting to guide Ranger. There were dim shapes in the gloom ahead, and always they gave Helen uneasiness until closer approach proved them to be rocks or low scrubby trees. These increased in both size and number as the horses progressed. Often Helen looked back into the gloom behind. This act was involuntary and occasioned her sensations of dread. Dorn expected to be pursued. And Helen experienced along with the dread, flashes of unfamiliar resentment. Not only was there an attempt afoot to rob her of her heritage but even her personal liberty. Then she shuddered at the significance of Dorn's words regarding her possible abduction by this hired gang. It seemed monstrous, impossible. Yet manifestly it was true enough to Dorn and his allies. The West then in reality was raw, hard, inevitable, a reality hateful to Helen.

Suddenly her horse stopped. He had come up alongside Bo's horse. Dorn had halted ahead and apparently was listening. Roy and the pack train were out of sight in the gloom.

"What is it?" whispered Helen.

"Reckon I heard a wolf," replied Dorn.

"Was that cry a wolf's?" asked Bo. "I heard. It was wild."

"We're gettin' up close to the foothills," said Dorn. "Feel how much colder the air is."

"I'm warm, too, but . . . ," Helen answered.

"If you had your choice of being here or back home, snug in bed . . . which would you take?" asked Bo.

"Bo!" exclaimed Helen, aghast.

"Well, I'd choose to be right here on this horse," rejoined Bo.

Dorn heard her, for he turned an instant, then slapped his horse and started on.

Helen now rode beside Bo, and for a long time they climbed steadily in silence. Helen knew when that dark hour before dawn had passed and she welcomed an almost imperceptible lightening in the east. Then the stars paled. Gradually a grayness absorbed all but the larger stars. The great blue white morning star, wonderful as Helen had ever seen it, lost its brilliance and life, and seemed to retreat into the dimming blue.

Daylight came gradually so that the gray desert became distinguishable by degrees. Rolling bare hills, half obscured by the gray lifting mantle of night, rose in the foreground, and behind was gray space, slowly taking form and substance. In the east there was a kindling of pale rose and silver that lengthened and brightened along a horizon growing visibly rugged.

"Reckon we'd better catch up with Roy," said Dorn, and he spurred his horse.

Ranger and Bo's mount needed no other urging, and they swung into a canter. Far ahead the pack animals showed with Roy driving them. The cold wind was so keen in Helen's face that tears blurred her eyes and froze her cheeks. And riding Ranger at that pace was like riding in a rocking chair. That ride, invigorating and exciting, seemed all too short.

"Oh, Nell, I don't care what becomes of . . . me!" exclaimed Bo breathlessly.

Her face was white and red, fresh as a rose, her eyes glanced darkly blue, her hair blew out in bright unruly strands. Helen knew she felt some of the physical stimulation that had so roused Bo, and seemed so irresistible, but somber thought was not deflected thereby.

It was clear daylight when Roy led off around a knoll from which patches of scrubby trees, cedars Dorn called them, straggled up one side of the foothills.

"The grass on the north slopes where the snow stays longest," said Dorn.

They descended into a valley that looked shallow but proved to be deep and wide, and then began to climb another foothill. Upon surmounting it, the sun had arisen and so glorious a view confronted Helen that she was unable to answer Bo's wild exclamations.

Bare yellow cedar-dotted slopes, apparently level, so gradual was the ascent, stretched away to a dense ragged line of forest that rose black over range after range, at last to fail near the bare summit of a magnificent mountain sunrise — flushed against the blue sky.

"Oh, beautiful!" cried Bo. "But they ought to be called Black Mountains."

"Old Baldy there is white half the year," replied Dorn.

"Look back an' see what you say," suggested Roy.

The girls turned to gaze silently. Helen imagined she looked down upon the whole wide world. How vastly different was the desert! Verily it yawned away from her, red and gold near at hand, growing softly flushed with purple far away, a barren void, borderless and immense, where dark green patches and black lines and upheaved ridges only served to emphasize distance and space.

"See thet little green spot," said Roy, pointing. "Thet's Snowdrop, an' the other one . . . way to the right . . . thet's Show Down."

"Where is Pine?" queried Helen eagerly.

"Farther still, up over the foothills at the edge of the woods."

"Then we're riding away from it."

"Yes. If we'd gone straight for Pine, thet gang could overtake us. Pine is four days' ride. An' by takin' to the mountain, Milt can hide his tracks. An' when he's thrown Anson off the scent, then he'll circle down to Pine."

"Mister Dorn, do you think you'll get us there safely . . . and soon?" asked Helen wistfully.

"I won't promise soon, but I promise safe. . . . An' I don't like bein' called 'mister,' " he replied.

"Are we ever going to eat?" inquired Bo demurely.

At this query Roy Beeman turned with a laugh to look at Bo. Helen saw his face fully in the light and it was thin and hard, darkly bronzed, with eyes like those of a hawk, and with square chin and lean jaws showing scant light beard.

"We shore are," he replied. "Soon as we reach the timber. Thet won't be long."

"Reckon we can rustle some, an' then take a good rest," said Dorn, and he urged his horse into a jog trot.

During a steady trot for a long hour Helen's roving eyes were everywhere, taking note of the things from near to far — the scant sage that soon gave place to as scanty a grass, and the dark blots that proved to be dwarf cedars, and the ravines opening out as if by magic from what had appeared level ground to wind away widening the gray stone walls, and, farther on, patches of lonely pine trees, two and three together, and then a straggling clump of yellow aspens, and up beyond the fringed border of forest, growing nearer all the while, the black sweeping benches rising to the noble dome of the dominant mountain of the range.

No birds or animals were seen in that long ride up toward the timber, which fact seemed strange to Helen. The air lost something of its cold cutting edge as the sun rose higher and it gained sweeter tang of forestland. The first faint suggestion of that fragrance was utterly new to Helen yet it brought a vague sensation of familiarity and with it an emotion as strange. It was as if she had smelled that keen pungent tang long ago and her physical sense caught it before her memory.

The yellow plain had only appeared to be level. Roy led down into a shallow ravine, where a tiny stream meandered, and he followed this around to the left, coming at length to a point where cedars and dwarf pines formed a little grove. Here, as the others rode up, he sat cross-legged in his saddle, and waited.

"We'll hang up a while," he said. "Reckon you're tired?"

"I'm hungry, but not tired yet," replied Bo.

Helen dismounted to find that walking was something she had apparently lost the power to do. Bo laughed at her, but she, too, was awkward when once more upon the ground.

Then Roy got down. Helen was surprised to find him lame. He caught her quick glance.

"A hoss threw me once an' rolled on me.

Only broke my collarbone, five ribs, one arm, an' my bowlegs in two places!"

Notwithstanding this evidence that he was a cripple as he stood there tall and lithe in his homespun ragged garments, he looked singularly powerful and capable.

"Reckon walkin' around would be good for you girls," advised Dorn. "If you ain't stiff yet, you'll be soon. An' walkin' will help. Don't go far. I'll call when breakfast's ready."

A little while later the girls were whistled in from their walk and found campfire and meal awaiting them. Roy was sitting cross-legged like an Indian in front of a tarpaulin upon which was spread a homely but substantial fare. Helen's quick eye detected a cleanliness and thoroughness she had scarcely expected to find in the camp cooking of men of the wilds. Moreover the fare was good. She ate heartily, and as for Bo's appetite she was inclined to be as much ashamed of that as amused at it. The young men were all eyes, assiduous in their service to the girls, but speaking seldom. It was not lost upon Helen how Dorn's gray gaze went often down across the open country. She divined apprehension from it rather than saw much expression in it.

"I . . . declare," burst out Bo, when she could not eat any more, "this isn't believable. I'm dreaming. . . . Nell, the black horse you rode is the prettiest I ever saw."

Ranger, with the other animals, was grazing along the little brook. Packs and saddles had been removed. The men sat leisurely. There was little evidence of hurried flight. Yet Helen could not cast off uneasiness. Roy might have been deep and careless with a motive to spare the girls anxiety, but Dorn seemed incapable of anything he did not absolutely mean.

"Rest or walk," he advised the girls. "We've got forty miles to ride before dark."

Helen preferred to rest, but Bo walked about, petting the horses and prying into the packs. She was curious and eager.

Dorn and Roy talked in low tones while they cleaned up the utensils and packed them away in a heavy canvas bag.

"You really expect Anson'll strike my trail this mornin'?" Dorn was asking.

"I shore do," replied Roy.

"An' how do you figure that so soon?"

"How'd you figure it . . . if you was Snake Anson?" queried Roy in reply.

"Depends on that rider from Magdalena," said Dorn soberly. "Although it's likely I'd've seen them wheel tracks an' hoss

119

tracks made where we turned off. But sup-posin' he does."

"Milt, listen. I told you Snake met us boys face to face day before yesterday in Show Down. An' he was plumb curious."

"But he missed seein' or hearin' about me," replied Dorn.

"Mebbe he did an' mebbe he didn't. Anyway what's the difference whether he finds out this mornin' or this evenin'?"

"Then you ain't expectin' a fight if Anson holds up the stage?"

"Wal, he'd have to shoot first, which ain't likely. John an' Hal, since thet shootin' scrape a year ago, have been sort of gun shy. Joe might get riled. . . . But I reckon the best we can be shore of is a delay. An' it'd be sense not to count on thet."

"Then you hang up here an' keep watch for Anson's gang . . . say long enough so's to be sure they'd be in sight if they find our tracks this mornin'. Makin' sure one way or another, you ride cross-country to Big Spring, where I'll camp tonight."

Roy nodded approval of that suggestion. Then without more words both men picked up ropes and went after the horses. Helen was watching Dorn so that, when Bo cried out in great excitement, Helen turned to see a savage yellow little mustang standing straight up on his hind legs and pawing the air. Roy had roped him and was now dragging him into camp.

"Nell, look at that for a wild pony!" exclaimed Bo.

Helen busied herself getting well out of the way of the infuriated mustang. Roy dragged him to a cedar nearby.

"Come now, Buckskin," said Roy soothingly, and he slowly approached the quivering animal. He went closer, hand over hand on the lasso. Buckskin showed the whites of his eyes and also his white teeth. But he stood while Roy loosened the loop and, slipping it down over his head, fastened it in a complicated knot around his nose.

"Thet's a hackamore," he said, indicating the knot. "He's never had a bridle an' never will have one, I reckon."

"You don't ride him?" queried Helen.

"Sometimes I do," replied Roy with a smile. "Would you girls like to try him?"

"Excuse me," answered Helen.

"Gee!" ejaculated Bo. "He looks like a devil. But I'd tackle him . . . if you think I could."

The wild leaven of the West had found quick root in Bo Rayner.

"Wal, I'm sorry, but I reckon I'll not let you . . . for a spell," replied Roy dryly. "He

121

pitches somethin' powerful bad."

"Pitches. You mean bucks."

"I reckon. . . . I was afraid he'd run off with you-all when you start."

In the next half hour Helen saw more and learned more about how horses of the open range were handled than she had ever heard of. Excepting Ranger, and Roy's bay, and the white pony Bo rode, the rest of the horses had actually to be roped and hauled in to camp to be saddled and packed. It was a job for fearless strong men, and one that called for patience as well as arms of iron. So that for Helen Rayner the thing succeeding the confidence she had placed in these men was respect. In an observing woman that half hour told much.

When all was in readiness for a start, Dorn mounted and said significantly: "Roy, I'll look for you about sundown. I hope no sooner."

"Wal, it'd be bad if I had to rustle along soon with bad news. Let's hope for the best. We've been shore lucky so far. Now you take to the pine mats in the woods an' hide your trail."

Dorn turned away. Then the girls bade Roy good bye and followed. Soon Roy and his buckskin-colored mustang were lost to sight round a clump of trees.

The unhampered horses led the way, scattered somewhat; the pack animals trotted after them, and the riders were close behind. All traveled at a jog trot. And this gait made the packs bob up and down and from side to side. The sun fell warmly at Helen's back and the wind lost its frosty coldness that almost appeared damp, for a dry sweet fragrance. Dorn drove up the shallow valley that showed timber on the levels above, and a black border of timber some few miles ahead. It did not take long to reach the edge of the forest.

Helen wondered why the big pines grew so far on that plain and no farther. Probably the growth had to do with snow, but as the ground was level she could not see why the edge of the woods should have come just there.

They rode into the forest.

To Helen it seemed a strange critical entrance into another world that she was destined to know and to love. The pines were big, brown-barked, seamed, and knotted, with no typical conformation except a majesty and beauty. They grew far apart. Few small pines and little underbrush flourished beneath them. The floor of this forest appeared remarkable in that it consisted of patches of high silvery grass and wide brown areas of pine needles. These manifestly were what Roy had meant by pine mats. Here and there a fallen monarch lay riven or rotting. Helen was presently struck with the silence of the forest and the strange fact that the horses seldom made any sound at all, and, when they did, it was a *cracking* of dead twig or *thud* of hoof on log. Likewise she became aware of a springy nature of the ground. And then she saw that the pine mats gave like rubber cushions under the hoofs of the horses and, after they had passed, sprang back to place again leaving no track. Helen could not see a sign of a trail they left behind. Indeed, it would take a sharp eye to follow Dorn through that forest. This knowledge was infinitely comforting to Helen, and for the first time since the flight had begun she felt a loosening of a weight upon mind and heart. It left her free for some of the appreciation she might have had in this wonderful ride under happier circumstances.

Bo, however, seemed too young, too wild, too intense to mind what the circumstances were. She responded to reality. Helen began to suspect that the girl would welcome any adventure, and Helen knew surely now that Bo was a true Auchincloss. For three long days Helen had felt a constraint with which

124

heretofore she had been unfamiliar, and for the last hours it had been submerged under dread. But it must be, she concluded, blood like her sister's, pounding at her veins to be set free, to race and to burn.

Bo loved action. She had an eye for beauty, but she was not contemplative. She was now helping Dorn drive the horses and hold them in rather close formation. She rode well and as yet showed no symptoms of fatigue or pain. Helen began to be aware of both, but not enough yet to limit her interest.

A wonderful forest without birds did not seem real to her. Of all living creatures in Nature, Helen liked birds best and she knew many and could imitate the songs of a few. But here under the stately pines there were no birds. Squirrels, however, began to be seen here and there and, in the course of an hour's travel, became abundant. The only one with which she was familiar was the chipmunk. All the others from the slim bright blacks to the striped russets and the white-tailed grays were totally new to her. They appeared tame and curious. The reds barked and scolded at the passing cavalcade; the blacks glided to some safe branch, there to watch; the grays paid no especial heed to this invasion of their domain.

Once, Dorn, halting his horse, pointed with long arm, and Helen, following the direction, descried several gray deer standing in a glade, motionless, with long ears up. They made a wild and beautiful picture. Suddenly they bounded away with remarkable, springy strides.

The forest on the whole held to the level open character, but there were swales and streambeds breaking up its regular conformity. Toward noon, however, it gradually changed, a fact that Helen believed she might have observed sooner had she been more keen. The general lay of the land began to ascend and the trees to grow denser.

She made another discovery. Ever since she had entered the forest, she had been aware of a fullness in her head and a something affecting her nostrils. She imagined, with regret, that she had taken cold. But presently her head cleared somewhat and she realized that the thick pine odor of the forest had clogged her nostrils as if with a sweet pitch. The smell was overpowering, and disagreeable because of its strength. Also, her throat and lungs seemed to burn.

When she began to lose interest in the forest and all pertaining to it, that regretful fact, she ascertained, owed its origin to aches and pains that would no longer be denied recognition. Thereafter she was not permitted to forget them and they grew worse. One especially was a pain beyond all her experience. It lay in the muscles of her side, above her hip, and it grew to be a treacherous thing. For it was not persistent. It came and went. After it did, she, with a terrible flash, found it could be borne by shifting or easing the body. But it gave no warning. When she expected it, she was mistaken; when she dared to breathe again, then, with piercing swiftness, it returned like a blade in her side. This then was one of the riding pains that made a victim of a tenderfoot on a long ride. It was almost too much to be borne. Presently to bear it any longer was not possible. She would fall off the horse and walk. The beauty of the forest, the living creatures to be seen scurrying away, the time, distance — everything faded before that stab-like pain. To her infinite relief she found that it was the trot that caused this torture. When Ranger walked, she did not have to suffer it. Thereupon she held him to a walk as long as she dared or until Dorn and Bo were almost out of sight, then she loped him ahead until he had caught up.

So the hours passed, the sun got around

low, sending golden shafts under the trees, and the forest gradually changed to a brighter, but a thicker color. This slowly darkened. Sunset was not far away.

She heard the horses splashing in water, and soon she rode up to see tiny streams of crystal water running swiftly over beds of green moss. She crossed a number of these and followed along the last one into a more open place in the forest where the pines were huge, towering, and far apart. A low gray bluff of stone rose to the right, perhaps one third as high as the trees. From somewhere came the rushing sound of running water.

"Big Spring," announced Dorn. "We camp here. You girls have done well."

Another glance proved to Helen that all those little streams poured from under this gray bluff.

"I'm dying for a drink!" cried Bo with her customary hyperbole.

"I reckon you'll never forget your first drink here," remarked Dorn.

Bo essayed to dismount and finally almost fell off, and, when she did get to the ground, her legs appeared to refuse their natural function and she fell flat. Dorn helped her up.

"What's wrong with me anyhow?" she

demanded in great amaze.

"Just stiff, I reckon," replied Dorn as he led her a few awkward steps.

"Bo, have you any hurts?" queried Helen, who still sat her horse, loath to try dismounting, yet wanting to beyond all words.

Bo gave her an eloquent glance. "Nell, did you have one in your side, like a wicked long darning needle, punching deep when you weren't ready?"

"That one I'll never get over!" exclaimed Helen softly. Then profiting by Bo's experience she dismounted cautiously and managed to keep upright. Her legs felt like wooden things.

Presently the girls went toward the spring.

"Drink slow!" called out Dorn.

Big Spring had its source somewhere deep inside the gray weathered bluff, from which came a hollow subterranean gurgle and roar of water. The fountainhead must have been a great well rushing up though the cold stone.

Helen and Bo lay flat on a mossy bank, seeing their faces as they bent over, and they sipped a mouthful, by Dorn's advice, and because they were so hot and parched and burning that they wanted to tarry a moment with a precious opportunity.

The water was so cold that it sent a shock

over Helen, made her teeth ache, and a singular revivifying current steal all through her, wonderful in its cool absorption of that dry heat of flesh, irresistible in its appeal to thirst. Helen raised her head to look at this water. It was colorless as she had found it tasteless.

"Nell . . . drink!" panted Bo. "Think of our . . . old spring . . . in the orchard . . . full of pollywogs!"

And then Helen drank thirstily, with closed eyes, while a memory of home stirred from Bo's gift of poignant speech.

CHAPTER SEVEN

The first camp duty Dorn performed was to throw a pack off one of the horses, and, opening it, he took out tarpaulin and blankets that he arranged on the ground under a pine tree.

"You girls rest," he said briefly.

"Can't we help?" asked Helen, although she could scarcely stand.

"You'll be welcome to do all you like after you're broke in."

"Broke in!" ejaculated Bo with a little laugh. "I'm all broke *up* now."

"Bo, it looks as if Mister Dorn expects us to have quite a stay with him in the woods."

"It does," replied Bo as slowly she sat down upon the blankets, stretched out with a long sigh, and laid her head on a saddle. "Nell, didn't he say not to call him mister?"

Dorn was throwing the packs off the other horses.

Helen lay down beside Bo and then for

once in her life she experienced the sweetness of rest.

"Well, Sister, what do you intend to call him?" queried Helen curiously.

"Milt, of course," replied Bo.

Helen had to laugh despite her weariness and aches.

"I suppose then . . . when your Las Vegas cowboy comes along, you will call him what he called you."

Bo blushed, which was a rather unusual thing for her. "I will if I like," she retorted. "Nell, ever since I could remember, you've raved about the West. Now you're *out* West, right in it, good and deep. So wake up!"

That was Bo's blunt and characteristic way of advising the elimination of Helen's superficialities. It sank deep. Helen had no retort. Her ambition, as far as the West was concerned, had most assuredly not been for such a wild unheard of jaunt as this. But possibly the West — a living from day to day — was one succession of adventures, trials, tests, troubles, and achievements. To make a place for others to live comfortably someday. That might be Bo's meaning, embodied in her forceful hint. But — Helen was too tired to think it out then. She found it interesting, and vaguely pleasant to watch Dorn.

He hobbled the horses and turned them loose. Then with axe in hand he approached a short dead tree standing among a few white-barked aspens. This dead stub was black, showing that fire had visited the forest. Dorn appeared to advantage swinging the axe. With his coat off, displaying his wide shoulders, straight back, and long powerful arms, he looked a young giant. He was lithe and supple, brawny but not bulky. The axe rang on the hard wood, reverberating through the forest. A few strokes sufficed to bring down the stub. Then he split it up. Helen was curious to see how he kindled a fire. First he ripped splinters out of the heart of the log, and laid them with coarser pieces on the ground. Then from saddlebag, which hung on a nearby branch, he took flint and steel, and a piece of what Helen supposed was rag or buckskin upon which powder had been rubbed. At any rate the first strike of the steel brought sparks, a blaze, and burning splinters. He put on larger pieces of wood, crosswise, and the fire roared.

That done, he stood erect, and, facing the north, he listened. Helen remembered now that she had seen him do the same thing twice before, since the arrival at Big Spring. It was Roy for whom he was listening and

133

watching. The sun had set and across the open space the tips of the pines were all losing their brightness.

The camp utensils, which the hunter emptied out of a sack, gave forth a *jangle* of iron and tin. Next he unrolled a large pack, the contents of which appeared to be numerous packs of all sizes. These evidently contained food supplies. The bucket looked as if a horse had rolled over it, pack and all. Dorn filled it at the spring. Upon returning to the campfire, he poured water into a wash basin and, getting down to his knees, proceeded to wash his hands thoroughly. The act seemed a habit, for Helen saw that, while he was doing it, he gazed off into the woods and listened. Then he dried his hands over the fire, and, turning to the spread-out pack, he began preparations for the meal.

Suddenly Helen thought of the man, and all that his actions implied. At Magdalena, on the stage ride, and last night, she had trusted this stranger, a hunter of the White Mountains, who appeared ready to befriend her. And she had felt an exceeding gratitude. Still she had looked at him impersonally. But it began to dawn upon her that chance had thrown her in the company of a remarkable man. That impression baffled her. It did not spring from the fact that he was brave and kind to help a young woman in peril, or that he appeared deft and quick at campfire chores. Most Western men were brave, her uncle had told her, and many were roughly kind, and all of them could cook. This hunter was physically a wonderful specimen of manhood with something leonine about his stature. But that did not give rise to her impression. Helen had been a schoolteacher and used to boys, and she sensed a boyish simplicity or vigor, a freshness in this hunter. She believed, however, that it was a mental and spiritual force in Dorn that had drawn her to think of it.

"Nell, I've spoken to you three times," protested Bo petulantly. "What're you mooning over?"

"I'm pretty tired . . . and far away, Bo," replied Helen. "What did you say?"

"I said I had an e-normous appetite."

"Really. That's not remarkable for you. I'm too tired to eat. And afraid to shut my eyes. They'd never come open. When did we sleep last, Bo?"

"Second night before we left home," declared Bo.

"Four nights! Oh, we've slept some."

"I'll bet I make some up in this woods. Do you suppose we'll sleep right here . . . right under this tree . . . with no covering?"

"It looks so," replied Helen dubiously.

"How perfectly lovely!" exclaimed Bo in delight. "We'll see the stars through the pines."

"Seems to be clouding over. Wouldn't it be awful if we had a storm?"

"Why, I don't know," answered Bo thoughtfully. "It must storm out West."

Again Helen felt a quality of inevitableness in Bo. It was something that had appeared only practical in the humdrum home life in St. Joseph. All of a sudden Helen received a flash of wondering thought, a thrilling consciousness that she and Bo had begun to develop in a new and wild environment. How strange, and fearful, perhaps, to watch that growth! Bo, being younger, more impressionable, with elemental rather than intellectual instincts, would grow stronger more swiftly. Helen wondered if she could yield to her own leaning to the primitive. But how could anyone with a thoughtful and grasping mind yield that way? It was the savage who did not think.

Helen saw Dorn stand erect once more and gaze into the forest.

"Reckon Roy ain't comin'," he soliloquized. "An' that's good." Then he turned to the girls. "Supper's ready."

The girls responded with a spirit greater

than their activity. And they ate like famished children that had been lost in the woods. Dorn attended them with a pleasant light upon his still face.

"Tomorrow night we'll have meat," he said.

"What kind?" asked Bo.

"Wild turkey or deer. Maybe both, if you like. But it's well to take wild meat slow. An' turkey . . . that'll melt in your mouth."

"Nummm," murmured Bo greedily. "I've heard of wild turkey."

When they had finished, Dorn ate his meal, listening to the talk of the girls and occasionally replying briefly to some query of Bo's. It was twilight when he began to wash the pots and pans, and almost dark by the time his duties appeared ended. Then he replenished the campfire and sat down on a log to gaze into the flames. The girls leaned comfortably propped against the saddles.

"Nell, I'll keel over in a minute," said Bo. "And I oughtn't . . . right on such a big supper."

"I don't see how I can sleep and I know I can't stay awake," rejoined Helen.

Dorn lifted his head alertly. "Listen."

The girls grew tense and still. Helen could not hear a sound, unless it was a low *thud* of hoof out in the gloom. The forest seemed sleeping. She knew from Bo's eyes, wide and shining in the campfire light, that she, too, had failed to catch whatever it was Dorn meant.

"Bunch of coyotes comin'," he explained.

Suddenly the quietness split to a chorus of snappy high-strung strange barks. They sounded wild, yet they held something of a friendly or inquisitive note. Presently gray forms could be descried just at the edge of the circle of light. Soft rustlings of stealthy feet surrounded the camp, and then barks and yelps broke out all around. It was a restless and sneaking pack of animals, thought Helen, and she was glad after the chorus ended, and, with a few desultory spiteful yelps, the coyotes went away.

Silence again settled down. If it had not been for the anxiety always present in Helen's mind, she would have thought this silence sweet and unfamiliarly beautiful.

"*Ah!* Listen to that fellow," spoke up Dorn. His voice was thrilling.

Again the girls strained their ears. That was not necessary, for presently, clear and cold out of the silence, pealed a mournful howl, long drawn, strange and full and wild.

"Oh! What's that?" whispered Bo.

"That's a big gray wolf . . . a timber wolf,

or loafer as he's sometimes called," replied Dorn. "He's high on some rocky ridge back there. He scents us an' he doesn't like it. . . . There he goes again. Listen. *Ah,* he's hungry."

While Helen listened to this exceedingly wild cry — so wild that it made her flesh creep and the most indescribable sensations of loneliness come over her — she kept her glance upon Dorn.

"You love him?" she murmured involuntarily, quite without understanding the motive of her query.

Assuredly Dorn had never had that question asked of him before, and it seemed to Helen, as he pondered, that he had never even asked it of himself.

"I reckon so," he replied presently.

"But wolves kill deer . . . and little fawns . . . and everything helpless in the forest," expostulated Bo.

The hunter nodded his head.

"Why then can you love him?" repeated Helen.

"Come to think of it, I reckon it's because of lots of reasons," returned Dorn. "He kills clean. He eats no carrion. He's no coward. He fights. He dies game. . . . An' he likes to be alone."

"Kills clean. What do you mean by that?"

"A cougar now, he mangles a deer. An' a silvertip, when killin' a cow or colt, he makes a mess of it. But a wolf kills clean, with sharp snaps."

"What are a cougar and a silvertip?"

"Cougar means mountain lion or panther, an' a silvertip is a grizzly bear."

"Oh, they're all cruel!" exclaimed Helen, shrinking.

"I reckon. Often I've shot wolves for re-layin' a deer."

"What's that?"

"Sometimes two or more wolves will run a deer, an', while one of them rests, the other will drive the deer around to his pardner, who'll take up the chase. That way they run the deer down. Cruel it is. But *Nature.* An' no worse than snow an' ice that starve deer, or a fox that kills turkey chicks breakin' out of the egg, or ravens that pick the eyes out of newborn lambs an' wait till they die. An' for that matter men are crueler than beasts of prey, for men add to Nature, an' have more than instincts."

Helen was silenced, as well as shocked. She had not only learned a new and striking point in natural history, but a clear intimation of the reason why she had vaguely imagined or divined a remarkable character in this man. A hunter was one

140

who killed animals for their fur, for their meat or horns, or for some lust for blood — that was Helen's definition of a hunter, and she believed it was held by the majority of people living in settled states. But the majority might be wrong. A hunter might be vastly different, and vastly more than a tracker and slayer of game. The mountain world of forest was a mystery to almost all men. Perhaps Dorn knew its secrets, its life, its terror, its beauty, its sadness and joy, and, if so, how full, how wonderful must be his mind! He spoke of men as no better than wolves. Could a lonely life in the wilderness teach a man that? Bitterness, envy, jealousy, spite, greed, and hate — these had no place in this hunter's heart. It was not Helen's shrewdness, but a woman's intuition that divined that.

Dorn rose to his feet and, turning his ear to the north, listened once more.

"Are you expecting Roy still?" inquired Helen.

"No, it ain't likely he'll turn up tonight," replied Dorn, and then he strode over to put a hand on the pine tree that soared above where the girls lay. His action and the way he looked up at the treetop and then at adjacent trees held more of that significance that so interested Helen.

141

"I reckon he's stood there some five hundred years an' will stand through to-night," muttered Dorn.

This pine was the monarch of that wide-spread group.

"Listen again," said Dorn.

Bo was asleep. And Helen, listening, at once caught a low distant roar.

"Wind. It's goin' to storm," explained Dorn. "You'll hear somethin' worthwhile. But don't be scared. Reckon we'll be safe. Pines blow down often. But this fellow will stand any fall wind that ever was. . . . Better slip under the blankets so I can pull the tarp up."

Helen slid down, just as she was, fully dressed except for boots, which she and Bo had removed, and she laid her head close to Bo's upon the saddle that served as pillow. Dorn pulled the tarpaulin up and folded it back just below their heads.

"When it rains, you'll wake, an' then just pull the tarp up over you," he said.

"Will it rain?" Helen asked. But she was thinking that this moment was the strangest that had ever happened to her. By the light of the campfire she saw Dorn's face, just as usual, still, darkly serene, expressing no thought. He was kind, but he was not thinking of these sisters as girls, alone with him in a pitch-black forest, helpless and defenseless. He did not seem to be thinking at all. But Helen had never before in her life been so keenly susceptible to experience.

"I'll be close by an' keep the fire goin' all night," he said.

She heard him stride off into the darkness. Presently there came a dragging, bumping sound, then a *crash* of a log dropped upon the fire. A cloud of sparks shot up, and many pattered down to *hiss* upon the damp ground. Smoke again curled upward along the great seamed tree trunk, and flames sputtered and crackled.

Helen listened again for the roar of wind. It seemed to come on a breath of air that fanned her cheek and softly blew Bo's curls, and it was stronger. But it died out presently only to come again, and still stronger. Helen realized then that the sound was that of an approaching storm. Her heavy eyelids almost refused to stay open, and she knew, if she let them close, she would instantly drop to sleep. And she wanted to hear the storm wind in the pines.

A few drops of cold rain fell upon her face, thrilling her with the proof that no roof stood between her and the elements. Then a breeze bore the smell of burned wood into her face, and somehow her quick mind flew to girlhood days, when she burned brush and leaves with her little brothers. The memory faded. The roar that had seemed distant was now back in the forest, coming swiftly, increasing in volume. Like a stream in flood it bore down. Helen grew amazed, startled. How rushing, oncoming, and heavy this storm wind! She likened its approach to the tread of an army. Then the roar filled the forest, yet it was back there behind her. Not a pine needle quivered in the light of the campfire. But the air seemed to be oppressed with a terrible charge. The roar augmented till it was no longer a roar, but an onsweeping crash, like an ocean torrent engulfing the earth. Bo awoke to cling to Helen in fright. The deafening storm blast was upon them. Helen felt the saddle pillow was under her head. The giant pine had trembled to its very roots. That mighty fury of wind was all aloft, in the treetops. And for a long moment it bowed the forest under its tremendous power. Then the deafening *crash* passed to roar, and that swept on and on, lessening in volume, deepening in low detonation, at last to die in the distance.

No sooner had it died than back to the north another low roar rose and ceased and rose again. Helen lay there, whispering to Bo, and heard again the great wave of wind come and crash and cease. That was the way of this storm wind of the mountain forest.

A soft *patter* of rain on the tarpaulin warned Helen to remember Dorn's directions, and, pulling up the heavy covering, she arranged it hood-like over the saddle. Then with Bo close and warm beside her she closed eyes that shut as if waxed tight, and the sense of the black forest and the wind and rain faded. Last of all sensations was the smell of smoke that blew under the tarpaulin.

When she opened her eyes, she remembered everything as if only a moment had elapsed. But it was daylight, although gray and cloudy. The pines were dripping mist. A fire *crackled* cheerily and blew curled smoke upward and a savory odor of hot coffee hung in the air. Horses were standing nearby, biting and kicking at each other. Bo was sound asleep. Dorn appeared busy around the campfire. As Helen watched the hunter, she saw him pause in his task, turn his ear to listen, and then look expectantly. And at that juncture a shout pealed from the forest. Helen recognized Roy's voice. Then she heard a splashing of water, and hoof beats coming closer. With that the buckskin mustang trotted into camp carrying Roy.

"Bad mornin' for ducks but good for us!" he called.

"Howdy, Roy," greeted Dorn, and his gladness was unmistakable. "I was lookin' for you."

Roy appeared to slide off the mustang without effort, and his swift hands slapped the straps as he unsaddled. Buckskin was wet with sweat and foam mixed with rain. He heaved and steam rose from him.

"Must have rode hard," observed Dorn.

"I shore did," replied Roy. Then he espied Helen, who had sat up, with hands to her hair, and eyes staring at him. " 'Mornin', miss. It's good news."

"Thank heaven," murmured Helen, and then she shook Bo. That young lady awoke but was loath to give up slumber. "Bo! Bo! Wake up. Mister Roy is back."

Whereupon Bo sat up, disheveled and sleepy-eyed.

"Oh-h, but I ache!" she moaned. But her eyes took in the camp scene to the effect that she added: "Is breakfast ready?"

"Almost. An' flapjacks this mornin'," replied Dorn.

Bo manifested active symptoms of health in the manner with which she laced her boots. Helen got their traveling bag and

146

with this they repaired to a flat stone beside the spring, not, however, out of earshot of the men.

"How long are you goin' to hang around camp before tellin' me?" inquired Dorn.

"Jest as I figgered, Milt," replied Roy. "Thet rider who passed you was a messenger to Anson. He an' his gang got on our trail quick. About ten o'clock I seen them comin'. Then I lit out for the woods. I stayed off in the woods close enough to see where they come in. An' shore they lost your trail. Then they spread through the woods workin' off to the south, thinkin' of course thet you would circle around to Pine on the south side of Old Baldy. There ain't a hoss tracker in Snake Anson's gang, thet's shore. Wal, I follered them for an hour till they'd rustled some miles off our trail. Then I went back to where you struck into the woods. An' I waited there all afternoon till dark, expectin' mebbe they'd back trail. But they didn't. I rode on a ways an' camped in the woods till jest before daylight."

"So far so good," declared Dorn.

"Shore. There's enough rough country south of Baldy an' along the two or three trails Anson an' his outfit will camp, you bet."

"It ain't to be thought of," muttered

Dorn, at some idea that had struck him.

"What ain't?"

"Goin' around the north side of Baldy."

"It shore ain't," rejoined Roy bluntly.

"Then I've got to hide tracks certain . . . rustle to my camp an' stay there till you say it's safe to risk takin' the girls to Pine?"

"Milt, you're talkin' the wisdom of the prophets."

"I ain't so sure we can hide tracks altogether. If Anson had any eyes for the woods, he'd not have lost me so soon."

"No. But you see he's figgerin' to cross your trail."

"If I could get fifteen or twenty mile farther on an' hide tracks certain, I'd feel safe from pursuit anyway," said the hunter reflectively.

"Shore is easy," responded Roy quickly. "I jest met up with some greaser sheepherders drivin' a big flock. They've come up from the south an' are goin' to fatten up at those Turkey *Parques*. Then they'll drive back south an' go on to Phoenix. Wal, you break camp quick an' make a plain trail out to thet sheep trail as if you was travelin' south. But, instead, you ride around ahead of thet flock of sheep. They'll keep to the open parks an' the trails through them necks of woods out here. An' passin' over your tracks they'll sure hide 'em."

"But supposin' Anson circles an' hits this camp. He'll track me easy out of that sheep trail. What then?"

"Jest what you want. Goin' south thet sheep trail is downhill an' muddy. It's goin' to rain hard. Your tracks would get washed out even if you did go south. An' Anson would keep on thet way till he was clear off the scent. Leave it to me, Milt. You're a hunter. But I'm a hoss tracker."

"All right. We'll rustle."

Then he called the girls to hurry.

CHAPTER EIGHT

Once astride the horse again Helen had to congratulate herself upon not being as crippled as she had imagined. Indeed, Bo made all the audible complaints.

Both girls had long waterproof coats, brand new, and of which they were considerably proud. New clothes had not been a common event in their lives.

"Reckon I'll have to slit these," Dorn had said, whipping out a huge knife.

"What for?" had been Bo's feeble protest.

"They wasn't made for ridin'. An' you'll get wet enough even if I do cut them. An' if I don't, you'll get soaked."

"Go ahead," had been Helen's reluctant permission.

So their long new coats were slit halfway up the back. The exigency of the case was manifest to Helen, when she saw how they came down over the cantles of the saddles and to their boot tops.

The morning was gray, and cold. A fine misty rain fell and the trees dripped steadily. Helen was surprised to see the open country again and that apparently they were to leave the forest behind for a while. The country was wide and flat on the right, and to the left it rolled and heaved along a black scalloped timberline. Above this bordering of the forest, low drifting clouds obscured the mountains. The wind was at Helen's back and seemed to be growing stronger. Dorn and Roy were ahead, traveling at a good trot, with the pack animals bunched before them. Helen and Bo had enough to do to keep up.

The first hour's ride brought little change in weather or scenery, but it gave Helen an inkling of what she must endure, if they kept that up all day. She began to welcome the places where the horses walked, but she disliked the levels. As for the descents, she hated those. Ranger would not go down slowly and the shake-up she received was unpleasant. Moreover, the spirited black horse insisted on jumping the ditches and washes. He sailed over them like a bird. Helen could not acquire the knack of sitting the saddle properly, and so, not only was her person bruised on these occasions, but her feelings were hurt. Helen had never before been conscious of vanity. Still she had never rejoiced in looking at a disadvantage, and her exhibitions here must have been frightful. Bo always would forge to the front, and she seldom looked back, facts for which Helen was grateful.

Before long they struck into a broad muddy belt full of innumerable small hoof tracks. This then was the sheep trail Roy had advised following. They rode upon it for three or four miles, and at length, coming to a gray-green valley, they saw a huge flock of sheep. Soon the air was full of bleats and *baas* as well as the odor of sheep, and a low soft roar of pattering hoofs. The flock held a compact formation, covering several acres, and grazed along rapidly. There were three herders on horses and several pack burros. Dorn engaged one of the Mexicans in conversation, and passed something to him, then pointed northward and down along the trail. The Mexican grinned from ear to ear, and Helen caught the quick: *"¡Sí, señor! Gracias, señor."* It was a pretty sight, that flock of sheep, as it rolled along, like a rounded woolly stream of grays and browns and here and there a black. They were keeping to a trail over the flats. Dorn headed into this trail, and, if anything, trotted a little faster.

Presently the clouds lifted and broke, showing blue sky, and one streak of sunshine. But the augury was without warrant. The wind increased. A huge black pall bore down from the mountains and it brought rain that could be seen falling in sheets from above and approaching like a swiftly moving wall. Soon it enveloped the fugitives.

With head bowed, Helen rode along for what seemed ages in a cold gray rain that blew almost on a level. Finally the heavy downpour passed, leaving a fine mist. The clouds scurried, low and dark, hiding the mountains altogether and making the gray wet plain a dreary sight. Helen's feet and knees were as wet as if she had waded in water. And they were cold. Her gloves, too, had not been intended for rain and they were wet through. The cold bit at her fingers so that she had to beat her hands together. Ranger misunderstood this to mean that he was to trot faster, which event was worse for Helen than freezing.

She saw another black scudding mass of clouds bearing down with its trailing sheets of rain, and this one appeared streaked with white. Snow! The wind was now piercingly cold. Helen's body kept warm, but her extremities and ears began to suffer exceedingly. She gazed ahead grimly. There was no help. She had to go on. Dorn and Roy were hunched down in their saddles, probably wet through, for they wore no rain-proof coats. Bo kept close behind them and plain it was that she felt the cold.

This second storm was not so bad as the first, because there was less rain. Still the icy keenness of the wind bit into the marrow. It lasted for an hour, during which the horses trotted on, trotted on. Again the gray torrent roared away, the fine mist blew, the clouds lifted and separated, and, closing again, darkened for another onslaught. This one brought sleet. The driving pellets stung Helen's neck and cheeks, and for a while they fell so thick and so hard upon her back that she was afraid she could not hold up under them. The bare places on the ground showed a sparkling coverlet of marbles of ice.

Thus storm after storm rolled over Helen's head. Her feet grew numb and ceased to hurt. But her fingers, because of her ceaseless efforts to keep up the circulation, retained the stinging pain. And now the wind pierced right through her. She marveled at her endurance, and there were many times that she believed she could not ride farther. Yet she kept on. All the winters she had ever lived had not brought such a day as this. Hard and cold, wet and windy, at an increasing elevation — that was the explanation. The air did not have sufficient oxygen for her blood.

Still, during all those interminable hours, Helen watched where she was traveling, and, if she ever returned over that trail, she would recognize it. The afternoon appeared far advanced when Dorn and Roy led down into an immense basin where a reedy lake spread over the flats. They rode along its margin, splashing up to the knees of the horses. Cranes and herons flew on with lumbering motion; flocks of duck winged swift flight from one side to the other. Beyond this depression the land sloped rather abruptly; outcroppings of rock circled along the edge of the highest ground, and again a dark fringe of trees appeared.

How many miles? wondered Helen. They seemed as many and as long as the hours. But at last, just as another hard rain came, the pines were reached. They proved to be widely scattered and afforded little protection from the storm.

Helen sat her saddle, a dead weight. Whenever Ranger quickened his gait or crossed a ditch, she held onto the pommel to keep from falling off. Her mind harbored only sensations of misery, and a persistent thought: why did she ever leave home for the West? Her solicitude for Bo had been forgotten. Nevertheless, any marked change in the topography of the country was registered, perhaps photographed in her memory by the torturing vividness of her experience.

The forest grew more level and denser. Shadows of twilight or gloom lay under the trees. Presently Dorn and Roy disappeared, going downhill, and likewise Bo. Then Helen's ears suddenly filled with a roar of rapid water. Ranger trotted faster. Soon Helen came to the edge of a great valley, black and gray, so full of obscurity that she could not see across or down into it. But she knew there was a rushing river at the bottom. The sound was deep, continuous, a heavy murmuring roar, singularly musical. The trail was steep. Helen had not lost all feeling as she had believed and hoped. Her poor mistreated body still responded excruciatingly to concussions, jars, wrenches, and all the other horrible movements making up a horse trot.

For long Helen did not look up. When she did so, there lay a green willow-bordered treeless space at the bottom of the valley through which a brown-white stream rushed with steady ear-filling roar.

Dorn and Roy drove the pack animals

across the stream and followed, going deep to the flanks of their horses. Bo rode into the foaming water as if she had been used to it all her days. A slip, a fall would have meant that Bo must drown in that mountain torrent.

Ranger trotted straight to the edge, and there, obedient to Helen's clutch on the bridle, he halted. The stream was fifty feet wide, shallow on the near side, deep on the opposite, with fast current and big waves. Helen was simply too frightened to follow.

"Let him come!" yelled Dorn. "Stick on now! Ranger!"

The big black plunged in, making the water fly. That stream was nothing for him, although it seemed impassable to Helen. She had not the strength left to lift her stirrups and the water surged over them. Ranger in two more plunges surmounted the bank, and then, trotting across the green to where the other horses stood steaming under some pines, he gave a great heave and halted.

Roy reached up to help her off.

"Thirty miles, Miss Helen," he said, and the way he spoke was a compliment.

He had to lift her off and help her to the tree where Bo leaned. Dorn had ripped off a saddle and was spreading saddle blankets on the ground under the pines.

"Nell . . . you swore . . . you loved me," was Bo's mournful greeting. The girl was pale, drawn, blue-lipped, and she could not stand up.

"Bo, I never did . . . or I'd never brought you to this . . . wretch that I am!" cried Helen. "Oh, what a horrible ride!"

Rain was falling; the trees were dripping; the sky was lowering. All the ground was soaking wet, with pools and puddles everywhere. Helen could imagine nothing but a heartless, dreary cold prospect. Just then home was vivid and poignant in her thoughts. Indeed so utterly miserable was she that the exquisite relief of sitting down, of a cessation of movement, of a release from that infernal perpetually trotting horse, seemed only a mockery. It could not be true that the time had come for rest.

Evidently this place had been a campsite for hunters or sheepherders, for there were remains of a fire. Dorn lifted the burned end of a log and brought it down hard upon the ground, splitting off pieces. Several times he did this. It was amazing to see his strength, his facility, as he split off handfuls of splinters. He collected a bundle of them, and, laying them down, he bent over them. Roy wielded the axe on another log, and each stroke split off a long strip. Then a tiny column of smoke drifted up over Dorn's shoulder as he leaned, bareheaded, sheltering the splinters with his hat. A blaze leaped up. Roy came with an armful of strips all white and dry, out of the inside of a log. Cross-wise these were laid over the blaze, and it began to roar. Then piece by piece the man built up a frame upon which they added heavier woods, branches, and stumps and logs, erecting a pyramid through which flames and smoke roared upward. It had not taken two minutes. Already Helen felt the warmth upon her icy face. She held up her bare numb hands.

Both Dorn and Roy were wet through to the skin, yet they did not tarry beside the fire. They relieved the horses. A lasso went up between two pines and a tarpaulin over it, V-shaped and pegged down at the four ends. The packs containing the baggage of the girls and the supplies and bedding were placed under this shelter.

Helen thought this might have taken five minutes more. In this short space of time the fire had leaped and flamed until it was huge and hot. Rain was falling steadily all around, but over and near that roaring blaze, ten feet high, no water fell. It evaporated. The ground began to steam and to dry. Helen suffered at first while the heat was driving out the cold. But presently the pain ceased.

"Nell, I never knew before how good a fire could feel," declared Bo.

And therein lay more food for Helen's reflection.

In ten more minutes Helen was dry and hot. Darkness came down upon the dreary sodden forest, but that great campfire made it a different world from the one Helen had anticipated. It blazed and roared, *cracked* like a pistol, *hissed* and *sputtered,* shot sparks everywhere, and sent aloft a dense yellow whirling column of smoke. It began to have a heart of gold.

Dorn took a long pole and raked out a pile of red embers upon which the coffee pot and oven soon began to steam.

"Roy, I promised the girls turkey tonight," said the hunter.

"Mebbe tomorrow, if the wind shifts. This's turkey country."

"Roy, a potato will do me!" exclaimed Bo. "Never again will I ask for cake and pie! I never appreciated good things to eat. And I've been a good little pig, always. I never . . . never knew what it was to be hungry . . . until now."

Dorn glanced up quickly.

"Lass, it's worth learnin'," he said.

Helen's thought was too deep for words. In such a brief space had she been transformed from misery to comfort.

The rain kept on falling, although it appeared to grow softer as night settled down black. The wind died away and the forest was still, except for the steady roar of the stream. A folded tarpaulin was laid between the pine and the fire, well within the light and warmth, and upon it the men set steaming pots and plates and cups the fragrance from which was strong and inviting.

"Fetch the saddle blankets an' set with your backs to the fire," said Roy.

Later, when the girls were tucked away snugly in their blankets and sheltered from the rain, Helen remained awake after Bo had fallen asleep. The big blaze made the improvised tent as bright as day. She could see the smoke, the trunk of the big pine towering aloft, and a blank space of sky. The stream hummed a song, seemingly musical at times, and then discordant and dull, now low, now roaring, and always rushing, gurgling, babbling, flowing, chafing in its hurry.

Presently the hunter and his friend returned from hobbling the horses and beside the fire they conversed in low tones.

"Wal, thet trail we made today will be hid, I reckon," said Roy with satisfaction.

"What wasn't sheeped over would be washed out. We've had luck. An' now I ain't worryin'," returned Dorn.

"Worryin'? Then it's the first I ever knowed you to do."

"Man, I never had a job like this," protested the hunter.

"Wal, thet's so."

"Now, Roy, when old Al Auchincloss finds out about this deal, as he's bound to when you or the boys get back to Pine, he's goin' to roar."

"Do you reckon folks will side with him against Beasley?"

"Some of them. But Al like as not will tell folks to go where it's hot. He'll bunch his men an' strike for the mountains to find his nieces."

"Wal, all you've got to do is to keep the girls hid till I can guide him up to your camp. Or failin' thet, till you can slip the girls down to Pine."

"No one but you an' your brothers ever seen my *parque.* But it could be found easy enough."

"Anson might blunder on it. But thet ain't likely."

"Why ain't it?"

"Because I'll stick to thet sheep thief's tracks like a wolf after a bleedin' deer. An' if he ever gets near your camp, I'll ride in ahead of him."

"Good," declared Dorn. "I was calculatin' you'd go down to Pine sooner or later."

"Not unless Anson goes. I told John thet in case there was no fight on the stage to make a beeline back to Pine. He was to tell Al an' offer his services along with Joe an' Hal."

"One way or another then there's bound to be blood spilled over this."

"Shore! An' high time. I jest hope I get a look down my old Forty-Four at thet Beasley."

"In that case I hope you hold straighter than times I've seen you."

"Milt Dorn, I'm a good shot," declared Roy stoutly.

"You're no good on movin' targets."

"Wal, mebbe so. But I'm not lookin' for a movin' target when I meet up with Beasley. I'm a hoss man, not a hunter. You're used to shootin' flies off deer's horns, jest for practice."

"Roy, can we make my camp by tomorrow night?" queried Dorn more seriously.

"We will if each of us has to carry one of

the girls. But they'll do it or die. Dorn, did you ever see a gamer girl than thet kid Bo?"

"Me! Where'd I ever see any girls?" ejaculated Dorn. "I remember some when I was a boy, but I was only fourteen then. Never had much use for girls."

"I'd like to have a wife like thet Bo," declared Roy fervidly.

There ensued a moment's silence.

"Roy, you're a Mormon an' you already got a wife," was Dorn's reply.

"Now, Milt, have you lived so long in the woods thet you never heard of a Mormon with two wives?" retorted Roy, and then he laughed heartily.

"I never could stomach what I did hear pertainin' to more than one wife for a man."

"Wal, my friend, you go an' get yourself *one*. An' see then if you wouldn't like to have *two*."

"I reckon one'd be more than enough for Milt Dorn."

"Milt, old man, let me tell you thet I always envied you your freedom," said Roy earnestly. "But it ain't life."

"You mean life is love of a woman?"

"No. Thet's only part. I mean a son . . . a boy thet's like you . . . thet you feel will go on with your life after you're gone."

"The thought of that . . . thought it all

out, watchin' the birds an' animals mate in the woods. . . . If I have no son, I'll never live hereafter."

"Wal," replied Roy hesitatingly, "I don't go in so deep as thet. I mean a son goes on with your blood an' your work."

"Exactly. . . . An', Roy, I envy you what you've got, because it's out of all bounds for Milt Dorn."

Those words, sad and deep, ended the conversation. Again the rumbling, rushing stream dominated the forest. An owl *hooted* dismally. A horse trod thuddingly nearby and from that direction came a cutting tear of teeth on grass.

A voice pierced Helen's deep dreams, and, awaking, she found Bo shaking and calling her.

"Are you dead?" came the gay voice.

"Almost. Oh, my back's broken," replied Helen. The desire to move seemed clamped in a vise, and, even if that came, she believed the effort would be impossible.

"Roy called us," said Bo. "He said hurry. I thought I'd die just sitting up, and I'd give you a million dollars to lace my boots. Wait, Sister, till you try to pull on one of those stiff boots!"

With heroic and violent spirit Helen sat

up to find that in the act her aches and pains appeared beyond number. Reaching for her boots, she found them cold and stiff. Helen unlaced one, opening it wide enough to get her sore foot down into it. But her foot appeared swollen and the boot appeared shrunken. She could not get it half on, although she expended what little strength seemed left to her aching arms. She groaned.

Bo laughed wickedly. Her hair was tousled, her eyes dancing, her cheeks red.

"Be game," she said. "Stand up like a real Western girl and *pull* your boot on."

Whether Bo's scorn or her advice made the task easier did not occur to Helen, the fact was that she got into her boots. Walking and moving a little appeared to loosen the stiff joints and ease that tired feeling. The water of the stream where the girls washed was colder than any ice Helen had ever felt. It almost paralyzed her hands. Bo mumbled, and blew like a porpoise. They had to run to the fire before being able to comb their hair. The air was wonderfully keen. The dawn was clear, bright, with a red glow in the east where the sun was about to rise.

"All ready, girls?" called Roy. "Reckon you can help yourselves. Milt ain't comin' in very fast with the hosses. I'll rustle off to help him. We've got a hard day before us. Yesterday wasn't nowhere to what today'll be."

"But the sun's going to shine!" implored Bo.

"Wal, you bet," rejoined Roy as he strode off.

Helen and Bo ate breakfast fast and had the camp to themselves for perhaps half an hour, then the horses came *thudding* down with Dorn and Roy riding bareback.

By the time all was in readiness to start, the sun was up melting the frost and ice so that a dazzling bright mist full of rainbows shone under the trees.

Dorn looked Ranger over and tried the cinches of Bo's horse. "What's your choice . . . a long ride behind the packs with me . . . or a short cut over the hills with Roy?" he asked.

"I choose the lesser of two rides," replied Helen, smiling.

"Reckon that'll be easiest, but you'll know you've had a ride," said Dorn significantly.

"What was that we had yesterday?" asked Bo archly.

"Only thirty miles, but cold an' wet. Today will be fine for ridin'?"

"Milt, I'll take a blanket an' some grub in case you don't meet us tonight," said Roy.

"An' I reckon we'll split up here where I'll have to strike out in thet short cut."

Bo mounted without a helping hand, but Helen's limbs were so stiff that she could not get astride the high Ranger without assistance. The hunter headed up the slope of the cañon which on that side was not steep. It was brown pine forest with here and there a clump of dark silver-pointed evergreens that Roy called spruce. By the time this slope was surmounted, Helen's aches were not so bad. The saddle appeared to fit her better and the gait of the horse was not so unfamiliar. She reflected, however, that she always had done pretty well uphill. Here it was beautiful forestland, uneven and wilder. They rode for a time along the rim, with the white rushing stream in plain sight far below, with its melodious roar ever thrumming in the ear.

Dorn reined in and peered down at the pine mat. "Fresh deer sign all along here," he said, pointing.

"Wal, I seen thet long ago," rejoined Roy.

Helen's scrutiny was rewarded by descrying several tiny depressions in the pine needles, dark in color and sharply defined.

"We may never get a better chance," said Dorn. "Those deer are workin' up our way. Get your rifle out."

Travel was resumed then, with Roy a little in advance of the pack train. Presently he dismounted, threw his bridle, and cautiously peered ahead. Then, turning, he waved his sombrero; the pack animals halted in a bunch. Dorn beckoned for the girls to follow and rode up to Roy's horse. This point, Helen saw, was at the top of an intersecting cañon. Dorn dismounted, without drawing his rifle from its saddle sheath, and approached Roy.

"Buck an' two deers," he said, low-voiced. "An' they've winded us, but don't see us yet. . . . Girls, ride up closer."

Following the direction indicated by Dorn's long arm, Helen looked down the slope. It was open, tall pines here and there, and clumps of silver spruce, and aspens shining like gold in the morning sunlight. Presently Bo exclaimed: "Oh, look! I see! I see!" Then Helen's roving glance passed something different from green and gold and brown. Shifting back to it, she saw a magnificent stag, with noble spreading antlers, standing like a statue, his head up in alert and wild posture. His color was gray. Beside him grazed two other deer of slighter and more graceful build, without horns.

"It's downhill," whispered Dorn. "An'

169

you're goin' to overshoot."

Then Helen saw that Roy had his rifle leveled. "Oh, don't!" she cried.

Dorn's remark evidently nettled Roy. He lowered the rifle.

"Milt, it's me lookin' over this gun. How can you stand there an' tell me I was goin' to shoot high? I had a dead bead on him."

"Boy, you didn't allow for downhill. . . . Hurry. He's seen us now."

Roy leveled the rifle, and, taking aim as before, he fired. The buck stood perfectly motionless as if he had indeed been stone. The does, however, jumped with a start and gazed in fright in every direction.

"Told you! I seen where your bullet hit thet pine . . . half a foot over his shoulder. Try again an' aim at his legs."

Roy now took a quicker aim and pulled trigger. A puff of dust right at the feet of the buck showed where Roy's lead had struck this time. With a single bound, wonderful to see, the big deer was out of sight behind trees and brush. The does leaped after him.

"Dog-gone the luck!" ejaculated Roy, red in the face, as he worked the lever of his rifle. "Never could shoot downhill nohow!"

His rueful apology to the girls for missing brought a merry laugh from Bo.

"Not for worlds would I have had you kill that beautiful deer!" she exclaimed.

"We won't have venison steak off him, that's certain," remarked Dorn dryly. "An' maybe none off any deer if Roy does the shootin'!"

They resumed travel, sheering off to the right, and keeping to the edge of the intersecting cañon. At length they rode down to the bottom where a tiny brook babbled through willows, and they followed this for a mile or so down to where it flowed into the larger stream. A dim trail overgrown with grass showed at this point.

"Here's where we part," said Dorn. "You'll beat me into my camp, but I'll get there sometime after dark."

"Hey, Milt, I forgot about thet darned pet cougar of yours an' the rest of your menagerie. Reckon they won't scare the girls? Especially old Tom?"

"You won't see Tom till I get home," replied Dorn.

"Ain't he corralled or tied up?"

"No. He has the run of the place."

"Wal, good bye then an' rustle along."

Dorn nodded to the girls, and, turning his horse, he drove the pack train before him up the open space between the stream and the wooded slope.

Roy stepped off his horse with that single action that appeared such a feat to Helen.

"Guess I'd better cinch up," he said as he threw a stirrup up over the pommel of his saddle. "You girls are goin' to see wild country."

"Who's old Tom?" queried Bo curiously.

"Why, he's Milt's pet cougar."

"Cougar? That's a panther . . . a mountain lion, didn't he say?"

"Shore is. Tom is a beauty. An' if he takes a likin' to you, he'll love you, play with you, maul you half to death."

Bo was all eyes. "Dorn has other pets, too?" she questioned eagerly.

"I never was up to his camp but what it was overrun with birds an' squirrels an' varmints of all kinds as tame . . . as tame as cows. Too darn' tame, Milt says. But I can't figger thet *parque* of his."

"What's a *parque*?" asked Helen as she shifted her foot to let him tighten the cinches on her saddle.

"Thet's Mexican for park, I guess," he replied. "These mountains are full of parks, an', say, I don't ever want to see no prettier places till I get to heaven. . . . There Ranger, old boy, thet's tight."

He slapped the horse affectionately, and, turning to his own, he stepped and swung his long length up.

"It ain't deep crossin' here. Come on!" he called, and spurred his bay.

The stream here was wide and it looked deep, but turned out to be deceptive.

"Wal, girls, here beginneth the second lesson," he drawled cheerily. "Ride one behind the other . . . stick close to me . . . do what I do . . . an' holler when you want to rest or if somethin' goes bad."

With that he spurred into the thicket. Bo went next, and Helen followed. The willows dragged at her so hard that she was unable to watch Roy, and the result was that a low-sweeping branch of a tree knocked her hard in the head. It hurt and startled her, and roused her mettle. Roy was keeping to the easy trot that covered ground so well, and he led up a slope to the open pine forest. Here the ride for several miles was straight, level, and open. Helen liked the forest today. It was brown and green, with patches of gold where the sun struck. She saw her first birds, big blue grouse that whirred up from under her horse, and little checkered gray quail that appeared awkward on the wing. Several times Roy pointed out deer flashing gray across some forest aisle, and often, when he pointed, Helen was not quick enough to see.

Helen realized that this ride would make up for the hideous one of yesterday. So far she had been only barely conscious of sore places and aching bones. These she would bear with. She loved the wild and the beautiful, both of which increased manifestly with every mile. The sun was warm, the air fragrant and cool, the sky blue as azure and so deep that she imagined she could look far up into it.

Suddenly Roy reined in so sharply that he pulled Bay up short. "Look!" he called sharply.

Bo screamed.

"Not thet way! Here! *Aw,* he's gone."

"Nell! It was a bear! I saw it. Oh, not like circus bears at all!"

Helen had missed her opportunity.

"Reckon he was a grizzly, an' I'm just as well pleased thet he loped off," said Roy. Altering his course somewhat, he led to an old rotten log that the bear had been digging in. "After grubs there . . . see his track. He was a whopper, shore enough."

They rode on, out to a high point that overlooked cañon and range, gorge and ridge, green and black as far as Helen could see. The ranges were bold and long, climbing to the central uplift where a number of fringed peaks raised their heads to the vast bare dome of Old Baldy. Far as vision could see to the right lay one rolling forest of pine, beautiful and serene. Somewhere down beyond must have lain the desert, but it was not in sight.

"I see turkeys way down there," said Roy, backing away. "We'll go down around an' mebbe I'll get a shot."

Descent beyond a rocky point was made through thick brush. This slope consisted of wide benches covered with copses and scattered pines and many oaks. Helen was delighted to see the familiar trees, although these were different from Missouri oaks. Rugged and gnarled, but not tall, these trees spread wide branches, the leaves of which were yellowing. Roy led into a grassy glade, and, leaping off his horse, rifle in hand, he prepared to shoot at something. Again Bo cried out, but this time it was with delight. Then Helen saw an immense flock of turkeys, apparently like the turkeys she knew at home, but these had bronze and checks of white, and they looked wild. There must have been a hundred in the flock, most of them hens. A few gobblers on the far side began the flight, running swiftly off. Helen plainly heard the *thud* of their feet. Roy shot once — twice — three times. Then rose a great commotion and *thumping,* and a loud roar of many wings. Dust and leaves whirling in the air were left where the turkeys had been.

"Wal, I got two," said Roy, and he strode forward to pick up his game. Returning, he tied two shiny plump gobblers back of his saddle and remounted his horse. "We'll have turkey tonight, if Milt gets to camp in time."

The ride was resumed. Helen never would have tired riding through those oak groves, brown and sear and yellow, with leaves and acorns falling.

"Bears have been workin' in here already," said Roy. "I see tracks all over. They eat acorns in the fall. An' mebbe we'll run into one yet."

The farther down he led the wilder and thicker grew the trees, so that dodging bunches was no light task. Ranger did not seem to care how close he passed a tree or under a limb, so that he missed them himself. But Helen thereby got some additional bruises. Particularly hard was it, when passing a tree, to get her knee out of the way in time.

Roy halted next at what appeared a large green pond full of vegetation and in places covered with a thick scum. But it had a current and an outlet, proving it to be a huge spring. Roy pointed down at a muddy place.

"Bear wallow. He heard us comin'. Look at thet little track. Cub track. An' look at these scratches on this tree, higher'n my head. An old she-bear stood up an' scratched them." Roy sat his saddle and reached up to touch fresh marks on the tree. "Woods's full of big bears," he said, grinning. "An' I take it particular kind of this old she rustlin' off with her cub. She-bears with cubs are dangerous."

The next place to stir Helen to enthusiasm was the glen at the bottom of this cañon. Beech trees, maples, aspens overtopped by lofty pines made dense shade over a brook where trout splashed in the brown swirling current and leaves drifted down, and stray flecks of golden sunlight lightened the gloom. Here was hard riding to and fro across the brook, between huge mossy boulders, and between aspens so close together that Helen could scarcely squeeze her knees through.

Once more Roy climbed, out of that cañon, over a ridge into another, down long wooded slopes and through scrub oak thickets, on and on till the sun stood straight overhead. Then he halted for a short rest, unsaddled the horses to let them roll, and gave the girls some cold lunch that he packed. He strolled off with his gun and, upon returning, resaddled and gave the word to start.

That was the last of rest and easy traveling for the girls. The forest that he struck into seemed ribbed like a washboard with deep ravines so steep of slope as to make precarious travel. Mostly he kept to the bottom where dry washes afforded a kind of trail. But it was necessary to cross those ravines when they were too long to be headed, and this crossing was work.

The locust thickets, characteristic of these slopes, were thorny and closely knit. They tore and scratched and stung both horses and riders. Ranger appeared to be the most intelligent of the horses and suffered less. Bo's white mustang dragged her through more than one brambly place. On the other hand, some of these steep slopes were comparatively free of underbrush. Great firs and pines loomed up on all sides. The earth was soft and the hoofs sank deep. Toward the bottom of a descent Ranger would brace his front hoofs, and then slide down on his haunches. This mode facilitated travel, but it frightened Helen. The climb out, then, on the other side had to be done on foot.

After half a dozen slopes surmounted in this way Helen's strength was spent and her breath was gone. She felt light-headed. She could not get enough air. Her feet felt like lead and her riding coat was a burden. A hundred times, hot and wet and throbbing, she was compelled to stop. Always she had been a splendid walker and climber. And here, to break up the long ride, she was glad to be on her feet. But she could only drag one foot up after the other. Then, when her nose began to bleed, she realized that it was the elevation that was causing all the trouble. Her heart, however, did not hurt her, although she was conscious of an oppression on her breast.

At length Roy led into a ravine so deep and wide and full of forest verdure that it appeared impossible to cross. Just the same he started down, after a little way dismounting. Helen found that leading Ranger down was worse than riding him. He came fast and he would step right in her tracks. She was not quick enough to get away from him. Twice he stepped on her foot and again his broad chest hit her shoulder and threw her flat. When he began to slide, near the bottom, Helen had to run for her life.

"Oh, Nell! Isn't . . . this . . . great?" panted Bo from somewhere ahead.

"Bo . . . your . . . mind's . . . gone," panted Helen in reply.

Roy tried several places to climb out and

failed in each. Leading down the ravine for 100 yards or more, he essayed another attempt. Here there had been a slide and in part the earth was bare. When he had worked up this, he halted above and called: "Bad place! Keep on the upside of the hosses!"

This appeared easier said than done. Helen could not watch Bo, because Ranger would not wait. He pulled at the bridle and snorted.

"Faster you come the better!" called Roy.

Helen could not see the sense of that, but she tried. Roy and Bo had dug a deep trail, zigzag, up that treacherous slide. Helen made the mistake of starting to follow in their tracks, and, when she realized this, Ranger was climbing fast, almost dragging her, and it was too late to get above. Helen began to labor. She slid down right in front of Ranger. The intelligent animal, with a snort, plunged out of the trail to keep from stepping on her. Then he was above her.

"Look out down there!" yelled Roy in warning. "Get on the upside!"

But that did not appear possible. The earth began to slide under Ranger and that impeded Helen's progress. He got in advance of her, straining on the bridle.

"Let go!" yelled Roy.

Helen dropped the bridle just as a heavy slide began to move with Ranger. He snorted fiercely, and, rearing high in a mighty plunge, he gained solid ground. Helen was buried to her knees, but, extricating herself, she crawled to a safe point and rested before climbing farther.

"Bad cave-in thet," was Roy's comment, when at last she joined him and Bo at the top.

Roy appeared at a loss as to which way to go. He rode to high ground and looked in all directions. To Helen one way appeared as wild and rough as another, and all was yellow, green, and black under the westering sun. Roy rode a short distance in one direction, then changed for another.

Presently he stopped. "Wal, I'm shore turned around," he said.

"You're not lost?" cried Bo.

"Reckon I've been thet for a couple of hours," he replied cheerfully. "Never did ride across here. I had the direction, but I'm blamed now if I can tell which way thet was."

Helen gazed at him in consternation. "Lost!" she echoed.

CHAPTER NINE

A silence ensued, fraught with poignant fear for Helen, as she gazed into Bo's whitening face. She read her sister's mind. Bo was remembering tales of lost people who never were found.

"Me an' Milt get lost every day," said Roy. "You don't suppose any man can know all this big country. It's nothin' for us to be lost."

"Oh! I was lost when I was little," said Bo.

"Wal, I reckon it'd been better not to tell you so offhand-like," replied Roy contritely. "Don't feel bad now. All I need is a peek at Old Baldy. Then I'll have my bearin'. Come on."

Helen's confidence returned as Roy led off at a fast trot. He rode toward the westering sun, keeping to the ridge they had ascended until once more he came out upon a promontory. Old Baldy loomed there, blacker and higher and closer. The dark forest showed round yellow bare spots like parks.

"Not so far off the track," said Roy as he wheeled his horse. "We'll make camp in Milt's *parque* tonight."

He led down off that ridge into a valley, and then up to higher altitude where the character of the forest changed. The trees were no longer pines, but fir and spruce, growing thin and exceedingly tall, with few branches below the topmost foliage. So dense was this forest that twilight seemed to have come.

Travel was arduous. Everywhere were windfalls that had to be avoided, and not a root was there without a fallen tree. The horses, laboring slowly, sometimes sank knee-deep into the brown duff. Gray moss festooned the tree trunks and an amber-green moss grew thickly on the rotting logs.

Helen loved this forest primeval. It was so still, so dark, so gloomy, so full of shadows and shade, and a dank smell of rotting wood and sweet fragrance of spruce. The great windfalls, where trees were jammed together in dozens, showed the savagery of the storms. Wherever a single monarch lay uprooted, there had sprung up a number of ambitious sons, jealous of each other, fighting for place. Even the trees fought each other. The forest was a place of mystery, but its strife could be read by any eye. Lightning had split firs clear to the roots, and others it had circled with ripping tear from top to trunk.

Time came, however, when the exceeding wildness of the forest, in density and fallen timber, made it imperative for Helen to put all her attention on ground and trees in her immediate vicinity. So the pleasure of gazing ahead at the beautiful wilderness was denied her. Thereafter travel became toil and the hours endless.

Roy led on and Ranger followed while the shadows darkened under the trees. She was reeling in her saddle, half blind and sick, when Roy called out cheerily that they were almost there.

Whatever his idea was, to Helen it seemed many miles that she followed him farther, out of the heavy timbered forest down upon slopes of low spruce, like evergreen, which descended sharply to another level, where dark shallow streams flowed gently and the solemn stillness held a low murmur of falling water, and at last the wood ended upon a wonderful park full of a thick rich golden light of fast-fading sunset.

"Smell the smoke," said Roy. "By Solomon, if Milt ain't here ahead of me!"

He rode on. Helen's weary gaze took in the round *parque,* the circling black slopes, leading up to craggy rims all gold and red in the last flare of the sun, and all the spirit left in her flashed up in thrilling wonder at this exquisite, wild, and colorful spot.

Horses were grazing out in the long grass and there were deer grazing with them. Roy led around a corner of the fringed bordering woodland, and there, under lofty trees, shone a campfire. Huge gray rocks loomed beyond, and then cliffs rose step by step to a notch in the mountain wall over which poured a thin lacy waterfall. As Helen gazed in rapture, the sunset gold faded to white, and all the western slope of the amphitheater darkened.

Dorn's tall form appeared. "Reckon you're late," he said as, with a comprehensive flash of eyes, he took in the three.

"Milt, I got lost," replied Roy.

"I feared as much. . . . You girls look like you'd've done better to ride with me," went on Dorn as he offered a hand to help Bo off. She took it, tried to get her feet out of the stirrups, and then she slid from the saddle into Dorn's arms. He placed her on her feet and, supporting her, said solicitously: "A hundred mile ride in three days for a tenderfoot is somethin' your Uncle Al won't believe. . . . Come, walk if it kills you."

Whereupon he led Bo, very much as if he were teaching a child to walk. The fact that the voluble Bo had nothing to say was significant to Helen, who was following with the assistance of Roy.

One of the huge rocks resembled a seashell in that it contained a hollow over which the wide-spreading shelf flared out. It reached toward branches of great pines. A spring burst from a crack in the solid rock. The campfire blazed under a pine, and the blue column of smoke rose just in front of the shelving rock. Packs were lying on the grass and some of them were open. There were no signs here of a permanent habitation of the hunter. But farther on were other huge rocks, leaning, cracked, and forming caverns, some of which perhaps he utilized.

"My camp is just back," said Dorn as if he had read Helen's mind. "Tomorrow we'll fix it up comfortable-like around here for you girls."

Helen and Bo were made as easy as blankets and saddles could make them, serving for resting places, and the men went about their tasks.

"Nell . . . isn't this . . . a dream?" murmured Bo.

"No, child. It's real . . . terribly real," replied Helen. "Now that we're here . . . with that awful ride over . . . we can think."

"It's so pretty . . . here." Bo yawned. "I'd just as lief Uncle Al didn't find us very soon."

"Bo! He's a sick man. Think what the worry will be to him."

"I'll bet if he knows Dorn, he won't be so worried."

"Dorn told us Uncle Al disliked him."

"*Pooh!* What difference does that make . . . ? Oh, I don't know which I am . . . hungrier or tireder!"

"I couldn't eat tonight," said Helen wearily.

When she stretched out, she had a vague delicious sensation that that was the end of Helen Rayner and she was glad. Above her, through the lacy fern-like pine needles, she saw blue sky and a pale star, just showing. Twilight was stealing down swiftly. The silence was beautiful, seemingly undisturbed by the soft silky dreamy fall of water. Helen closed her eyes, ready for sleep, with the physical commotion within her body gradually yielding. In some places her bones felt as if they had come out through her flesh; in others throbbed deep-seated aches; her muscles appeared slowly to subside, to relax with the quivering twinges ceasing one by one, and through muscle and bone, through all her body, pulsed a burning current.

Bo's head dropped on Helen's shoulder. Sense became vague to Helen. She lost the low murmur of the waterfall, and then the sound or feeling of someone at the campfire, and her last conscious thought was that she tried to open her eyes and could not.

When she awoke, all was bright. The sun shone almost directly overhead. Helen was astounded. Bo lay wrapped in deep sleep, her face flushed, with beads of perspiration on her brow and the chestnut curls damp. Helen threw down the blankets, and then, gathering courage, for she felt as if her back was broken, she endeavored to sit up. In vain! Her spirit was willing, but her muscles refused to act. It must take a violent spasmodic effort. She tried it with shut eyes and, succeeding, sat there trembling. The commotion she had made in the blankets awoke Bo, and she blinked her surprised blue eyes in the sunlight.

"Hello . . . Nell . . . do I have to . . . get up?" she asked sleepily.

"Can you?" queried Helen.

"Can I what?" Bo was now thoroughly awake and lay there staring at her sister.

"Why . . . get up."

"I'd like to know why not," retorted Bo as she made the effort. She got one arm and shoulder up only to flop back like a crippled thing. And she uttered the most piteous little moan. "I'm dead. I know . . . I am."

"Well, if you're going to be a Western girl, you'd better have spunk enough to move."

"Uhn-huh!" ejaculated Bo. Then she rolled over, not without groans, and, once upon her face, she raised herself on her hands and turned to a sitting posture. "Where's everybody? Oh, Nell, it's perfectly lovely here. Paradise!"

Helen looked around. A fire was smoldering. No one was in sight. Wonderful distant colors seemed to strike her glance as she tried to fix it upon nearby objects. A beautiful little green tent or shack had been erected out of spruce boughs. It had a slanting roof that sloped all the way from a ridge pole to the ground; half of the opening in front was closed as were the sides. The spruce boughs appeared all to be laid in the same direction, giving it a smooth compact appearance, actually as if it had grown there.

"That lean-to wasn't there last night?" inquired Bo.

"I didn't see it. Lean-to? Where'd you get that name?"

"It's Western, my dear. . . . I'll bet they put it up for us. . . . Sure, I see our bags inside. Let's get up. . . . Say, it must be late."

The girls had considerable fun as well as pain in getting up and keeping each other erect until their limbs would hold them firmly. They were delighted with the spruce lean-to. It faced the open and stood just under the wide-spreading shelf of rock. The tiny outlet from the spring flowed beside it and spilled its clear water over a stone to fall into a little pool. The floor of this woodland habitation consisted of tips of spruce boughs, to about a foot in depth, all laid one way, smooth and springy, and so sweetly odorous that the air seemed intoxicating. Helen and Bo opened their baggage, and, what with use of the cold water, and brush and comb, and clean blouses, they made themselves feel as comfortable as possible, considering the excruciating aches. Then they went out to the campfire.

Helen's eye was attracted by moving objects near at hand. Then, simultaneously with Bo's cry of delight, Helen saw a beautiful doe approaching under the trees. Dorn walked beside it.

"You sure had a long sleep," was the hunter's greeting. "I reckon you both look better."

"Good morning. Or is it afternoon? We're just able to move about," said Helen.

"I could ride," declared Bo stoutly "Oh, Nell, look at the deer! It's coming to me."

The doe had hung back a little as Helen reached the campfire. It was a gray slender creature, smooth as silk, with great dark eyes. It stood a moment, long ears erect, and then with a graceful little trot came up to Bo and reached a slim nose for her outstretched hand. All about it, except the beautiful soft eyes, seemed wild, and yet it was as tame as a kitten. Then, suddenly, as Bo fondled the long ears, it gave a start and, breaking away, ran back out of sight under the pines.

"What frightened it?" asked Bo.

Dorn pointed up at the wall under the shelving roof of rock. There twenty feet from the ground, curled up on a ledge, lay a huge tawny animal with a face like that of a cat.

"She's afraid of Tom," replied Dorn. "Recognizes him as a hereditary foe, I guess. I can't make friends of them."

"Oh . . . so that's Tom . . . the pet lion!" exclaimed Bo. "*Ugh!* No wonder that deer ran off!"

"How long has he been up there?" queried Helen, gazing fascinatedly at Dorn's famous pet.

"I couldn't say. Tom comes an' goes," replied Dorn. "But I sent him up there last night."

"And he was there . . . perfectly free . . . right over us . . . while we slept!" burst out Bo.

"Yes. An' I reckon you slept the safer for that." •

"Of all things! Nell, isn't he a monster? But he doesn't look like a lion . . . an African lion. He's a panther. I saw his like at the circus once."

"He's a cougar," said Dorn. "The panther is long and slim. Tom is not only long but thick an' round. I've had him four years. An' he was a kitten no bigger'n my fist when I got him."

"Is he perfectly tame . . . safe?" asked Helen anxiously.

"I've never told anybody that Tom was safe, but he is," replied Dorn. "You can absolutely believe it. A wild cougar wouldn't attack a man unless cornered or starved. An' Tom is like a big cat."

The beast raised his great cat-like face, with its sleepy half-shut eyes, and looked down upon them.

"Shall I call him down?" inquired Dorn.

For once Bo did not find her voice.

"Let us . . . get a little more used to

192

him . . . at a distance," replied Helen with a little laugh.

"If he comes to you, just rub his head an' you'll see how tame he is," said Dorn. "Reckon you're both hungry?"

"Not so very," returned Helen, aware of his penetrating gray gaze upon her.

"Well, I am," vouchsafed Bo.

"Soon as the turkey's done we'll eat. My camp is around between the rocks. I'll call you."

Not until his broad back was turned did Helen notice that the hunter looked different. Then she saw he wore a lighter, cleaner suit of buckskin, with no coat, and instead of the high-heeled horseman's boots he wore moccasins and leggings. The change made him appear more lithe.

"Nell, I don't know what you think, but *I* call him handsome," declared Bo.

Helen had no idea what she thought. "Let's try to walk some," she suggested.

So they assayed that painful task and got as far as a pine log some few rods from their camp. This point was close to the edge of the park from which there was an unobstructed view.

"My! What a place!" exclaimed Bo, with eyes wide and round.

"Oh, beautiful!" breathed Helen.

An unexpected blaze of color drew her gaze first. Out of the black spruce slopes shone patches of aspens, gloriously red and gold, and low down along the edge of timber troops of aspens ran out into the park, not yet so blazing as those above, but purple and yellow and white in the sunshine. Masses of silver spruce, like trees in the moonlight, bordered the park, sending out here and there an isolated tree, sharp as a spear, with under branches close to the ground. Long golden-green grass, resembling half-ripe wheat, covered the entire floor of the park, gently waving to the wind. Above sheered the black, gold-patched slopes, steep and unscalable, rising to buttresses of dark iron-hued rock. And to the east circled the rows of cliff bench, gray and old and fringed, splitting at the top in the notch where the lacy slumberous waterfall, like white smoke, fell and vanished to re-appear in wider sheet of lace, only to fall and vanish again in the green depths.

It was a verdant valley, deep-set in mountain walls, wild and sad and lonesome. The waterfall dominated the spirit of the place, dreamy and sleepy and tranquil, and it murmured sweetly in one breath of wind, and lulled with another, and sometimes died out altogether, only to come again in soft strange roar.

"Paradise Park," whispered Bo to herself.

A call from Dorn disturbed their raptures. Turning, they hobbled with eager but painful steps in the direction of a larger campfire, situated to the right of the great rock that sheltered their lean-to. No hut or house showed there and none was needed. Hiding places and homes for 100 hunters were there in the sections of caverned cliffs, split off in bygone ages from the mountain wall above. A few stately pines stood out from the rocks, and a clump of silver spruces ran down to a brown brook. This camp was only a step from the lean-to, around the corner of a huge rock, yet it had been out of sight. Here indeed was evidence of a hunter's home — pelts and skins and antlers, a neat pile of split firewood, a long ledge of rock, well-sheltered, and loaded with bags like a huge pantry shelf, packs and ropes and saddles, tools and weapons, and a platform of dry brush as shelter for a fire around which hung on poles a various assortment of utensils for camp.

"Hyar . . . you git!" shouted Dorn, and he threw a stick at something. A bear cub scampered away in haste. He was small and woolly and brown, and he grunted as he ran. Soon he halted.

"That's Bud," said Dorn as the girls came up. "Guess he near starved in my absence. An' now he wants everythin', especially the sugar. We don't have sugar often up here."

"Isn't he dear? Oh, I love him!" cried Bo. "Come back, Bud. Come, Buddie."

The cub, however, kept his distance, watching Dorn with bright little eyes.

"Where's Mister Roy?" asked Helen.

"Roy's gone. He was sorry not to say good bye. But it's important he gets down in the pines on Anson's trail. He'll hang to Anson, an', in case they get near Pine, he'll ride in to see where your uncle is."

"What do you expect?" questioned Helen gravely.

"Most anythin'," he replied. "Al, I reckon, knows now. Maybe he's rustlin' into the mountains by this time. If he meets up with Anson, well an' good, for Roy won't be far off. An' sure if he runs across Roy, why they'll soon be here. But, if I were you, I wouldn't count on seein' your uncle very soon. I'm sorry. I've done my best. It sure is a bad deal."

"Don't think me ungracious," replied Helen hastily. How plainly he had intimated that it must be privation and annoyance for her to be compelled to accept his hospitality. "You are good . . . kind. I owe you much. I'll be eternally grateful."

Dorn straightened as he looked at her. His glance was intent, piercing. He seemed to be receiving a strange or unusual portent. No need for him to say he had never before been spoken to like that.

"You may have to stay here with me . . . for weeks . . . maybe months . . . if we've the bad luck to get snowed in," he said slowly, as if startled at this deduction. "You're safe here. No sheep thief could ever find this camp. I'll take risks to get you safe into Al's hands. But I'm goin' to be pretty sure about what I'm doin'. . . . So . . . there's plenty to eat an' it's a pretty place."

"Pretty! Why, it's grand!" exclaimed Bo. "I've called it Paradise Park."

"Paradise Park," he repeated, weighing the words. "You've named it an' also the creek. Paradise Creek! I've been here twelve years with no fit name for my home till you said that."

"Oh, that pleases me," returned Bo, with shining eyes.

"Eat now," said Dorn. "An' I reckon you'll like that turkey."

There was a clean tarpaulin upon which were spread steaming fragrant pans — roast turkey, hot biscuits and gravy, mashed potatoes as white as if prepared at home, stewed dried apples, and butter and coffee. This bounteous repast surprised and delighted the girls, and, when they had once tasted the roast wild turkey, then Milt Dorn had reason to blush at their encomiums.

"I hope . . . Uncle Al . . . doesn't come . . . for a month," declared Bo as she tried to get her breath. There was a brown spot on her nose and one in each cheek, suspiciously close to her mouth.

Dorn laughed. It was pleasant to hear him, for his laugh seemed unused and deep, as if it came from tranquil depths.

"Won't you eat with us?" asked Helen.

"Reckon I will," he said. "It'll save time an' hot grub tastes better."

Quite an interval of silence ensued, which presently was broken by Dorn.

"Here comes Tom."

Helen observed with a thrill that the cougar was magnificent, seen erect on all fours, approaching with slow sinuous grace. His color was tawny with spots of whitish gray. He had bowlegs, big and round and furry, and a huge head with great tawny eyes. No matter how tame he was said to be, he looked wild. Like a dog he walked right up and it so happened that he was directly behind Bo, within reach of her when she turned.

"Oh, Lord!" cried Bo, and up went both of her hands, in one of which was a huge piece of turkey. Tom took it, not viciously, but nevertheless with a *snap* that made Helen jump. As if by magic the turkey vanished. And Tom took a closer step toward Bo. Her expression of fright changed to consternation.

"He stole my turkey."

"Tom, come here," ordered Dorn sharply. The cougar glided around rather sheepishly. "Now lie down an' behave."

Tom crouched on all fours, his head resting on his paws, with his beautiful tawny eyes, light and piercing, fixed upon the hunter.

"Don't grab," said Dorn, holding out a piece of turkey. Whereupon Tom took it less voraciously.

As it happened the little bear cub saw this transaction, and he plainly indicated his opinion of the preference showed to Tom.

"Oh, the dear!" exclaimed Bo. "He means it's not fair. . . . Come, Bud . . . come on."

But Bud would not approach the group until called by Dorn. Then he scrambled to them with every manifestation of delight. Bo almost forgot her own needs in feeding him, and getting acquainted with him. Tom plainly showed his jealousy of Bud, and Bud likewise showed his fear of the great cat.

Helen could not believe the evidence of her eyes — that she was in the woods, calmly and hungrily partaking of sweet, wild-flavored meat — that a full-grown mountain lion lay on one side of her and a baby brown bear sat on the other — that a strange hunter, a man of the forest, there in his lonely and isolated fastness, appealed to the romance in her and interested her as no one else she had ever met.

When the wonderful meal was at last finished, Bo enticed the bear cub around to the camp of the girls, and there soon became great comrades with him. Helen, watching Bo play, was inclined to envy her. No matter where Bo was placed, she always got something out of it. She adapted herself. She who could have a good time with almost anyone or anything would find the hours sweet and fleeting in this beautiful park of wild wonders.

But merely objective actions — merely physical movements had never yet contented Helen. She could run and climb and ride and play with hearty and healthy abandon, but those things would not suffice long for her, and her mind needed food. Helen was a thinker. One reason she had desired to make her home in the West was that by taking up a life of the open, of action, she might think and dream and brood less. And here she was in the wild West, after the three most strenuously active days of her career, and still the same old giant revolved her mind and turned it upon herself and upon all she saw.

"What can I do?" she asked Bo almost helplessly.

"Why rest, you silly," retorted Bo. "You walk like an old crippled woman with only one leg."

Helen hoped the comparison was undeserved, but the advice was sound. The blankets spread out in the grass looked inviting and they felt comfortably warm in the sunshine. The breeze was slow, languorous, fragrant, and it brought the low *hum* of the murmuring waterfall, like a melody of bees. Helen made a pillow and lay down to rest. The green pine needles, so thin and fine in their criss-crossed network, showed clearly against the blue sky. She looked in vain for birds. Then her gaze went wonderingly to the lofty fringed rim of the great amphitheater, and, as she studied it, she began to grasp its remoteness, how far away it was in the rarified atmosphere. A black eagle, sweeping along, looked of tiny size, and yet he was far under the heights above.

How pleasant she fancied it to be up there. And drowsy fancy lulled her to sleep.

Helen slept all afternoon and, upon awakening toward sunset, found Bo curled beside her. Dorn had thoughtfully covered them with a blanket; also he had built a campfire. The air was growing keen and cold.

Later, when they had put on their coats and made comfortable seats beside the fire, Dorn came over, apparently to visit them.

"I reckon you can't sleep all the time," he said. "An' bein' city girls you'll get lonesome."

"Lonesome!" echoed Helen. The idea of her being lonesome here had not occurred to her.

"I've thought that all out," went on Dorn as he sat down, Indian fashion, before the blaze. "It's natural you'd find time drag up here, bein' used to lots of people an' goin's on, an' work, an' all girls like."

"I'd never be lonesome here," replied Helen with her direct force.

Dorn did not betray surprise, but he showed that his mistake was something to ponder over.

"Excuse me," he said presently, as his gray eyes held hers. "That's how I had it. As I remember girls . . . an' it doesn't seem long

202

since I left home . . . most of them would die of lonesomeness up here." Then he addressed himself to Bo. "How about you? You see I figured you'd be the one that liked it, an' your sister the one who wouldn't."

"I won't get lonesome very soon," replied Bo.

"I'm glad. It worried me some . . . not ever havin' girls as company before. An' in a day or so, when you're rested, I'll help you pass the time."

Bo's eyes were full of flashing interest, and Helen asked him: "How?"

It was a sincere expression of her curiosity and not either a doubtful or ironic challenge of an educated woman to a man of the forest. But as a challenge he took it.

"How?" he repeated, and a strange smile flitted across his face. "Why, by givin' you rides an' climbs to beautiful places. An' then, if you're interested, to show you how little so-called civilized people know of Nature."

Helen realized then that whatever his calling, hunter or wanderer or hermit, he was not uneducated, even if he appeared illiterate.

"I'll be happy to learn from you," she said.

"Me, too!" chimed in Bo. "You can't tell too much to anyone from Missouri."

He smiled then, and that warmed Helen to him, for then he seemed less removed from other people. About this hunter there began to be something of the very nature of which he spoke — a stillness, aloofness, an unbreakable tranquility, a cold clear spirit like that in the mountain air, a physical something not unlike the tamed wildness of his pets, or the strength of the pines.

"I'll bet I can tell you more'n you'll ever remember," he said.

"What'll you bet," retorted Bo.

"Well, more roast turkey against . . . say somethin' wise when you're safe an' home to your Uncle Al's, runnin' his ranch."

"Agreed. Nell, you hear?"

Helen nodded her head.

"All right. We'll leave it to Nell," began Dorn half seriously. "Now I'll tell you, first, for the fun of passin' time we'll ride an' race my horses out in the park. An' we'll fish in the brooks an' hunt in the woods. There's an old silvertip around that you can see me kill. An' we'll climb to the peaks an' see wonderful sights. . . . So much for that. Now, if you really want to learn . . . or if you only want me to tell you . . . well, that's no matter. Only I'll win the bet. You'll see how this park lies on the crater of a volcano an' was once full of water . . . an' how the snow blows in on one side in winter, a hundred feet deep, when there's none in the other. . . . An' the trees . . . how they grow an' live an' fight one another an' depend on each other, an' protect the forest from storm winds. . . . An' how they hold the water that is the fountains of the great rivers. . . . An' how the creatures an' things that live in them or on them are good for them, an' neither could live without the other. . . . An' then I'll show you my pets tame an' untamed, an' tell you how it's man that makes any creature wild . . . how easy they are to tame . . . an' how they learn to love you. . . . An' there's the life of the forest, the strife of it . . . how the bear lives, an' the cats, an' the wolves, an' the deer. . . . You'll see how cruel Nature is . . . how savage an' wild the wolf or cougar tears down the deer . . . how a wolf loves fresh hot blood an' how a cougar unrolls the skin of a deer back from his neck. . . . An' you'll see that this cruelty of Nature . . . this work of the wolf an' cougar is what makes the deer so beautiful an' healthy an' swift an' sensitive. Without his deadly foes the deer would deteriorate an' die out. . . . An' you'll see how this principle works out among all creatures of the forest. Strife! It's the meanin' of all creation an' the salvation. . . . If you're quick to see, you'll learn that the Nature here in the wilds is the same as that of men . . . only men are no longer cannibals. Trees fight to live . . . birds fight . . . animals fight . . . men fight. . . . They all live off one another. An' it's this fightin' that brings them all closer an' closer to bein' perfect. But nothin' will ever be perfect."

"But how about religion?" interrupted Helen earnestly.

"Nature has a religion an' it's to live . . . to grow . . . to reproduce, each of its kind."

"But that is not God in the immortality of the soul," declared Helen.

"Well, it's as close to God an' immortality as Nature ever gets."

"Oh, you would rob me of my religion!"

"No, I just talk as I see life," replied Dorn reflectively, as he poked a stick into the red embers of the fire. "Maybe I have a religion. I don't know. But it's not the kind you have . . . not the Bible kind. . . . That kind doesn't keep the men in Pine an' Snowdrop an' all over . . . sheepmen an' ranchers an' farmers n' travelers, such as I've known . . . the religion they prefer doesn't keep them from lyin', cheatin', stealin', an' killin'. . . . I reckon no man who lives as I do, which perhaps is my religion, will lie or cheat or kill, unless it's to kill in self-defense or like

I'd do if Snake Anson would ride up here now. . . . My religion, maybe, is love of life . . . wild life as it was in the beginnin' . . . an' the wind that blows secrets from everywhere, an' the water that sings all day an' night, an' the stars that shine constant, an' the trees that speak somehow, an' the rocks that aren't dead. . . . I'm never alone here or on the trails. There's somethin' unseen, but always with me. An' that's it. Call it God if you like. . . . But what stalls me is . . . where was that spirit when this earth was a ball of fiery gas? Where will that spirit be when all life is frozen out or burned out on this globe an' it hangs dead in space like the moon? That time will come. . . . There's no waste in Nature. Not the littlest atom is destroyed. It changes, that's all, as you see this pine wood go up in smoke an' feel somethin' that's heat come out of it. Where does that go? It's not lost. Nothin' is lost. . . . So, the beautiful an' savin' thought is, maybe all rock an' wood, water an' blood an' flesh are resolved back into the elements to come to life somewhere again sometime."

"Oh, what you say is wonderful, but it's terrible!" exclaimed Helen. He had struck deep into her soul.

"Terrible? I reckon," he replied sadly.

Then ensued a little interval of silence.

207

"Milt Dorn, I lose the bet," declared Bo with earnestness behind her frivolity.

"I'd forgotten that. Reckon I talked a lot," he said apologetically. "You see I don't get much chance to talk, except to myself or Tom. Years ago, when I found the habit of silence settlin' down on me, I took to thinkin' out loud an' talkin' to anythin'."

"I could listen to you all night," returned Bo dreamily.

"Do you read . . . do you have books?" inquired Helen suddenly.

"Yes. I read tolerable well, a good deal better than I talk or write," he replied. "I went to school till I was fifteen. Always hated study, but liked to read. . . . Years ago an old friend of mine down here at Pine . . . Widow Cass . . . she gave me a lot of old books. An' I packed them up here. Winter's the time I read."

Conversation lagged after that, except for desultory remarks, and presently Dorn bade the girls good night and left them.

Helen watched his tall form vanish in the gloom under the pines, and, after he had disappeared, she still stared.

"Nell!" called Bo shrilly. "I've called you three times. I want to go to bed."

"Oh! I . . . I was thinking," rejoined Helen, half embarrassed, half wondering at herself. "I didn't hear you."

"I should smile you didn't," retorted Bo. "Wish you could just have seen your eyes. . . . Nell, do you want *me* to tell *you* something?"

"Why . . . yes," said Helen rather feebly. She did not at all, when Bo talked like that.

"You're going to fall in love with that wild hunter," declared Bo in a voice that rang like a bell.

Helen was not only amazed, but enraged. She caught her breath, preparatory to giving this incorrigible sister a piece of her mind.

Bo went calmly on. "I can feel it in my bones."

"Bo, you're a little fool . . . a sentimental, romancing, gushy little fool!" retorted Helen. "All you seem to hold in your head is some rot about love. To hear you talk one would think there's nothing else in the world but love."

Bo's eyes were bright, shrewd, affectionate, and laughing as she bent their steady gaze upon Helen.

"Nell, that's just it. There *is* . . . nothing else!"

CHAPTER TEN

After a few days of riding the grassy level of that wonderfully gold and purple park, and dreamily listening by day to the ever low and ever changing murmur of the waterfall, and by night to the wild lonely mourn of a hunting wolf, and climbing to the dizzy heights where the wind stung sweetly, Helen Rayner lost track of time and forgot her peril.

Roy Beeman did not return. If occasionally Dorn mentioned Roy and his quest, the girls had little to say beyond a recurrent anxiety for the old uncle, and then they forgot again. Paradise Park, lived in a little while at that season of the year, would have claimed anyone, and ever afterward haunted sleeping or waking dreams.

Bo took at once to the wild life, to the horses and rides, to the camp work, for the girls had insisted on doing their share, to the many pets, and especially to the cougar,

Tom. The big cat followed Bo everywhere, played with her, rolling and pawing, kitten-like, and he would lay his massive head in her lap to purr his content. Bo had little fear of anything. And here in the wilds she soon lost that.

One of Dorn's pets was a half-grown black bear named Muss. He was abnormally jealous of little Bud and he had a well-developed hatred of Tom; otherwise, he was a very good-tempered bear and enjoyed Dorn's impartial regard. Tom, however, chased Muss out of camp whenever Dorn's back was turned, and sometimes Muss stayed away, shifting for himself. With the advent of Bo, who spent a good deal of time on the animals, Muss manifestly found the camp more attractive. Whereupon Dorn predicted trouble between Tom and Muss.

Bo liked nothing better than a rough and tumble frolic with the black bear. Muss was not very big or very heavy, and in a wrestling bout with the strong and wiry girl he sometimes came out second best. It spoke well of him that he seemed to be careful not to hurt Bo. He never bit or scratched, although he sometimes gave her sounding slaps with his paws. Whereupon Bo would clench her gauntleted fists and sail into him in earnest.

One afternoon, before the early supper they always had, Dorn and Helen were watching Bo teasing the bear. She was in her most vixenish mood, full of life and fight. Tom lay all his long length on the grass, watching with narrow gleaming eyes.

When Bo and Muss locked in an embrace and went down to roll over and over, Dorn called Helen's attention to the cougar. "Tom's jealous. It's strange how animals are like people. Pretty soon I'll have to corral Muss or there'll be a fight."

Helen could not see anything wrong with Tom except that he did not look playful.

During suppertime both bear and cougar disappeared, although this was not remarkable until afterwards. Dorn whistled and called, but the rival pets did not return. Next morning Tom was there, curled up snugly at the foot of Bo's bed, and, when she arose, he followed her around as usual. But Muss did not return.

The circumstance made Dorn anxious. He left camp, taking Tom with him and, upon returning, stated that he had followed Muss's tracks as far as possible, and then had tried to put Tom on the trail, but the cougar would not or could not follow it. Dorn said Tom never liked a bear trail, anyway — cougars and bears being common enemies. So whether by accident or design Bo lost one of her playmates.

The hunter searched some of the slopes next day and even went up on one of the mountains. He did not discover any sign of Muss, but he said he had found something else.

"Do you girls want some real excitement?" he asked.

Helen smiled her acquiescence and Bo replied with one of her forceful speeches.

"Don't mind bein' good an' scared?" he went on.

"You can't scare me," bantered Bo. But Helen looked doubtful.

"Up in one of the parks I run across one of my horses . . . a lame bay you haven't seen. Well, he had been killed by that old silvertip I told you was hangin' around. Hadn't been dead over an hour. Blood was still runnin' an' only a little meat eaten. That bear heard me or saw me an' made off into the woods. But he'll come back tonight. I'm goin' up there, lay for him, an' kill him. . . . Reckon you'd better go, because I don't want to leave you here alone at night."

"Are you going to take Tom?" asked Bo.

"No. The bear might get his scent. An' besides Tom ain't reliable on bears."

When they had hurried supper, and Dorn

213

had gotten in the horses, the sun had set and the valley was shadowing low down while the ramparts were still golden.

The long zigzag trail Dorn followed up the slope took nearly an hour to climb, so that, when that was surmounted and he led out of the woods, twilight had fallen. A rolling park extended as far as Helen could see, bordered by forest that in places sent out straggling stretches of trees. Here and there like islands were isolated patches of timber.

At 10,000 feet elevation the twilight of this clear and cold night was a rich and rare atmospheric effect. It looked as if it was seen through perfectly clear smoked glass. Objects were singularly visible, even at long range, and seemed magnified. In the west, where the afterglow of sunset lingered over the dark ragged spruce-speared horizon line, there was such a transparent golden line melting into vivid star-fired blue that Helen could only gaze and gaze in wondering admiration.

Dorn spurred his horse into a lope and the spirited mounts of the girls kept up with him. The ground was rough, with tufts of grass growing close together, yet the horses did not stumble. Their action and snorting betrayed excitement. Dorn led around several clumps of timber, up a long grassy swale, and then straight westward across an open flat toward where the dark-fringed forest line raised itself, wild and clear, against the cold sky. The horses went swiftly, and the wind cut like a blade of ice. Helen could barely get her breath and she panted as if she had just climbed a laborsome hill. The stars began to blink out of the blue, and the gold paled somewhat, and yet twilight lingered. It seemed long across that flat, but really was short. Coming to a thin line of trees that led down over a slope to deeper, but still isolated patch of woods, Dorn dismounted and tied his horse. When the girls got off, he halted their horses, also.

"Stick close to me an' put your feet down easy," he whispered. How tall and dark he loomed in the fading light! Helen thrilled, as she had often of late, at the strange potential physical force of the man. Stepping softly, without the least sound, Dorn entered this straggly bit of woods, which appeared to have narrow byways and nooks. Then presently he came to the top of a well-wooded slope, dark as pitch, apparently. But as Helen followed, she perceived the trees, and they were thin dwarf spruce, partly dead. The slope was exposed — springy, easy to step upon without noise. Dorn went so cautiously that Helen could not hear him, and sometimes in the gloom she could not see him. Then the chill thrills ran over her. Bo kept holding on to Helen, which fact hampered Helen as well as worked somewhat to disprove Bo's boast. At last level ground was reached. Helen made out a light-gray background crossed by black bars. Another glance showed this to be the dark tree trunks against the open park.

Dorn halted and with a touch brought Helen to a straining pause. He was listening. It seemed wonderful to watch him bend his head and stand as silently and motionlessly as one of the dark trees.

"He's not there yet," Dorn whispered, and he stepped forward very slowly. Helen and Bo began to come up against thin dead branches that were invisible, and they cracked. Then Dorn knelt down, seemed to melt into the ground.

"You'll have to crawl," he whispered.

How strange and thrilling that was for Helen, and hard work! The ground bore twigs and dead branches, which had to be carefully crawled over, and lying flat, as was necessary, it took prodigious effort to drag her body inch by inch. Like a huge snake Dorn wormed his way along.

Gradually the wind lightened. They were nearing the edge of the park. Helen now saw a strip of open with a high black wall of spruce beyond. The afterglow flashed or changed, like a diminishing northern light, and then failed. Dorn crawled on farther to halt at length between two tree trunks at the edge of the wood.

"Come up beside me," he whispered.

Helen crawled on, and presently Bo was beside her, panting, with pale face and great staring eyes, plain to be seen in the wan light.

"Moon's comin' up. We're just in time. The old grizzly's not there yet, but I see coyotes. Look." Dorn pointed across the open neck of park to a dim blurred patch standing apart some little distance from the black wall.

"That's the dead horse," whispered Dorn. "An' if you watch close, you can see the coyotes. They're gray an' they move. . . . Can't you hear them?"

Helen's excited ears, so full of throbs and imaginings, presently registered low snaps and snarls. Bo gave her arm a squeeze.

"I hear them. They're fighting. . . . Oh . . . gee," she panted, and drew a long full breath of unutterable excitement.

"Keep quiet now an' watch an' listen," said the hunter.

Slowly the black ragged forest line seemed

to grow blacker and lift; slowly the gray neck of park lightened under some invisible influence; slowly the stars paled and the sky filmed over. Somewhere the moon was rising. And slowly that vague blurred patch grew a little clearer.

Through the tips of the spruce, now seen to be rather close at hand, shone a slender silver crescent moon, darkening, hiding, shining again, climbing until its exquisite sickle point topped the trees, and then, magically it cleared them, radiant and cold. While the eastern black wall shaded still blacker, the park blanched and the borderline opposite began to stand out as trees.

"Look! Look!" cried Bo very low and fearfully, as she pointed.

"Not so loud," whispered Dorn.

"But I see something!"

"Keep quiet," he admonished.

Helen, in the direction Bo pointed, could not see anything but moon-blanched bare ground, rising close at hand to a little ridge.

"Lie still," whispered Dorn. "I'm goin' to crawl around to get a look from another angle. I'll be right back." He moved noiselessly backward and disappeared.

With him gone, Helen felt a palpitating of her heart and a prickling of her skin.

"Oh, my, Nell. Look," whispered Bo in

fright. "I know I saw something."

On top of the little ridge a round object moved slowly, getting farther out into the light. Helen watched with suspended breath. It moved out to be silhouetted against the sky — apparently a huge round bristling animal frosty in color. Helen's tongue clove to the roof of her mouth. That frosty color proved the thing to be a grizzly bear. One instant it seemed huge — the next small — then close at hand and far away. It swerved to come directly toward them. Suddenly Helen realized that the beast was not a dozen yards distant. She was just beginning a new experience — a real and horrifying terror in which her blood curdled, her heart gave a tremendous leap and then stood still, and she wanted to fly, but was rooted to the spot — when Dorn returned to her side.

"That's a pesky porcupine," he whispered. "Almost crawled over you. He sure would have stuck you full of quills."

Whereupon, he threw a stick at the animal. It bounced straight up to turn around with startling quickness, and it gave forth a rattling sound, then it crawled out of sight.

"Por-cu-pine?" whispered Bo pantingly. "It might . . . as well . . . have been . . . an elephant."

Helen uttered a long eloquent sigh. She would not have cared to describe her emotions at sight of a harmless hedgehog.

"Listen," warned Dorn, very low. His big hand closed over Helen's gauntleted one. "There you have the real cry of the wild."

Sharp and cold on the night air split the cry of a wolf, distant yet wonderfully distinct. How wild and mournful and hungry! How marvelously pure! Helen shuddered through all her frame with the thrill of its music, the wild and unutterable and deep emotions it aroused. Again a sound of this forest had pierced beyond her life, back into the dim remote past from which she had come.

The cry was not repeated. The coyotes were still. And a silence fell, absolutely unbroken.

Dorn nudged Helen, and then reached out to give Bo a tap. He was peering keenly ahead and his strained intensity could be felt. Helen looked with all her might and she saw the shadowy gray forms of the coyotes skulk away, out of the moonlight into the gloom of the woods, where they disappeared. Not only Dorn's intensity but the very silence, the wildness of the moment and place, seemed fraught with wonderful potency. Bo must have felt it, too, for she was trembling all over, and holding tightly on to Helen, and breathing quickly and fast.

"Ahuh," muttered Dorn under his breath.

Helen caught the relief and certainty in his exclamation, and she divined then something of what the moment must have been to a hunter. Then her roving alert glance was arrested by a looming gray shadow coming out of the forest. It moved, but surely that huge thing could not be a bear. It passed out of gloom into silver moonlight. Helen's heart bounded. For it was a great frosty-coated bear lumbering along toward the dead horse. Instinctively Helen's hand sought the arm of the hunter. It felt like iron under a rippling surface. The touch eased away the oppression over her lungs, the tightness of her throat. What must have been fear left her, and only a powerful excitement remained. A sharp expulsion of breath from Bo and a violent jerk of her frame were signs that she had sighted the grizzly.

In the moonlight he looked of immense size and that wild park with the gloomy blackness of forest furnished a fit setting for him. Helen's quick mind, so taken up with emotions, still had a thought for the wonder and the meaning of that scene. She wanted the bear killed, yet that seemed a pity.

He had a wagging, rolling slow walk that took several moments to reach his quarry. When at length he reached it, he walked around with sniffs, plainly heard, and then a cross growl. Evidently he had discovered that his meal had been messed over. As a whole the big bear could be seen distinctly, but only in outline and color. The distance was perhaps 200 yards. Then it looked as if he had begun to tug at the carcass. Indeed he was dragging it, very slowly but surely.

"Look at that," whispered Dorn. "If he ain't strong. Reckon I'll have to stop him."

The grizzly, however, stopped of his own accord, just outside of the shadow line of the forest. Then, hunched in a big frosty heap over his prey, he began to tear and rend.

"Jess was a mighty good horse," muttered Dorn grimly. "Too good to make a meal for a hog silvertip." Then the hunter silently rose to a kneeling position, swinging the rifle in front of him. He glanced up into the low branches of the tree overhead. "Girls, there's no tellin' what a grizzly will do. If I yell, you climb up in this tree an' do it quick."

With that he leveled the rifle, resting his left elbow on his knee. The front end of the rifle, reaching out of the shade, shone silver in the moonlight. Man and weapon became still as stone. Helen held her breath. But Dorn relaxed, lowering the barrel.

"Can't see the sights very well," he whispered, shaking his head. "Remember now . . . if I yell, you climb!"

Again he aimed and slowly grew rigid. Helen could not take her fascinated eyes off him. He knelt bareheaded and in that shadow she could make out the gleam of his clear-cut profile, stern and cold.

A streak of fire and heavy report startled her. Then she heard the bullet hit. Shifting her glance, she saw the bear lurch with convulsive action, rearing on his hind legs. Loud *clicking* snaps must have been a clenching of his jaws in rage. But there was no other sound. Then again Dorn's heavy gun *boomed.* Helen heard again that singular spatting *thud* of striking lead. The bear went down with a flop as if he had been dealt a terrific blow. But just as quickly he was up on all fours and began to whirl with hoarse savage bawls of agony and fury. His action quickly carried him out of the moonlight into the shadow, where he disappeared. There the bawls gave place to gnashing snarls, and crashings in the brush, and snapping of branches as he made his way into the forest.

"Sure he's mad," said Dorn, rising to his feet. "An' I reckon hard hit. But I won't follow him tonight."

Both the girls got up, and Helen found she was shaky on her feet and very cold.

"Oh-h, wasn't . . . it . . . won- . . . wonder . . . ful!" cried Bo.

"Are you scared? Your teeth are chatterin'," queried Dorn.

"I'm . . . cold."

"Well, it sure is cold all right," he responded. "Now the fun's over you'll feel it. . . . Nell, you're froze, too."

Helen nodded. She was indeed as cold as she had ever been before. But that did not prevent a strange warmness along her veins and a quickened pulse, the cause of which she did not conjecture.

"Let's rustle," said Dorn, and led the way out of the wood and skirted its edge around to the slope. There they climbed to the flat, and went through the straggling line of trees to where the horses were tethered.

Up here the wind began to blow, not hard through the forest, but still strong and steady out in the open, and bitterly cold. Dorn helped Bo to mount, and then Helen.

"I'm . . . numb," she said. "I'll fall off . . . sure."

"No. You'll be warm in a jiffy," he replied, "because we'll ride some, goin' back. Let your horse pick the way an' you hang on."

With Ranger's first jump Helen's blood began to run. Out he shot, his lean dark head beside Dorn's horse. The wild park lay, clear and bright, in the moonlight, with strange silvery radiance on the grass. The patches of timber, like spired black islands in a moon-blanched lake, seemed to harbor shadows, and places for bears to hide, ready to spring out. As Helen neared each little grove, her pulses shook and her heart beat. Half a mile of rapid riding burned out the cold. And all seemed glorious — the sailing moon, white in a dark-blue sky, the white passionless stars, so solemn, so far away, the beckoning fringe of forestland, at once mysterious and friendly, and the fleet horses, running with soft rhythmic *thuds* over the grass, leaping the ditches and the hollows, making the bitter wind sting and cut. Coming up that park, the ride had been long; going back was as short as it was thrilling. In Helen experiences gathered realization slowly, and it was this swift ride, the horses neck and neck, and all the wildness and beauty, that completed the slow insidious work of years. The tears of excitement froze on her cheeks and her heart heaved full. All that pertained to this night got into her blood. It was only to feel, to live now, but it could be understood and remembered forever afterward.

Dorn's horse, a little in advance, sailed over a ditch. Ranger made a splendid leap, but he alighted among some grassy tufts, and fell. Helen shot over his head. She struck lengthwise, her arms stretched, and slid hard to a shocking impact that stunned her. Bo's scream rang in her ears; she felt the wet grass under her face, and then the strong hands that lifted her. Dorn loomed over her, bending down to look into her face; Bo was clutching her with frantic hands. And Helen could only gasp. Her breast seemed caved in. The need to breathe was torture.

"Nell . . . you're not hurt. You fell light, like a feather. All grass here. . . . You can't be hurt!" said Dorn sharply.

His anxious voice penetrated beyond her hearing, and his strong hands went swiftly over her arms and shoulders feeling for broken bones.

"Just had the wind knocked out of you," went on Dorn. "It feels awful, but it's nothin'."

Helen got a little air that was like hot pinpoints in her lungs, and then a deeper breath, and then full gasping respiration.

"I guess . . . I'm not hurt . . . not a bit," she choked out.

"You sure had a header. Never saw a prettier spill. Ranger doesn't do that often. I reckon we were travelin' too fast. . . . But it was fun, don't you think?"

It was Bo who answered. "Oh, glorious! But, gee, I was scared."

Dorn still held Helen's hands. She released them, while looking up at him. The moment was realization for her, of what for days had been a vague sweet uncertainty becoming near and strange, disturbing and present. This accident had been a sudden violent end to the wonderful ride. But its effect, the knowledge of what had got into her blood, would never change. And inseparable from it was this man of the forest.

CHAPTER ELEVEN

On the next morning Helen was awakened by what she imagined had been a dream of someone shouting. With a start she sat up. The sunshine showed pink and gold on the ragged spruce line of the mountain ruins. Bo was on her knees, braiding her hair with shaking hands, and at the same time trying to peep out.

And the echoes of a ringing cry were cracking back from the cliffs. That had been Dorn's voice.

"Nell! Nell! Wake up!" called Bo wildly. "Oh, someone's come! Horses and men!"

Helen got to her knees and peered out over Bo's shoulder. Dorn, standing tall and striking beside the campfire, was waving his sombrero. Way down the open edge of the park came a string of pack burros with mounted men behind. In the foremost rider Helen recognized Roy Beeman.

"That first one's Roy!" she exclaimed. "I'd

never forget him on a horse. . . . Bo, it must mean Uncle Al's come!"

"Sure. We're born lucky. Here we are safe and sound . . . and all this grand camp trip. . . . Look at the cowboys. . . . *Look!* Oh, maybe this isn't great!" babbled Bo.

Dorn wheeled to see the girls peeping out. "It's time you're up!" he called. "Your Uncle Al is here."

For an instant after Helen sank back out of Dorn's sight, she sat there perfectly motionlessly, so struck was she by the singular tone of Dorn's voice. She imagined that he regretted what this visiting cavalcade of horsemen meant — they had come to take her to her ranch in Pine. Helen's heart suddenly began to beat fast, but thickly, as if muffled within her breast.

"Hurry now, girls!" called Dorn.

Bo was already out, kneeling on the flat stone at the little brook, splashing water in a great hurry. Helen's hands trembled so that she could scarcely lace her boots or brush her hair, and she was long behind Bo in making herself presentable. When Helen stepped out, a short powerfully built man in coarse garb and heavy boots stood holding Bo's hands.

"Wal, wal! You favor the Rayners," he was saying. "I remember your Dad an' a fine

229

feller he was."

Beside them stood Dorn and Roy, and beyond was a group of horses and riders.

"Uncle, here comes Nell," said Bo softly.

"Aw!" The old cattleman breathed hard as he turned.

Helen hurried. She had not expected to remember this uncle, but one look into the brown beaming face, with the blue eyes flashing, yet sad, and she recognized him, at the same instant recalling her mother.

He held out his arms to receive her.

"Nell Auchincloss all over again!" he exclaimed in deep voice, as he kissed her. "I'd have knowed you anywhere!"

"Uncle Al!" murmured Helen. "I remember you . . . though I was only four."

"Wal, wal, thet's fine," he replied. "I remember you straddled my knee once, an' your hair was brighter . . . an' curly. It ain't neither now. . . . Sixteen years! An' you're twenty now? What a fine broad-shouldered girl you are! An', Nell, you're the handsomest Auchincloss I ever seen!"

Helen found herself blushing, and withdrew her hands from his as Roy stepped forward to pay his respects. He stood bareheaded, lean and tall, with neither his clear eyes nor his still face, or the proffered hand expressing anything of the proven quality of fidelity, of achievement that Helen sensed in him.

"Howdy Miss Helen. . . . Howdy Bo," he said. "You-all both look fine an' brown. . . . I reckon I was shore slow rustlin' your Uncle Al up here. But I was figgerin' you'd like Milt's camp for a while."

"We shore did," replied Bo archly.

"*Aw!*" breathed Auchincloss heavily. "Lemme set down." He drew the girls to the rustic seat Dorn had built for them under the big pine.

"Oh! You must be tired! How . . . how are you?" asked Helen anxiously.

"Tired! Wal, if I am, it's jest this here minnit. When Joe Beeman rode in on me with thet news of you . . . wal, I jest forgot I was a worn-out old hoss. Haven't felt so good in years. . . . Mebbe two such young an' pretty nieces will make a new man of me."

"Uncle Al, you look strong and well to me," said Bo, "and young, too, an'. . . ."

"*Haw! Haw!* Thet'll do," interrupted Al. "I see through you. What you'll do to Uncle Al will be aplenty. . . . Yes, girls, I'm feelin' fine. But strange . . . strange! Mebbe thet's my joy at seein' you safe . . . safe when I feared so thet damned greaser Beasley. . . ."

In Helen's grave gaze his face changed swiftly — and all the several years of toil

231

and battle and privation showed, with something that was not age, or resignation, yet as tragic as both.

"Wal, never mind him . . . now," he added slowly, and the warmer light returned to his face. "Dorn . . . come here."

The hunter stepped closer.

"I reckon I owe you more'n I can ever pay," said Auchincloss, with an arm around each niece.

"No, Al, you don't owe me anythin'," returned Dorn thoughtfully as he looked away.

"Ahuh!" grunted Al. "You hear him, girls. . . . Now listen, you wild hunter. An' you girls listen. . . . Milt, I never thought you much good, 'cept for the wilds. But I reckon I'll have to swallow thet. I do. Comin' to me as you did . . . an' after bein' drove off . . . keepin' your council an' savin' my girls from thet hold-up, wal, it's the biggest deal any man ever did for me. . . . An' I'm ashamed of my hard feelin's an' here's my hand."

"Thanks, Al," replied Dorn with his fleeting smile, and he met the proffered hand. "Now, will you be makin' camp here?"

"Wal, no. I'll rest a bit, an' you can pack the girls' outfit . . . then we'll go. Sure you're goin' with us?"

"I'll call the girls to breakfast," replied Dorn, and he moved away without answering Auchincloss's query.

Helen divined that Dorn did not mean to go down to Pine with them, and the knowledge gave her a blank feeling of surprise. Had she expected him to go?

"Come here, Jeff," called Al to one of his men.

A short, bowlegged horseman with dusty garb and sun-bleached face hobbled forth from the group. He was not young, but he had a boyish grin and bright little eyes. Awkwardly he doffed his slouch sombrero.

"Jeff, shake hands with my nieces," said Al. "This's Helen, an' your boss from now on. An' this's Bo . . . fer short. Her name was Nancy, but, when she lay a baby in her cradle, I called her Bo-Peep an' the name's stuck. . . . Girls, this here's my foreman, Jeff Mulvey, who's been with me twenty years."

The introduction caused embarrassment to all three principals, particularly to Jeff.

"Jeff, throw the packs an' saddles fer a rest," was Al's order to his foreman.

"Nell, reckon you'll have fun bossin' thet outfit." Al chuckled. "None of 'ems got a wife. Lot of scallywags they are, no woman would have them!"

"Uncle, I hope I'll never have to be their

233

boss," replied Helen.

"Wal, you're goin' to be, right off," declared Al. "They ain't a bad lot, after all. . . . An' I got a likely new man."

With that, he turned to Bo, and, after studying her pretty face, he asked in apparently severe tone.

"Did you send a cowboy named Carmichael to ask me for a job?"

Bo looked quite startled. "Carmichael! Why, Uncle, I never heard that name before," replied Bo bewilderedly.

"Ahuh! Reckoned the young rascal was lyin'," said Auchincloss. "But I liked the fellar's looks an' so let him stay." Then the rancher turned to the group of lounging riders. "Las Vegas, come here," he ordered in a loud voice.

Helen thrilled at sight of a tall superbly built cowboy reluctantly detaching himself from the group. He had a red-bronze face, young like a boy's. Helen recognized it, and the flowing red scarf, and the swinging gun, and the slow, spur-*clinking* gait. No other than Bo's Las Vegas cowboy admirer!

Then Helen flashed a look at Bo, which look gave her a delicious almost irresistible desire to laugh. That young lady also recognized the reluctant individual approaching with flushed and downcast face. Helen

234

recorded her first experience of Bo's utter discomfiture. Bo turned white — then red as a rose.

"Say, my niece said she never heard of the name Carmichael," declared Al severely, as the cowboy halted before him. Helen knew her uncle had the repute of dealing hard with his men, but here she was reassured and pleased at the twinkle in his eye.

"Shore, boss, I can't help thet," drawled the cowboy. "It's good old Texas stock."

He did not appear shame-faced now, but just as cool, easy, clear-eyed, and lazy as the day Helen had liked his warm young face and intent gaze.

"Texas! You fellows from the Panhandle are always hollerin' Texas. I never seen thet Texans had anyone else beat . . . say from Missouri," returned Al testily.

Carmichael maintained a discreet silence, and carefully avoided looking at the girls.

"Wal, I reckon we'll all call you Las Vegas, anyway," continued the rancher. "Didn't you say my niece sent you to me for a job?"

Whereupon Carmichael's easy manner vanished. "Now, boss, shore my memory's pore," he said. "I only says. . . ."

"Don't tell me thet. My memory's not p-o-r-e," replied Al, mimicking the drawl. "What you said was thet my niece would

235

speak a good word for you."

Here Carmichael stole a timid glance at Bo, the result of which was to render him utterly crestfallen. Not improbably he had taken Bo's expression to mean something it did not, for Helen read it as a mingling of consternation and fright. Her eyes were big and blazing; a red spot was growing in each cheek as she gathered strength from his confusion.

"Wal, didn't you?" demanded Al.

From the glance the old rancher shot from the cowboy to the others of his employ it seemed to Helen that they were having fun at Carmichael's expense.

"Yes, sir, I did," suddenly replied the cowboy.

"Ahuh! All right, here's my niece. Now see thet she speaks the good word."

Carmichael looked at Bo and Bo looked at him. Their glances were strange, wondering, and they grew shy. Bo dropped hers. The cowboy apparently forgot what had been demanded of him.

Helen put a hand on the old rancher's arm.

"Uncle, what happened was my fault," she said. "The train stopped at Las Vegas. This young man saw us at the open window. He must have guessed we were lonely, homesick girls, getting lost in the West. For he spoke to us . . . nice and friendly. He knew of you. And he asked, in what I took for fun, if we thought you would give him a job. And I replied, just to tease Bo, that she would surely speak a good word for him."

"*Haw! Haw!* So thet's it," replied Al, and he turned to Bo with merry eyes. "Wal, I kept this here Las Vegas Carmichael on his say-so. Come in with your good word, unless you want to see him lose his job."

Bo did not grasp her uncle's bantering because she was seriously gazing at the cowboy. But she had grasped something.

"He . . . he was the first person . . . out West . . . to speak kind to us," she said, facing her uncle.

"Wal, thet's a pretty good word, but it ain't enough," responded Al.

Subdued laughter came from the listening group. Carmichael shifted from side to side.

"He . . . he looks as if he might ride a horse well," ventured Bo.

"Best horseman I ever seen," agreed Al heartily.

"And . . . and shoot?" added Bo hopefully.

"Bo, he packs thet gun low, like Jim Wilson, an' all them Texas gunfighters. Reckon thet ain't no good word."

"Then . . . I'll vouch for him," said Bo

with finality.

"That settles it." Auchincloss turned to the cowboy. "Las Vegas, you're a stranger to us. But you're welcome to a place in the outfit an' I hope you won't never disappoint me."

Auchincloss's tone, passing from jest to earnest, betrayed to Helen the old rancher's need of new and true men, and hinted of trying days to come.

Carmichael stood before Bo, sombrero in hands, rolling it around and around, manifestly bursting with words he could not speak. And the girl looked very young and sweet with her flushed face and shining eyes. Helen saw in the moment more than that little byplay of confusion.

"Miss . . . Miss Rayner . . . I shore . . . am obliged," he stammered presently.

"You're very welcome," she replied softly.

"I . . . I got on the next train," he added.

When he said that, Bo was looking straight at him, but she seemed not to have heard.

"What's your name?" suddenly she asked.

"Carmichael."

"I heard that. But didn't Uncle call you Las Vegas?"

"Shore. But it wasn't my fault. That cow-punchin' outfit saddled it on me, right off. They don't know no better. Shore, I jest

238

won't answer to that handle. . . . Now . . . Miss Bo . . . my real name is Tom."

"I simply could not call you . . . any name but Las Vegas," replied Bo very sweetly.

"But . . . beggin' your pawdon . . . I . . . I don't like thet," blustered Carmichael.

"People often get called names . . . they don't like," she said with deep intent.

The cowboy blushed scarlet. Helen, as well as he, got Bo's inference to that last audacious epithet he had boldly called out as the train was leaving Las Vegas. She also sensed something of the disorder in store for Mr. Carmichael. Just then the embarrassed young man was saved by Dorn's call to the girls to come to breakfast.

That meal, the last for Helen in Paradise Park, gave rise to a strange and inexplicable restraint. She had little to say. Bo was in the highest spirits, teasing the pets, joking with her uncle and Roy, and even poking fun at Dorn. The hunter seemed somewhat somber; Roy was his usual dry genial self. And Auchincloss, who sat nearby, was an interested spectator. When Tom put in an appearance, lounging with his feline grace into the camp, as if he knew he was a privileged pet, then the rancher could scarcely contain himself.

"Dorn, it's thet damn' cougar!" he ejaculated.

"Sure, that's Tom."

"He ought to be corralled or chained. I've no use for cougars," protested Al.

"Tom is as tame an' safe as a kitten."

"Ahuh! Wal, you tell thet to the girls if you like. But not me! I'm an old hoss, I am."

"Uncle, Tom sleeps curled up at the foot of my bed," said Bo.

"*Aw* . . . what?"

"Honest Injun," she responded. "Nell, isn't it so?"

Helen smilingly nodded her corroboration. Then Bo called Tom to her, and made him lie with his head on his stretched paws, right beside her, and beg for bits to eat.

"Wal! I'd never have believed thet!" exclaimed Al, shaking his big head. "Dorn, it's one on me. I've had them big cats foller me on the trails, through the woods, moonlight an' dark. An' I've heard 'em let out that awful cry. They ain't any wild sound on earth that can beat a cougar's. Does this Tom ever let out one of them wails?"

"Sometimes at night," replied Dorn.

"Wal, excuse me. Hope you don't fetch the yaller rascal down to Pine."

"I won't."

"What'll you do with this menagerie?"

Dorn regarded the rancher attentively. "Reckon, Al, I'll take care of them."

"But you're goin' down to my ranch."

"What for?"

Al scratched his head and gazed perplexedly at the hunter. "Wal, ain't it customary to visit friends?"

"Thanks, Al. Next time I ride down Pine way . . . in the spring, perhaps . . . I'll run over an' see how you are."

"Spring!" ejaculated Auchincloss. Then he shook his head sadly and a faraway look filmed his eyes. "Reckon you'd call some late."

"Al, you'll get well now. These girls . . . now. . . . They'll cure you. Reckon I never saw you look so good."

Auchincloss did not press his point further at that time, but after the meal, when the other men came to see Dorn's camp and pets, then Helen's quick ears caught the renewal of the subject.

"I'm askin' you, will you come?" Auchincloss said, low and eagerly.

"No. I couldn't fit in down there," replied Dorn.

"Milt, talk sense. You can't go on forever huntin' bear an' tamin' cats," protested the old rancher.

"Why not?" asked the hunter thoughtfully.

Auchincloss stood up and shaking himself, as if to ward off his testy temper, he put a hand on Dorn's arm. "One reason is you're needed in Pine."

"How? Who needs me?"

"I do. I'm playin' out fast. An' Beasley's my enemy. The ranch an' all I got will go to Nell. . . . Thet ranch will have to be run by a man an' *held* by a man. . . . Do you savvy? It's a big job. An' I'm offerin' to make you my foreman right now."

"Al, you sort of take my breath," replied Dorn. "An' I'm sure grateful. . . . But the fact is, even if I could handle the job, I . . . I don't believe I'd want to."

"Make yourself want to, then. Thet'd soon come. You'd get interested. This country will develop. I seen thet years ago. The government is goin' to chase the Apaches out of here. Soon homesteaders will be flockin' in. . . . Big future, Dorn. You want to get in now. . . . An'. . . ." Here Auchincloss hesitated, then spoke lower. "An' take your chance with the girl. I'll be on your side."

A slight vibrating start ran over Dorn's stalwart form. "Al . . . you're plumb dotty!" he exclaimed.

"Dotty! Me? Dotty!" ejaculated Auchincloss. Then he swore. "In a minnit I'll tell you what you are."

"But, Al, that talk's so . . . so . . . like an old fool's."

"Ahuh. An' why so?"

"Because that wonderful girl would never look at me," Dorn replied simply.

"I seen her lookin' already," declared Al bluntly.

Dorn shook his head as if arguing with the old rancher was hopeless.

"Never mind thet," went on Al. "Mebbe I am a dotty old fool . . . 'specially for takin' a shine to you. . . . But I say again . . . will you come down to Pine an' be my foreman?"

"No," replied Dorn.

"Milt, I've no son . . . an' I'm . . . afraid of Beasley." This was uttered in an agitated whisper.

"Al, you make me ashamed," said Dorn hoarsely. "I can't come. I've no nerve."

"You've no what?"

"Al, I don't know what's wrong with me. But I'm afraid I'd find out if I came down there."

"A-huh! It's the girl!"

"I don't know, but I'm afraid so. . . . An' I won't come."

"*Aw,* yes you will. . . ."

Helen rose with beating heart and tingling ears, and moved away out of hearing. She had listened too long to what had not been intended for her ears, yet she could not be sorry. She walked a few rods along the brook, out from under the pines, and, standing in the open edge of the park, she felt the beautiful scene still her agitation. The following moments, then, were the happiest she had spent in Paradise Park, and the profoundest of her whole life.

Presently her uncle called her. "Nell, this here hunter wants to give you thet black hoss! An' I say you take him!"

"Ranger deserves better care than I can give him," said Dorn. "He runs free in the woods most of the time. . . . I'd be obliged if she'd have him."

Bo swept a saucy glance from Dorn to her sister. "Sure she'll have Ranger. . . . Just offer him to *me!*"

Dorn stood there expectantly, holding a blanket in his hand, ready to saddle the horse.

Carmichael walked around Ranger with that appraising eye so keen in cowboys.

"Las Vegas, do you know anything about horses?" asked Bo.

"Me? Wal, if you ever buy or trade a hoss, you shore have me there," replied Carmichael.

"What do you think of Ranger?" went on Bo.

"Shore I'd buy him sudden, if I could."

"Mister Las Vegas, you're too late," asserted Helen as she advanced to lay a hand on the horse. "Ranger is mine."

Dale smoothed out the blanket, and, folding it, he threw it over the horse, and then with one powerful swing he set the saddle in place.

"Thank you very much for him," said Helen softly.

"You're welcome, an' I'm sure glad," responded Dorn, and then, after a few deft strong pulls at the straps, he continued: "There, he's ready for you." With that he laid an arm over the saddle and faced Helen, as she stood patting and smoothing Ranger.

Helen, strong and calm now, in feminine possession of her secret and his, as well as her composure, looked frankly and steadily at Dorn. He seemed composed, too, yet the bronze of his fine face was a trifle pale.

"But I can't thank you . . . I'll never be able to repay you . . . for your service to me and my sister," said Helen.

"I reckon you needn't try," Dorn returned. "An' my service, as you call it, has been good for me."

245

"Are you going down to Pine with us?"

"No."

"But you will come soon?"

"Not very soon, I reckon," he replied, and averted his gaze.

"When?"

"Hardly before spring."

"Spring? That is a long time. Won't you come to see me sooner than that?"

"If I can get down to Pine."

"You're the first friend I've made in the West," said Helen earnestly.

"You'll make many more . . . an' I reckon soon forget him you called the man of the forest."

"I never forget any of my friends. And you've been the . . . the biggest friend I ever had."

"I'll be proud to remember."

"But will you remember . . . will you promise to come to Pine?"

"I reckon."

"Thank you. All's well then. . . . My friend, good bye."

"Good bye," he said, clasping her hand. His glance was clear, warm, beautiful, yet it was sad.

Auchincloss's hearty voice broke the spell. Then Helen saw that the others were mounted. Bo had ridden up close, and her face was earnest and happy and grieved all at once as she bade good bye to Dorn. The pack burros were bobbing along toward the green slope. Helen was the last to mount, but Roy was the last to leave the hunter.

It was a merry singing train that climbed that brown odorous trail, under the dark spruces. Helen assuredly was happy, yet a pang abided in her breast. She remembered that halfway up the slope there was a turn in the trail where it came out upon an open bluff. The time seemed long, but at last she got there. And she checked Ranger so as to have a moment's gaze down into the park.

It yawned there, a dark-green and bright-gold gulf, asleep under a westering sun, exquisite, wild, lonesome. Then she saw Dorn standing in the open space between the pines and the spruces. He waved to her. And she returned the salute.

Roy caught up with her then and halted his horse. He waved his sombrero to Dorn and let out a piercing yell that awoke the sleeping echoes, splitting strangely from cliff to cliff.

"Shore Milt never knowed what it was to be lonesome," said Roy as if thinking aloud. "But he'll know now."

Ranger stepped out of his own accord and, turning off the ledge, entered the spruce forest. Helen lost sight of Paradise Park. For hours then she rode along a shady fragrant trail, seeing the beauty of color and wildness, hearing the murmur and rush and roar of water, but all the while her mind revolved the sweet and momentous realization that had thrilled her — that the hunter, this strange man of the forest, so deeply versed in Nature and so unfamiliar with emotion, aloof and simple and strong like the elements that had developed him, had fallen in love with her and did not know it.

CHAPTER TWELVE

Dorn stood with face and arm upraised, and he watched Helen ride off the ledge to disappear in the forest. That vast spruce slope seemed to have swallowed her. She was gone! Slowly Dorn lowered his arm with a gesture expressive of a strange finality, an eloquent despair, of which he was unconscious. He turned to the park, to his camp, and the many duties of a hunter. The park did not seem the same, nor did his home, nor his work.

"I reckon this feelin's natural," he soliloquized resignedly, "but it's sure queer for me. That's what comes of makin' friends. . . . Nell an' Bo, now, they made a difference, an' a difference I never knew before."

He calculated that this difference had been simply one of responsibility, and then the charm and liveliness of the companionship of girls, and finally friendship. These would pass now that the causes were re-moved.

Before he had worked an hour around camp, he realized a change had come but it was not the one anticipated. Always before he had put his mind on his tasks, whatever they might be; now he worked while his thoughts were strangely involved.

The little bear cub whined at his heels; the tame deer seemed to regard him with deep questioning eyes; the big cougar pad-ded softly here and there as if searching for something.

"You all miss Bo . . . now . . . I reckon," said Dorn. "Well, she's gone an' you'll have to get along with me."

Some vague approach to irritation with his pets surprised him. Presently he grew both irritated and surprised with himself — a state of mind totally unfamiliar. Several times as old habit brought momentary abstraction he found himself suddenly look-ing around for Helen and Bo. And each time the shock grew stronger. They were gone, but their presence lingered. After his camp chores were completed, he went over to pull down the lean-to that the girls had utilized as a tent. The spruce boughs had dried out brown and sear; the wind had blown the roof away; the sides were leaning in. As there was now no further use for this little habitation, he might better pull it down. Dorn did not acknowledge that his gaze had involuntarily wandered toward it many times. Therefore he strode over with the intention of destroying it.

For the first time since Roy and he had built the lean-to, he stepped inside. Nothing was more certain than the fact that he experienced a strange sensation, perfectly incomprehensible to him. The blankets lay there on the spruce boughs, disarranged and thrown back by hurried hands, yet still holding something of round folds where the slender forms had nestled. A black scarf often worn by Bo lay covering the pillow of pine needles, a red ribbon that Helen had worn on her hair hung from a twig. These articles were all that had been forgotten. Dorn gazed at them attentively, then at the blankets and all around the fragrant little shelter, and he stepped outside with an uncomfortable knowledge that he could not destroy the place where Helen and Bo had spent so many hours.

Whereupon, in studious mood, Dorn took up his rifle and strode out to hunt. His winter supply of venison had not yet been laid in. Action suited his mood; he climbed far and passed by many a watching buck to slay, which seemed murder, and at last he jumped one that was wild and bounded away. This he shot, and set himself a Herculean task in packing the whole carcass back to camp. Burdened thus he staggered under the trees, sweating freely, many times laboring for breath, aching with toil, until at last he had reached camp. There he slid the deer carcass off his shoulders, and, standing over it, he gazed down while his breast labored. It was one of the finest young bucks he had ever seen. But neither in stalking it, or making a wonderful shot, or in packing home a weight that would have burdened two men, or in gazing down at his beautiful quarry, did Dorn experience any of the old joy of the hunter.

"I'm a little off my feed," he mused as he wiped the sweat from his heated face. "Maybe a little dotty, as I called Al. . . . But that'll pass."

Whatever his state, it did not pass. As of old after a long day's hunt he reclined beside the campfire and watched the golden sunset glows change on the ramparts; as of old he lay a hand on the soft furry head of the pet cougar; as of old he watched the gold change to red and then to dark, and twilight fall like a blanket; as of old he listened to the dreamy lulling murmur of the waterfall. The old familiar beauty, wildness, silence, and loneliness were there, but the old content seemed strangely gone.

Soberly he confessed then that he missed the happy company of the girls. He did not distinguish Helen from Bo in his slow introspection. When he sought his bed, he did not at once fall to sleep. Always after a few moments of wakefulness, while the silence settled down or the wind moaned through the pines, he had fallen asleep. This night he found different. Although he was tired, sleep would not soon come. The wilderness, the mountains, the park, the camp — all seemed to have lost something. Even the darkness seemed empty. And when at length Dorn fell asleep, it was to be troubled by restless dreams.

Up with the keen-edged, steely bright dawn he went at his tasks with the springy stride of the deerstalker.

At the end of that strenuous day, which was singularly full of the old excitement and action and danger, and of new observations, he was bound to confess that no longer did the chase suffice for him. Many times on the heights that day, with the wind keen in his face and the vast green billows of spruce below him, he had found that he was gazing without seeing, halting without object, dreaming as he had never dreamed before.

Once, when a magnificent elk came out upon a rocky ridge, and whistling a challenge to invisible rivals, stood there a target to stir any hunter's pulse, Dorn did not even raise his rifle. Into his ear just then rang Helen's voice: *Milt Dorn, you are no Indian. Giving yourself to a hunter's wild life is selfish. It is wrong. You love this lonely life, but it is not work. Work that does not help others is not a real man's work.*

From that moment conscience tormented him. It was not what he loved, but what he ought to do that counted in the sum of good achieved in the world. Old Al Auchincloss had been right. Dorn was wasting strength and intelligence that should go to do his share in the development of the West. Now that he had reached maturity, if through his knowledge of Nature's laws he had come to see the meaning of the strife of men for existence, for place, for possession, and to hold them in contempt, that was no reason why he should keep himself aloof from them, from some work that was needed in an incomprehensible world.

Dorn did not hate work, but he loved freedom. To be alone, to live with Nature, to feel the elements, to labor and dream and idle and climb and sleep unhampered by duty, by worry, by restriction, by the petty interests of men — this had always been his ideal of living. Cowboys, riders, sheepherders, farmers — these toiled on from one place and one job to another for the little money doled out to them. Nothing beautiful, nothing significant had ever existed in that for him. He had worked as a boy at every kind of range work, and of all that humdrum waste of effort he had liked sawing wood best. Once he had quit a job of branding cattle because the smell of burning hide, the bawl of the terrified calf had sickened him. If men were honest, there would be no need to scar cattle. He had never in the least desired to own land and droves of stock, and make deals with ranchmen, deals advantageous to himself. Why should a man want to make a deal or trade a horse or do a piece of work to another man's disadvantage? Self-preservation was the first law of life. But as the plants and trees and birds and beasts interpreted that law, merciless and inevitable as they were, they had neither greed nor dishonesty. They lived by the grand rule of what was best for the greatest number.

But Dorn's philosophy, cold and clear and inevitable, like Nature itself, began to be pierced by the human appeal in Helen Rayner's words. What did she mean? Not that he should lose his love of wilderness, but that he realize himself! Many chance words of that girl had depth. He was young, strong, intelligent, free from taint of disease, or the fever of drink. He could do something for others. Who? If that mattered, there for instance was poor old Mrs. Cass, aged and lame now, and there was Al Auchincloss, dying in his boots, afraid of enemies, and wistful for his blood and his property to receive the fruit of his labors, and there were the two girls, Helen and Bo, new and strange to the West, about to be confronted by a big problem of ranch life and rival interests. Dorn thought of still more people in the little village of Pine — of others who had failed, whose lives were hard, who could have been made happier by kindness and assistance.

What then was the duty of Milt Dorn to himself? Because men preyed on each other and on the weak, should he turn his back upon a so-called civilization or should he grow like them? Clear as a bell came the answer that his duty was to do neither. And then he saw how the little village of Pine, as well as the whole world, needed men like him. He had gone to Nature, to the forest, to the wilderness for his development, and all the judgments and efforts of his future would be a result of that education.

Thus Dorn, lying in the darkness and silence of his lonely park, arrived at a conclusion that he divined was but the beginning of a struggle.

It took long introspection to determine the exact nature of that struggle, but at length it evolved into the paradox that Helen Rayner had opened his eyes to his duty as a man, that he accepted it, yet found a strange obstacle in the perplexing, tumultuous, sweet fear of ever going near her again.

Suddenly, then, all his thought revolved around the girl, and, thrown off his balance, he weltered in a wilderness of unfamiliar ideas.

When he awoke next day, the fight was on in earnest. In his sleep his mind had been active. The idea that greeted him, beautiful as the sunrise, flashed in memory of Auchincloss's significant words: *Take your chance with the girl.*

The old rancher was in his dotage. He hinted of things beyond the range of possibility. That idea of a chance for Dorn remained before his consciousness only an instant. Stars were unattainable; life could not be fathomed; the secrets of Nature did not abide alone on the earth — these theories were not any more impossible of proving than that Helen Rayner might be for him.

Nevertheless her strange coming into his life had played havoc, the extent of which he had only begun to realize.

For a month he tramped through the forest. It was October, a still golden fulfilling season of the year, and everywhere in the vast dark green a glorious blaze of oak and aspen made beautiful contrast. He carried his rifle, but he never used it. He would climb miles and go this way and that with no object in view. Yet his eye and ear had never been keener. Hours he would spend on a promontory, watching the distance, where the golden patches of aspen shone brightly out of dark-green mountain slopes. He loved to fling himself down in an aspen grove at the edge of a *parque,* and there lie in that radiance like a veil of gold and purple and red, with the white tree trunks striping the shade. Always, whether there were breeze or not, the aspen leaves quivered, ceaselessly, wonderfully, like his pulse, beyond his control. Often he reclined against a mossy rock beside a mountain stream to listen, to watch, to feel all that was there, while his mind held a haunting, dark-eyed vision of a girl. On the lonely heights, like an eagle, he sat gazing down into Paradise Park, which was more and more beautiful, but would never again be the same, never fill him with content, never be all and all to him.

Late in October the first snow fell. It melted at once on the south side of the park, but the north slopes and the rims and domes above stayed white.

Dorn had worked quick and hard at curing and storing his winter supply of food, and now he spent days chopping and splitting wood to burn during the months he would be snowed-in. He watched for the dark gray, fast-scudding storm clouds, and welcomed them when they came. Once there lay ten feet of snow on the trails he would be snowed-in until spring. It would be impossible to go down to Pine. And perhaps during the long winter he would be cured of this strange nameless disorder of his feelings.

November brought storms up on the peaks. Flurries of snow fell in the park every day, but the sunny south side, where Dorn's camp lay, retained its autumnal color and warmth. Not till late in winter did the snow creep over this secluded nook.

The morning came at last, piercingly keen and bright, when Dorn saw that the heights were impassable, and the realization brought him a poignant regret. He had not guessed how he had wanted to see Helen Rayner again until it was too late. That opened his eyes. A raging frenzy of action followed, in which he only tired himself physically without helping himself spiritually.

It was sunset when he faced the west, looking up at the pink snow domes and the dark golden fringe of spruce, and in that moment he found the truth.

"I love that girl. I love that girl!" he spoke aloud to the distant white peaks, to the winds, to the loneliness and silence of his prison, to the great pines and to the murmuring streams, and to his faithful pets. It was his tragic confession of weakness, of amazing truth, of hopeless position, of pitiful excuse for the transformation wrought in him.

Dorn's struggle ended there when he faced his soul. To understand himself was to be released from strain, worry, ceaseless importuning doubt, and wonder and fear.

But the fever of unrest, of uncertainty had been nothing compared to a sudden upflashing torment of love.

With somber deliberation he set about the tasks needful, and others that he might make — his campfires and meals, the care of his pets and horses, the mending of saddles and pack harness, the curing of buckskin for moccasins and hunting suits. So his days were not idle. But all this work was habit for him and needed no application of mind.

And Dorn, like some men of lonely wilderness lives who did not retrograde toward the savage, was a thinker. Love made him a sufferer.

The surprise and shame of his unconscious surrender, the certain hopelessness of it, the long years of communion with all that was wild, lonely, and beautiful, the wonderfully developed insight into Nature's secrets, and the sudden dawning revelation that he was no omniscient being exempt from the ruthless ordinary destiny of man — all these showed him the strength of his manhood and of his passion, and that the life he had chosen was of all lives the one calculated to make love sad and terrible.

Helen Rayner haunted him. In the sunlight there was not a place around camp that did not picture her lithe vigorous body, her dark thoughtful eyes, her eloquent resolute lips, and the smile that was so sweet and strong. At night she was there like a slender specter, pacing beside him under the moaning pines. Every campfire held in its heart the glowing white radiance of her spirit.

Nature had taught Dorn to love solitude and silence, but love itself taught him their meaning. Solitude had been created for the eagle on his crag, for the blasted mountain fir, lovely and gnarled on its peak, for the elk and the wolf. But it had not been intended for man. And to live always in the silence of wild places was to become obsessed with self — to think and dream — to be happy, which state however pursued by man was not good for him. Man must be given imperious longings for the unattainable.

It needed then only the memory of an unattainable woman to render solitude passionately desired by a man, yet almost unendurable. Dorn was alone with his secret, and every pine, every thing in that park saw him shaken and undone.

In the dark pitchy deadness of night, when there was no wind and the cold on the peaks had frozen the waterfall, then the silence seemed insupportable. Many hours that should have been given to slumber were paced out under the cold white pitiless stars, under the lonely pines.

Dorn's memory betrayed him, mocked his restraint, cheated him of any peace, and his imagination, sharpened by love, created pictures, fancies, feelings that drove him frantic.

He thought of Helen Rayner's strong shapely brown hand. In a thousand different actions it haunted him. How quick and deft in campfire tasks! How graceful and swift as she plaited her dark hair! How tender and skilful in its ministration when one of his pets had been injured! How eloquent when pressed tightly against her breast in a moment of fear on the dangerous heights! How expressive of unthinkable things when laid on his arm!

Dorn saw that beautiful hand slowly creep up his arm, across his shoulder, and slide round his neck to clasp there. He was powerless to inhibit the picture. And what he felt then was boundless, unutterable. No woman had ever yet so much as clasped his hand, and heretofore no such imaginings had ever crossed his mind, yet deep in him, somewhere hidden, had been this waiting, sweet, and imperious need. In the bright day he appeared to ward off such fancies, but at night he was helpless. And every fancy left him weaker, wilder.

When at the culmination of this phase of his passion, Dorn, who had never known the touch of a woman's lips, suddenly yielded to the illusion of Helen Rayner's kisses, he found himself quite mad, filled with rapture and despair, loving her as he hated himself. It seemed as if he had experienced all these terrible feelings in some former life, and had forgotten them in this life. He had no right to think of her, but he could not resist it. Imagining the sweet surrender of her lips was a sacrilege, yet here, in spite of will and honor and shame, he was lost.

Dorn, at length, was vanquished, and he ceased to rail at himself, or restrain his fancies. He became a dreamy sad-eyed campfire gazer, like many another lonely man, separated by chance or error, from what the heart hungered for most. But this great experience, when all its significance had clarified in his mind, immeasurably broadened his understanding of the principles of Nature applied to life.

Love had been in him, stronger than in most men, because of his keen vigorous lonely years in the forest, where health of mind and body were intensified and preserved. How simple, how natural, how inevitable! He might have loved any fine-spirited, healthy-bodied girl. Like a tree shooting its branches and leaves, its whole entity, toward the sunlight, so had he grown toward a woman's love. Why? Because the thing he revered in Nature, the spirit, the universal, the life that was God, had created at his birth or before his birth the three tremendous instincts of Nature — to fight for life, to feed himself, to reproduce his kind. That was all there was to it. But, oh, the mystery, the beauty, the torment, and the terror of this third instinct — this hunger for the sweetness and the glory of a woman's love!

CHAPTER THIRTEEN

Helen Rayner dropped her knitting into her lap and sat pensively gazing out of the window over the bare yellow ranges of her uncle's ranch.

The winter day was bright, but steely, and the wind that whipped down from the white-capped mountains had a keen frosty edge. A scant snow lay in protected places; cattle stood bunched in the lea of ridges; low sheets of dust scurried across the flats.

The big living room of the ranch house was warm and comfortable with its red adobe walls, its huge stone fireplace where cedar logs blazed, and its many-colored blankets. Bo Rayner sat before the fire, curled up in an armchair, absorbed in a book. On the floor lay a greyhound, his racy fine head stretched toward the warmth.

"Did Uncle call?" asked Helen, with a start out of her reverie.

"I didn't hear him," replied Bo.

Helen rose to tiptoe across the floor, and, softly parting some curtains, she looked into the room where her uncle lay. He was asleep. Sometimes he called out in his slumbers. For weeks now he had been confined to his bed, slowly growing weaker. With a sigh Helen returned to her window seat and took up her work.

"Bo, the sun is bright," she said. "The days are growing longer. I'm so glad."

"Nell, you're always wishing time away. For me it passes quickly enough," replied the sister.

"But I love spring and summer and fall . . . and I guess I hate winter," returned Helen thoughtfully.

The yellow ranges rolled away up to the black ridges and they in turn swept up to the cold white mountains. Helen's gaze seemed to go beyond that snowy barrier. And Bo's keen eyes studied her sister's earnest sad face.

"Nell, do you ever think of Dorn?" suddenly she queried.

The question startled Helen. A slow blush suffused neck and cheek. "Of course," she replied as if surprised that Bo should ask such a thing.

"I . . . I shouldn't have asked that," said Bo softly, and then bent again over her book.

Helen gazed tenderly at that bright bowed head. In this swift flying eventful busy winter, during which the management of the ranch had devolved slowly upon Helen, the little sister had grown away from her. Bo had insisted upon her own free will and she had followed it, to the amusement of her uncle, to the concern of Helen, to the dismay and bewilderment of the faithful Mexican housekeepers, and to the undoing of all the young men on the ranch.

Helen had always been hoping and waiting for a favorable hour in which she might find this willful sister once more susceptible to wise and loving influence. But while she hesitated to speak, slow footsteps and a *jingle* of spurs sounded without, and then came a timid knock. Bo looked up brightly and ran to open the door.

"Oh . . . it's only you," she uttered in withering scorn to whomever had knocked.

Helen thought she could guess who it was.

"How are you-all?" asked a drawling voice.

"Well, Mister Carmichael, if that interests you . . . I'm quite ill," replied Bo freezingly.

"Ill . . . ? *Aw,* no, now?"

"It's a fact. If I don't die right off, I'll have to be taken back to Missouri," said Bo casually.

"Are you goin' to ask me in?" queried

Carmichael bluntly. "It's cold . . . an' I've got somethin' to say to. . . ."

"To *me?* Well, you're not backward, I declare," retorted Bo.

"Miss Rayner, I reckon it'll be strange to you . . . findin' out I didn't come to see you."

"Indeed! No. But what *was* strange was the deluded idea I had that you meant to apologize to me . . . like a gentleman. Come in, Mister Carmichael. My sister is here."

The door closed as Helen turned around. Carmichael stood just inside with his sombrero in hand, and, as he gazed at Bo, his lean face seemed hard. In the few months since autumn he had changed — aged it seemed, and the once young frank, alert, and careless cowboy traits had merged into the making of a man. Helen knew just how much of a man he really was. He had been her mainstay during all the complex working of the ranch that had fallen upon her shoulders.

"Wal, I reckon you was deluded all right . . . if you thought I'd crawl like them other lovers of yours," he said with cool deliberation.

Bo turned pale and her eyes fairly blazed, yet even in what must have been her fury, Helen saw amaze and pain.

269

"*Other* lovers? I think the biggest delusion here is the way you flatter yourself," replied Bo stingingly.

"Me . . . flatter myself? Nope. You don't savvy me. I'm shore hatin' myself these days."

"Small wonder. *I* certainly hate you . . . with all my heart."

At this retort the cowboy dropped his head and did not see Bo flaunt herself out of the room. But he heard the door close, and then slowly came toward Helen.

"Cheer up, Las Vegas," said Helen, smiling. "Bo's hot-tempered."

"Miss Nell, I'm just like a dog. The meaner she treats me the more I love her," he replied dejectedly.

To Helen's first instinct of liking for this cowboy there had been added admiration, respect, and a growing appreciation of strong faithful developing character. Carmichael's face and hands were red and chapped from winter winds; the leather of wrist bands, belt, and boots was all worn and shining and thin; little streaks of dust fell from him as he breathed heavily. He no longer looked the dashing cowboy, ready for a dance or lark or fight.

"How in the world did you offend her so?" asked Helen. "Bo is mad. I never saw her so mad as that."

"Miss Nell, it was just this way," began Carmichael. "Shore Bo's knowed I was in love with her. I asked her to marry me an' she wouldn't say yes or no. . . . An' mean as it sounds, she never run away from it, that's shore. We've had some quarrels . . . two of them bad, an' this last's the worst."

"Bo told me about one quarrel," said Helen. "It was because you drank . . . that time."

"Shore it was. She took one of her cold spells an' I just got drunk."

"But that was wrong," protested Helen.

"I ain't so shore. You see I used to get drunk often . . . before I come here. An' I've been drunk only once. But at Las Vegas, the outfit would never believe that. Wal, I promised Bo I wouldn't do it again, an' I've kept my word."

"That is fine of you. But tell me, why is she angry now?"

"Bo makes up to all the fellars," confessed Carmichael, hanging his head. "I took her to the dance last week over in the town hall. That's the first time she'd gone anywhere with me. I shore was proud. . . . But that dance was hell. Bo carried on somethin' terrible, an' I. . . ."

"Tell me. What did she do?" demanded

271

Helen anxiously. "I'm responsible for her. I've got to see that she behaves."

"*Aw,* I ain't sayin' she didn't behave like a lady," replied Carmichael. "It was . . . she . . . wal, all them fellars are fools over her . . . an' Bo wasn't true to me."

"My dear boy, is Bo engaged to you?"

"Lord . . . if she only was!" He sighed.

"Then how can you say she wasn't true to you? Be reasonable."

"I reckon now, Miss Nell, that no one can be in love and act reasonable," rejoined the cowboy. "I don't know how to explain, but the fact is I felt that Bo has played the . . . the devil with me an' all the other fellars."

"You mean she has flirted?"

"I reckon."

"Las Vegas, I'm afraid you're right," said Helen with growing apprehension. "Go on. Tell me what's happened."

"Wal, that Turner boy, who rides for Beasley, he was hot after Bo," returned Carmichael, and he spoke as if the memory hurt him. "Reckon I've no use for Turner. He's a fine-lookin', strappin' big cowpuncher, an' calculated to win the girls. He brags that he can, an' I reckon he's right. Wal, he was always hangin' around Bo. An' he stole one of my dances with Bo. I only had three, an' he comes up to say this one was his. Bo,

very innocent . . . oh, she's a cute one . . .
she says . . . 'Why, Mister Turner, is it really
yours?' An' she looked so full of joy that,
when he says to me . . . 'Excuse us, friend
Carmichael,' . . . I sat there like a locoed
jackass and let them go. But I wasn't mad
at thet. He was a better dancer than me, an'
I wanted her to have a good time. What
started the hell was I seen him put his arm
round her when it wasn't just time, accordin' to the dance, an' Bo . . . she didn't
break any records gettin' away from him.
She pushed him away after a little . . . after
I near died. Wal, on the way home I had to
tell her. I shore did. An' she said what I'd
love to forget. Then . . . then, Miss Nell, I
grabbed her . . . it was outside here by the
porch an' all bright moonlight . . . I grabbed
her an' hugged an' kissed her good. When I
let her go, I says, sorta brave, but I was
plumb scared . . . I says . . . 'Wal, are you
goin' to marry me now?' "

He concluded with a gulp and looked at
Helen with woe in his eyes.

"Oh! What did Bo do?" breathlessly queried Helen.

"She slapped my face," he replied. "An'
then she says . . . 'I *did* like you best, but
now I hate you!' An' she slammed the door
in my face."

"I think you made a great mistake," said Helen gravely.

"Wal, if I thought so, I'd beg her forgiveness. But I reckon I don't. What's more I feel better than before. I'm only a cowboy an' never was much good till I met her. Then I braced. I got to havin' hopes, studyin' books, an' you know how I've been lookin' into this ranchin' game. I stopped drinkin' an' saved my money. Wal, she knows all that. Once she said she was proud of me. But it didn't seem to count big with her. An' if it can't count big, I don't want it to count at all. I reckon the madder Bo is at me, the more chance I've got. She knows I love her . . . that I'd die for her . . . that I'm a changed man. An' she knows I never before thought of darin' to touch her hand. An' she knows she flirted with Turner."

"She's only a child," replied Helen. "And all this change . . . the West . . . the wildness . . . and you boys making much of her . . . why, it's turned her head. But Bo will come out of it true blue. She is good, loving. Her heart is gold."

"I reckon I know, an' my faith can't be shook," rejoined Carmichael simply. "But she ought to believe that she'll make bad blood out here. The West is the West. Any kind of girls are scarce. An' one like Bo. . . .

274

Lord! We cowboys never seen one to compare with her. She'll make bad blood an' some of it will be spilled."

"Uncle Al encourages her," said Helen apprehensively. "It tickles him to hear how the boys are after her. Oh, she doesn't tell him. But he hears. And I, who must stand in Mother's place to her, what can I do?"

"Miss Nell, are you on my side?" asked the cowboy wistfully. He was strong and elemental, caught in the toils of some power beyond him.

Yesterday Helen might have hesitated at that question. But today Carmichael brought some proven quality of loyalty, some strange depth of rugged sincerity, as if he had learned his future worth.

"Yes, I am," Helen replied earnestly, and she offered her hand.

"Wal, then it'll shore all turn out happy," he said, squeezing her hand. His smile was grateful, but there was nothing in it of the victory he hinted at. Some of his ruddy color had gone. "An' now I want to tell you why I came." He had lowered his voice. "Is Al asleep?" he whispered.

"Yes," replied Helen. "He was a little while ago."

"Reckon I'd better shut his door."

Helen watched the cowboy glide across

275

the room and carefully close the door, then return to her with intent eyes. She sensed events in his look, and she divined suddenly that he must feel as if he were her brother.

"Shore I'm the one that fetches all the bad news to you," he said regretfully.

Helen caught her breath. There had indeed been many little calamities to mar her management of the ranch — loss of cattle, horses, sheep — the desertion of herders to Beasley — failure of freighters to arrive when most needed — fights among the cowboys — and disagreements over long-arranged deals.

"Your Uncle Al makes a heap of this here Jeff Mulvey," asserted Carmichael.

"Yes, indeed. Uncle absolutely relies on Jeff," replied Helen.

"Wal, I hate to tell you, Miss Nell," said the cowboy bitterly, "that Mulvey ain't the man he seems."

"Oh, what do you mean?"

"When your uncle dies, Mulvey is goin' over to Beasley an' he's goin' to take all the fellars who'll stick to him."

"Could Jeff be so faithless . . . after so many years my uncle's foreman? Oh, how do you know?"

"Reckon I guessed long ago. But wasn't shore. Miss Nell, there's a lot in the wind lately, as poor old Al grows weaker. Mulvey has been particularly friendly to me an' I've nursed him along, 'cept I wouldn't drink. An' his pards have been particular friends with me, too, more an' more as I loosened up. You see they was shy of me when I first got here. Today the whole deal showed clear to me like a hoof track in soft ground. Bud Lewis, who's bunked with me, come out an' tried to win me over to Beasley . . . soon as Auchincloss dies. I palavered with Bud an' I wanted to know. But Bud would only say he was goin' along with Jeff an' others of the outfit. I told him I'd reckon over it an' let him know. He thinks I'll come around."

"Why . . . why will these men leave me when . . . when . . . ? Oh, poor Uncle! They bargain on his death. But why . . . tell me why?"

"Beasley has worked on them . . . won them over," replied Carmichael grimly. "After Al dies, the ranch will go to you. Beasley means to have it. He an' Al was pards once, an' now Beasley has most folks here believin' he got the short end of that deal. He'll have papers, shore, an' he'll have most of the men. So he'll just put you off an' take possession. That's all, Miss Nell, an' you can rely on it's bein' true."

"I . . . believe you . . . but I can't believe such . . . such robbery possible," gasped Helen.

"It's simple as two an' two. Possession is law out here. Once Beasley gets on the ground, it's settled. What could you do with no men to fight for your property?"

"But surely some of the men will stay with me."

"I reckon. But not enough."

"Then I can hire more. The Beeman boys. And Dorn would come to help me."

"Dorn would come. An' he'd help a heap. I wish he was here," replied Carmichael soberly. "But there's no way to get him. He's snowed-up till May."

"I dare not confide in Uncle," said Helen with agitation. "The shock might kill him. Then to tell him of the unfaithfulness of his men . . . that would be cruel. . . . Oh, it can't be so bad as you think."

"I reckon it couldn't be no worse. An', Miss Nell, there's only one way to get out of it . . . an' that's the way of the West."

"How?" queried Helen eagerly.

Carmichael lunged himself erect and stood gazing down at her. He seemed completely detached now from that frank, amiable cowboy of her first impressions. The redness was totally gone from his face.

Something strange and cold and sure looked out of his eyes.

"I seen Beasley go in Fisher's saloon as I rode past. Suppose I go down there, pick a quarrel with Beasley, an' kill him?"

Helen sat bolt upright with a cold shock. "Carmichael, you're not serious?" she exclaimed.

"Serious? I shore am. That's the only way, Miss Nell. An' I reckon it's what Al would want. An' between you an' me, it would be easier than ropin' a calf. These fellars around Pine don't savvy guns. Now I come from where guns mean somethin'. An' when I tell you I can throw a gun slick an' fast, why I shore ain't braggin'. You needn't worry none about me, Miss Nell."

Helen grasped that he had taken the signs of her shocked sensibility to mean she feared for his life. But what had sickened her was the mere idea of bloodshed in her behalf.

"You'd . . . kill Beasley . . . just because there are rumors of his treachery?" gasped Helen.

"Shore. It'll have to be done anyhow," replied the cowboy.

"No! No! It's too dreadful to think of. Why, that would be murder. I . . . I can't understand how you speak of it so . . . so calmly."

"Reckon I ain't doin' it calmly. I'm as mad as hell," said Carmichael with a reckless smile.

"Oh, if you are serious, then I say no . . . no. . . . No! I forbid you. I don't believe I'll be robbed of my property."

"Wal, supposin' Beasley does put you off . . . an' takes possession. What're you goin' to say then?" demanded the cowboy in slow cool deliberation.

"I'd say the same then as now," she replied.

He bent his head thoughtfully while his red hands smoothed his sombrero. "Shore you girls haven't been West very long," he muttered as if apologizing for them. "An' I reckon it takes time to learn the ways of a country."

"West or no West, I won't have fights deliberately picked and men shot, even if they do threaten me," declared Helen positively.

"All right, Miss Nell, shore I respect your wishes," he returned. "But I'll tell you this. If Beasley turns you an' Bo out of your home . . . wal, I'll look him up on my own account."

Helen could only gaze at him as he backed to the door, and she thrilled and shuddered at what seemed his loyalty to her, his love for Bo, and that which was inevitable in himself.

"Reckon you might save us all some trouble now if you'd just get mad an' let me go after that greaser."

"Greaser! Do you mean Beasley?"

"Shore. He's a half-breed. He was born in Magdalena, where I heard folks say nary one of his parents was no good."

"That doesn't matter. I'm thinking of humanity . . . of law and order. Of what is right."

"Wal, Miss Nell, I'll wait till you get real mad . . . or till Beasley. . . ."

"But, my friend, I'll not get mad," interrupted Helen. "I'll keep my temper."

"I'll bet you don't," he retorted. "Mebbe you think you've none of Bo in you. But I'll bet you could get so mad, once you started, that you'd be terrible. What've you got those eyes for, Miss Nell, if you're an Auchincloss?"

He was smiling, yet he meant every word. Helen felt the truth as something she feared.

"Las Vegas, I won't bet. But you . . . you will always come to me . . . first . . . if there's trouble."

"I promise," he replied soberly, and then

went out.

Helen found that she was trembling and that there was commotion in her breast. Carmichael had frightened her. No longer did she hold doubt of the gravity of the situation. She had seen Beasley often, several times close at hand, and once she had been forced to meet him. That time had convinced her that he had evinced personal interest in her. And on this account, coupled with the fact that Riggs appeared to have nothing else to do but shadow her, she had been slow in developing her intention of organizing and teaching a school for the children of Pine. Riggs had become rather a doubtful celebrity in the settlements. He had spread notoriety, about the truth of which there was doubt in the minds of many. Yet his bold apparent badness had made its impression. From all reports he spent his time gambling, drinking, and bragging. It was no longer news in Pine what his intentions were toward Helen Rayner. Twice he had ridden up to the ranch house, upon one occasion securing an interview with Helen. In spite of her contempt and indifference, he was actually influencing her life there in Pine. And it began to appear that the other man, Beasley, might soon direct stronger significance upon the liberty of her actions.

The responsibility of the ranch had turned out to be a heavy burden. It could not be managed, at least by her, in the way Auchincloss wanted it done. He was old, irritable, irrational, and hard. Almost all the neighbors were set against him, and naturally did not take kindly to Helen. She had not found the slightest evidence of unfair dealing on the part of her uncle, but he had been a hard driver. Then his shrewd far-seeing judgment had made all his deals fortunate for him, which fact had not brought a profit of friendship.

Of late, since Auchincloss had grown weaker and less dominating, Helen had taken many decisions upon herself, with gratifying and hopeful results. But the wonderful happiness that she had expected to find in the West still held aloof. That dream of Paradise Park seemed only a dream, sweeter and more intangible as time passed, and fuller of vague regrets. Bo was a comfort, but also a very considerable source of anxiety. She might have been a help to Helen if she had not assimilated Western ways so swiftly. Helen wished to decide things in her own way, which was yet quite far from Western. So Helen had been thrown more and more upon her own resources, with the cowboy Carmichael the only one who had come forward involuntarily to her aid.

For an hour Helen sat alone in the room, looking out of the window and facing stern reality with a colder, graver, keener sense of intimacy than ever before. To hold her property, to live her life in this community, according to her ideas of honesty, justice, and law might well be beyond her powers. Today she had been convinced that she could not do so without fighting for them, and to fight she must have friends. That conviction warmed her toward Carmichael, and a thoughtful consideration of all he had done for her proved that she had not fully appreciated him. She would make up for her oversight.

There were no Mormons in her employ, for the good reason that Auchincloss would not hire them. But in one of his kindlier hours, growing rare now, he had admitted that the Mormons were the best and most sober, faithful workers on the ranges, and that his sole objection to them was just this fact of their superiority. Helen decided to hire the four Beemans, and any of their relatives or friends who would come, and, to do this, if possible, without letting her uncle know. His temper now, as well as his judgment, was a hindrance to efficiency. This decision regarding the Beemans brought Helen back to Carmichael's fervent wish for Dorn, and then to her own.

Soon spring would be at hand, with its multiplicity of range tasks. Dorn had promised to come to Pine then, and Helen knew that promise would be kept. Her heart beat a little faster, in spite of her business-centered thoughts. Dorn was there, over the black-sloped, snow-tipped mountain, shut away from the world. Helen almost envied him. No wonder he loved loneliness, solitude, the sweet, wild silence and beauty of Paradise Park! But he was selfish and Helen meant to show him that. She needed his help. When she recalled his physical prowess with animals, and imagined what it must be in relation to men, she actually smiled at the thought of Beasley forcing her off her property, if Dorn were there. Beasley could only force disaster upon himself. Then Helen experienced a quick shock. Would Dorn answer to this situation as Carmichael had answered? It afforded her relief to assure herself to the contrary. The cowboy was one of a blood-letting breed; the hunter was a man of thought, gentleness, humanity. This situation was one of the kind that had made him despise the littleness of men. Helen assured herself that he was different from her uncle and from the cowboy, in all the relations of life which she had observed while with him. But a doubt lingered in her mind. She remembered his calm reference to Snake Anson, and that caused a reoccurrence of the little shiver Carmichael had given her. When the doubt augmented to a possibility that she might not be able to control Dorn, then she tried not to think of it any more. It confused and perplexed her that into her mind should flash a thought that, although it would be dreadful for Carmichael to kill Beasley, for Dorn to do it would be a calamity — a terrible thing. Helen did not analyze that strange thought. She was as afraid of it as she was of the stir in her blood when she visualized Dorn.

Her meditation was interrupted by Bo, who entered the room, rebellious-eyed and very lofty. Her manner changed, which apparently owed its cause to the fact that Helen was alone.

"Is that . . . cowboy gone?" she asked.

"Yes. He left quite some time ago," replied Helen.

"I wondered if he made your eyes shine . . . your color burn so. . . . Nell, you're just beautiful."

"Is my face burning?" asked Helen with a little laugh. "So it is. Well, Bo, you've no cause for jealousy. Las Vegas can't be blamed for my blushes."

"Jealous! Me? Of that wild-eyed, soft-voiced, two-faced cowpuncher? I guess not, Nell Rayner. What'd he say about me?"

"Bo, he said a lot," replied Helen reflectively. "I'll tell you presently. First I want to ask you . . . has Carmichael ever told you he's helped me?"

"No. When I see him . . . which hasn't been often lately he . . . I . . . well, we fight. Nell, has he helped you?"

Helen smiled in faint amusement. She was going to be sincere, but she meant to keep her word to the cowboy. The fact was that reflection had acquainted her with her indebtedness to Carmichael.

"Bo, you've been so wild to ride half-broken mustangs and carry on with cowboys . . . and read and sew . . . and keep your secrets that you've had no time for your sister or her troubles."

"Nell!" burst out Bo in amaze and pain. She flew to Helen and seized her hands. "What're you saying?"

"It's all true," replied Helen, thrilling and softening. This sweet sister, once aroused, would be hard to resist. Helen imagined she should hold to her tone of reproach and severity.

"Sure it's true," cried Bo fiercely. "But what's my . . . my fooling got to do with the . . . the rest you said? Nell, are you keeping things from me?"

"My dear, I never get any encouragement to tell you my troubles."

"But I've . . . I've nursed Uncle . . . sat up with him . . . just the same as you," said Bo with quivering lips.

"Yes, you've been good to him."

"We've no other trouble, have we, Nell?"

"You haven't, but I have," responded Helen reproachfully.

"Why . . . why didn't you tell me?" cried Bo passionately. "What are they? Tell me now. You must think me a . . . selfish, hateful cat."

"Bo, I've had much to worry me . . . and the worst is yet to come," replied Helen. Then she told Bo how complicated and bewildering was the management of a big ranch when the owner was ill, testy, defective in memory, and hard as steel — when he had hoards of gold and notes, but could not or would not remember his obligations — when the neighbor ranchers had just claims — when cowboys and sheepherders were discontented, and wrangled among

288

themselves — when great herds of cattle and flocks of sheep had to be fed in winter — when supplies had to be continually freighted across a muddy desert — and lastly, when an enemy rancher was slowly winning away the best hands with the end in view of deliberately taking over the property when the owner died. Then Helen told her she had only that day realized the extent of Carmichael's advice and help and labor; how, indeed, he had been a brother to her — how. . . .

But at this juncture Bo buried her face in Helen's breast and began to cry wildly. "I . . . I . . . don't want . . . to hear . . . any more," she sobbed.

"Well, you've got to hear it," replied Helen inexorably. "I want you to know how he's stood by me."

"But I hate him."

"Bo, I suspect that is not true."

"I do. I do."

"Well, you act and talk very strangely then."

"Nell Rayner . . . are . . . you . . . you sticking up for that . . . that devil?"

"I am, yes, so far as it concerns my conscience," rejoined Helen earnestly. "I never appreciated him as he deserved . . . not until now. He's a man, Bo, every inch of him.

I've seen him grow up to that in three months. I'd never have gotten along without him. I think he's fine, manly, big. I. . . ."

"I'll bet he's made love to you, too," replied Bo woefully.

"Talk sense," said Helen sharply. "He has been a brother to me. But, Bo Rayner, if he *had* made love to me, I might have appreciated it more than you."

Bo raised her face, flushed in part and also pale, with tear-wet cheeks and the telltale blaze in the blue eyes.

"I've been wild about that fellow. But I hate him, too," she said with flashing spirit. "And I want to go on hating him. So don't tell me any more."

Whereupon Helen briefly and graphically related how Carmichael had offered to kill Beasley, as the only way to save her property, and how, when she refused, that he threatened he would do it anyhow.

Bo fell over with a gasp and clung to Helen. "Oh, Nell . . . oh, now I love him more than . . . ever!" she cried, in mingled rage and despair.

Helen clasped her closely and tried to comfort her as in the old days, not so very far back when troubles were not so serious as now. "Of course, you love him," she concluded. "I guessed that long ago. And

I'm glad. But you've been willful, foolish. You wouldn't surrender to it. You wanted your fling with the other boys. You've . . . oh, Bo, I fear you have been a sad little flirt."

"I wasn't very bad till . . . till he got bossy. Why, Nell, he acted . . . right off . . . just as if he *owned* me. But he didn't. . . . And to show him . . . I really did flirt with that Turner fellow. Then he . . . he insulted me. . . . Oh, I hate him!"

"Nonsense, Bo. You can't hate anyone while you love him," protested Helen.

"Much you know about that," flashed Bo. "You just can! Look here. Did you ever see a cowboy rope and throw and tie up a mean horse?"

"Yes, I have."

"Do you have any idea how strong a cowboy is . . . how his hands and arms are like iron?"

"Yes, I'm sure I know that, too."

"And how savage he is?"

"Yes."

"And how he *goes* at anything he wants to do?"

"I must admit cowboys are abrupt," responded Helen with a smile.

"Well, Miss Rayner, did you ever . . . when you were standing quiet like a lady . . . did you ever have a cowboy dive at you with a terrible lunge . . . grab you and hold you so you couldn't move or breathe or scream . . . hug you till all your bones cracked . . . and kiss you so fierce and so hard that you wanted to kill him and die?"

Helen had gradually drawn back from this blazing-eyed eloquent sister, and, when the end of that remarkable question came, it was impossible to reply.

"There! I see you never had that done to you," resumed Bo with satisfaction. "So don't ever talk to me."

"I've heard his side of the story," said Helen constrainedly.

With a start Bo sat up straighter, as if better to defend herself. "Oh, so you have? And I suppose you'll take his part . . . even about that . . . that bearish trick."

"No. I think that rude and bold. But, Bo, I don't believe he meant to be either rude or bold. From what he confessed to me, I gather that he believed he'd lose you outright or win you outright by that violence. It seems girls can't play at love, not here in the wild West. He said there would be blood shed over you. I begin to realize what he meant. He's not sorry for what he did. Think how strange that is. For he has the instincts of a gentleman. He's kind, gentle, chivalrous. Evidently he had tried every way to win your favor except any familiar advance. He did that as a last resort. In my opinion his motives were to force you to accept or refuse him, and, in case you refused him, he'd always have those forbidden stolen kisses to assuage his self-respect when he thought of Turner or anyone else daring to be familiar with you. Bo, I see though Carmichael, even if I don't make him clear to you. You've got to be honest with yourself. Did that mad act of his win or lose you? In other words do you love him or not?"

Bo hid her face. "Oh, Nell! It made me *see* how I loved him . . . and that made me so . . . so sick I hated him. . . . But now . . . the hate is all gone."

CHAPTER FOURTEEN

When spring came at last and the willows drooped, green and fresh, over the brook and the range rang with brays of burro and whistles of stallion, old Al Auchincloss had been a month in his grave.

To Helen it seemed longer. The month had been crowded with work, events, and growing, more hopeful duties, so that it contained a world of living. The uncle had not been forgotten, but the innumerable restrictions to development and progress were no longer manifest. Beasley had not presented himself or any claim upon Helen, and she, gathering confidence day by day, began to believe all that purport of trouble had been exaggerated.

In this time she had come to love her work and all that pertained to it. The estate was large. She had no accurate knowledge of how many acres she owned, but it was more than 2,000. The fine, old rambling ranch house, set like a fort on the last of the foothills, corrals and field and barn and meadows, and the rolling green range beyond, and innumerable sheep, horses, cattle — all these belonged to Helen, to her ever-wondering realization and ever-growing joy. Still, she was afraid to let herself go and be perfectly happy. Always there was the fear that had been too deep and strong to forget so soon.

This bright fresh morning in March, Helen came out upon the porch to revel a little in the warmth of sunshine and the crisp pine-scented wind that swept down from the mountains. There was never a morning that she did not gaze mountain-ward, trying to see, with a folly she realized, if the sun had melted more perceptibly away on the bold white ridge. For all she could see it had not melted an inch, and she would not confess why she sighed. The desert had become green and fresh, stretching away there far below her range, growing dark and purple in the distance with vague buttes rising. The air was full of sound — notes of blackbirds and the *baas* of sheep, and blasts from the corrals, and the *clatter* of light hoofs on the court.

Bo was riding in from the stables. Helen loved to watch her on one of those fiery little mustangs, but the sight was likewise given to rouse apprehensions. This morning Bo appeared particularly bent on frightening Helen. Down the lane, Carmichael appeared waving his arms, and Helen at once connected him with Bo's manifest desire to fly away from that particular place. Since that day, a month back, when Bo had confessed her love for Carmichael, she and Helen had not spoken of it or of the cowboy. The boy and girl were still at odds. But this did not worry Helen. Bo had changed much for the better, especially in that. She devoted herself to Helen, and to her work. Helen knew that all would turn out well in the end, and so she had been careful of her rather precarious position between the two young firebrands.

Bo reined in the mustang at the porch steps. She wore a buckskin riding suit that she had made herself, and its soft gray with the touches of red beads was mightily becoming to her. Then she had grown considerably during the winter and now looked too flashing and pretty to resemble a boy, yet singularly healthy and strong and lithe. Red spots shone in her cheeks and her eyes held that ever-dangerous blaze.

"Nell, did you give me away to that cowboy?" she demanded.

"Give you away!" exclaimed Helen blankly.

"Yes. You know I told you a while back that I was wildly in love with him. Did you give me away . . . tell on me?" She might have been furious, but she certainly was not confused.

"Why, Bo! How could you? No, I did not," replied Helen.

"Never gave him a hint?"

"Not even a hint. You have my word for that. Why? What's happened?"

"He makes me sick."

Bo would not say any more, which fact might have been owing to the near approach of the cowboy.

" 'Mawnin', Miss Nell," he drawled. "I was just tellin' this here Miss Bo-Peep Rayner. . . ."

"Don't call me that!" broke in Bo with fire in her voice.

"Wal, I was just tellin' her that she wasn't goin' off on any more of them long rides. Honest now, Miss Nell, it ain't safe, an'. . . ."

"You're not my boss," retorted Bo.

"Indeed, Sister, I agree with him. You won't obey me."

"Reckon someone's got to be your boss," drawled Carmichael. "Shore I ain't hankerin' for the job. You could ride to Kingdom Come or off among the Apaches . . . or over here a ways" — at this he grinned knowingly — "or anywhere for all I care. But I'm workin' for Miss Nell, an' she's boss. An' if she says you're not to take them rides . . . you won't. Savvy that, miss?"

It was a treat for Helen to see Bo look at the cowboy.

"Mis-ter Carmichael, may I ask how you are going to prevent me from riding where I like?"

"Wal, if you're goin' off locoed this way I'll keep you offen a hoss if I have to rope you an' tie you up. By golly, I will!" His dry humor was gone and manifestly he meant what he said.

"Wal," she drawled it very softly and sweetly, but deadly venomous, "if . . . you . . . ever . . . touch . . . me again!"

At this he flushed, then made a quick passionate gesture with his hand, expressive of heat and shame.

"You an' me will never get along," he said with a dignity full of pathos. "I seen that a month back when you changed sudden-like to me. But nothin' I say to you was any reckonin' of mine. I'm talkin' for your sister. It's for her sake. An' your own. . . . I never told her an' I never told you that I've seen

Riggs sneakin' after you twice on them desert rides. Wal, I tell you now."

The intelligence apparently had not the slightest effect on Bo. But Helen was astounded and alarmed.

"Riggs! Oh, Bo, I've seen him myself . . . riding around. He does not mean well. You must be careful."

"If I ketch him again," went on Carmichael with his mouth forming a hard line, "I'm goin' after him." He gave her a cool, intent, piercing look, then he dropped his head and turned away to stride back toward the corrals.

Helen could make little of the manner in which her sister watched the cowboy pass out of sight.

"A month back . . . when I changed sudden-like?" mused Bo. "I wonder what he meant by that. Nell, did I change . . . right after the talk you had with me about him?"

"Indeed you did, Bo," replied Helen. "But it was for the better. Only he can't see it. How proud and sensitive he is! You wouldn't guess it at first. Bo, your reserve has wounded him more than your flirting. He thinks it's indifference."

"Maybe that'll be good for him," declared Bo. "Does he expect me to fall on his neck? He's that thick-headed! Why, he's the locoed one, not me."

"I'd like to ask you, Bo, if you've seen how *he* has changed?" queried Helen earnestly. "He's older. He's worried. Either his heart is breaking for you or else he fears trouble for us. I fear it's both. How he watches you! Bo, he knows all you do . . . where you go. That about Riggs sickens me."

"If Riggs follows me and tries any of his four-flush desperado games, he'll have his hands full," said Bo grimly. "And that without my cowboy protector. But I just wish Riggs would do something. Then we'll see what Las Vegas Tom Carmichael cares. Then we'll see!" Bo bit out the last words passionately and jealously, then she lifted her bridle to the spirited mustang. "Nell, don't you fear for me," she said. "I can take care of myself."

Helen watched her ride away, all but willing to confess that there might be truth in what Bo said. Then Helen went about her work, which consisted of routine duties as well as an earnest study to familiarize herself with continually new and complex conditions of ranch life. Every day brought new problems. She made notes of all that she observed and all that was told her, which task she had found, after a few weeks of trial, was going to be exceedingly valuable to her. She did not intend always to be dependent upon the knowledge of hired men, however faithful some of them might be.

This morning on her rounds she had expected developments of some kind, owing to the presence of Roy Beeman and two of his brothers, who had arrived yesterday. And she was to discover that Jeff Mulvey, accompanied by six of his co-workers and associates, had deserted her without a word or even sending for their pay. Carmichael had predicted this. Helen had half doubted. It was a relief now to be confronted with facts, however disturbing. She had fortified herself to withstand a great deal more trouble than had happened. At the gateway of the main corral, a huge enclosure fenced high with peeled logs, she met Roy Beeman, lasso in hand, the same tall, lean, limping figure she remembered so well. Sight of him gave her an inexplicable thrill — a flashing memory of an unforgettable night ride. Roy was to have charge of the horses on the ranch, of which there were several hundred, not counting many lost on range and mountain or the unbranded colts.

Roy took off his sombrero and greeted her. This Mormon had a courtesy for women that spoke well for him. Helen wished she had more employees like him.

"It's jest as Las Vegas told us it'd be," he said regretfully. "Mulvey an' his pards lit out this mornin'. I'm sorry, Miss Helen. Reckon that's all because I come over."

"I heard the news," replied Helen. "You needn't be sorry, Roy, for I'm not. I'm *glad.* I want to know who I can trust."

"Las Vegas says we're shore in for it now."

"Roy, what do you think?"

"I reckon so. Still, Las Vegas is powerful cross these days an' always lookin' on the dark side. With us boys now, it's sufficient unto the day is the evil thereof. But, Miss Helen, if Beasley forces the deal, there will be serious trouble. I've seen that happen. Four or five years ago Beasley rode some greasers off their farms and no one ever knowed if he had a just claim."

"Beasley has no claim on my property. My uncle solemnly swore that on his deathbed. And I find nothing in his books or papers of those years when he employed Beasley. In fact, Beasley was never Uncle's partner. The truth is that my uncle took Beasley up when he was a poor homeless boy."

"So my old dad says," replied Roy. "But what's right don't always prevail in these parts."

"Roy, you're the keenest man I've met

302

since I came West. Tell me what you think will happen."

Beeman appeared flattered, but he hesitated to reply. Helen had long been aware of the reticence of these outdoor men.

"I reckon you mean cause and effect, as Milt Dorn would say," responded Roy thoughtfully.

"Yes. If Beasley attempts to force me off my ranch, what will happen?"

Roy looked up and met her gaze. Helen remembered that singular stillness, intentness of his face.

"Wal, if Dorn an' John get here in time, I reckon we can bluff that Beasley outfit."

"You mean my friends . . . my men would confront Beasley . . . refuse his demands . . . and if necessary fight him off?"

"I shore do," replied Roy.

"But suppose you're not all here? Beasley would be smart enough to choose an opportune time. Suppose he did put me off and take possession? What then?"

"Then it'd only be a matter of how soon Dorn or Carmichael . . . or I . . . got to Beasley."

"Roy! I feared just that. It haunts me. Carmichael asked me to let him go pick a fight with Beasley . . . asked me, just as he would ask me about his work! I was shocked. And now you say Dorn . . . and you. . . ." Helen choked in her agitation.

"Miss Helen, what else could you look for? Las Vegas is in love with Miss Bo. Shore he told me so. An' Dorn's in love with you! Why you couldn't stop them any more'n you could stop the wind from blowin' down a pine when it got ready. . . . Now it's some different with me. I'm a Mormon an' I'm married. But I'm Dorn's pard, these many years. I care a powerful sight for you and Miss Bo. So I reckon I'd draw on Beasley the first chance I got."

Helen strove for utterance, but it was denied her. Roy's simple statement of Dorn's love had magnified her emotions by completely changing its direction. She forgot what she had felt wretched about. She could not look at Roy.

"Miss Helen, don't feel bad," he said kindly. "Shore you're not to blame. Your comin' West hasn't made any difference in Beasley's fate, except mebbe to hurry it a little. My dad is old, an', when he talks, it's like history. He looks back on happenin's. Wal, it's the nature of happenin's that Beasley passes away before his prime. Men of his breed don't live old in the West. So I reckon you needn't feel bad or worry. You've got friends."

Helen incoherently thanked him, and, forgetting her usual round of corrals and stables, she hurried back toward the house, deeply stirred, throbbing and dim-eyed with a feeling she could not control. Roy Beeman had made a statement that had upset her equilibrium. It seemed simple and natural, yet momentous and staggering. To hear that Dorn loved her — to hear it spoken frankly, earnestly by Dorn's best friend was strange, sweet, terrifying. But was it true? Her own consciousness had admitted it. Yet that was vastly different from a man's open statement. No longer was it a dear dream, a secret that seemed hers alone. How she had lived on that secret hidden deep in her breast!

Something burned the dimness from her eyes as she looked toward the mountains and her sight became clear, telescopic with its intensity. Magnificently the mountains loomed. Black inroads and patches on the slopes showed where a few days back all had been white. The snow was melting fast. Dorn would soon be free to ride down to Pine. And that was an event Helen prayed for, yet feared as she had never feared anything.

The noonday dinner bell startled Helen

from a reverie that was a pleasant aftermath of her unrestraint. How the hours had flown! This morning at least must be credited to indolence.

Bo was not in the dining room, or in her own room, nor was she in sight from window or door. This absence had occurred before, but not particularly to disturb Helen. In this instance, however, she grew worried. Her nerves presaged strain. There was an overcharge of sensibility in her feelings or a strange pressure in the very atmosphere. She ate dinner alone, looking her apprehension, which was not mitigated by the expressive fears of old María, the Mexican woman who served her.

After dinner she sent word to Roy and Carmichael that they had better ride out to look for Bo. Then Helen applied herself resolutely to her books until a rapid *clatter* of hoofs out in the court caused her to jump up and hurry to the porch. Roy was riding in.

"Did you find her?" queried Helen hurriedly.

"Wasn't no track or sign of her up the north range," replied Roy as he dismounted and threw his bridle. "An' I was ridin' back to take up her tracks from the corral an' trail her. But I seen Las Vegas comin' an' he waved his sombrero. He was comin' up from the south. . . . There he is now."

Carmichael appeared swinging into the lane. He was mounted on Helen's big black Ranger, and he made the dust fly.

"Wal, he's seen her, that's shore," vouch-safed Roy with relief as Carmichael rode up.

"Miss Nell, she's comin'," said the cowboy as he reined in, and slid down with his graceful single motion. Then in a violent action, characteristic of him, he slammed his sombrero down on the porch and threw up both arms. "I've a hunch it's come off!"

"Oh, what?" exclaimed Helen.

"Now, Las Vegas, talk sense," expostulated Roy. "Miss Helen is shore serious today. Has anything happened?"

"I reckon, but I don't know what," replied Carmichael, drawing a long breath. "Folks, I must be gettin' old. For I shore felt awful queer till I seen Bo. She was ridin' down the ridge across the valley. Ridin' some fast, too, an' she'll be here right off, if she doesn't stop in the village."

"Wal, I hear her comin' now," said Roy. "An, if you asked me, I'd say she *was* ridin' some fast."

Helen heard the light swift rhythmic beat of hoofs, and then out on the curve of the

307

road that led down to Pine she saw Bo's mustang, white with lather, coming on a dead run.

"Las Vegas, do you see any Apaches?" asked Roy quizzingly.

The cowboy made no reply, but he strode out from the porch, directly in front of the mustang. Bo was pulling hard on the bridle, and had him slowing down but not controlled. When he reached the house, it could easily be seen that Bo had pulled him to the limit of her strength, which was not enough to halt him. Carmichael lunged for the bridle and, seizing it, hauled him to a standstill.

At close sight of Bo, Helen uttered a startled cry. Bo was white and her sombrero was gone and her hair undone; there was blood and dirt on her face, and her riding suit was torn and muddy. She had evidently sustained a fall. Roy gazed at her in admiring consternation, but Carmichael never looked at her at all. Apparently he was examining the horse.

"Nell, help me off . . . somebody," cried Bo peremptorily. Her voice was weak, but not her spirit.

Roy sprang to help her off, and, when she was down, it developed that she was lame.

"Oh, Bo! You've had a tumble!" exclaimed

Helen anxiously, and she ran to assist Roy. They led her up the porch and to the door. There she turned to look at Carmichael who was still examining the spent mustang.

"Tell him . . . to come in," she whispered.

"Hey, there, Las Vegas!" called Roy. "Rustle hyar, will you?"

When Bo had been led into the sitting room and seated in a chair, Carmichael entered. His face was a study, as slowly he walked up to Bo.

"Girl, you ain't hurt?" he asked huskily.

"It's no fault of yours that I'm not crippled . . . or dead . . . or worse," retorted Bo. "You said the south range was the only safe ride for me. And there . . . I . . . it happened." She panted a little and her bosom heaved. One of her gauntlets was gone, and the bare hand, that was bruised and bloody, trembled as she held it out.

"Dear, tell us . . . are you badly hurt?" queried Helen with hurried gentleness.

"Not much. I've had a spill," replied Bo. "But, oh, I'm mad . . . I'm boiling." She looked as if she might have exaggerated her doubt of injuries, but certainly she had not overestimated her state of mind. Any blaze Helen had heretofore seen in those quick eyes was tame compared to this one. It actually leaped. Bo was more than pretty then.

Manifestly Roy was admiring her looks, but Carmichael saw beyond her charm. And slowly he was growing pale.

"I rode out the south range . . . as I was told," began Bo, breathing hard and trying to control her feelings. "That's the ride you usually take, Nell, and you bet . . . if you'd taken it today, you'd not be here now. . . . About three miles out I climbed off the range up that cedar slope. I always keep to high ground. When I got up, I saw two horsemen ride out of some broken rocks off to the east. They rode as if to come between me and home. I didn't like that. I circled south. About a mile farther in I spied another horseman and he showed up directly in front of me and came along slow. That I liked still less. It might have been accident, but it looked to me that these riders had some intent. All I could do was head off to the southeast and ride. You bet I did ride. But I got into rough ground where I'd never been before. It was slow going. At last I made the cedars and there I cut loose, believing I could circle ahead of these strange riders, and come around through Pine . . . I had it wrong."

Here she hesitated, perhaps for breath, for she had spoken rapidly, or perhaps to get better hold on her subject. Not improbably the effect she was creating on her listeners began to be significant. Roy sat absorbed, perfectly motionless, eyes keen as steel, his mouth open. Carmichael was gazing over Bo's head, out of the window, and it seemed that he must know the rest of her narrative. Helen knew that her own wide-eyed attention alone would have been all-compelling inspiration to Bo Rayner.

"Sure I had it wrong," resumed Bo. "Pretty soon I heard a horse behind. I looked back. I saw a big bay riding down on me. Oh, but he was running. He just tore through the cedars. . . . I was scared half out of my senses. But I spurred and beat my mustang. Then began a race! Rough going . . . thick cedars . . . washes and gullies! I had to make him run . . . to keep my saddle . . . to pick my way. Oh-h-h, but it was glorious! To race for fun . . . that's one thing . . . to race for your life is another! My heart was in my mouth . . . choking me. I couldn't have yelled. I was as cold as ice . . . dizzy sometimes . . . blind others . . . then my stomach turned . . . and I couldn't get my breath. Yet the wild thrills I had. . . . But I stuck on and held my own for several miles . . . to the edge of the cedars. There the big horse gained on me. He came pounding closer . . . perhaps as close as a hundred yards . . . I could hear him plain enough. Then I had my spill. Oh! My mustang tripped . . . threw me way over his head. I hit light, but slid far . . . and that's what scraped me. So, I know my knee is raw. . . . When I got to my feet, the big horse dashed up, throwing gravel all over me . . . and his rider jumped off. . . . Now who do you think he was?"

Helen knew, but she did not voice her conviction. Carmichael knew positively, yet he kept silent. Roy was smiling as if the narrative told did not seem so alarming to him. "Wal, the fact of you bein' here, safe an' sound, sorta makes no difference who that son-of-a-gun was," he said.

"Riggs! Harve Riggs!" blazed Bo. "The instant I recognized him, I got over my scare. I was so mad I burned all through like fire. I don't know what I said, but it was wild . . . and it was a whole lot, you bet.

" 'You sure can ride,' he said.

"I demanded why he had dared to chase me and he said he had an important message for Nell. This was it . . . 'Tell your sister that Beasley means to put her off an' take the ranch. If she'll marry me, I'll block his deal. If she won't marry me, I'll go in with Beasley.' Then he told me to hurry home

312

and not to breathe a word to anyone except Nell. Well, here I am . . . and I seem to have been breathing rather fast."

She looked from Helen to Roy and from Roy to Las Vegas. Her smile was for him, and to anyone not overexcited by her story that smile would have told volumes.

"Wal, I'll be dog-goned!" ejaculated Roy feelingly.

Helen laughed. "Indeed the working of that man's mind is beyond me. . . . Marry him to save my ranch? I wouldn't marry him to save my life!"

Carmichael suddenly broke his silence. "Bo, did you see the other men?"

"Yes. I was coming to that," she replied. "I caught a glimpse of them back in the cedars. The three were together, or at least three horsemen were there. They had halted behind some trees. Then on the way home I began to think. Even in my fury I had received impressions. Riggs was *surprised* when I got up. I'll bet he had not expected me to be who I was. He thought I was *Nell!* I look bigger in the buckskin outfit. My hair was up till I lost my hat and that was when I had the tumble. He took me for Nell. Another thing I remember, he made some sign . . . some motion while I was calling him names, and I believe that was to keep

313

those other men back. . . . I believe Riggs had a plan with these other men to waylay Nell and make off with her. I absolutely know it."

"Bo, you're so . . . so . . . you jump at wild ideas so," protested Helen, trying to believe in her own assurance. But inwardly she was trembling.

"Miss Helen, that ain't a wild idee," said Roy seriously. "I reckon your sister is pretty close on the trail. Las Vegas, don't you savvy it that way?"

Carmichael's answer was to stalk out of the room.

"Call him back!" cried Helen apprehensively.

"Hold on, boy!" called Roy sharply.

Helen reached the door simultaneously with Roy. The cowboy picked up his sombrero, jammed it on his head, gave his belt a vicious hitch that made the gun sheath jump, and then in one giant step he was astride Ranger.

"Carmichael! Stay!" cried Helen.

The cowboy spurred the black and the stones rang under iron-shod hoofs.

"Bo! Call him back! Please call him back!" importuned Helen in distress.

"I won't," declared Bo Rayner. Her face shone whiter now and her eyes were like fiery flint. That was her answer to a loving gentle-hearted sister; that was her answer to the call of the West.

"No use," said Roy quietly. "An' I reckon I'd better trail him up."

He, too, strode out and, mounting his horse, galloped swiftly away.

It turned out that Bo was more bruised and scraped and shaken that she had imagined. One knee was rather badly cut, which injury alone would have kept her from riding again very soon. Helen, who was somewhat skilled at bandaging wounds, worried a great deal over the sundry blotches on Bo's fair skin, and it took considerable time to wash and dress them. Long after this was done, and during the early supper and afterward, Bo's excitement remained unabated. The whiteness stayed on her face and the blaze in her eyes. Helen ordered and begged her to go to bed, for the fact was Bo could not stand up and her hands shook.

"Go to bed? Not much," she said. "I want to know what he does to Riggs."

It was that possibility that had Helen in dreadful suspense. If Carmichael killed Riggs, it seemed to Helen, that the bottom would drop out of this structure of Western life she had begun to build so earnestly and fearfully. She did not believe that he would do so. But the uncertainty was torturing.

"Dear Bo," appealed Helen, "you don't want. . . . Oh! You do want Carmichael to . . . to kill Riggs?"

"No, I don't, but I wouldn't care if he did," replied Bo bluntly.

"Do you think . . . he will?"

"Nell, if that cowboy really loves me, he read my mind right here before he left," declared Bo. "And he knew what I thought he'd do."

"And what's . . . that?" faltered Helen.

"I want him to round Riggs up down in the village . . . somewhere in a crowd. I want Riggs shown up as the coward, braggart, four-flush that he is. And insulted, slapped, kicked . . . driven out of Pine!"

Her passionate speech still rang throughout the room when there came footsteps on the porch. . . . Helen hurried to raise the bar from the door and open it, just as a tap sounded on the door post. Roy's face stood white out of the darkness. His eyes were bright. And his smile made Helen's fearful query needless.

"How are you-all this evenin'?" he drawled as he came in.

A fire blazed on the hearth and a lamp burned on the table. By their light Bo

316

looked white and eager-eyed as she reclined in the big armchair.

"What'd he do?" she asked with all her amazing force.

"Wal, now, ain't you goin' to tell me how you are?"

"Roy, I'm all bunged up. I ought to be in bed. But I just couldn't sleep till I hear what Las Vegas did. I'd forgive anything except his getting drunk."

"Wal, I shore can ease your mind on thet," replied Roy. "He never drank a drop."

Roy was distractingly slow about beginning the tale any child could have guessed he was eager to tell. For once the hard intent quietness, the soul of labor, pain, and endurance so plain in his face was softened by pleasurable emotion. He poked at the burning logs with the toe of his boot. Helen observed that he had changed his boots and now wore no spurs. Then he had gone to his quarters after whatever had happened down in Pine.

"Where *is* he?" asked Bo.

"Who? Riggs? Wal, I don't know. But I reckon he's somewhere out in the woods nursin' hisself."

"Not Riggs. First tell me where *he* is."

"Shore then you must mean Las Vegas. I just left him down at the cabin. He was gettin' ready for bed, early as it is. All tired out he was an' thet white thet you wouldn't have knowed him. But he looked happy at thet, an' the last words he says, more to himself than to me I reckon, was . . . 'I'm some locoed gent, but, if she doesn't call me Tom now, she's no good!' "

Bo actually clapped her hands, notwithstanding that one of them was bandaged.

"Call him Tom? I should smile I will," she declared in delight. "Hurry now . . . what'd . . . ?"

"It's shore powerful strange how he hates that handle Las Vegas," went on Roy imperturbably.

"Roy, tell me what he did . . . what *Tom* did . . . or I'll scream!" cried Bo.

"Miss Helen, did you ever see the likes of that girl?" asked Roy, appealing to Helen.

"No, Roy, I never did," agreed Helen. "But please . . . please tell us what has happened."

Roy grinned and rubbed his hands together in a dark delight, almost fiendish in its sudden revelation of a gulf of strange emotion deep within him. Whatever had happened to Riggs had not been too much for Roy Beeman. Helen remembered hearing her uncle say that a real Westerner hated nothing so hard as the swaggering desperado, the make-believe gunman who pretended to sail under the true, wild, and reckoning colors of the West.

Roy leaned his lithe tall form against the stone mantelpiece and faced the girls.

"When I rode out after Las Vegas, I seen him 'way down the road," began Roy rapidly. "An' I seen another man ridin' down into Pine from the other side. Thet was Riggs, only I didn't know it then. Las Vegas rode up to the store, where some fellars was hangin' around, an' he spoke to them. When I came up, they was all headin' for Turner's saloon. I seen a dozen horses hitched to the rails. Las Vegas rode on. But I got off at Turner's an' went in with the bunch. Whatever it was Las Vegas said to them fellars, shore they didn't give him away. Pretty soon more men strolled into Turner's an' there got to be 'most twenty altogether, I reckon. Jeff Mulvey was there with his pards. They had been drinkin' sorta free. An' I didn't like the way Mulvey watched me. So I went out an' into the store, but kept a-lookin' for Las Vegas. He wasn't in sight. But I seen Riggs ridin' up. Now Turner's is where Riggs hangs out an' does his braggin'. He looked powerful deep an' thoughtful, dismounted slow without seein' the onusual number of horses there, an' then he slouches into Turner's. No more'n a minute after thet Las Vegas rode down like a streak. An' just as quick he was off an' through that door."

Roy paused as if to gain force or to choose his words. His tale now appeared all directed to Bo, who gazed at him, spellbound, a fascinated listener.

"Before I got to Turner's door . . . an' that was only a little ways . . . I heard Las Vegas yell. Did you ever hear him? Wal, he's got the wildest yell of any cowpuncher I ever heard. Quick-like I opened the door an' slipped in. There was Riggs an' Las Vegas alone in the center of the big saloon, with the crowd edgin' to the walls an' slidin' back of the bar. Riggs was whiter'n a dead man. I didn't hear an' I don't know what Las Vegas yelled at him. But Riggs knew an' so did the gang. All of a sudden every man there shore seen in Las Vegas what Riggs had always bragged *he* was. Thet time comes to every man like Riggs.

" 'What'd you call me?' he asked, his jaw shakin'.

" 'I ain't called you yet,' answered Las Vegas. 'I just whooped.'

" 'What d'ye want?'

" 'You scared my girl.'

" 'The hell ye say. Who's she?' blustered Riggs, an' he began to take quick looks

320

around. But he never moved a hand. There was somethin' tight about the way he stood. Las Vegas had both arms half out, stretched as if he meant to leap. But he didn't. I never seen Las Vegas do that, an', when I seen him then, I understood it.

" 'You know. An' you threatened her an' her sister. Go for your gun,' called Las Vegas, low and sharp.

"That put the crowd right an' nobody moved. Riggs turned green then. I almost felt sorry for him. He began to shake so he'd've dropped a gun if he had pulled one.

" 'Hyar, you're off . . . some mistake. . . . I ain't seen no girls . . . I. . . .'

" 'Shut up an' draw!' yelled Las Vegas. His voice just pierced holes in the roof an' it might have been a bullet from the way Riggs collapsed. Every man seen in a second more thet Riggs wouldn't an' couldn't draw. He was afraid for his life. He was not what he had claimed to be. I don't know if he had any friends there. But, in the West, good men an' bad men, all alike, have no use for Riggs's kind. An' thet stony quiet broke with haw-haw. It shore was as pitiful to see Riggs as it was fine to see Las Vegas.

"When he dropped his arms then I knowed there would be no gun play. An' then Las Vegas got red in the face. He slapped Riggs with one hand, then with the other. An' he began to cuss Riggs. I shore never knowed thet nice spoken Las Vegas Carmichael could use such language. It was a stream of the baddest names known out here, an' I caught somethin' like low-down an' sneak an' four-flush an' long-haired skunk, but for the most part they was just the cussedest kind of names. An' Las Vegas spouted them till he was black in the face, an' foamin' at the mouth, an' hoarser'n a bawlin' cow.

"When he got out of breath from cussin', he punched Riggs all about the saloon, threw him outdoors, knocked him down, an' kicked him till he got up, an' then kept kickin' him down the road with the whole haw-hawin' gang behind. An' he drove him out of town!"

CHAPTER FIFTEEN

For two days Bo was confined to her bed, suffering considerable pain, and subject to fever during which she talked irrationally. Some of this talk afforded Helen as vast an amusement as she was certain it would have lifted Tom Carmichael to a seventh heaven.

The third day, however, Bo was better, and, refusing to remain in bed, she hobbled to the sitting room, where she divided her time between staring out of the window toward the corrals and pestering Helen with questions she tried to make appear casual. But Helen saw through her case and was in a state of glee. What she hoped most for was that Carmichael would suddenly develop a little less inclination for Bo. It was that kind of treatment the young lady needed. And now was the great opportunity. Helen almost felt tempted to give the cowboy a hint.

Neither this day, nor the next, however,

did he put in an appearance at the house, although Helen saw him twice on her rounds. He was busy, as usual, and greeted her as if nothing particular had happened.

Roy called twice, once in the afternoon, and again during the evening. He grew more likeable upon longer acquaintance. This last visit he rendered Bo speechless by teasing her about another girl Carmichael was going to take to a dance. Bo's face showed that her vanity could not believe this statement, but that her intelligence of young men credited it with being possible. Roy evidently was as penetrating as he was kind. He made a dry, casual little remark about the snow never melting on the mountains during the latter part of March, and the look with which he accompanied this remark brought a blush to Helen's cheek.

After Roy had departed, Bo said to Helen: "Confound that fellow! He sees right through me."

"My dear, you're rather transparent these days," murmured Helen.

"You needn't talk. He gave you a dig," retorted Bo. "He just knows you're dying to see the snow melt."

"Gracious! I hope I'm not as bad as that. Of course, I want the snow melted and spring to come and flowers. . . ."

"Ha! Ha! Ha!" taunted Bo. "Nell Rayner, do you see any green in my eyes? Spring to come! Yes, the poet said in the spring a young man's fancy lightly turns to thought of love. But that poet meant a young woman."

Helen gazed out of the window at the white stars.

"Nell, have you seen him . . . since I was hurt?" continued Bo with an effort.

"Him? Who?"

"Oh, who do you suppose? I mean *Tom!*" she responded, and the last word came with a burst.

"Tom! Who's he? *Ah,* you mean Las Vegas. Yes, I've seen him."

"Well, did he ask a— . . . about me?"

"I believe he did ask how you were . . . something like that."

"*Humph!* Nell, I don't always trust you" After that she relapsed into silence, read a while, and dreamed a while, looking into the fire, and then she limped over to kiss Helen good night and left the room.

Next day she was rather quiet, seeming upon the verge of one of the dispirited spells she got infrequently. Early in the evening just after the lights had been lit, and she had joined Helen in the sitting room, a familiar step sounded on the loose boards of the porch.

Helen went to the door to admit Carmichael. He was clean-shaven, dressed in his dark suit, which presented such marked contrast from his riding garb, and he wore a flower in his buttonhole. Nevertheless, despite all this style, he seemed more than usually the cool, easy, careless cowboy.

" 'Evenin', Miss Helen," he said as he stalked in. " 'Evenin', Miss Bo. How are you-all?"

Helen returned his greeting with a welcoming smile.

"Good evening . . . *Tom,*" said Bo demurely.

That assuredly was the first time she had ever called him Tom. As she spoke, she looked distractingly pretty and tantalizing. But if she had calculated to floor Carmichael with that initial, half-promising, wholly mocking use of his name, she had reckoned without cause. The cowboy received that greeting as if he had heard her use it a thousand times or had not heard it at all. Helen decided if he was acting a part, he was certainly a clever actor. He puzzled her somewhat, but she liked his look, and his easy manner, and the something about him that must have been his unconscious sense of pride. He had gone far enough, perhaps too far in his overtures to Bo.

"How are you feelin'?" he asked.

"I'm better today," she replied with down-cast eyes. "But I'm lame yet."

"Reckon that bronc' piled you up. Miss Helen said that shore wasn't any joke about the cut on your knee. Now a fellar's knee is a bad place to hurt, if he has to keep on ridin'."

"Oh, I'll be well soon. How's Sam? I hope he wasn't crippled."

"Thet Sam . . . why he's so tough he never knowed he had a fall."

"Tom . . . I . . . I want to thank you for giving Riggs what he deserved." She spoke it earnestly, eloquently, and for once she had no sly little intonation or pert allure-ment, such as was her wont to use on this infatuated young man.

"*Aw,* you heard about that," replied Car-michael with a wave of his hand to make light of it. "Nothin' much. It had to be done. An' shore I was afraid of Roy. He'd've been mad. An' so would any of the other boys. I'm sorta lookin' out for all of them, you know, actin' as Miss Helen's foreman now."

Helen was unutterably tickled. The effect of his speech upon Bo was stupendous. He had disarmed her. He had, with the firmness and tact and suavity of a diplomat, removed himself from obligation, and the detachment of self, the casual thing he apparently made out of his magnificent championship was bewildering and humiliating to Bo. She sat silently for a moment or two while Helen tried to fit easily into the conversation. It was not likely that Bo would long be at a loss for words, and also it was immensely probable that with a flash of her wonderful spirit she would turn the tables on her perverse lover in a twinkling. Anyway, plain it was that a lesson had sunk deep. She looked startled, hurt, wistful, and finally sweetly defiant.

"But . . . you told Riggs I was your girl!" Thus Bo unmasked her battery. And Helen could not imagine how Carmichael would ever resist that and the soft arch glance that accompanied it.

Helen did not yet know the cowboy, any more than did Bo.

"Shore. I had to say that. I had to make it strong before that gang. I reckon it was presumin' of me, an' I shore apologize."

Bo stared at him, and then, giving a little gasp, she drooped.

"Wal, I just run in to say howdy an' to inquire after you-all," said Carmichael. "I'm goin' to the dance, an' as Flo lives out of town a ways, I'd shore better rustle. . . . Good night, Miss Bo, I hope you'll be ridin' Sam soon. An' good night, Miss Helen."

Bo roused to a very friendly and laconic little speech, much overdone. Carmichael strode out, and Helen, bidding him good bye, closed the door after him.

The instant he had departed Bo's transformation was tragic.

"Flo! He meant Flo Stubbs . . . that ugly crossed-eyed bold little frump!"

"Bo!" expostulated Helen. "The young lady is not beautiful, I grant, but she's very nice and pleasant. I like her."

"Nell Rayner, men are no good! And cowboys are the worst!" declared Bo terribly.

"Why didn't you appreciate Tom when you had him?" asked Helen.

Bo had been growing furious, but now the allusion, in the past tense, to the conquest she had suddenly and amazingly found dear, quite broke her spirit. It was a very pale, unsteady, and miserable girl who avoided Helen's gaze and left the room.

Next day Bo was not approachable from any direction. Helen, running often in upon Bo, found her victim to a multiplicity of moods, ranging from woe to dire dark broodings, from them to wistfulness, and at last to a pride that sustained her.

Late in the afternoon, at Helen's leisure hour, when she and Bo were in the sitting room, horses tramped into the court, and footsteps mounted the porch. Opening to a loud knock, Helen was surprised to see Beasley. And out in the court were several mounted horsemen. Helen's heart sank. This visit indeed had been foreshadowed.

" 'Afternoon, Miss Rayner," said Beasley, doffing his sombrero. "I've called on a little business deal. Will you see me?"

Helen acknowledged his greeting while she thought rapidly. She might just as well see him, and have that inevitable interview done with.

"Come in," she said, and, when he had entered, she closed the door. "My sister, Mister Beasley."

"How d'you do, miss," said the rancher in bluff loud voice.

Bo acknowledged the introduction with a frigid little bow.

At close range Beasley seemed a forceful personality as well as a rather handsome man of perhaps thirty-five, heavy of build, swarthy of skin, and sloe-black of eye, like that of a Mexican whose blood was reported to be in him. He looked crafty, confident, and self-centered. If Helen had never heard of him before that visit, she would have distrusted him.

"I'd've called sooner, but I was waitin' for old José, the Mexican who herded for me when I was pardner to your uncle," said Beasley, and he sat down to put his huge gloved hands on his knees.

"Yes?" queried Helen interrogatively.

"José rustled over from Magdalena, an' now I can back up my claim. . . . Miss Rayner, this hyar ranch ought to be mine an' is mine. It wasn't so big or so well stocked when Al Auchincloss beat me out of it. I reckon I'll allow for that. I've paper, and old José for witness. An' I calculate you'll pay me eighty thousand dollars, or else I'll take over the ranch."

Beasley spoke in an ordinary matter-of-fact tone that certainly seemed sincere, and his manner was blunt, but perfectly natural.

"Mister Beasley, your claim is no news to me," responded Helen quietly. "I've heard about it. And I questioned my uncle. He swore on his deathbed that he did not owe you a dollar. Indeed, he claimed the indebtedness was yours to him. I could find nothing in his papers. So I must repudiate your claim. I will not take it seriously."

"Miss Rayner, I can't blame you for takin'

Al's word against mine," said Beasley. "An' your stand is natural. But you're a stranger here an' you know nothin' of struck deals in these ranges. It ain't fair to speak bad of the dead, but the truth is that Al Auchincloss got his start by stealin' sheep an' unbranded cattle. Thet was the start of every rancher I know. It was mine. An' we none of us ever thought of it as rustlin'."

Helen could only stare her surprise and doubt at this statement.

"Talk's cheap anywhere, an' in the West talk ain't much at all," continued Beasley. "I'm no talker. I jest want to tell my case an' make a deal if you'll have it. I can prove more in black an' white, an' with witness, than you can. Thet's my case. The deal I'd make is this. . . . Let's marry an' settle a bad deal that way."

The man's direct assumption, absolutely without a qualifying consideration for her woman's attitude, was amazing, ignorant, and base, but Helen was so well prepared for it that she hid her disgust.

"Thank you, Mister Beasley. But I can't accept your offer," she replied.

"Would you take time an' consider?" he asked, spreading wide his huge gloved hands.

"Absolutely no."

Beasley rose to his feet. He showed no disappointment or chagrin, but the bold pleasantness left his face. And slight as that change was, it stripped him of the only redeeming quality he showed.

"That means I'll force you to pay me the eighty thousand, or put you off," he said.

"Mister Beasley, even if I owed you that, how could I raise so enormous a sum? I don't owe it. And I certainly won't be put off my property. You can't put me off."

"An' why can't I?" he demanded, with lowering dark gaze.

"Because your claim is dishonest. And I can prove it," declared Helen forcibly.

"Who're you goin' to prove it to . . . that I'm dishonest?"

"To my men . . . to your men . . . to the people of Pine . . . to everybody. There's not a person who won't believe me."

He seemed curious, discomfited, surlily annoyed, and yet fascinated by her statement or else by the quality and appearance of her as she spiritedly defended her cause.

"An' how're you goin' to prove all that?" he growled.

"Mister Beasley, do you remember last fall when you met Snake Anson with his gang up in the woods . . . and hired him to make

333

off with me?" asked Helen in swift ringing words.

The dark olive of Beasley's bold face shaded to a dirty white. "Wha-at?" he jerked out hoarsely.

"I see you remember. Well, Milt Dorn was hidden in the loft of that cabin where you met Anson. He heard every word of your deal with the outlaw."

Beasley swung his arm in sudden violence, so hard that he flung his glove to the floor. As he stooped to snatch it up, he uttered a sibilant hiss. Then, stalking to the door, he jerked it open, and slammed it behind him. His loud voice, hoarse with passion, preceded the scrape and crack of hoofs.

Shortly after supper that day, when Helen was just recovering her composure, Carmichael presented himself at the open door. Bo was not there. In the dimming twilight Helen saw that the cowboy was pale, somber, grim.

"Oh, what's happened?" cried Helen.

"Roy's been shot. It come off in Turner's saloon. But he ain't dead. We packed him over to Widow Cass's. An' he said for me to tell you he'd pull through."

"Shot! Pull through!" repeated Helen in slow unrealizing exclamation. She was

334

conscious of a deep internal tumult and a cold checking of blood in all her external body.

"Yes, shot," replied Carmichael fiercely. "An', whatever he says, I reckon he won't pull through."

"Oh, heaven, how terrible!" burst out Helen. "He was so good . . . such a man! What a pity! Oh, he must have met that in my behalf. Tell me, what happened? Who shot him?"

"Wal, I don't know. An' that's what's made me hoppin' mad. I wasn't there when it came off. An' he won't tell me."

"Why not?"

"I don't know that, either. I reckoned first it was because he wanted to get even. But after thinkin' it over, I guess he doesn't want me lookin' up anyone right now for fear I might get hurt. An' you're goin' to need your friends. That's all I can make of Roy."

Then Helen hurriedly related the event of Beasley's call on her that afternoon and all that had occurred.

"Wal, the half-breed son-of-a-greaser!" ejaculated Carmichael in utter befuddlement. "He wanted you to marry him?"

"He certainly did. I must say it was a . . . a rather abrupt proposal."

Carmichael appeared to be laboring with

speech that had to be smothered behind his teeth. At last he let out an explosive breath. "Miss Nell, I've shore felt in my bones thet I'm the boy slated to brand thet big bull."

"Oh, he must have shot Roy. He left here in a rage."

"I reckon you can coax it out of Roy. Fact is, all I could learn was thet Roy come in the saloon alone. Beasley was there, an' Riggs. . . ."

"Riggs!" interrupted Helen.

"Shore, Riggs. He came back again. But he'd better keep out of my way. And Jeff Mulvey with his outfit. Turner told me he heard an argument an' then a shot. The gang cleared out, leavin' Roy on the floor. I came in a little later. Roy was still layin' there. Nobody was doin' anythin' for him. An' nobody had. I hold thet against Turner. Wal, I got help an' packed Roy over to Widow Cass's. Roy seemed all right. But he was too bright an' talky to suit me. The bullet hit his lung, thet's shore. An' he lost a sight of blood before we stopped it. Thet skunk Turner might have lent a hand. An' if Roy croaks, I reckon I'll. . . ."

"Tom, why must you always be reckoning to kill somebody?" demanded Helen angrily.

" 'Cause somebody's got to be killed around here. Thet's why!" he snapped back.

"Even so . . . should you risk leaving Bo and me without a friend?" asked Helen reproachfully.

At that Carmichael wavered and lost something of his sullen deadliness.

"*Aw*, Miss Nell, I'm only mad. If you'll just be patient with me . . . an' mebbe coax me. . . . But I can't see no other way out."

"Let's hope and pray," said Helen earnestly. "You spoke of my coaxing Roy to tell who shot him. When can I see him?"

"Tomorrow, I reckon. I'll come for you. Fetch Bo along with you. We've got to play safe from now on. An' what do you say to me an' Hal sleepin' here at the ranch house?"

"Indeed, I'd feel safer," she replied. "There are rooms. Please come."

"All right. An' now I'll be goin' to fetch Hal. Shore wish I hadn't made you pale and scared like this."

About 10:00 a.m. the next morning Carmichael drove Helen and Bo in to Pine, and tied up the team before Widow Cass's cottage.

The peach and apple trees were mingling blossoms of pink and white; a drowsy *hum* of bees filled the fragrant air; rich dark green alfalfa covered the small orchard flat;

a wood fire sent up a lazy column of blue smoke, and birds were singing sweetly.

Helen could scarcely believe that amid all this tranquility a man lay perhaps fatally injured. Assuredly Carmichael had been somber and reticent enough to raise the gravest fears.

Widow Cass appeared on the little porch, a gray, bent, worn, but cheerful old woman who Helen had come to know as her friend.

"My land! I'm that glad to see you, Miss Helen," she said. "And you've fetched the little lass as I've not got acquainted with yet."

"Good morning, Missus Cass. How . . . how is Roy?" replied Helen anxiously, scanning the wrinkled face.

"Roy? Now don't you look so scared. Roy's 'most ready to git on his hoss an' ride home, if I let him. He knowed you was a-comin'. An' he made me hold a lookin' glass for him to shave. How's thet for a man with a bullet hole through him. You can't kill them Mormons, nohow."

She led them into a little sitting room, where on a couch underneath a window Roy Beeman lay. He was wide awake and smiling, but haggard. He lay partly covered with a blanket. His gray shirt was open at the neck disclosing bandages.

" 'Mornin', girls," he drawled. "Shore is good of you now, comin' down."

Helen stood beside him, bent over him in her earnestness, as she greeted him. She saw a shade of pain in his eyes and his immobility struck her, but he did not seem badly off. Bo was pale, round-eyed, and apparently too agitated to speak. Carmichael placed chairs beside the couch for the girls.

"Wal, what's ailin' you this nice mornin'?" asked Roy, eyes on the cowboy.

"Huh! Would you expect me to be wearin' the smile of a fellar goin' to be married?" retorted Carmichael.

"Shore you haven't made up with Bo yet," returned Roy.

Bo blushed rosy red. And the cowboy's face lost something of its somber hue.

"I allow it's none of you d— . . . darn' bizness if *she* ain't made up with me," he said.

"Las Vegas, you're a wonder with a hoss an' a rope, an' I reckon with a gun, but when it comes to girls, you shore ain't there."

"I'm no Mormon, by golly. . . . Come, Missus Cass, let's get out of here, so they can talk."

"Folks, I was jest a-goin' to say that Roy's got fever an' he oughtn't t'talk too much," said the old woman. Then she and Carmichael went into the kitchen and closed the door.

Roy looked up at Helen with his keen eyes, more kindly piercing than ever. "My brother John was here. He'd just left when you come. He rode home to tell my folks I'm not so bad hurt, an' then he's goin' to ride a beeline into the mountains."

Helen's eyes asked what her lips refused to utter.

"He's goin' after Dorn. I sent him. I reckoned us-all sorta needed sight of thet dog-gone' hunter."

Roy had averted his gaze quickly to Bo. "Don't you agree with me, lass?"

"I sure do," replied Bo heartily.

All within Helen had been stilled for the moment of her realization, and then came swell and beat of heart, and inconceivable chafing of a tide at its restraint.

"Can John . . . fetch Dorn out . . . when the snow's so deep?" she asked unsteadily.

"Shore. He's takin' two hosses up to the snowline. Then, if necessary, he'll go over the pass on snowshoes. But I bet him Dorn would ride out. Snow's about gone except on the north slopes an' on the peaks."

"Then . . . when may I . . . we except to see Dorn?"

"Three or four days, I reckon. I wish he

340

was here now. . . . Miss Helen, there's trouble afoot."

"I realize that. I'm ready. Did Las Vegas tell you about Beasley's visit to me?"

"No. You tell me," replied Roy.

Briefly Helen began to acquaint him with the circumstances of that visit, and before she had finished she made sure Roy was swearing to himself.

"He asked you to marry him! Jerusalem! Thet I'd never have reckoned. The . . . low-down coyote of a greaser! Wal, Miss Helen, when I met up with *Señor* Beasley last night, he was shore spoilin' from somethin' . . . now I see what thet was. An' I reckon I picked out the bad time."

"For what? Roy, what did you do?"

"But, Miss Helen, thet's the only way. To be afraid *makes* more danger. Beasley 'peared civil enough, first off. Him an' me kept edgin' off, an' his pards kept edgin' after us, till he got me in a corner of the saloon. I don't know all I said to him. Shore I talked a heap. I told him what my old man thought. An' Beasley knowed as well as I thet my old man's not only the oldest inhabitant hereabout, but he's the wisest, too. An' he wouldn't tell a lie. Wal, I used all his sayin's in my argument to show Beasley thet, if he didn't haul up short, he'd end almost as short. Beasley's thick-headed, an' powerful conceited. Vain as a peacock! He couldn't see it, an' he got mad. I told him he was rich enough without robbin' you of your ranch, an' . . . wal, I shore put up a big talk for your side. By this time he an' his gang had me crowded in a corner, an', from their look, I begun to get cold feet. But I was in it an' had to make the best of it. The argument worked down to his pin-nin' me to my word thet I'd fight for you when thet fight come off. An' I shore told him for my own sake I wished it'd come off quick. . . . When . . . wal . . . then somethin' did come off quick!"

"Roy! Then he shot you!" exclaimed Helen passionately.

"Now, Miss Helen, I didn't say who done it," replied Roy with his engaging smile.

"Tell me then . . . who did?"

"Wal, I reckon I sha'n't tell you unless you promise not to tell Las Vegas. Thet cowboy is plumb off his head. He thinks he knows who shot me an' I've been lyin' somethin' scandalous. You see, if he learns . . . then he'll go gunnin'! An', Miss Helen, thet Texan is bad. He might get plugged as I did . . . an' there would be another man put off your side when the big trouble comes."

"Roy, I promise you I will not tell Las Vegas," replied Helen earnestly.

"Wal, then . . . it was Riggs!" Roy grew still paler as he confessed this, and his voice, almost a whisper, expressed shame and hate. "Thet four-flush did it. Shot me from behind Beasley! I had no chance. I couldn't even see him draw. But when I fell an' lay there an' the others dropped back, then I seen the smokin' gun in his hand. He looked powerful important. An' Beasley began to cuss him an' was cussin' him as they all run out."

"Oh, the coward! The despicable coward!" cried Helen.

"No wonder Tom wants to find out!" exclaimed Bo, low and deep. "I'll bet he suspects Riggs."

"Shore he does. But I wouldn't give him no satisfaction."

"Roy, you know that Riggs can't last out here."

"Wal, I hope he lasts till I get on my feet again."

"There you go! Hopeless, all you boys! You must spill blood!"

"Dear Miss Helen, don't take on so. I'm like Dorn . . . no man to hunt up trouble. But out here there's a sort of unwritten law . . . an eye for an eye . . . a tooth for a tooth. I believe in God Almighty, an' killin's against my religion. But Riggs shot me . . . the same as shootin' me in the back."

"Roy, I'm only a woman . . . I fear, faint-hearted and unequal to this West."

"Wait till somethin' happens to you. Supposin' Beasley comes an' grabs you with his own dirty big paws an', after maulin' you some, throws you out of your home! Or supposin' Riggs chases you into a corner!"

Helen felt the start of all her physical being — a violent leap of blood. But she could only judge of her looks from the grim smile of the wounded man as he watched her with his keen intent eyes.

"My friend, anythin' can happen," he said. "But let's hope it won't be the worst."

He had begun to show signs of weakness, and Helen, rising at once, said that she and Bo had better leave him then, but would come to see him the next day. At her call, Carmichael entered again with Mrs. Cass, and, after a few remarks, the visit was terminated. Carmichael lingered in the doorway.

"Wal, cheer up, you old Morman!" he called.

"Cheer up yourself, you cross, old bachelor!" retorted Roy, quite unnecessarily loud. "Can't you raise enough nerve to make up with Bo!"

Carmichael evacuated the doorway as if he had been spurred. He was quite red in the face while he unhitched the team and silent during the ride up to the ranch house. There he got down and followed the girls into the sitting room. He appeared still somber, although not sullen, and had fully regained his composure.

"Did you find out who shot Roy?" he asked abruptly of Helen.

"Yes. But I promised Roy I would not tell," replied Helen nervously. She averted her eyes from his searching gaze, intuitively fearing his next query.

"Was it thet . . . Riggs?"

"Las Vegas, don't ask me. I will not break my promise."

He strode to the window and looked out a moment, and presently, when he turned toward Bo, he seemed a stronger, loftier, more impelling man with all his emotions under control.

"Bo, will you listen to me . . . if I swear to speak the truth . . . as I know it?"

"Why certainly," replied Bo with the color coming swiftly to her face.

"Roy doesn't want me to know because he wants to meet thet fellar himself. An' I want to know because I want to stop him

345

before he can do more dirt to us or our friends. Thet's Roy's reason an' mine. An' I'm askin' you to tell me."

"But, Tom . . . I oughtn't," replied Bo haltingly.

"Did you promise Roy not to tell?"

"No."

"Or your sister?"

"No, I didn't promise either."

"Wal, then you tell me. I want you to trust me in this here matter. But not because I love you an' once had a wild dream you might care for me. . . ."

"Oh . . . Tom!" faltered Bo.

"Listen. I want you to trust me because trouble's comin' an' because I'm the one who knows what's best. I wouldn't lie an' I wouldn't say so if I didn't know shore. I swear Dorn will back me up. But he can't be here for some days. An' thet gang has got to be bluffed. You ought to see this. I reckon you've been quick in savvyin' Western ways. I couldn't pay you no higher compliment, Bo Rayner. Now will you tell me?"

"Yes, I will," replied Bo with the blaze leaping to her eyes.

"Oh, Bo . . . please don— . . . please don't. . . . Wait!" implored Helen.

"Bo . . . it's between you an' me," said

Carmichael.

"Tom, I'll tell you," whispered Bo. "It was a low-down cowardly trick. . . . Roy was surrounded . . . and shot from behind Beasley . . . by that four-flush Riggs!"

CHAPTER SIXTEEN

The memory of a woman had ruined Milt Dorn's peace, had confounded his philosophy of self-sufficient lonely happiness in the solitude of the wilds, had forced him to come face to face with his soul and the fatal significance of life. When he realized his defeat, that things were not as they seemed, that there was no joy for him in the coming of spring, that he had been blind in his free sensorial Indian relations to existence, he fell into an inexplicably strange state of despondency, a gloom as deep as the silence of his home. Dorn reflected that the stronger an animal, the keener its nerves, the higher its intelligence, the greater must be its suffering under restraint or injury. He thought of himself as a high order of animal whose great physical need was action, and now the incentive to action seemed dead. He grew lax. He did not want to move. He performed his diminishing duties under compulsion.

He watched for spring as a liberation, but not so that he could leave the valley. He hated the cold, he grew weary of wind and snow; he imagined the warm sun, the park once more green with grass and bright with daisies, the return of birds and squirrels and deer to their old haunts would be the means whereby he could break this spell upon him. Then he might gradually return to past contentment, although it would never be the same.

But spring, coming early to Paradise Park, brought a fever to Dorn's blood — a fire of unutterable longing. It was good, perhaps, that this was so, because he seemed driven to work, climb, tramp, and keep ceaselessly on the move from dawn to dark. That action strengthened his lax muscles and kept him from those motionless, senseless hours of brooding. He at least need not be ashamed of longing for that which could never be his — the sweetness of a woman — a house full of light, joy, hope, the meaning and beauty of children. But those dark moods were sinking into a pit of hell.

Dorn had not kept track of days and weeks. He did not know when the snow melted off three slopes of Paradise Park. All he knew was that an age had dragged over his head and that spring had come. During his restless waking hours, and even when he was asleep, there seemed always in the back of his mind a growing consciousness that soon he would emerge from this trial, a changed man, ready to sacrifice his chosen lot to give up his lonely life of selfish indulgence in lazy affinity with Nature, and to go wherever his strong hands might perform some real service to people. Nevertheless he wanted to linger in this mountain fastness until his ordeal was over — until he could meet her, and the world, knowing himself more of a man than ever before.

One bright morning, while he was at his campfire, the tame cougar gave low growling warning. Dorn was startled. Tom did not act like that because of a prowling grizzly or a straying stag. Presently Dorn espied a horseman riding slowly out of the straggling spruces. And with that sight Dorn's heart gave a leap, recalling to him a divination of his future relations to his kind. Never had he been so glad to a see a man!

This visitor resembled one of the Beemans, judging from the way he sat his horse, and presently Dorn recognized him to be John.

At this juncture the jaded horse was spurred into a trot, soon reaching the pines and the camp.

"Howdy there, you ole b'ar hunter!" called John, waving his hand.

For all his hearty greeting his appearance checked a like response from Dorn. The horse was mud to his flanks and John was mud to his knees, wet, bedraggled, worn, and white. The hue of his face meant more than fatigue.

"Howdy, John," replied Dorn.

They shook hands. John wearily swung his leg over the pommel, but did not at once dismount. His clear gray eyes were wonderingly riveted upon the hunter.

"Milt . . . what'n hell's wrong?" he queried.

"Why?"

"Bust me if you ain't changed so I hardly knowed you. You've been sick . . . all alone here!"

"Do I look sick?"

"Wal, I should smile. Thin an' pale an' down in the mouth. Milt, what ails you?"

"I've gone to seed."

"You've gone off your head, jest as Roy said, livin' alone here. You overdid it, Milt. An' you look sick."

"John, my sickness is here," replied Dorn soberly as he lay a hand on his heart.

"Lung trouble!" ejaculated John. "With thet chest an' up 'n this air? Get out!"

"No . . . not lung trouble," said Dorn.

"I savvy. Had a hunch from Roy, anyhow."

"What kind of a hunch?"

"Easy now, Dorn, ole man. . . . Don't you reckon I'm ridin' in on you pretty early? Look at that lion!" John slid off and waved a hand at his drooping beast, then began to unsaddle him. "Wal, he done great. He bogged some comin' over. An' I climbed the pass at night on the frozen snow."

"You're welcome as the flower in May. . . . John, what month is it?"

"By spades! Are you as bad as thet? Let's see. It's the Twenty-Third of March."

"March! Well, I'm beat. I've lost any reckonin' . . . an' a lot more, maybe."

"Thar!" declared John, slapping the mustang. "You can jest hang up here till my next trip. Milt, how're your hosses?"

"Wintered fine."

"Wal, thet's good. We'll need two big stray hosses right off."

"What for?" queried Dorn sharply. He dropped a stick of wood and straightened up from the campfire.

"You're goin' to ride down to Pine with me . . . thet's what for."

Familiarly then came back to Dorn the quiet, intent suggestiveness of the Beemans in moments foreboding trial.

352

At this certain assurance of John's, too significant and dark to be doubted, Dorn's thought of Pine gave slow birth to a strange sensation, as if he had been dead and was vibrating back to life.

"Tell me what you got to tell!" he broke out.

Quick as a flash the Mormon replied. "Roy's been shot. But he won't die. He sent for you. Bad deals afoot. Beasley means to force Helen Rayner out an' steal her ranch."

A tremor ran all through Dorn. It seemed another painful yet thrilling connection between his past and this vaguely calling future. His emotions had been broodings, dreams, longings. This thing his friend said had the sting of real life.

"Then old Al's dead?" he asked.

"Long ago . . . I reckon around the middle of February. The property went to Helen. She's been doin' fine. An' many folks say it's a pity she'll lose it."

"She won't lose it," declared Dorn. How strange his voice sounded to his own ears. It was hoarse and unreal, as if from disuse.

"Wal, we-all have our ideas. I say she will. My father says so. Carmichael says so."

"Who's he?"

"Reckon you remember thet cowpuncher who came up with Roy an' Auchincloss after the girls . . . last fall?"

"Yes. They called him Las . . . Las Vegas. I liked his looks."

"*Humph!* You'll like him a heap when you know him. He's kept the ranch goin' for Miss Helen all along. But the deals comin' to a head. Beasley's got thick with that Riggs. You remember him?"

"Yes."

"Wal, he's been hangin' out at Pine all winter, watchin' for some chance to get at Miss Helen or Bo. Everybody's seen thet. An' jest lately he chased Bo on hossback . . . gave the kid a nasty fall. Roy says Riggs was after Miss Helen. But I think one or t'other of the girls would do thet varmint. Wal, thet sorta started goin's on. Carmichael beat Riggs an' drove him out of town. But he came back. Beasley called on Miss Helen an' offered to marry her so's not to take the ranch from her, he said."

Dorn awoke with a thundering curse.

"Shore!" exclaimed John. "I'd say the same . . . only I'm religious. Don't thet beady-eyed greaser's gall make you want to spit all over yourself? My God, but Roy was mad! Roy's powerful fond of Miss Helen an' Bo. . . . Wal, then, Roy first chance he got, braced Beasley an' give him some straight talk. Beasley was foamin' at the mouth, Roy said. It was then Riggs shot Roy. Shot him from behind Beasley when Roy wasn't lookin'! An' Riggs brags of bein' a gunfighter. . . . Mebbe thet wasn't a bad shot for him!"

"I reckon," replied Dorn as he swallowed hard. "Now just what was Roy's message to me?"

"Wal, I can't remember all Roy said," answered John dubiously. "But Roy shore was excited an' dead in earnest. He says . . . 'Tell Milt what's happened. Tell him Helen Rayner's in more danger than she was last fall. Tell him I've seen her look away acrost the mountains toward Paradise Park with her heart in her eyes. Tell him she needs him most of all.' "

Dorn shook all over as with an attack of ague. He was seized by a whirlwind of exquisite passionate terrible sweetness of sensation when what he wildly wanted was to curse Roy and John for the simple-minded conclusions.

"Roy's crazy!" panted Dorn.

"Wal, now, Milt, thet's downright surprisin' of you. Roy's the level-headedest of any fellars I know."

"Man! If he *made* me believe him. . . . and it turned out untrue . . . I'd . . . I'd kill him," replied Dorn.

"Untrue! Do you think Roy Beeman would lie?"

"But, John, you fellows can't see my case. Nell Rayner wants me . . . needs me! It can't be true!"

"Well, my love-sick pard . . . it jest is true!" exclaimed John feelingly. "Thet's the hell of life . . . never knowin'. But here it's joy for you. You can believe Roy Beeman about women as quick as you'd trust him to track your lost hoss. Roy's married three girls. I reckon he'll marry some more. Roy's only twenty-eight an' he has two big farms. He said he'd seen Nell Rayner's heart in her eyes, lookin' for you . . . an' you can jest bet your life thet's true. An' he said it because he means you to rustle down there an' fight for thet girl."

"I'll go," said Dorn in a shaky whisper as he sat down on a pine log near the fire. He stared unseeingly at the bluebells in the grass by his feet while storm after storm possessed his breast. They were fierce and brief because driven by his will. In those few moments of contending strife Dorn was immeasurably removed from that dark gulf of self that had made his winter a nightmare. And when he stood erect again, it seemed that the old earth had a stirring electrifying impetus for his feet. Something black, bitter, melancholy, and morbid, always unreal to him, had passed away forever. The great moment had been forced upon him. He did not believe Roy Beeman's preposterous hint regarding Helen, but he had gone back or soared onward, as if by magic, to his old true self.

Mounted on Dorn's strongest horses, with only a light pack, an axe, and their weapons, the two men had reached the snowline on the pass by noon that day. Tom, the tame cougar, trotted along in the rear.

The crust of the snow, now half thawed by the sun, would not hold the weight of a horse, although it upheld the men on foot. They walked, leading the horses. Travel was not difficult until the snow began to deepen, then progress slackened materially. John had not been able to pick out the line of the trail, so Dorn did not follow his tracks. An old blaze on the trees enabled Dorn to keep fairly well to the trail, and, at length, the height of the pass was reached where the snow was deep. Here the horses labored, plowing through foot by foot. When finally they sank to their flanks, they had to be dragged and goaded on, and helped by thick flat bunches of spruce boughs placed under their hoofs. It took three hours of breaking toil to do the few hundred yards of deep snow at the height of the pass. The cougar did not have great difficulty in following, although it was evident he did not like such traveling.

That behind them, the horses gathered heart and worked on to the edge of the steep descent where they had all they could do to hold back from sliding and rolling. Fast time was made on this slope, at the bottom of which began a dense forest with snow still deep in places and windfalls hard to locate. The men here performed Herculean labors, but they got through to a park where the snow was gone. The ground, however, soft and boggy in places, was more treacherous than the snow, and the travelers had to skirt the edge of the park to a point opposite, and then go on through the forest. When they reached bare and solid ground, just before dark that night, it was high time, for the horses were ready to drop and the men likewise.

Camp was made in an open wood. When darkness fell and the men were resting on bough beds, feet to the fire, with Tom curled up close by, the horses still drooped where they had been unsaddled. Morning, however, discovered them grazing on the long, bleached grass. John shook his head when he looked at them.

"You reckoned to make Pine by nightfall. How far is it . . . the way you'll go?"

"Fifty mile or thereabouts," replied Dorn.

"Wal, we can't ride it on these critters."

"John, we'd do more than that if we had to."

They were saddled and on the move before sunrise, leaving snow and bog behind. Level parks and level forests led one after another too long slopes and steep descents, all growing sunnier and greener as the altitude diminished. Squirrels and grouse, turkeys and deer, and less tame denizens of the forest grew more abundant as the travel advanced. In this game zone, however, Dorn had trouble with Tom. The cougar had to be watched and called often to keep him off of trails.

"Tom doesn't like a long trip," said Dorn. "But I'm goin' to take him. Some way or other he may come in handy."

"Sic him onto Beasley's gang," replied John. "Some men are powerful scared of cougars. But I never was."

"Nor me. Though I've had cougars give me a darn' uncanny feelin'."

The men talked but little. Dorn led the way, with Tom trotting noiselessly beside his horse. John followed close behind. They loped the horses across parks, trotted through the forests, walked slowly up what few inclines they met, and slid down the soft, wet pine-matted descents. So they averaged from six to eight miles an hour. The horses held up well under that steady travel, and this without any rest at noon.

Dorn seemed to feel himself in an emotional trance. Yet, despite this, the same old sensorial perceptions crowded, thick and fast, upon him, strangely sweet and vivid after the past dead months when neither sun nor wind or cloud or scent of pine or anything in Nature could stir him. His mind, his heart, his soul seemed steeped in an intoxicating wine of expectation, while his eyes and ears and nose had never been keener to register the facts of the forestland. He saw the black thing far ahead that resembled a burned stump, but he knew it was a bear before it vanished; he saw the gray flash of deer and wolf and coyote, and the red of fox, and the small wary heads of old gobblers just sticking above the grass, and he saw deep tracks of game as well as the slow-rising blades of bluebells where some soft-footed beast had just trod. And he heard the melancholy notes of birds, the twitter of grouse, the sough of the wind, the light dropping of pine cones, the near and distant bark of squirrels, the deep gobble of a turkey close at hand and the challenge from a rival far away, the *cracking* of twigs in the thickets, the murmur of running water, the scream of an eagle, and the shrill cry of a hawk, and always the soft dull steady pads of the hoofs of the horses.

The smells, too, were the sweet stinging ones of spring, warm and pleasant — the odor of the clean fresh earth cutting its way through that thick, strong fragrance of pine, the smell of logs rotting in the sun, and of fresh new grass and flowers along a brook of snow water.

"I smell smoke," said Dorn suddenly as he reined in, and turned for corroboration from his companion.

John sniffed the warm air. "Wal, you're more of an Injun than me," he replied, shaking his head.

They traveled on, and presently came out upon the rim of the last slope. A long league of green slanted below them, breaking up into straggling lines of trees and groves that joined the cedar, and these in turn stretched on and down in gray-black patches to the desert, that glittering and bare, with streaks of somber hue, faded into the obscurity of distance.

The village of Pine appeared to nestle in a

curve on the edge of the great forest, and the cabins looked like tiny white dots set in green.

"Look there," said Dorn, pointing.

Some miles to the right a gray escarpment of rock cropped out of the slope, forming a promontory, and from it a thick, pale column of smoke curled upward to be lost from sight as soon as it had no background of green.

"They's your smoke, shore enough," replied John thoughtfully. "Now, I jest wonder who's campin' there. No water near or grass for horses."

"John, that point's been used for smoke signals many a time."

"Was jest thinkin' of thet same. Shall we ride around there an' take a peek?"

"No. But we'll remember that. If Beasley's got his deep scheme goin', he'll have Snake Anson's gang somewhere close."

"Roy said thet same. Wal, it's some three hours till sundown. The hosses keep up. I reckon I'm fooled, for we'll make Pine all right. But old Tom there, he's tired or lazy."

The big cougar was lying down, panting, and his half-shut eyes were on Dorn.

"Tom's not lazy an' fat. He could travel at this gait for a week. But let's rest a half hour an' watch that smoke before movin' on. We can make Pine before sundown."

When travel had been resumed, halfway down the slope Dorn's sharp eyes caught a broad track where shod horses had passed, climbing in a long slat toward the promontory. He dismounted to examine them, and John, coming up, proceeded with alacrity to get off and do likewise. Dorn made his deductions after which he stood in a brown study beside his horse, waiting for John.

"Wal, what'd you make of them here tracks?" asked that worthy.

"Some horses an' a pony went along here yesterday, an' today a single horse made that fresh track."

"Wal, Milt, for a hunter you ain't so bad at hoss tracks," observed John. "But how many horses went yesterday?"

"I couldn't make out . . . several . . . maybe four or five."

"Six hosses an' a colt or little mustang, unshod, to be strict correct. Wal, supposin' they did. What's it mean to us?"

"I don't know as I'd thought anythin' unusual, if it hadn't been for that smoke we saw off the rim, an' then this here fresh track made along today. Looks queer to me."

"Wish Roy was here," replied John,

scratching his head. "Milt, I've a hunch, if he was, he'd foller them tracks."

"Maybe. But we haven't time for that. We can back trail them, though, if they keep clear as they are here. An' we'll not lose any time, either."

That broad track led straight toward Pine, down to the edge of the cedars where, amid some jagged rocks, evidence showed that men had camped there for days. Here it ended as a broad trail. But from the north came the single fresh track made that very day, and from the east, more in a line with Pine, came two tracks made the day before. And there were imprints of big and little hoofs. Manifestly these interested John more than they did Dorn, who had to wait for his companion.

"Milt, it ain't a colt's . . . thet little track," avowed John.

"Why not . . . an' what if it isn't?" queried Dorn.

"Wal, it ain't, because a colt always straggles back, an' from one side to another. This little track keeps close to the big one. An', by George, it was made by a led mustang."

John resembled Roy Beeman then with that leaping intent fire in his gray eyes. Dorn's reply was to spur his horse into a trot and call sharply to the lagging cougar.

When they turned into the broad, blossom-bordered road that was the only thoroughfare of Pine, the sun was setting red and gold behind the mountains. The horses were too tired for any more than a walk. Natives of the village, catching sight of Dorn and Beeman, and the huge gray cat following like a dog, called excitedly to one another. A group of men in front of Turner's gazed intently down the road, and soon manifested signs of excitement. Dorn and his comrade dismounted in front of Widow Cass's cottage. And Dorn called as he strode up the little path. Mrs. Cass came out. She was white and shaking, but appeared calm. At sight of her, John Beeman drew a sharp breath.

"Wal, now . . . ," he began hoarsely, and left off.

"How's Roy?" queried Dorn.

"Lord knows, I'm glad to see you, boys. Milt, you're thin an' strange-lookin'. . . . Roy's had a little setback. He got a shock today an' it throwed him off. Fever . . . an' now he's out of his head. It won't do no good for you to waste time seein' him. Take my word for it, he's all right. But there's others as. . . . For the land's sake, Milt Dorn, you fetched thet cougar back! Don't let him near me!"

"Tom won't hurt you, auntie," said Dorn as the cougar came padding up the path. "You were sayin' somethin' . . . about others. Is Miss Helen safe? Hurry!"

"Ride up to see her . . . an' waste no more time here."

Dorn was quick in the saddle, followed by John, but the horses had to be severely punished to force them even to a trot. And that was a lagging trot that now did not leave Tom behind.

The ride up to Auchincloss's ranch house seemed endless to Dorn. Natives came out in the road to watch after he had passed. Stern as Dorn was in dominating his feelings, he could not wholly subordinate his mounting joy to a waiting terrible anticipation of catastrophe. But no matter what fateful events might hinge upon this nameless circumstance about to be disclosed, the wonderful and glorious fact of the present was that in a moment he would see Helen Rayner.

There were saddled horses in the courtyard, but no riders. A Mexican boy sat on the porch bench in the seat where Dorn remembered he had encountered Al Auchincloss. The door of the big sitting room was open. The scent of flowers, the murmur of bees, the pounding of hoofs came vaguely to Dorn. His eyes dimmed, so that the ground, when he slid out of his saddle, seemed far below him. He stepped upon the porch. His sight suddenly cleared. A tight fullness at his throat made incoherent the words he said to the Mexican boy. But they were understood as the boy ran back around the house. Dorn knocked sharply and stepped over the threshold.

Outside, John, true to his habits, was thinking, even in that moment of surprise, about the faithful, exhausted horses. As he unsaddled them, he talked. "For soft an' fat hosses, winterin' high up, wal, you've done somethin'."

Then Dorn heard a voice in another room, a step, a *creak* of the door. It opened. A woman in white appeared. He recognized Helen. But instead of the rich brown bloom and dark-eyed beauty so hauntingly limned on his memory, he saw a white, beautiful face, strained and quivering in anguish, and eyes that pierced his heart. He could not speak.

"Oh! My friend . . . you've come," she whispered.

Dorn put out a shaking hand. But she did not see it. She clutched his shoulders, as if to feel whether or not he was real, and then her arms went up around his neck.

"Oh, thank God! I knew you would come," she said, and her head sank to his shoulder.

Dorn divined what he had suspected. Helen's sister had been carried off. Yet while his quick mind grasped Helen's broken spirit — the unbalance that was reason for this marvelous and glorious act — he did not take other meaning of the embrace to himself. He just stood there, transported, charged like a tree stuck by lightning, making sure with all his keen senses, so that he could feel forever how she was clinging around his neck, her face over his bursting heart, her quivering form close — pressed to his.

"It's . . . Bo," he said unsteadily.

"She went riding yesterday . . . and . . . never . . . came . . . back," replied Helen brokenly.

"I've seen her trail. She's been taken into the woods. I'll find her. I'll fetch her back," he replied rapidly.

With a shock she seemed to absorb his meaning. With another shock she raised her face — leaned back a little to look at him.

"You'll find her . . . fetch her back?"

"Yes," he answered instantly.

With that ringing word it seemed to Dorn

she realized how she was standing. He felt her shake as she dropped her arms and stepped back while the white anguish of her face was flooded out by a wave of scarlet. But she was brave in her confusion. Her eyes never fell, although they changed swiftly, darkening with shame, amaze, and with feeling he could not read.

"I'm almost . . . out of my head," she faltered.

"No wonder. I saw that. . . . Your meetin' me as if I was your brother. . . . But now you must get clear-headed. I've no time to lose." He led her to the door. "John, it's Bo that's gone!" he called. "Since yesterday. . . . Send the boy to get me a bag of meat an' bread. You run to the corral an' get me a fresh horse. My old horse, Ranger, if you can find him quick. An' rustle."

Without a word, John leaped bareback on one of the horses he had just unsaddled and spurred him across the courtyard.

Then the big cougar, seeing Helen, got up from where he lay on the porch, and came to her.

"Oh, it's Tom!" cried Helen, and, as he rubbed her knees, she patted his head with trembling hand. "You big, beautiful pet. Oh, how I remember! Oh, how Bo would love to. . . ."

"Where's Carmichael?" interrupted Dorn. "Out huntin' Bo?"

"Yes. It was he who missed her first. He rode everywhere yesterday. Last night when he came back, he was wild. I've not seen him today. He made all the other men, but Hal and Joe, stay home at the ranch."

"Right. An' John must stay, too," declared Dorn. "But it's strange. Carmichael ought to have found the girl's tracks. She was ridin' a pony."

"Bo rode Sam. He's a little bronc', very strong and fast."

"I came across his tracks. How'd Carmichael miss them?"

"He didn't. He found them . . . trailed them all along the north range. That's where he forbid Bo to go. You see they're in love with each other. They've been at odds. Neither will give in. Bo disobeyed him. There's hard ground off the north range, so he said. He was able to follow her tracks only so far."

"Were there any other tracks along with hers?"

"No."

"Miss Helen, I found them 'way southeast of Pine. Up on the slope of the mountain. There were seven other horses makin' that trail . . . when we run across it. On the way down we found a camp where men had waited. An' Bo's pony, led by a rider on a big horse, come into that camp from the east . . . maybe north a little. An' that tells the story."

"Riggs ran her down . . . made off with her?" cried Helen passionately. "Oh, the villain! He had men in waiting. That's Beasley's work. They were after me."

"It may not be just what you said, but that's close enough. An' Bo's in a bad fix. You must face that an' try to bear up under . . . fears of the worst."

"My friend . . . you will save her!"

"I'll fetch her back, alive or dead."

"Dead! Oh, my God!" Helen cried, and closed her eyes an instant, to open them burning black. "But Bo isn't dead. I know that . . . I feel it. She'll not die very easily. She's a little savage. She has no fear. She'd fight like a tigress for her life. She's strong. You remember how strong. She can stand anything. Unless they murder her outright, she'll live . . . a long time . . . through any ordeal. . . . So I beg you, my friend, don't lose an hour . . . don't ever give up."

Dorn trembled under the clasp of her hands. Loosing his own from her clinging hold, he stepped out on the porch. At that moment John appeared on Ranger down the lane, coming at a gallop.

"Nell, I'll never come back without her," said Dorn. "I reckon you can hope . . . only be prepared. That's all. It's hard. But these damned deals are common out here in the West."

"Suppose Beasley comes . . . here?" exclaimed Helen, and again her hand went out toward him.

"If he does, you refuse to get off," replied Dorn. "But don't let him or his greasers put a dirty hand on you. Should he threaten force . . . why pack some clothes . . . an' your valuables . . . an' go down to Missus Cass's. An' wait till I come back."

"Wait . . . till you . . . come back," she faltered, slowly turning white again. Her dark eyes dilated. "Milt . . . you're like Las Vegas! You'll kill Beasley!"

Dorn heard himself laugh, very cold and strange, foreign to his ears. A grim deadly hate of Beasley vied with the tenderness and pity he felt for this distressed girl. It was a sore trial to see her leaning there against the door — to be compelled to leave her alone. Abruptly he stalked off the porch. Tom followed him. The black horse whinnied his recognition of Dorn and snorted at sight of the cougar. Just then the Mexican boy returned with a bag. Dorn tied this, with the small pack, behind the saddle.

"John, you stay here with Miss Helen," said Dorn. "An' if Carmichael comes back, keep him, too! An' tonight, if anyone rides in to Pine from the way we come, you be sure to spot him."

"I'll do that, Milt," responded John.

Dorn mounted, and, turning for a last word to Helen, he felt the words of cheer halt on his lips as he saw her standing, white and broken-hearted, with her hands to her bosom. He could not look twice.

"Come on there, you Tom!" he called to the cougar. "Reckon on this track you'll pay me for all my trainin' of you."

"Oh . . . my friend," came Helen's sad voice, almost a whisper to his throbbing ears. "Heaven help you . . . to save her. I. . . ."

Then Ranger started and Dorn heard no more. He could not look back. His eyes were full of tears and his breast ached. By a tremendous effort he shifted that emotion — called on all the spiritual energy of his being to the duty of this grim task before him.

He did not ride down through the village, but skirted the northern border, and marked around to the south, where, coming to the trail he had made an hour past, he headed on it, straight for the slope now darkening in the twilight. The big cougar showed more willingness to return on this trail than he had shown in the coming. Ranger was fresh and wanted to go, but Dorn held him in.

A cool wind blew down from the mountain with the coming of night. Against the brightening stars Dorn saw the promontory lift its bold outline. It was miles away. It haunted him, strangely calling. A night, and perhaps a day, separated him from the gang that held Bo Rayner prisoner. Dorn had no plan as yet. He had only a motive as great as the love he bore Helen Rayner.

Beasley's evil genius had planned this abduction. Riggs was a tool, a cowardly knave dominated by a stronger will. Snake Anson and his gang had lain in wait at that cedar camp, had made that broad hoof track leading up the mountain. Beasley had been there with them that very day. All this was as assured to Dorn as if he had seen the men.

But the matter of Dorn's recovering the girl and doing it speedily strung his mental strength to its highest pitch. Many outlines of action flashed through his mind as he rode on, peering keenly through the night, listening with practiced ears. All were rejected. And at the outset of every new branching of thought he would gaze down at the gray form of the cougar, long, graceful, heavy, as he padded beside the horse. From the first thought of returning to help Helen Rayner he had conceived an undefined idea of possible value in the qualities of his pet. Tom had performed wonderful feats of trailing, but he had never been tried on men. Dorn believed he could make him trail anything, yet he had no proof of this. One fact stood out of all Dorn's conjectures, and it was that he had known men, and brave men, to fear cougars.

Far up on the slope, in a little hollow where water ran and there was a little grain for Ranger to pick, Dorn haltered him, and made ready to spend the night. He was sparing with his food, giving Tom more than he took himself. Curled close up to Dorn, the big cat went to sleep.

But Dorn lay awake for long.

The night was still, with only a faint moan of wind on this sheltered slope. Dorn saw hope in the stars. He did not seem to have promised himself or Helen that he could save her sister, and then her property. He seemed to have stated something unconsciously settled, outside of his thinking. Strange how this certainty was not vague, yet irreconcilable with any plans he created!

Behind it, somehow nameless with inconceivable power, surged all his wonderful knowledge of forest, of trails, of scents, of night, of the nature of men lying down to sleep in the dark lonely woods, of the nature of this great cat that lived its every action in accordance with his will.

He grew sleepy, and gradually his mind stilled, with his last conscious thought a portent that he would awaken to accomplish his desperate task.

CHAPTER SEVENTEEN

Young Burt possessed the keenest eyes of any man in Snake Anson's gang, for which reason he was given the post as look-out from the lofty promontory. His instructions were to keep sharp watch over the open slopes below and to report any sight of a horse.

A cedar fire with green boughs on top of dead wood sent up a long pale column of smoke. This signal fire had been kept burning since sunrise.

The preceding night, camp had been made on a level spot in the cedars back of the promontory. But manifestly Anson did not expect to remain there long. For after breakfast the packs had been made up and the horses stood saddled and bridled. They were restless and uneasy, tossing bits and fighting flies. The sun, now halfway to meridian, was hot and no breeze blew in that sheltered spot.

Shady Jones had ridden off early to fill the water bags, and had not yet returned. Anson, thinner and scalier and more snake-like than ever, was dealing a greasy, dirty deck of cards, his opponent being the square-shaped, black-visaged Moze. In lieu of money the gamblers wagered with cedar berries, each of which berries represented a pipeful of tobacco. Jim Wilson brooded under a cedar tree, his unshaven face a dirty dust line, a smoldering fire in his light eyes, a sullen set to his jaw. Every little while he would raise his eyes to glance at Riggs and it seemed that a quick glance was enough. Riggs paced to and fro in the open, coatless and hatless, his black broadcloth trousers and embroidered vest dusty and torn. An enormous gun bumped outwardly in its sheath swinging below his hip. Riggs looked perturbed. His face was sweating freely, yet it was far from red in color. He did not appear to mind the sun or the flies. His eyes were staring, dark, wild, shifting in gaze from everything they encountered. But often that gaze shot back to the captive girl sitting under a cedar some yards from the men.

Bo Rayner's little booted feet were tied together with one end of a lasso and the other end trailed off over the ground. He hands were free. Her riding habit was dirty and disordered. Her eyes blazed defiantly out of a small pale face.

"Harve Riggs, I wouldn't be standing in those cheap boots of yours for a million dollars," she said sarcastically.

Riggs took no notice of her words.

"You pack that gun sheath wrong end out. What have you got the gun for, anyhow?" she added tauntingly.

Snake Anson let out a hoarse laugh and Moze's black visage opened in a huge grin. Jim Wilson seemed to drink in the girl's words. Sullen and somber he bent his lean head, very still, as if listening.

"You'd better shut up," said Riggs darkly.

"I will not shut up," declared Bo.

"Then I'll gag you," he threatened.

"Gag me! Why, you dirty, low-down two-bit of a bluff!" she exclaimed hotly. "I'd like to see you try it. I'll tear that long hair of yours right off your head."

Riggs advanced toward her with his hands clutching as if eager to throttle her. The girl leaned forward, her face reddening, her eyes fierce.

"You damned little cat!" muttered Riggs thickly. "I'll gag you . . . if you don't stop squallin'."

"Come on, I dare you to lay a hand on

me. . . . Harve Riggs, I'm not the least afraid of you. Can't you savvy that? You're a liar, a four-flush, a sneak! Why, you're not fit to wipe the feet of any of these outlaws."

Riggs took two long strides and bent over her, his teeth protruding in a snarl, and he cuffed her hard on the side of the head.

Bo's head jerked back with the force of the blow, but she uttered no cry.

"Are you goin' to keep your jaw shut?" he demanded stridently, and a dark tide of blood surged up into his neck.

"I should smile I'm not," retorted Bo in cool deliberate anger of opposition. "You've roped me! And you've struck me! Now get a club . . . stand off there . . . out of my reach . . . and beat me! Oh, if I only knew cuss words fit for you . . . I'd call you them!"

Snake Anson had stopped playing cards and was watching, listening, with a half-disgusted, half-amused expression on his serpent-like face. Jim Wilson slowly rose to his feet. If anyone had observed him, it would have been to note that he now seemed singularly fascinated by this scene, yet all the while absorbed in himself. Once, he loosened the neckband of his blouse.

Riggs swung his arm more violently at the girl. But she dodged.

380

"You dog," she hissed. "Oh, if I only had a gun!"

Her face then, with its dead whiteness and the eyes of flame, held a tragic impelling beauty that stung Anson into remonstrance.

"*Aw*, Riggs, don't beat up the kid," he protested. "Thet won't do any good. Let her alone."

"But she's got to shut up," replied Riggs.

"How'n hell air you goin' to shet her up? Mebbe if you git out of her sight, she'll be quiet. . . . How about thet, girl?"

Anson gnawed his drooping mustache as he eyed Bo.

"Have I made any kick to you or your men yet?" she queried.

"It strikes me you ain't," replied Anson.

"You won't hear me make any so long as I'm treated decent," said Bo. "I don't know what you've got to do with Riggs. He ran me down . . . roped me . . . dragged me to your camp. . . . Now I've a hunch you're waiting for Beasley."

"Girl, your hunch is correct," said Anson.

"Well, do you know I'm the wrong girl?"

"What's thet? I reckon you're Nell Rayner, who got left all old Auchincloss's property."

"No, I'm Bo Rayner. Nell is my sister. She owns the ranch. Beasley wanted her."

Anson cursed, deep and low. Under his

sharp bristling eyebrows he bent cunning green eyes upon Riggs.

"Say, you! Is what this kid says so?"

"Yes. She's Nell Rayner's sister," replied Riggs doggedly.

"Ahuh! Wal, why the hell did you drag her into my camp an' off up here to signal Beasley? He ain't wantin' her. He wants the girl who owns the ranch. . . . Did you take one fer the other . . . same as that day we was with you?"

"Guess I must have," replied Riggs sullenly.

"But you knowed her from her sister afore you come to my camp?"

Riggs shook his head. He was paler now and sweating more freely. The lank hair hung wetly over his forehead. His manner was that of a man suddenly realizing he had gotten into a tight place.

"Oh, he's a liar!" exclaimed Bo with contemptuous ring in her voice. "He comes from my country. He has known Nell and me for years."

Snake Anson turned to look at Wilson.

"Jim, now hyar's a queer deal this fellar has rung in on us. . . . I thought thet kid was pretty young. Don't you remember Beasley told me Nell Rayner was a handsome woman?"

"Wal, pard Anson, if this heah girl ain't shore handsome, my eyes have gone pore," drawled Wilson.

"Ahuh! So your Texas chivalree over the ladies is some operatin'," retorted Anson with fine sarcasm. "But thet ain't tellin' me what you think?"

"Wal, I ain't tellin' you what I think yet. . . . But I know thet kid ain't Nell Rayner. For I've seen her."

Anson studied his right-hand man for a moment, then, taking out his tobacco pouch, he sat himself down upon a stone and proceeded leisurely to roll a cigarette. He put it between his thin lips and apparently forgot to light it. For a few moments he gazed at the yellow ground and some scant sagebrush.

Riggs took to pacing up and down. Wilson leaned as before against the cedar. The girl slowly recovered from her excess of anger.

"Kid, see hyar," said Anson, addressing the girl, "if Riggs knowed you wasn't Nell an' fetched you along anyhow . . . what'd he do thet fur?"

"He chased me . . . caught me. Then he saw someone after us and he hurried to your camp. . . . He was afraid . . . the cur!"

Riggs heard her reply, for he turned a malignant glance upon her.

"Anson, I fetched her because I know Nell Rayner will give up anythin' on earth for her," he said in loud voice.

Anson pondered this statement with an air of considering its apparent sincerity.

"Don't you believe him," declared Bo Rayner bluntly. "He's a liar. He's double-crossing Beasley and all of you."

Riggs raised a shaking hand to clench it at her. "Keep still or it'll be the worse for you."

"Riggs, shut up yourself," put in Anson as he leisurely rose. "Mebbe it ain't occurred to you thet she might have some talk interestin' to me. An' I'm runnin' this hyar camp. . . . Now, kid, talk up an' say what you like."

"I said he was double-crossing you all," replied the girl instantly. "Why, I'm surprised you'd be caught in his company. My Uncle Al and my sweetheart Carmichael and my friend Dorn . . . they all told me what Western men are, even down to outlaws, robbers, cut-throat rascals like you. And I know the West well enough now to be sure that four-flusher doesn't belong here and can't last here. He went to Dodge City once, and, when he came back, he made a bluff at being a badman. He was a swaggering, bragging, drinking gunfighter. He talked of the men he'd shot, of the fights he'd had. He dressed like some of those gun-throwing gamblers. . . . He was in love with my sister Nell. She hated him. He followed us out West and he has hung on my actions like a sneaking Indian. Why, Nell and I couldn't even walk to the store in the village. He rode after us out on the range . . . chased me. . . . For that, Carmichael called Riggs's bluff down in Turner's saloon. Dared him to draw! Cussed him every name on the range! Slapped and beat and kicked him! Drove him out of Pine! And now, whatever he has said to Beasley or you, it's a dead sure bet he's playing his own game. That's to get hold of Nell, and if not her . . . then me. . . . Oh, I'm out of breath . . . and I'm out of . . . names to call him. If I talked forever . . . I'd never be . . . able to . . . do him justice. . . . But lend me . . . a gun . . . a minute."

Jim Wilson's quiet form vibrated with a start. Anson, with an admiring smile, pulled his gun and, taking a couple of steps forward, held it out butt first. She stretched eagerly for it and he jerked it away.

"Hold on there!" yelled Riggs in alarm.

"Damn, Jim, if she didn't mean bizness!" exclaimed the outlaw.

"Wal, now . . . see heah, miss. Would you bore him . . . if you hed a gun?" inquired

Wilson curious interest. There was more of respect in his demeanor than admiration.

"No. I don't want his cowardly blood on my hands," replied the girl. "But I'd make him dance . . . I'd make him run."

"Shore you can handle a gun?"

She nodded her answer while her eyes flashed hate and her resolute lips twitched.

Then Wilson made a singularly swift motion and his gun was pitched butt first to within a foot of her hand. She snatched it up, cocked it, aimed it, all before Anson could move. But he yelled. "Drop thet gun, you little devil!"

Riggs turned ghastly as the big blue gun lined on him. He also yelled, but that yell was different from Anson's.

"Run or dance!" cried the girl.

The big gun *boomed,* and leaped almost out of her hand. She took both hands, and called derisively as she fired again. The bullet hit at Riggs's feet, scattering the dust and fragments of stone all over him. He bounded here — there — then darted for the rocks. A third time the heavy gun spoke and this bullet must have ticked Riggs for he let out a hoarse bawl and leaped sheerly for the protection of a rock.

"Plug him! Shoot off a leg!" yelled Snake Anson, whooping and stamping, as Riggs got out of sight.

Jim Wilson watched the whole performance with the same quietness that had characterized his manner toward the girl. Then, as Riggs disappeared, Wilson stepped forward and took the gun from the girl's trembling hands. She was whiter than ever, but still resolute and defiant. Wilson took a glance over in the direction Riggs had hidden, and then proceeded to reload the gun. Snake Anson's roar of laughter ceased rather suddenly.

"Hyar, Jim, she might have held up the whole gang with thet gun," he protested.

"Ahuh. You know a lot about wimmen now, don't you . . . but, by God, thet did my heart good. . . ."

"Jim, what'n earth would you have did if thet'd been you, instead of Riggs?"

The query seemed important and amazing. Wilson pondered.

"Shore I'd stood there . . . stick still . . . an' never moved an eye winker."

"An' let her shoot!" ejaculated Anson, nodding his long head. "Me, too!"

So these rough outlaws, inured to all the violence and baseness of their dishonest calling, rose to the challenging courage of a slip of a girl. She had the one thing they respected — nerve.

Just then a halloo from the promontory brought Anson up with a start. Muttering to himself, he strode out toward the jagged rocks that hid the outlook. Moze shuffled his burly form after Anson.

"Miss, it shore was grand . . . thet performance of Mister Gunman Riggs," remarked Jim Wilson, attentively studying the girl.

"Much obliged to you for lending me your gun," she replied. "I . . . I hope I hit him . . . a little."

"Wal, if you didn't sting him, then Jim Wilson knows nothin' about lead."

"Jim Wilson? Are you the man . . . the outlaw my Uncle Al knew?"

"Reckon I am, miss. Fer I knowed Al shore enough. . . . What'd he say about me?"

"I remember once he was telling me about Snake Anson's gang. He mentioned you. Said *you* were a real gunfighter. And what a damn' shame it was you had to be an outlaw."

"Wal! An' so old Al spoke thet nice of me. . . . It's tolerable likely I'll remember. . . . An' now, miss, can I do anythin' for you?"

Swift as a flash she looked at him. "What do you mean?"

"Wal, shore I don't mean much, I'm sorry to say. Nothin' to make you look like

388

thet. . . . I hev to be an outlaw, shore as you're born. But . . . mebbe there's a difference in outlaws."

She understood him and paid him the compliment not to voice her sudden up-flashing hope that he might be one to betray his leader.

"Please take this rope off my feet. Let me walk a little. Let me have a . . . a little privacy. That fool watched every move I made. I promise not to run away. . . . And, oh, I'm thirsty."

"Shore you've got sense." He freed her feet and helped her get up. "There'll be some fresh water any minnit now, if you'll wait." Then he turned his back and walked over to where Riggs sat nursing a bullet burn on his leg.

"Say, Riggs, I'm takin' the responsibility of loosin' the girl for a little spell. She can't get away, an' there ain't any sense in bein' mean."

Riggs made no reply, and went on rolling down his trouser leg, lapped a fold over at the bottom, and pulled on his boot. Then he strode out toward the promontory. Halfway there he encountered Anson, tramping back.

"Beasley's comin' one way an' Shady's comin' another. We'll be off this hot point of rock by noon," said the outlaw leader.

Riggs went to the promontory to look for himself.

"Where's the girl?" demanded Anson, in surprise, when he got back to the camp.

"Wal, she's walkin' around between heah an' Pine," drawled Wilson.

"Jim, you let her loose?"

"Shore I did. She's been hawg-tied all the time. An' she said she'd not run off. I'd take that girl's word even to a sheep thief."

"Ahuh! So would I, for all of thet. But, Jim, somethin' workin' in you. Ain't you sort of rememberin' a time when you was young . . . an' mebbe knowed pretty kids like this one?"

"Wal, if I am, it'll shore turn out damn' bad for somebody."

Anson gave him a surprised stare and suddenly lost the bantering tone. "Ahuh! So thet's how it's workin'," he replied, and flung himself down in the shale.

Young Burt made his appearance then, wiping his sallow face. His deep-set hungry eyes, upon which his comrades set such store, roved around the camp.

"Whar's the gurl?" he queried.

"Jim let her go out fer a stroll," replied Anson.

"I seen Jim was gittin' softy over her. *Haw!*

390

Haw! Haw!"

But Snake Anson did not crack a smile. The atmosphere appeared not to be congenial for jokes, a fact Burt rather suddenly divined. Riggs and Moze returned from the promontory, the latter reporting that Shady Jones was riding up close. Then the girl walked slowly into sight and approached to find a seat within ten yards of the group. They waited in silence until the expected horseman rode up with water bottles slung on both sides of his saddle. His advent was welcome. All the men were thirsty. Wilson took water to the girl before drinking himself.

"Thet's an all-fired hot ride fer water," declared the outlaw Shady, who somehow fitted his name in color and impression. "An', boss, if it's the same to you, I won't take it ag'in."

"Cheer up, Shady. We'll be rustlin' back in the mountains before sundown," said Anson.

"Hang me, if thet ain't the cheerfulest news I've had in some days. Hey, Moze?"

The black-faced Moze nodded his shaggy head.

"I'm sick an' sore of this deal," broke out Burt, evidently encouraged by his elders. "Ever since last fall we've been hangin'

391

around . . . till jest lately freezin' in camps . . . no money . . . no drink . . . no grub worth havin'. All on promises!"

Not improbably this young and reckless member of the gang had struck the note of discord. Wilson seemed most detached from any sentiment prevailing there. Some strong thoughts were revolving in his brain.

"Burt, you ain't insinuatin' thet I made promises?" inquired Anson ominously.

"No, boss, I ain't. You allus said we might hit it rich. But them promises was made to you. An' it'd be jest like thet greaser to go back on his word, now we got the gurl."

"Son, it happens we got the wrong one. Our long-haired pard hyar . . . Mister Riggs . . . him with the big gun . . . he waltzes up with this sassy kid instead of the woman Beasley wanted."

Burt snorted his disgust while Shady Jones, roundly swearing, pelted the smoldering campfire with stones. Then they all lapsed into surly silence. The object of their growing scorn, Riggs, sat a little way apart, facing none of them, but maintaining as bold a front as apparently he could muster.

Presently a horse shot up his ears, the first indication of scent or sound imperceptible to the men. But with this cue they all, except Wilson, sat up attentively. Soon the *crack* of iron-shod hoofs on stone broke the silence. Riggs nervously rose to his feet. And the others, still excepting Wilson, one by one followed suit. In another moment a rangy bay horse trotted out of the cedars, up to the camp, and his rider jumped off nimbly for so heavy a man.

"Howdy, Beasley," was Anson's greeting.

"Hello, Snake, old man," replied Beasley as his bold snapping black eyes swept the group. He was dusty and hot, and wet with sweat, yet evidently too excited to feel discomfort. "I seen your smoke signal first off, an' jumped my hoss quick. But I rode north of Pine before I headed around this way. . . . Did you corral the girl or did Riggs? Hello, Riggs. . . . Say! You look queer! What's wrong here? You haven't signaled me for nothin'?"

Snake Anson beckoned to Bo.

"Come out of the shade. Let him look you over."

The girl walked out from under the spreading cedar that had hidden her from sight.

Beasley stared aghast — his jaw dropped.

"Thet's the kid sister of the woman I wanted!" he ejaculated.

"So we've jest been told."

Astonishment still held Beasley. "Told?"

393

he echoed. Suddenly his big body leaped with a start. "Who got her? Who fetched her?"

"Why, Mister Gunman Riggs, hyar," replied Anson with a subtle scorn.

"Riggs, you got the wrong girl!" shouted Beasley. "You made thet mistake once before. What're you up to?"

"I chased her an', when I got her, seein' it wasn't Nell Rayner . . . why . . . I kept her anyhow," replied Riggs. "An' I've got a word for your ear alone."

"Man, you're crazy . . . queerin' my deal thet way!" roared Beasley. "You heard my plans. . . . Riggs, this girl stealin' can't be done twice. . . . Was you drinkin' or locoed or what?"

"Beasley, he was giving you the double-cross," cut in Bo Rayner's cool voice.

The rancher stared speechlessly at her, then at Anson, then at Wilson, and last at Riggs when his brown visage shaded dark with rush of purple blood. With one lunge he knocked Riggs flat, then stood over him with a convulsive hand at his gun.

"You white-livered cardsharp! I've a notion to bore you. . . . They told me you had a deal of your own an' now I believe it."

"Yes . . . I had," replied Riggs, cautiously getting up. He was ghastly. "But I wasn't double-crossin' you. Your deal was to get the girl away from home so you could take possession of her property. An' I wanted her."

"What for did you fetch the sister then?" demanded Beasley, his big jaw bulging.

"Because I've a plan to. . . ."

"Plan, hell! You've spoiled my plan an' I've seen about enough of you." Beasley breathed hard; his lowering gaze boded uncertain will toward the man who had crossed him; his hand still hung low and clutching.

"Beasley, tell them to get my horse. I want to go home," said Bo Rayner.

Slowly Beasley turned. Her words enjoined a silence. What to do with her now appeared a problem.

"I had nothin' to do with fetchin' you here an' I'll have nothin' to do with sendin' you back or whatever's done with you," declared Beasley.

Then the girl's face flashed white again and her eyes changed to fire. "You're as big a liar as Riggs!" she cried passionately. "And you're a thief, a bully who picks on defenseless girls. . . . Oh, we know your game. Milt Dorn heard you plot with this outlaw Anson to steal my sister. . . . You ought to be hanged . . . you half-breed greaser!"

"Cat-eyed slut! I'll cut out your tongue!" hissed Beasley.

"Yes, I'll bet you would if you had me alone. But these outlaws . . . these sheep thieves . . . these tools you hire are better than you and Riggs. . . . What do you suppose Carmichael will do to you? Carmichael! He's my sweetheart . . . that cowboy. You know what he did to Riggs. . . . Have you brains enough to know what he'll do to you?"

"He'll not do much," growled Beasley. But the thick purplish blood was receding from his face. "Your cowpuncher. . . ."

"Bah!" she interrupted, and she snapped her fingers in his face. "He's from Texas! He's from Texas!"

"Supposin' he is from Texas," demanded Beasley in angry irritation. "What's thet? Texans are all over. There's Jim Wilson, Snake Anson's right-hand man. He's from Texas. But thet ain't scarin' anyone." He pointed toward Wilson who shifted uneasily from foot to foot.

The girl's flaming glance followed his hand. "Are you from Texas?" she asked.

"Yes, miss, I am . . . an' I reckon I don't deserve it," replied Wilson. It was certain that a vague shame attended his confession.

"Oh! I believed even a bandit from Texas

396

would fight for a helpless girl," she replied in withering scorn of disappointment.

Jim Wilson dropped his head. If anyone there suspected a serious turn to Wilson's attitude toward that situation, it was the keen outlaw leader.

"Beasley, you're courtin' death," he broke in.

"You bet you are!" added Bo with a passion that made her listeners quiver. "You've put me at the mercy of a gang of outlaws. You may force my sister out of her home. But your day will come. Tom Carmichael will *kill* you!"

Beasley mounted his horse. Sullen, livid, furious he sat shaking in the saddle to glare down at the outlaw leader.

"Snake, thet's no fault of mine the deal's miscarried. I was square. I made my offer for the workin' out of my plan. It ain't been done. Now there's hell to pay an' I'm through."

"Beasley, I reckon I couldn't hold you to anythin'," replied Anson slowly. "But if you was square, you ain't square now. We've hung around an' tried hard. My men are all sore. An' we're broke, with no outfit to speak of. Me an' you never fell out before. But I reckon we might."

"Do I owe you any money . . . accordin'

to the deal?" demanded Beasley.

"No, you don't," responded Anson sharply.

"Then thet's square. I wash my hands of the whole deal. Make Riggs pay up. He's got money an' he's got plans. Go in with him."

With that Beasley spurred his horse, wheeled, and rode away. The outlaws gazed after him until he disappeared in the cedars.

"What'd you expect from a greaser?" queried Shady Jones.

"Anson, didn't I say so?" added Burt.

The black-visaged Moze rolled his eyes like a mad bull and Jim Wilson studiously examined a stick he held in his hands. Riggs showed immense relief.

"Anson, stake me to some of your outfit an' I'll ride off with the girl," he said eagerly.

"Where'd you go now?" queried Anson curiously.

Riggs appeared at a loss for a quick answer; his wits were no more equal to this predicament than his nerve.

"You're no woodsman. An' unless you're plumb weird, you'd never risk goin' near Pine or Show Down. . . . There'll be real trackers huntin' your trail."

The listening girl suddenly appealed to Wilson. "Don't let him take me off . . .

alone . . . in the woods," she faltered. That was the first indication of her weakening.

Jim Wilson broke into gruff reply: "I'm not bossin' this gang."

"But you're a man!" she importuned.

"Riggs, you fetch along your precious firebrand an' come with us," said Anson craftily. "I'm particular curious to see her brand you."

"Snake, lemme take the girl back to Pine," said Jim Wilson.

Anson swore his amaze.

"It's sense," continued Wilson. "We've shore got our own troubles, an' keepin' her'll only add to them. I've a hunch. Now you know I ain't often givin' to buckin' your say-so. But this deal ain't tastin' good to me. That girl ought to be sent home."

"But mebbe there's somethin' in it for us. Her sister'd pay to git her back."

"Wal, I shore hope you'll recollect I offered . . . thet's all," concluded Wilson.

"Jim, if we wanted to git rid of her, we'd let Riggs take her off," remonstrated the outlaw leader. He was perturbed and undecided. Wilson worried him.

The long Texan veered around, full-faced. What subtle transformation in him.

"Like hell we would!" he said mildly.

It could not have been the tone that

caused Anson to quail. He might have been leader here but he was not the greater man. His face clouded.

"Break camp," he ordered.

Riggs had probably not heard that last exchange between Anson and Wilson, for he had walked a few rods aside to get his horse.

In a few moments, when they started off, Burt, Jones, and Moze were in the lead driving the pack horses, Anson rode next, the girl came between him and Riggs, and significantly it seemed Jim Wilson brought up the rear.

This start was made a little after the noon hour. They zigzagged up the slope, took to a deep ravine, and followed it up to where it headed in the level forest. From there, travel was rapid, the pack horses being driven at a jog trot. Once when a troop of deer burst out of a thicket into a glade to stand with ears high, young Burt halted the cavalcade. His well-aimed shot brought down a deer. Then the men rode on, leaving him behind to dress and pack the meat. The only other halt made was at the crossing of the first water, a clear swift brook, where both horses and men drank thirstily. Here Burt caught up with his comrades.

They traversed glade and park, and wended a crooked trail through the deepening forest, and climbed bench after bench to higher ground, while the sun sloped to the westward, lower and redder. Sunset had gone, and the twilight was momentarily brightening to the afterglow when Anson, breaking his silence of the afternoon, ordered a halt.

The place was wild, dismal, a shallow vale between dark slopes of spruce. Grass, firewood, and water were there in abundance. All the men were off, throwing saddles and packs, before the tired girl made an effort to get down. Riggs, observing her, made a not ungentle move to pull her off. She gave him a sounding slap with her gloved hand.

"Keep your paws to yourself," she said. No evidence of exhaustion was there in her spirit.

Wilson had observed this by-play, but Anson had not.

"What come off?" he asked.

"Wal, the Honorable Gunman Riggs jest got caressed by the lady . . . as he was doin' the elegant," replied Moze, who stood nearest.

"Jim, was you watchin'?" queried Anson. His curiosity had held through the afternoon.

"He tried to yank her off an' she biffed

him," replied Wilson.

"Thet Riggs is jest daffy or plain locoed," said Snake in an aside to Moze.

"Boss, you mean plain cussed. Mark my words he'll hoodoo this outfit. Jim was figgerin' correct."

"Hoodoo . . . ," cursed Anson under his breath.

Many hands made quick work. In a few moments a fire was burning brightly, water was boiling, pots were steaming, the odor of venison permeated the cool air. The girl had at last slipped off her saddle to the ground where she sat while Riggs led the horse away. She sat there apparently forgotten, a pathetic droop to her head.

Wilson had taken an axe and was vigorously wielding it among the spruces. One by one they fell with swish and soft crash. Then the sliding ring of the axe told how he was slicing off the branches with long sweeps. Presently he appeared in the semi-darkness dragging half-trimmed spruces behind him. He made several trips, the last of which was to stagger under a huge burden of spruce boughs. These he spread under a low projecting branch of an aspen. Then he leaned the bushy spruces slantingly against this branch on both sides, quickly improvising a V-shaped shelter with narrow aperture in front. Next, from one of the packs, he took a blanket and threw that inside the shelter.

Then touching the girl on the shoulder, he whispered: "When you're ready, slip in there. . . . An' don't lose no sleep by worryin', for I'll be layin' right here."

He made a motion to indicate his length across the front of the narrow aperture.

"Oh, thank you. Maybe you really are a Texan," she whispered back.

"Mebbe," was his gloomy reply.

Chapter Eighteen

The girl refused to take food proffered her by Riggs, but she ate and drank a little that Wilson brought her, then she disappeared in the spruce lean-to.

Whatever loquacity and companionship that had previously existed in Snake Anson's gang, they were not manifest in this camp. Each man seemed preoccupied, as if pondering the dawn in his mind of an ill omen not clear to him yet and not yet dreamed of by his fellows. They all smoked. Then Moze and Shady played cards a while by the light of the fire, but it was a dull game, in which they seldom spoke. Riggs sought his blanket first, and the fact was significant that he lay down some distance from the spruce shelter that contained Bo Rayner. Presently young Burt went off grumbling to his bed. And not long afterward the card players did likewise.

Snake Anson and Jim Wilson were left

brooding in silence beside the dying camp-fire.

The night was dark with only a few stars showing. A fitful wind moaned unearthily through the spruce. An occasional *thump* of hoof sounded from the dark woods. No cry of wolf or coyote or cat gave reality to the wildness of forestland.

By and by those men who had rolled in their blankets were breathing deeply and slowly in heavy slumber.

"Jim, I take it this hyar Riggs has queered our deal," said Snake Anson in low voice.

"I reckon," replied Wilson.

"An' I'm feared he's queered this hyar White Mountain country fer us."

"Shore I ain't got so far as thet. What d'ye mean, Snake?"

"Damn' if I savvy," was the gloomy reply. "I only know what was bad looks growin' worse. Last fall . . . an' winter . . . an' now it's near April. We've got no outfit to make a long stand in the woods. . . . Jim, jest how strong is thet Beasley down in the settle-ments?"

"I've a hunch he ain't half as strong as he bluffs."

"Me, too. I got thet idee yesterday. He was scared of the kid . . . when she fired up an' sent thet hot shot about her cowboy sweetheart killin' him. . . . He'll do it, Jim. I seen that Carmichael at Magdalena some years ago. Then he was only a youngster. But *whew!* Mebbe he wasn't bad after toyin' with a little red liquor."

"Shore. He was from Texas, she said."

"Jim, I savvied your feelin's was hurt . . . by thet talk about Texas . . . an' when she up an' asked you."

Wilson had no rejoinder for this remark.

"Wal, Lord knows, I ain't wonderin'. You wasn't a hunted outlaw all your life. An' neither was I. . . . Jim, I never was keen on this girl deal . . . now was I?"

"I reckon it's honest to say no to thet," replied Wilson. "But it's done. Beasley'll get plugged sooner or later. Thet won't help us any. Chasin' sheepherders out of the country an' stealin' sheep . . . thet ain't stealin' gurls by a damn' sight. . . . Beasley'll blame thet onto us an' be greaser enough to send some of his men out to hunt us. For Pine an' Show Down won't stand thet long. There's them Mormons. They'll be hell when they wake up. Suppose Carmichael got thet hunter Dorn an' them hawk-eyed Beemans on our trail?"

"Wal, we'd cash in . . . damn' quick," replied Anson gruffly.

"Then why didn't you let me take the girl

back home?"

"Wal, come to think of thet, Jim, I'm sore, an' I need money . . . an' I knowed you'd never take a dollar from her sister. . . . An' I've made up my mind to get somethin' out of her."

"Snake, you're no fool. How'll you do thet same an' do it quick?"

"Ain't reckoned it out yet."

"Wal, you got aboot tomorrow an' thet's all," returned Wilson gloomily.

"Jim, what's ailin' you?"

"I'll let you figger thet out."

"Wal, damn, somethin' ails the whole gang," declared Anson savagely. "With them it's nothin' to eat . . . no whiskey . . . no money to bet with . . . no tobacco. . . . But thet's not what's ailin' you, Jim Wilson, nor me!"

"Wal, what is, then?" queried Wilson.

"With me, it's a strange feelin' thet my day's over on these ranges. I can't explain, but it jest feels so. Somethin' in the air. I don't like them dark shadows out there under the spruces. Savvy? An' as fer you, Jim, wal, you allus was half decent, an' my gang's got too low-down fer you."

"Snake, did I ever fail you?"

"Damn, no, you never did. You're the best pard I ever knowed. . . . In the years we've rustled together we never had a contrary word till I let Beasley fill my ears with his promises. Thet's my fault. . . . But, Jim, it's too late."

"It mightn't have been too late yesterday."

"Mebbe not. But it is now, an' I'll hang onto the girl or git her worth in gold," declared the outlaw grimly.

"Snake, I've seen stronger gangs than yours come an' go. Them Big Bend gangs in my country . . . them rustlers . . . they were all badmen. You have no likes of them gangs out heah. If they didn't get wiped out by Rangers or cowboys, why they jest naturally wiped out themselves. Thet's a law I recognize in relation to gangs like them. An' as for yours . . . why, Anson, it wouldn't hold water against one real gunslinger."

"Ahuh! Then if we run up ag'in' Carmichael or some such fellar . . . would you be suckin' your finger like a baby?"

"Wal, I wasn't takin' count of myself. I was talkin' generalities."

"*Aw,* what'n hell are them?" asked Anson disgustedly. "Jim, I know as well as you thet this hyar gang is hard put. We're goin' to be trailed an' chased. We've got to hide . . . be on the go all the time . . . here and there . . . all over, in the roughest woods. An' wait our chance to work south."

"Shore. . . . But, Snake, you ain't takin' no count of the feelin's of the men . . . an' of mine an' yours. . . . I'll bet you my hoss thet in a day or so this gang will go to pieces."

"I'm feared you spoke what's been crowdin' to git in my mind," replied Anson. Then he threw up his hands in a strange gesture of resignation. The outlaw was brave, but all men of the wilds recognized a force stronger than themselves. He sat there resembling a brooding snake with basilisk eyes upon the fire. At length he arose, and, without another word to his comrade, he walked wearily to where lay the dark quiet forms of the sleepers.

Jim Wilson remained beside the flickering fire. He was reading something in the red embers, perhaps the past. Shadows were on his face, not all from the fading flames or the towering spruces. Ever and anon he raised his head to listen, not apparently that he expected any unusual sound, but as if involuntarily. Indeed, as Anson had said, there was something nameless in the air. The black forest breathed heavily, in fitful moans of wind. It had its secrets. The glances Wilson threw on all sides betrayed that any hunted man did not love the dark night, although it hid him. Wilson seemed

409

fascinated by the life enclosed there by the black circle of spruce. He might have been reflecting on the strange reaction happening to every man in that group, since a girl had been brought among them. Nothing was clear, however; the forest kept its secret as did the melancholy wind; the outlaws were sleeping like tired beasts, with their dark secrets locked in their hearts.

After a while Wilson put some sticks on the red embers, then pulled the end of a log over them. A blaze sputtered up, changing the dark circle, and showing the sleepers with their set shadowed faces upturned. Wilson gazed on all of them, a sardonic smile on his lips, and then his look fixed upon the sleeper apart from the others — Riggs. It might have been the false light of flame and shadows that created Wilson's expression of dark and terrible hate. Or it might have been the truth, expressed in that lonely unguarded hour, from the depths of a man born in the South — a man who by his inheritance of race had reverence for all womanhood — by whose strange, wild, outlawed bloody life of a gunfighter he must hate with the deadliest hate this type that aped and mocked his fame.

It was a long gaze Wilson rested upon Riggs — as strange and secretive as the forest wind, moaning down the great aisles — and, when that dark gaze was withdrawn, Wilson stalked away to make his bed with the stride of one in whom spirit had liberated force.

He laid his saddle in front of the spruce shelter where the girl had entered, and his tarpaulin and blankets likewise, and then wearily stretched his long length to rest.

The campfire blazed up, showing the exquisite green and brown-flecked festooning of the spruce branches, so symmetrical and perfect, yet so irregular, and then it burned out and died down, leaving all in the dim gray starlight. The horses were not moving around; the moan of night wind had grown fainter; the low *hum* of insects was dying away; even the *tinkle* of the brook had diminished. And that growth toward absolute silence continued, yet absolute silence was never attained. Life abided in the forest, only it had changed its form for the dark hours.

Anson's gang did not bestir themselves at the usual early sunrise hour, common to all woodsmen, hunters, or outlaws to whom the break of day was welcome. These companions, Anson and Riggs included, might have hated to see the dawn come. It meant only another meager meal, then the weary packing and the long, long ride to nowhere in particular, and another meager meal — all toiled for without even the necessities of satisfactory living, and assuredly without the thrilling hopes that made their life significant, and certainly with a growing sense of approaching calamity.

The outlaw leader rose, surly and cross-grained. He had to boot Burt to drive him out for the horses. Riggs followed him. Shady Jones did nothing except grumble. Wilson, by common consent, always made the sourdough bread, and he was slow about it this morning. Anson and Moze did the rest of the work, without alacrity. The girl did not appear.

"Is she dead?" growled Anson.

"No, she ain't," replied Wilson, looking up. "She's sleepin'. Let her sleep. . . . She'd shore be a damn' sight better off if she was daid."

"Ahah! So would all of this hyar outfit," was Anson's response.

"Wal, Sna-ake, I shore reckon we'll all be thet there soon," drawled Wilson in his familiar cool and irritating tone that said so much more than the content of the words.

Anson did not address the Texas member of his party again.

Burt rode bareback into camp driving half the number of the horses; Riggs followed shortly with several more. But three were unused, one of them being Anson's favorite. He would not have budged without that horse. During breakfast he growled about his lazy men and after the meal tried to urge them off. Riggs went unwillingly. Burt refused to go at all.

"Nix. I footed them hills all I'm a-goin' to," he said. "An' from now on I rustle my own hoss."

The leader glared his reception of this opposition. Perhaps his sense of fairness actuated him once more, for he ordered Shady and Moze out to do their share.

"Jim, you're the best tracker in this outfit. Suppose you go," suggested Anson. "You allus used to be the first one off."

"Times has changed, Snake," was the imperturbable reply.

"Wal, won't you go?" demanded the leader impatiently.

"I shore won't."

Wilson did not look or intimate in any way that he would not leave the girl in camp with one or any or all of Anson's gang, but the truth was as significant as if he had shouted it. The slow-thinking Moze gave Wilson a sinister look.

"Boss, ain't it funny how a pretty wench . . . ?" began Shady Jones sarcastically.

"Shut up, you fool!" broke in Anson. "Come on, I'll help rustle them hosses."

After they had gone, Burt took his rifle and strolled off into the forest. Then the girl appeared. Her hair was down, her face pale, with dark shadows. She asked for water to wash her face. Wilson pointed to the brook, and, as she walked slowly toward it, he took a comb and a clean scarf from his pack, and carried them to her.

Upon her return to the campfire she looked very different with her hair arranged and the red stains in her cheeks.

"Miss, air you hungry?" asked Wilson.

"Yes, I am," she replied.

He helped her to portions of bread, venison and gravy, and a cup of coffee. Evidently she relished the meat, but she had to force down the rest.

"Where are they all?" she asked.

"Rustlin' the hosses."

Probably she divined that he did not want to talk, for the fleeting glance she gave him attested to a thought that his voice or demeanor had changed. Presently she sought a seat under the aspen tree out of the sun, and the smoke continually blowing in her face, and there she stayed, a forlorn little figure, for all the resolute lips and defiant eyes.

The Texan paced to and fro beside the campfire with bent head and hands locked behind him. But for the swinging gun he would have resembled a lanky farmer, coatless and hatless, with his brown vest open, his trousers stuck in the top of the high boots.

And neither he nor the girl changed their positions relatively for a long time. At length, however, after peering into the woods and listening, he remarked to the girl that he would be back in a moment, and then walked off around the spruces.

No sooner had he disappeared, in fact so quickly, that afterward it presupposed design instead of accident, than Riggs came running from the opposite side of the glade. He ran straight to the girl, who sprang to her feet.

"I hid . . . two of the horses," he panted, husky with excitement. "I'll take . . . two saddles. You grab some grub. . . . We'll run for it."

"No!" she cried, stepping back.

"But it's not safe . . . for us . . . here," he said hurriedly, glancing all around. "I'll take you . . . home. I swear. . . . Not safe . . . I tell you . . . this gang's after me. Hurry!"

He laid hold of two saddles, one with each hand. The moment had reddened his face, brightened his eyes, made his action strong.

"I'm safer here with this outlaw gang," she replied.

"You won't come?" His color began to lighten then and his face to distort. He dropped his hold on the saddles.

"Harve Riggs, I'd rather become a toy and a rag for these ruffians than spend an hour alone with you," she flashed at him in unquenchable hate.

"By God, I'll drag you!"

He seized her, but could not hold her. Breaking away she screamed.

"Help!"

That whitened his face, drove him to frenzy. Leaping forward, he struck her a hard blow across the mouth. It staggered her. And tripping on a saddle, she fell. His hands flew to her throat, ready to choke her. But she lay still and held her tongue. Then he dragged her to her feet.

"Hurry now . . . grab that pack . . . an' follow me." Again Riggs laid hold of the two saddles. A desperate gleam, baleful and vainglorious, flashed over his face. He was living his one great adventure.

The girl's eyes dilated. They looked beyond him. Her lips opened.

"Scream again an' I'll kill you!" he cried hoarsely and swiftly. The very opening of her lips had terrified him.

A step sounded behind Riggs.

"Reckon one scream was enough," spoke a voice, slow, but without the drawl, easy and cool, yet incalculable in some terrible sense.

Riggs wheeled with inarticulate cry. Wilson stood a few paces off with his gun half leveled, low down. His face seemed as usual, only his eyes held a quivering light intensity, like boiling molten silver.

"Girl, what made thet blood in your mouth?"

"Riggs hit me," she whispered. Then at something she feared or saw or divined, she shrank back, dropped on her knees, and crawled into the spruce shelter.

"Wal, Riggs, I'd invite you to draw if thet'd be any use," said Wilson. This speech was reflective, yet it hurried a little.

Riggs could not draw or move or speak. He seemed turned to stone, except his jaw, which slowly fell.

"Harve Riggs, gunman from down Missouri way!" continued the voice of incalculable intent. "Reckon you've looked into a heap of gun barrels in your day. . . . Shore.

417

Wal, look in this heah one!" Wilson deliberately leveled the gun on a line with Riggs's starting eyes. "Wasn't you heard to brag in Turner's saloon . . . thet you could see lead comin' . . . an' dodge it? Shore you must be swift! Dodge this heah bullet!"

The gun spouted flame and *boomed.* One of Riggs's starting, popping eyes — the right one — went out, like a lamp. The other rolled horribly, then set in blank dead fixedness. Riggs swayed in slow motion until a lost balance felled him heavily, an inert mass.

Wilson bent over the prostrate form. Strange violent contrast to the cool scorn of the preceding moment! Hissing, spitting, as if poisoned by passion, he burst with the hate that his character had forbidden him to express on a living counterfeit. Wilson was shaken as if by a palsy. He choked over passionate incoherent invective. It was class hate first, then the hate of real manhood for a craven bastard, then the hate of disgrace for a murder. No man so fair as a gunfighter in the Western creed of an "even break"!

Wilson's terrible cataclysm of passion passed. Straightening up, he sheathed his weapon and began a slow pace before the fire. Not many moments afterward he jerked his head high and listened. Horses were softly *thudding* through the forest. Soon Anson rode into sight with his men, and one of the strayed horses. It chanced, too, that young Burt appeared on the other side of the glade. He walked quickly as one who anticipated news.

Snake Anson, as he dismounted, espied the dead man.

"Jim! I thought I heard a shot."

The others exclaimed and leaped off their horses to view the prostrate form with that curiosity and strange fear common to all men confronted by sight of sudden death.

That emotion was only momentary.

"Shot his lamp out!" ejaculated Moze.

"Wonder how gunman Riggs liked thet plumb center peg!" exclaimed Shady Jones with a hard laugh.

"Back of his head's all gone!" gasped young Burt. Not improbably he had not seen a great many bullet-marked men.

"Jim! Damn if the long-haired fool didn't try to draw on you!" exclaimed Snake Anson, astounded.

Wilson neither spoke nor sensed his pacing.

"What was it over?" added Anson curiously.

"He hit the gurl," replied Wilson.

Then there were long drawn exclamations

all around and glance met glance.

"Jim, you saved me the job," continued the outlaw leader. "An' I'm much obliged. . . . Fellars, search Riggs an' we'll divvy. . . . Thet all right, Jim?"

"Shore, an' you can have my share."

They found banknotes in the man's pocket and considerable gold worn in a money belt around his waist. Shady Jones appropriated his boots and Moze his gun. Then they left him as he had fallen.

"Jim, you'll have to track them lost horses. Two still missin' an' one of them's mine!" called Anson as Wilson paced to the end of his beat.

The girl heard Anson, for she put her head out of the spruce shelter and said: "Riggs said he'd hid two of the horses. They must be close. He came that way."

"Howdy, kid. Thet's good news," replied Anson. His spirits were rising. "He must hev wanted you to slope with him?"

"Yes. I wouldn't go."

"An' then he hit you?"

"Yes."

"Wal, recallin' your talk of yestiddy, I can't see as Mister Riggs lasted much longer hyar than he'd hev lasted in Texas. . . . We've some of thet great country right in our outfit."

The girl withdrew her white face.

"It's break camp, boys," was the leader's order. "A couple of you look up them horses. They'll be hid in some thick spruces. The rest of us'll pack."

Soon the gang was on the move, heading toward the height of land, and swerving from it only to find soft and grassy ground that would not leave any tracks.

They did not travel more than a dozen miles during the afternoon, but they climbed bench after bench until they reached the timbered plateau that stretched in sheer black slope up to the peaks. Here rose the great and gloomy forest of firs and pines, with the spruce overshadowed and thinned out. The last hour of travel was tedious and toilsome, a zigzag, winding, breaking, climbing hunt for the kind of campsite suited to Anson's fancy. He seemed to be growing strangely irrational about selecting places to camp. At last, for no reason that could have been manifest to a good woodsman, he chose a gloomy bowl in the center of the densest forest that had been traversed. The opening, if such it could have been called, was not a park or even a glade. A dark cliff, with strange holes, rose to one side, but not so high as the lofty pines that brushed it. Along its base babbled a brook, running over such formation of rock that from different points near at hand it gave forth different sounds, some singing, others melodious, and one at least of a hollow weird deep sound, not loud, but strangely penetrating.

"Damn' spooky, I say," observed Shady sentiently.

The little uplift of mood, coincident with the rifling of Riggs's person, had not won over to this evening camp. What talk the outlaws indulged in was necessary and conducted in low tones. The place enjoined silence.

Wilson performed for the girl very much the same service as he had the night before. Only he advised her not to starve herself; she must eat to keep up her strength. She complied at the expense of considerable effort.

As it had been a back-breaking day in which all of them, except the girl, had climbed miles on foot, they did not linger awake long enough after supper to learn what a wild, weird, and pitch-black spot the outlaw leader had chosen. The little spaces of open ground between the huge-trunked pine trees had no counterpart up in the lofty spreading foliage. Not a star could blink a wan ray of light into that Stygian pit. The wind cutting down over abrupt heights farther up sung in the pine needles as if they were strings vibrant with chords. Dismal *creaks* were audible. They were the forest sounds of branch or tree rubbing one another, but which needed the corrective medium of daylight to convince any human that they were other than ghostly. Then, despite the wind and despite the changing murmur of the brook, there seemed to be a silence insulating them, as deep and impenetrable as the darkness.

But the outlaws, who were fugitives now, slept the sleep of the weary, and heard nothing. They awoke with the sun, when the forest seemed smoky in a golden gloom, when light and bird and squirrel proclaimed the day.

The horses had not strayed out of this basin during the night, a circumstance that Anson was not slow to appreciate.

"It ain't no cheerful camp, but I never seen a safer place to hole up in," he remarked to Wilson.

"Wal, yes . . . if any place is safe," replied that ally dubiously.

"We can watch our back tracks. There ain't any other way to git in hyar thet I see."

"Snake, we was tolerable fair sheep rustlers, but we're no good woodsmen."

Anson grumbled his disdain of this comrade who had once been his mainstay. Then he sent Burt out to hunt fresh meat and engaged his other men at cards. As they now had the means to gamble, they at once became absorbed. Wilson smoked and divided his thoughtful gaze between the gamblers and the drooping figure of the girl. The morning air was keen, and she, evidently not caring to be near her captors beside the campfire, had sought the only sunny spot in this gloomy dell. A couple of hours passed; the sun climbed high; the air grew warmer. Once, the outlaw leader raised his head to scan the heavy timbered slopes that enclosed the camp.

"Jim, them hosses are strayin' off," he observed.

Wilson leisurely rose and stalked off across the small open patches in the direction of the horses. They had grazed around from the right toward the outlet of the brook. Here headed a ravine, dense and green. Two of the horses had gone down. Wilson evidently heard them, although they were not in sight, and he circled somewhat so as to get ahead of them and drive them back. The invisible brook ran down over the rocks with murmur and babble. He halted with instinctive action. He listened. Forest sounds, soft, lulling, came on the warm pine-scented breeze. It would have taken no keen ear to hear soft and rapid padded footfalls. He moved on cautiously and turned into a little open mossy spot, brown-matted and odorous, full of ferns and bluebells. In the middle of this, deep in the moss, he espied a huge round track of a cougar. He bent over it. Suddenly he stiffened, then straightened guardedly. At that instant he received a hard prod in the back. Throwing up his hands, he stood still, then slowly turned. A tall hunter in gray buckskin, gray-eyed and square-jawed, had him covered with a cocked rifle. And beside this hunter stood a monster cougar, snarling and blinking.

Chapter Nineteen

"Howdy, Dorn," drawled Wilson. "Reckon you're a little previous on me."

"*Shsssh!* Not so loud," said the hunter in low voice. "You're Jim Wilson?"

"Shore am. . . . Say, Dorn, you showed up soon. Or did you jest happen to run acrost us?"

"I've trailed you. . . . Wilson, I'm after the girl."

"Hell, I knowed thet when I seen you."

The cougar seemed actuated by the threatening position of his master, and he opened his mouth, showing great yellow fangs, and spat at Wilson. The outlaw apparently had no fear of Dorn or the cocked rifle, but that huge snarling cat occasioned him uneasiness.

"Wilson, I've heard you spoken of as a white outlaw," said Dorn.

"Mebbe I am. But shore I'll be a scared one in a minnit. . . . Dorn, he's goin' to jump me."

"The cougar won't jump you unless I make him. . . . Wilson, if I let you go, will you get the girl for me?"

"Wal, lemme see. . . . supposin' I refuse?" queried Wilson shrewdly.

"Then, one way or another, it's all up with you."

"Reckon I ain't got much choice. Yes, I'll do it. . . . But, Dorn, are you goin' to take my word for thet an' let me go back to Anson?"

"Yes, I am. You're no fool. An' I believe you're square. I've got Anson an' his gang corralled. You can't slip me . . . not in these woods. I could run off your horses . . . pick you off one by one . . . or turn the cougar loose on you at night."

"Shore. It's your game. Anson dealt himself this hand. . . . Between you an' me, Dorn, I never liked the deal."

"Who shot Riggs?"

"Wal, yours truly was around when thet come off," replied Wilson with an involuntary little shudder. Some thought made him sick.

"The girl? Is she safe . . . unharmed?" queried Dorn hurriedly.

"She's shore jest as safe an' sound as when she was home. . . . Dorn, she's the gamest kid thet ever breathed. Why, no one could hev ever made me believe a girl, a kid like her, could hev the nerve she's got. . . . Nothin's happened to her 'cept Riggs hit her in the mouth. . . . I killed him fer thet. . . . An' so help me God, I believe it's been workin' in me to save her somehow. Now it'll not be so hard."

"But how?" demanded Dorn.

"Lemme see. . . . Wal, I've got to sneak her out of camp an' meet you. Thet's all."

"It must be done quick."

"But, Dorn, listen," remonstrated Wilson earnestly. "Too quick'll be as bad as too slow. Snake is sore these days, gittin' sorer all the time. He might savvy somethin', if I ain't careful, an' kill the girl, or do her harm. I know these fellars. They're all ready to go to pieces. An' shore I must play safe. Shore it'd be safer to have a plan."

Wilson's shrewd light eyes gleamed with an idea. He was about to lower one of his upraised hands, evidently to point to the cougar, when he thought better of that.

"Anson's scared of cougars. Mebbe we can scare him an' the gang so it'd be easy to sneak the girl off. . . . Can you make thet big brute do tricks? Rush the camp at night an' squall an' chase off the hosses?"

"I'll guarantee to scare Anson out of ten

428

years' growth," replied Dorn.

"Shore it's a go then," resumed Wilson, as if glad. "I'll post the girl . . . give her a hunch to do her part. . . . You sneak up tonight jest before dark. I'll hev the gang worked up. An' then you put the cougar to his tricks . . . whatever you want. When the gang gits wild, I'll grab the girl an' pack her off down heah or somewheres aboot, an' whistle fer you. . . . But mebbe thet ain't so good. If thet cougar comes pilin' into camp, he might jump me, instead of one of the gang. An' another hunch. He might slope up on me in the dark when I was tryin' to find you. Shore thet ain't appealin' to me."

"Wilson, this cougar is a pet," replied Dorn. "You think he's dangerous, but he's not. No more than a kitten. He only looks fierce. He has never been hurt by a person an' he's never fought anythin' himself but deer an' bear. I can make him trail any scent. But the truth is, I couldn't make him hurt you or anybody. . . . All the same he can be made to scare the hair off anyone who doesn't know him."

"Shore thet settles me. I'll be havin' a grand joke while them fellars is scared to death. . . . Dorn, you can depend on me. An' I'm beholdin' to you fer what'll square me some with myself. . . . Tonight, and if it won't work then, tomorrow night shore!"

Dorn lowered the rifle. The big cougar spat again. Wilson dropped his hands and, stepping forward, split the green wall of intersecting spruce branches. Then he hurried up the ravine toward the glen. Once there, in sight of his comrades, his action and expression changed.

"Hosses all there, Jim?" asked Anson as he picked up his cards.

"Shore. They act awful queer, them hosses," replied Wilson. "They're afraid of somethin'?"

"Ahuh! Silvertip mebbe," muttered Anson. "Jim, you jest keep watch on them hosses. We'd be done if some tarnal varmint stampeded them."

"Reckon I'm elected to do all the work now," complained Wilson, "while you cardsharps cheat each other. . . . Rustle the hosses . . . an' water an' firewood. Cook an' wash. Hey?"

"No one I ever seen can do them camp tricks any better'n Jim Wilson," replied Anson.

"Jim, you're a lady's man an' thar's our pretty hoodoo over thar to feed an' amoose," remarked Shady Jones with a smile that disarmed his speech.

The outlaws guffawed.

"Git out, Jim, you're breakin' up the game," said Moze, who appeared loser.

"Wal, thet gurl would starve if I wasn't fer me," replied Wilson genially, and he walked over toward her, beginning to address her, quite loudly, as he approached. "Wal, miss, I'm elected cook, an' I'd shore like to heah what you . . . fancy fer dinner."

The outlaws heard, for they guffawed again. "Damn if Jim ain't funny!" exclaimed Anson.

The girl looked up amazed. Wilson was winking at her, and, when he got near, he began to speak rapidly and low.

"I jest met Dorn down in the woods with his pet cougar. He's after you. I'm goin' to help him git you safe away. Now you do your part. I want you to pretend you've gone crazy. Savvy? Act out of your head. Shore I don't care what you do or say, only act crazy. . . . An' don't be scared. Understand? No matter what you heah or see don't you be scared. We're goin' to scare the gang, so I'll hev a chance to sneak you away. Tonight or tomorrow . . . shore."

Before he began to speak, she was pale, sad, dull of eye. Swiftly with his words she was transformed, and, when he had ended, she did not appear the same girl. She gave him one blazing flash of comprehension and nodded her head rapidly.

"Yes, I understand. I'll do it," she whispered.

The outlaw turned slowly away with the most abstract air, confounded amidst his shrewd acting, and he did not collect himself until halfway back to his comrades. Then, beginning to hum an old darky tune, he stirred up and replenished the fire, and set about preparation for the midday meal. But he did not miss anything going on around him. He saw the girl go into her shelter and come out with her hair all down over her face. Wilson, back to his comrades, grinned his glee, and he wagged his head as if he thought the situation was developing well.

The gambling outlaws, however, did not at once see the girl preening herself and smoothing her long hair in a way calculated to startle.

"Busted!" ejaculated Anson with a curse, as he slammed down his cards. "If I ain't hoodooed, I'm a two-bit of a gambler!"

"Sartin' you're hoodooed," said Shady Jones in scorn. "Is that jest dawnin' on you?"

"Boss, you play like a cow stuck in the mud," remarked Moze laconically.

"Fellars, it ain't funny," declared Anson with pathetic gravity. "I'm jest gittin' on to myself. Somethin's damn' wrong. Since my last fall, no luck . . . nothin' but the wurst end of everythin'. I ain't blamin' anybody. I'm the boss. It's me thet's off."

"Snake, shore it was the girl deal you made," rejoined Wilson, who had listened. "I told you. Our troubles hev only begun. An' I can see the wind up. . . . Look!"

Wilson pointed to where the girl stood, her hair flying wildly all over her face and shoulders. She was making most elaborate bows to an old stump, sweeping the ground with her tresses in her obeisance.

Anson stared. He grew utterly astounded. His amaze was ludicrous. And the other two men looked to stare, to equal their leader's bewilderment.

"What'n hell's come over her?" asked Anson dubiously. "Must hev perked up. . . . But she isn't feelin' thet gay!"

Wilson tapped his forehead with a significant finger. "Shore I was scared of her this mornin'," he whispered.

"Naw!" exclaimed Anson incredulously.

"If she hain't queer, I never seen no queer wimmin'," vouchsafed Shady Jones, and it would have been judged, by the way he wagged his head, that he had been all his days familiar with women.

Moze looked beyond words and quite alarmed.

433

"I seen it comin'," declared Wilson, very much excited. "But I was scared to say so. You-all made fun of me aboot her. . . . Now I shore wish I had spoke up."

Anson nodded solemnly. He did not believe the evidence of his sight, but the facts seemed stunning. As if the girl were a dangerous and incomprehensible thing, he approached her step by step. Wilson followed, and the others appeared drawn irresistibly.

"Hey, thar . . . kid!" called Anson hoarsely.

The girl drew her slight form up haughtily. Through her spreading tresses, her eyes gleamed unnaturally upon the outlaw leader. But she deigned not to reply.

"Hey, thar . . . you, Rayner girl," added Anson lamely. "What's ailin' you?"

"My lord. Did you address me?" she asked loftily.

Shady Jones got over his consternation and evidently extracted some humor from the situation, as his dark face began to break its strain.

"*Aww*," breathed Anson heavily.

"Ophelia awaits your command, my lord. I've been gathering flowers," she said sweetly, holding up her empty hands as if they contained a bouquet.

Shady Jones exploded in convulsed laughter. But his merriment was not shared. And suddenly it brought disaster upon him. The girl flew at him.

"Why do you croak, you toad? I will have you whipped and put in irons, you scullion!" she cried passionately.

Shady underwent a remarkable change, and stumbled in his backward retreat. Then she snapped her fingers in Moze's face.

"You black devil! Get hence! Avaunt!"

Anson plucked up courage enough to touch her.

"*Aww!* Now Opheyar. . . ."

Probably he meant to try to humor her, but she screamed and he jumped back as if she might burn him. She screamed shrilly in wild staccato notes.

"You! You!" She pointed her finger at the outlaw leader. "You brute to women! You ran off from your wife!"

Anson turned plum color, and then slowly white. The girl must have sent a random shot home.

"And now the devil's turned you into a snake. A long scaly snake with green eyes! *Uugh!* You'll crawl on your belly soon . . . when my cowboy finds you. And he'll tramp you in the dust."

She floated away from them and began to whirl gracefully, arms spread, and hair flying, and then, apparently oblivious of the staring men, she broke into a low sweet song. Next she danced around a pine, then danced into her little green enclosure. From which presently she sent out the most doleful moans.

"*Aww!* What a damn' shame!" burst out Anson. "Thet fine healthy nervy kid! Clean gone! Daffy! Crazier'n a bedbug!"

"Shore it's a shame," protested Wilson. "But it's wuss for us. . . . Lord! If we was hoodooed before, what will we be now? Didn't I tell you, Snake Anson? You was warned. Ask Shady an' Moze . . . they see what's up."

"No luck'll ever come our way ag'in," predicted Shady mournfully.

"It beats me, boss, it beats me," muttered Moze.

"A crazy woman on my hands! My God, if thet ain't the last straw!" broke out Anson, tragically, as he turned away. Ignorant, superstitious, worked upon by things as they seemed, the outlaw imagined himself at last beset by malign forces. When he flung himself down on one of the packs, his big red-haired hands shook. Shady and Moze resembled two other men at the end of their ropes.

Wilson's tense face twitched and he

averted it, as apparently he fought off a paroxysm of some nature. Just then Anson swore a thundering oath. "Crazy or not I'll git gold out of thet kid!" he roared.

"But, man, talk sense. Are you gittin' daffy, too? I declare this outfit's been eatin' loco. . . . You can't git gold fer her," said Wilson deliberately.

"Why can't I?"

" 'Cause we're bein' tracked. We can't make no dickers. Why, in another day or so, we'll be dodgin' lead."

"Tracked! Whar'd you git thet idee? As soon as this?" queried Anson, lifting his head like a striking snake. His men, likewise, betrayed sudden interest.

"Shore it's no idee. I ain't seen anyone. But I feel it in my senses. I hear somebody comin' . . . a step on our trail . . . all the time . . . night in particular. . . . Reckon there's a big posse after us."

"Wal, if I see or hear anythin', I'll knock the girl on the head an' we'll dig out of hyar," replied Anson sullenly.

Wilson executed a swift forward motion, violent and passionate, so utterly unlike what might have been looked for from him that the three outlaws gaped.

"Then you'll shore hev to knock Jim Wilson on the haid first," he said in a voice as strange as his action.

"Jim! You wouldn't go back on me?" implored Anson, with uplifted hands, in a dignity of pathos.

"I'm losin' my haid, too, an' you shore might as well knock it in, an' you'll hev to before I'll stand your murdurin' thet poor little gurl you've drove crazy."

"Jim, I was only mad," replied Anson. "Fer thet matter, I'm growin' daffy myself. . . . *Aw!* We-all need a good stiff drink of whiskey."

So he tried to throw off gloom and apprehension, but he failed. His comrades did not rally to his help. Wilson walked away, nodding his head.

"Boss, let Jim alone," whispered Shady. "It's orful the way you buck ag'in' him . . . when you seen he's stirred up. Jim's true blue. But you gotta be careful."

Moze corroborated this statement by gloomy nods.

When the card playing was resumed, Anson did not join the game, and both Moze and Shady evinced little of that wholehearted obsession that usually attended their gambling. Anson lay at length, his head in a saddle, scowling at the little shelter where the captive girl kept herself out of sight. At times a faint song or laugh, very unnatural, was wafted across the space. Wilson plodded at the cooking and apparently heard no sounds. Presently he called the men to eat, which office they surlily and silently performed as if it was a favor bestowed upon the cook.

"Snake, hadn't I ought to take a bite of grub over to the gurl?" asked Wilson.

"Do you hev to ask me that?" snapped Anson. "She's gotta be fed, if we hev to stuff it down her throat."

"Wal, I ain't stuck on the job," replied Wilson. "But I'll tackle it, seein' you-all got cold feet."

With plate and cup he reluctantly approached the little lean-to, and, kneeling, he put his head inside. The girl, quick-eyed and alert, had evidently seen him coming. At any rate she greeted him with a cautious smile.

"Jim, was I pretty good?" she whispered.

"Miss, you was shore the finest actress I ever seen," he responded in a low voice. "But you darn' near overdid it. I'm goin' to tell Anson you're sick now . . . like you been poisoned. Dorn shore will help us out."

"Oh, I'm on fire to get away!" she exclaimed. "Jim Wilson, I'll never forget you so long as I live!"

He seemed greatly embarrassed. "Wal . . .

miss . . . I . . . I'll do my best licks. But I ain't gamblin' none on results. Be patient. I reckon between me an' Dorn, you'll git away from heah."

Withdrawing his head, he got up and returned to the campfire where Anson was waiting curiously.

"I left the grub. But she didn't touch it. Seems sort of sick to me, like she was poisoned."

"Jim, didn't I hear you talkin'?" asked Anson.

"Shore. I was coaxin' her. Reckon she ain't so ranty as she was. But she shore is doubled up an' sickish."

"Wuss and wuss all the time," said Anson between his teeth. "An' where's Burt? Hyar it's noon an' he left early. He never was no woodsman. He's got lost."

"Either that or he's run into somethin'," replied Wilson thoughtfully.

Anson doubled a huge fist and cursed deep under the breath — the reaction of a man whose accomplices and partners and tools, whose luck, whose faith in himself had failed him. He flung himself down under a tree, and after a while, when his rigidity relaxed, he probably fell asleep. Moze and Shady kept at their game. Wilson paced to and fro, sat down, and then got up to bunch the horses again, walked around the dell, and back to camp. The afternoon hours were long. And they were waiting hours. The act of waiting appeared on the surface of all these outlaws did.

At sunset the golden gloom of the glen changed to a vague thick twilight. Anson rolled over, yawned, and sat up. As he glanced around, evidently seeking Burt, his face clouded. "No sign of Burt?" he asked.

Wilson expressed a mild surprise. "Wal, Snake, you ain't expectin' Burt now?"

"I am. 'Course I am. Why not?" demanded Anson. "Any other time we'd look fer him, wouldn't we?"

"Any other time ain't now. . . . Burt won't ever come back." Wilson spoke it with a positive finality.

"Ahuh! Some more of them queer feelin's of your'n . . . operatin' again, hey? Them unnatural kind thet you can't explain, hey?"

Anson's queries were bitter and rancorous.

"Yes. . . . An' Snake, I tax you with this heah. . . . Ain't any of them queer feelin's operatin' in you?"

"By God, no!" rolled out the leader savagely. But his passionate denial was a proof that he lied. From the moment of this outburst, which was a fierce clinging to the old brave instincts of his character, unless a sudden change marked the nature of his fortunes, he would rapidly deteriorate to the breaking point and in such brutal unrestrained natures as his, this breaking point meant a desperate stand, a desperate forcing of events, a desperate accumulation of passions that stalked out to deal and to meet disaster and blood and death.

Wilson put a little wood on the fire and he munched a biscuit. No one asked him to cook. No one made any effort to do so. One by one each man went to the pack to get some bread and meat. Then they waited as men who knew not what they waited for, yet hated and dreaded it.

Twilight in that glen was naturally a strange veiled condition of the atmosphere. It was a merging of shade and light, which two seemed to make gray creeping shadows.

Suddenly a snorting and stamping of the horses startled the men.

"Somethin' scared the hosses," said Anson, rising. "Come on."

Moze accompanied him, and they disappeared in the gloom. More trampling of hoofs was heard, then a *cracking* of brush and the deep voices of men. At length the two outlaws returned, leading three of the horses, which they haltered in the open glen.

The campfire light showed Anson's face dark and serious.

"Jim, them hosses are wilder'n deer," he said. "I ketched mine, an' Moze got two. But the rest worked away whenever we come close. . . . Some varmint has scared them bad. We all gotta rustle out thar quick."

Wilson rose, shaking his head doubtfully. And at that moment the quiet air split to a piercing horrid neigh of a terrified horse. Prolonged to a screech, it broke and ended. Then followed snorts of fright, pound and *crack* and *thud* of hoofs, and *crash* of brush, then a gathering thumping crashing roar, split by piercing sounds.

"Stampede!" yelled Anson, and he ran to hold his own horse, which he had haltered right in camp. It was big and wild-looking and now reared and plunged to break away. Anson just got there in time, and then it took all his weight to pull the horse down. Not until the crashing, snorting, pounding mêlée had subsided and died away over the rim of the glen did Anson dare leave his frightened favorite.

"Gone! Our hosses are gone! Did you hear 'em?" he exclaimed blankly.

"Shore they're a cut-up an' crippled bunch by now," replied Wilson.

"Boss, we'll never git 'em back, not in a hundred years," declared Moze.

"Thet settles us, Snake Anson," stridently added Shady Jones. "Them hosses are gone! You can kiss your hand to them. . . . They wasn't hobbled. They hed an orful scare. They split on thet stampede an' they'll never git together. . . . See what you've fetched us to!"

Under the force of this triple arraignment the outlaw leader dropped to his seat, staggered and silenced. In fact, silence fell upon all the men and likewise enfolded the glen.

Night set in jet black, dismal, lonely, without a star. Faintly the wind moaned. Weirdly the brook babbled through its strange chords to end in that sound that was hollow. It was never the same — a rumble, as of faint distant thunder — a deep gurgle, as of water drawn into a vortex — a rolling, as of a stone in swift current. The black cliff was invisible yet seemed to have many weird faces; the giant pines loomed spectrally; the shadows were thick, moving, changing. Flickering lights from the campfire circled the huge trunks and played fantastically over the brooding men. This campfire did not blaze or burn cheerily; it had no glow, no sputter, no white heart, no red living embers. One by one the outlaws, as if with common consent, tried their hands at making the fire burn aright. What little wood had been collected was old; it would burn up with false flare, only to die quickly.

After a while not one of the outlaws spoke or stirred. Not one smoked. Their gloomy eyes fixed on the fire. Each one was concerned with his own thoughts, his own lonely soul, unconsciously full of a doubt of the future. That brooding hour severed him from comrade.

At night nothing seemed the same that it was by day. With success and plenty, with full-blooded action past and more in store, these outlaws were as different from their present state as this black night was different from the bright day they waited for. Wilson, although he played a deep game of deceit for the sake of the helpless girl and thus did not have haunting and superstitious fears on her account, was probably more conscious of impending catastrophe than any of them.

The evil they had done spoke in the voice of Nature, out of the darkness, and was interpreted by each, according to his hopes and fears. Fear was their predominating sense. For years they had lived with some species of fear — of honest men or ven-

445

geance, of pursuit, of starvation, of lack of drink or gold, of blood and death, of stronger men, of luck, of chance, of fate, of mysterious nameless force. Wilson was the type of fearless spirit, but he endured the most gnawing and impossible fear of all — that of himself — that he must inevitably fall to deeds beneath his manhood.

So they hunched around the campfire, brooding because hope was at lowest ebb, listening because the weird black silence with its moan of wind and hollow laugh of brook compelled them to hear, waiting for sleep, for the hours to pass, for whatever was to come.

And it was Anson who caught the first intimation of an impending doom.

Chapter Twenty

"Listen!" Anson whispered tensely. His poise was motionless, his eyes roved everywhere. He held up a shaking finger to command silence.

A third and stranger sound accompanied the low weird moan of the wind and the hollow mockery of the brook — and it seemed a barely perceptible, exquisitely delicate wail or whine. It filled in the lulls between the other sounds.

"If thet's some varmint, he's damn' close," whispered Anson.

"But shore it's far off," said Wilson.

Shady Jones and Moze divided their opinions in the same way.

All breathed freer when the wail ceased, relaxing to their former lounging positions around the fire. An impenetrable wall of blackness circled the pale space lighted by the campfire, and this circle contained the dark somber group of men in the center, the dying campfire, and a few spectral trunks of pines and the tethered horses out in the outer edge. The horses scarcely moved from their tracks and their erect alert heads attested to their sensitivities to the peculiarities of the night.

Then, at an unusually quiet lull, the strange sound gradually arose to a wailing whine.

"It's thet crazy wench cryin'," declared the outlaw leader.

Apparently his allies accepted that statement with as much relief as they had expressed for the termination of the sound.

"Shore thet must be it," agreed Jim Wilson gravely.

"We'll git a lot of sleep with that gurl whinin' all night," growled Shady Jones.

"She gives me the creeps," said Moze.

Wilson got up to resume his pondering walk, head bent, hands behind his back, a grim realistic figure of perturbation.

"Jim . . . set down. You make me nervous," said Anson irritably.

Wilson actually laughed, but low, as if to keep his strange mirth well confined.

"Snake, I'll bet you my hoss an' my gun ag'in' a look-out thet in aboot six seconds more or less I'll be stampedin' like them hosses."

Anson's lean jaw dropped. The other two outlaws stared with round eyes. Wilson was not drunk, they evidently knew, but what he really was appeared a mystery.

"Jim Wilson, are you showin' yellow?" queried Anson hoarsely.

"Mebbe. The Lord only knows. But listen heah. . . . Snake, you've seen an' heard people croak."

"You mean cash in . . . die?"

"Shore."

"Wal, yes . . . a couple or so," replied Anson grimly.

"But you never seen no one die of shock . . . of an orful scare?"

"No, I reckon I never did."

"I have. An' thet's what's ailin' Jim Wilson." And he resumed his dogged steps.

Anson and his two comrades exchanged bewildered glances with one another.

"Ahuh! Say, what's thet got to do with us hyar?" asked Anson presently.

"Thet gurl is dyin'!" retorted Wilson in a voice cracking like a whip.

The three outlaws stiffened in their seats, incredulous, yet irresistibly swayed by emotions that stirred to this dark lonely ill-omened hour.

Wilson trudged to the edge of the lighted circle, muttering to himself, and came back

449

again; then he trudged farther, this time almost out of sight, but only to return; the third time he vanished in the impenetrable wall of night. The three men scarcely moved a muscle as they watched the place where he had disappeared. In a few moments he came stumbling back.

"Shore she's almost gone," he said dismally. "It took my nerve, but I felt of her face. . . . Thet orful wail is her breath chokin' in her throat. . . . Like a death rattle, only long instead of short."

"Wal, if she's gotta croak, it's good she gits it over quick," replied Anson. "I ain't hed sleep fer three nights. . . . An' what I need is whiskey."

"Snake, thet's gospel you're spoutin'," remarked Shady Jones morosely.

The direction of sound in the glow was difficult to be assured of, but any man not stirred to a high pitch of excitement could have told that the difference in volume of this strange wail must have been caused by different distance and positions from whence it came. Also, when it was loudest, it was most like a whine. But these outlaws heard with their consciences.

At last it ceased abruptly.

Wilson again left the group to be swallowed up by the night. His absence was longer than usual, but he returned hurriedly.

"She's daid!" he exclaimed solemnly. "Thet innocent kid . . . who never harmed no one . . . an' who'd make any man better for seein' her . . . she's daid! Anson, you've shore a heap to answer fer when your time comes."

"What's eatin' you?" demanded the leader angrily. "Her blood ain't on my hands."

"It shore is!" shouted Wilson, shaking his hand at Anson. "An' you'll hev to take your medicine. I felt thet comin' all along. An' I feel some more."

"*Aw!* She's jest gone to sleep," declared Anson, shaking his long frame as he rose. "Gimme a light."

"Boss, you're plumb off to go near a dead gurl thet's jest died crazy," protested Shady Jones.

"Off! *Haw! Haw!* Who ain't off in this outfit, I'd like to know?" Anson possessed himself of a stick blazing at one end, and with this he stalked off toward the lean-to where the girl was supposed to lie dead. His gaunt figure lighted by the torch certainly fitted the weird black surroundings. And it was seen that once near the girl's shelter he proceeded more slowly until he halted. He bent to peer inside.

"She's . . . gone!" he yelled in harsh, shaken accents.

Then the torch burned out, leaving only a red glow. He whirled it about, but the blaze did not rekindle. His comrades, peering intently, lost sight of his tall form and the end of the red-ended stick. Darkness like pitch swallowed him. For a moment no sound intervened. Again the moan of wind, the strange little mocking hollow roar, dominated the place. Then there came a rush of air, of something, perhaps of air, like the soft *swishing* of spruce branches swinging aside. Dull *thudding* footsteps followed it. Anson came running back to the fire. His aspect was wild, his face pale, his eyes were fierce and starting from their sockets. He had drawn his gun.

"Did . . . ye . . . see or hear . . . anythin'?" he panted, peering back, then all around, and at last at his men.

"No, an' I shore was lookin' an' listenin'," replied Wilson.

"Boss, there wasn't nothin'," declared Moze.

"I ain't so sartin," said Shady Jones with doubtful, staring eyes. "I believe I heerd a rustlin'?"

"She wasn't there!" ejaculated Anson, in wondering awe. "She's gone! My torch went

452

out. I couldn't see. An' jest then I felt somethin' was passin'! Fast! I jerked around. . . . All was black, an' yet, if I didn't see a big gray streak, I'm crazier'n thet girl. But I couldn't swear to anythin' but a rushin' of wind. I felt thet."

"Gone!" exclaimed Wilson in great alarm. "Fellars, if thet's so, then mebbe she wasn't daid an' she wandered off. . . . But she was daid! Her heart had quit beatin'. I'll swear to thet."

"I move to break camp," said Shady Jones gruffly, and he stood up. Moze seconded that move by an expressive flash of his black visage.

"Jim, if she's dead . . . an' gone . . . what in hell's come off?" huskily asked Anson. "It only seems thet way. . . . We're all worked up. . . . Let's talk sense."

"Anson, shore there's a heap you an' me don't know," replied Wilson. "The world come to an end once. Wal, it can come to another end. . . . I tell you I ain't surprised. . . ."

"*Thar!*" cried Anson, whirling, with his gun leaping out.

Something huge, shadowy, gray against the black rushed behind the men and trees, and following it came a perceptible acceleration of the air.

"Shore, Snake, there wasn't nothin'," said Wilson presently.

"I heerd," whispered Shady Jones.

"It was only a breeze blowin' thet smoke," rejoined Moze.

"I'd bet my soul somethin' went back of me," declared Anson, glaring into the void.

"Listen an' let's make shore," suggested Wilson.

The guilty agitated faces of the outlaws showed plainly enough in the flickering light for each to see a connecting dread in his fellows. Like statues they stood, watching and listening.

Few sounds stirred in the strange silence. Now and then the horses heaved heavily, but stood still; a dismal dreary note of wind in the pines vied with a hollow laugh of the brook. And these low sounds only fastened attention upon the quality of the silence. A breathing lonely spirit of solitude permeated the black dell. Like a pit of unplumbed depths the dark night yawned. An evil conscience, listening there, could have heard the most peaceful, beautiful, and mournful sounds of Nature only as strains of a calling hell.

Suddenly the silent oppressive surcharged air split to a short piercing scream.

Anson's big horse stood straight up, pawing the air, and came down with a *crash.* The other horses shook with terror.

"Wasn't . . . thet . . . a cougar?" whispered Anson thickly.

"Thet was a woman's scream," replied Wilson, and he appeared to be shaking like a leaf in the wind.

"Then . . . I figgered right . . . the kid's alive . . . wanderin' around . . . an' she let out thet awful scream," said Anson.

"Wanderin' around, yes . . . but she's daid!"

"My God! It ain't possible!"

"Wal, if she ain't wanderin' around daid, she's almost daid," replied Wilson. And he began to whisper to himself.

"If I'd only knowed what thet deal meant, I'd hev plugged Beasley instead of listenin'. . . . An' I ought to hev knocked thet kid on the head an' made sartin she'd croaked. If she goes screamin' around thet way. . . ."

His voice failed as there rose a thin, splitting, high-pointed shriek, somewhat resembling the first scream only less wild. It came apparently from the cliff. From another point in the pitch-black glen rose the wailing terrible cry of a woman in agony. Wild, haunting, mournful wail!

Anson's horse, losing the halter, plunged

back, almost falling over a slight depression in the rocky ground. The outlaw caught him and dragged him nearer the fire. The other horses stood shaking and straining. Moze ran between them and held them. Shady Jones threw green brush on the fire. With *sputter* and *crackle* a blaze started, showing Wilson standing tragically, his arms out, facing the black shadows.

The strange live shriek was not repeated. But the cry like that of a woman in her death throes pierced the silence again. It left a quivering ring that softly died away. Then the stillness clamped down once more and the darkness seemed to thicken. The men waited, and, when they had begun to relax, the cry burst out appallingly close, right behind the trees. It was human — the personification of pain and terror — the tremendous struggle of precious life against horrible death. So pure, so exquisite, so wonderful was the cry that the listeners writhed as if they saw an innocent, tender, beautiful girl torn frightfully before their eyes. It was full of suspense; it thrilled for death; its marvelous potency was the wild note — that beautiful and ghastly note of self-preservation.

In sheer desperation the outlaw leader fired his gun at the black wall whence the cry came. Then he had to fight his plunging horse to keep him from breaking away. Following the shot was an interval of silence; the horses became tractable; the men gathered closer to the fire, with the halters still held firmly.

"If it was a cougar . . . thet'd scare him off," said Anson.

"Shore, but it ain't a cougar," replied Wilson. "Wait an' see!"

They all waited, listening with ears turned to different points, eyes roving everywhere, afraid of their very shadows. Once more the moan of wind, the mockery of brook, deep gurgle, laugh, and babble, dominated the silence of the glen.

"Boss, let's shake this spooky hole," whispered Moze.

The suggestion attracted Anson and he pondered it while slowly shaking his head.

"We've only three hosses. An' mine'll take ridin' . . . after them squalls, damn' if he won't," replied the leader. "We've got packs, too. An' hell ain't nothin' on this place fer bein' dark."

"No matter. Let's go. I'll walk an' lead the way," said Moze eagerly. "I got sharp eyes. You fellars can ride an' carry a pack. We'll git out of here an' come back in daylight fer the rest of the outfit."

457

"Anson, I'm keen fer thet myself," declared Shady Jones.

"Jim, what d'ye say to thet?" queried Anson. "Rustlin' out of this black hole?"

"Shore it's a grand idee," agreed Wilson.

"Thet was a cougar," avowed Anson, gathering courage as the silence remained unbroken. "But jest the same it was as tough on me as if it had been a woman screamin' over a blade twistin' in her gizzards."

"Snake, shore you seen a woman heah lately?" deliberately asked Wilson.

"Reckon I did. Thet kid," replied Anson dubiously.

"Wal, you seen her go crazy, didn't you?"

"Yes."

"An' she wasn't heah when you went huntin' fer her?"

"Correct."

"Wal, if thet's so, what do you want to blab aboot cougars fer?"

Wilson's argument seemed incontestable. Shady and Moze nodded gloomily and shifted restlessly from foot to foot. Anson dropped his head.

"No matter . . . if only we don't hear . . . ," he began, suddenly to grow mute.

Right upon them, from some place, just out of the circle of light, rose a scream, by reason of its proximity the most piercing and agonizing yet heard, simply petrifying the group until the peal passed. Anson's huge horse reared and with snort of terror lunged in tremendous leap, straight out. He struck Anson with *thudding* impact, knocking him over the rocks into the depression back of the campfire, and plunging after him. Wilson had made a flying leap just in time to avoid being struck, and he turned to see Anson go down. There came a crash, a groan, and then the strike and pound of hoofs as the horse struggled up. Apparently he had rolled over his master.

"Help, fellars!" yelled Wilson, quick to leap down over the little bank, and in the dim light to grasp the halter. The three men dragged the horse out and securely tied him close to a tree. That done, they peered down into the depression. Anson's form could just barely be distinguished in the gloom. He lay stretched out. Another groan escaped him.

"Shore I'm scared he's hurt," said Wilson.

"Hoss rolled right on top of him. An' thet hoss's heavy," declared Moze.

They got down and knelt beside their leader. In the darkness his face looked dull gray. His breathing was not right.

"Snake, old man, you ain't . . . hurt?" asked Wilson with a tremor in his voice. Receiving no reply, he said to his comrades:

"Lay hold an' we'll heft him up where we can see."

The three then carefully lifted Anson up on the bank and laid him near the fire in the light. Anson was conscious. His face was ghastly. Blood showed on his lips.

Wilson knelt beside him. The other outlaws stood up and with one dark gaze at each other damned Anson's chance of life. And on the instant rose that terrible distressing scream of acute agony — like that of a woman being dismembered. Shady Jones whispered something to Moze. Then they stood gazing down at their fallen leader.

"Tell me where you're hurt?" asked Wilson.

"He . . . smashed . . . my chest," said Anson in broken, strangled whisper.

Wilson's deft hands opened the outlaw's shirt and felt of his chest.

"No. Shore your breastbone ain't smashed," replied Wilson hopefully. And he began to run his hands around one side of Anson's body and then the other. Abruptly he stopped, averted his gaze, then slowly ran the hand all along that side. Anson's ribs had been broken and crushed in by the weight of the horse. He was bleeding at the mouth and his slow painful expulsions of breath brought on bloody froth, which

460

showed that the broken bones had penetrated the lungs. An injury sooner or later fatal!

"Pard, you busted a rib or two," said Wilson.

"*Aw,* Jim . . . it must be . . . wuss'n thet," he whispered. "I'm . . . in orful . . . pain. An' I can't . . . git . . . any . . . breath."

"Mebbe you'll be better," said Wilson with a cheerfulness his face belied.

Moze bent close over Anson, took a short scrutiny of that ghastly face, at the blood-stained lips, and the lean hands plucking at nothing. Then he jerked erect.

"Shady, he's goin' to cash. Let's clear out of this."

"I'm yours pertickler previous," replied Jones.

Both turned away. They untied the two horses and led them up to where the saddles lay. Swiftly the blankets went on, swiftly the saddles swung up, swiftly the cinches snapped. Anson lay gazing up at Wilson, comprehending this move. And Wilson stood strangely grim and silent, somehow detached coldly from that self of the past few hours.

"Shady, you grab some bread an' I'll pack a hunk of meat," said Moze. Both men came near to the fire, into the light within ten feet of where the leader lay.

"Fellars . . . you ain't . . . slopin'?" he whispered in husky amaze.

"Boss, we air thet same. We can't do you any good, an' this hole ain't healthy," replied Moze.

Shady Jones swung himself astride his horse, all about him sharp, eager, strung.

"Moze, I'll tote the grub an' you lead out of hyar, till we git past the wust timber," he said.

"*Aw,* Moze . . . you wouldn't leave . . . Jim hyar . . . alone," implored Anson.

"Jim can stay an' be damned," retorted Moze. "I've had enough of this hole."

"But, Moze . . . it ain't square . . . ," panted Anson. "Jim wouldn't . . . leave me. I'd . . . stick . . . by . . . you. . . . I'll make it . . . all up to you."

"Snake, you're goin' to cash," sardonically returned Moze.

A current leaped all through Anson's stretched frame. His ghastly face blazed. That was the great and the terrible moment that for long had been in abeyance. Wilson had known grimly that it would come, by one means or another. Anson had doggedly and faithfully struggled against the tide of fatal issues. Moze and Shady Jones, deep-locked in their self-centered motives, had

462

not realized the inevitable trend of their dark lives.

Anson, prostrate as he was, swiftly drew his gun and shot Moze. Without sound or movement of hand, Moze fell. Then the plunge of Shady's horse caused Anson's second shot to miss. A quick third shot brought no apparent result, but Shady's cursing resort to his own weapon. He tried to aim from the plunging horse. His bullets spattered dust and gravel over Anson. Then Wilson's long arm stretched and his heavy gun *banged.* Shady collapsed in the saddle, and the frightened horse, throwing him, plunged out of the circle of light. *Thudding* hoofs, *crashings* of brush, quickly ceased.

"Jim . . . did you . . . git him?" whispered Anson.

"Shore did, Snake," was the slow halting response. Jim Wilson must have sustained a sick shudder as he replied. Sheathing his gun, he folded a blanket and put it in under Anson's head.

"Jim . . . my feet . . . air orful cold," whispered Anson.

"Wal, it's gittin' chilly," replied Wilson, and, taking a second blanket, he lay that over Anson's limbs. "Snake, I'm feared Shady hit you once."

"Ahuh! But not so I'd care . . . much . . .

if I hed . . . no wuss hurt."

"You lay still now. Reckon Shady's hoss stopped out heah a ways. An' I'll see."

"Jim . . . I ain't heerd . . . thet scream fer . . . a little."

"Shore it's gone. . . . Reckon now thet was a cougar."

"Damn . . . I knowed it!"

Wilson stalked away into the darkness. That inky wall did not seem so impenetrable and black after he had gotten out of the circle of light. He proceeded carefully and did not make any missteps. He groped from tree to tree toward the cliff and presently brought up against a huge flat rock, as high as his head. Here the darkness was blackest, yet he was able to see a slight form on the rock.

"Miss, are you there . . . all right?" he called softly.

"Yes, but I'm scared to death," she whispered in reply.

"Shore it wound up sudden. . . . Come now. I reckon your trouble's over."

He helped her off the rock, and, finding her unsteady on her feet, he supported her with one arm, and held the other out in front of him to feel for objects. Foot by foot they worked out from under the dense shadow of the cliff, following the course of the little brook. It babbled and gurgled, and almost drowned the low whistle Wilson sent out. The girl dragged heavily upon him now, evidently weakening. At length he reached the little open patch at the head of the ravine. Halting here, he whistled again. An answer came from somewhere behind him and to the right. Wilson waited with the girl hanging on his arm.

"Dorn's heah," he said. "An' don't you keel over now . . . after all the nerve you hed."

A swishing of brush, a step, a soft padded footfall, a looming dark figure, and a long, slow, gray shape stealthily moving — it was the last of these that made Wilson jump.

"Wilson!" came Dorn's subdued voice.

"Heah. I've got her, Dorn. Safe an' sound," replied Wilson, stepping toward the tall form. And he put the drooping girl into Dorn's arms.

"Bo! Bo! You're all right?" Dorn's deep voice was tremulous.

She roused up to seize him and to utter little cries of joy.

"Oh, Dorn! Oh, thank heaven! I'm ready to drop now . . . Hasn't it been a night . . . an adventure? I'm well . . . safe . . . sound. . . . Dorn, we owe it to this Jim Wilson."

"Bo, I . . . we'll all thank him . . . all our lives," replied Dorn. "Wilson, you're a man! If you'll shake that gang. . . ."

"Dorn, shore there ain't much of a gang left, unless you let Burt git away," replied Wilson.

"I didn't kill him . . . or hurt him. But I scared him so, I'll bet he's runnin' yet. . . . Wilson, did all the shootin' mean a fight?"

"Tolerable."

"Oh, Dorn, it was terrible. I saw it all. I. . . ."

"Wal, miss, you can tell him after I go. . . . I'm wishin' you good luck." His voice was a cool easy slow drawl, slightly tremulous.

The girl's face flashed white in the gloom. She pressed against the outlaw, wrung his hands.

"Heaven help you, Jim Wilson! You *are* from Texas! I'll remember you . . . pray for you all my life!"

Wilson moved away, out toward the pale glow of light under the black pines.

466

CHAPTER
TWENTY-ONE

The sunset hour while Helen Rayner watched Dorn ride away on a quest perilous to him and which meant almost life or death for her, it was surpassing strange that she could think of nothing except the thrilling tumultuous moment when she had put her arms around his neck.

It did not matter that Dorn — splendid fellow that he was! — had made the ensuing moment free of shame by taking her action as sisterly — the fact that she had actually done it was enough. How utterly impossible for her to anticipate her impulses or to understand them once they were acted upon! Confounding and terrible realization then was that, if Dorn returned with her sister, Helen knew she would do the same thing over again!

"If I do . . . I won't be two-faced about it," she soliloquized, and a hot blush flamed her cheeks.

She watched Dorn until he rode out of sight.

When he had gone, worry and dread replaced this other confusing emotion, and she turned to the business of meeting events. Before supper she packed her valuables and books, papers, and clothes together with Bo's, and had them in readiness so, if she was forced to vacate the premises, she would have their personal possessions.

The Mormon boys and several others of her trusted men slept in their tarpaulin beds on the porch of the ranch house that night, so that Helen at least would not be surprised. But the day came with its usual manifold duties undisturbed by any event. And it passed slowly with the leaden feet of listening, watching vigilance.

Carmichael did not come back, nor was there news of him to be had. The last known of him had been late the afternoon of the preceding day when a sheepherder had seen him far out on the north range, headed for the hills. The Beemans reported that Roy's condition had improved, and also that there was a subdued excitement of suspense down in the village.

This second lonely night was almost unendurable for Helen. When she slept, it was to dream horrible dreams; when she lay awake, it was to have her heart leap to her throat at a rustle of leaves near the window, and to lay in torture of imagination as to poor Bo's plight. A thousand times Helen said to herself that Beasley could have had the ranch and welcome, if only Bo had been spared. Helen absolutely connected her enemy with her sister's disappearance. Riggs might have been a means to it.

Daylight was not attended by so many fears: there were things to do that demanded attention. And thus it was that the next morning, shortly before noon, she was recalled to her perplexities by a shouting out at the corrals and a galloping of horses somewhere near. From the window she saw a big smoke.

"Fire! That must be one of the barns . . . the old one, farthest out," she said, gazing out of the window. "Some careless Mexican with his everlasting cigarette!"

Helen resisted an impulse to go out and see what had happened. She had decided to stay in the house. But when footsteps sounded on the porch and a rap on the door, she unhesitatingly opened it. Four Mexicans stood close. One of them, quick as thought, flashed a hand in to grasp her, and in a single motion, pull her across the threshold.

"No hurt, *señorita*," he said, and pointed — making motions she must go.

Helen did not need to be told what this visit meant. Many as her conjectures had been, however, she had not thought of Beasley subjecting her to this outrage. And her blood boiled.

"How dare you!" she said, trembling in her effort to control her temper. But class, authority, voice availed nothing with these swarthy Mexicans. They grinned. Another laid hold of Helen with dirty brown hand. She shrank from the contact.

"Let go!" she burst out furiously. And instinctively she began to struggle to free herself. Then they all lay hold of her. Helen's dignity might never have been. A burning, choking rush of blood was her first acquaintance with the terrible passion of anger that was her inheritance from the Auchinclosses. She who had resolved not to lay herself open to any indignity now fought like a tigress. The Mexicans, jabbering in their excitement, had all they could do, until they lifted her bodily from the porch. They handled her as if she had been a half-empty sack of corn. One holding each hand and foot they packed her, with dress disarranged and half torn off, down the path to the lane and down the lane to the road. There they stood her upright and pushed her off her property.

Through half-blinded eyes Helen saw them guarding the gateway, ready to prevent her entrance. She staggered down the road toward the village. It seemed she made her way through a red dimness — that there was a congestion in her brain — that the distance to Mrs. Cass's cottage was insurmountable. But she got there, to stagger up the path, to hear the old woman's cry. Dizzy, faint, sick, with a blackness enveloping all she looked at, Helen felt herself led into the sitting room and placed in the big chair.

Presently sight and clearness of mind returned to her. She saw Roy, white as a sheet, questioning her with terrible eyes. The old woman hung murmuringly over her, trying to comfort her as well as fasten the disordered dress.

"Four greasers . . . packed me down . . . the hill . . . threw me off my ranch . . . into the road," panted Helen. She seemed to tell this also to her own consciousness and to realize the mighty wave of anger that shook her whole body. "If I'd known . . . I would have killed them!" She exclaimed that, full voiced and hard, with dry hot eyes on her friends.

Roy reached out to take her hand, speaking huskily. Helen did not distinguish what he said. The frightened old woman knelt with unsteady fingers fumbling over the rents in Helen's dress. The moment came when Helen's quivering began to subside, when her blood quieted to let reason sway, when she began to do battle with her rage, and slowly to take fearful stock of this consuming peril that had been a sleeping tigress in her veins.

"Oh, Miss Helen, you looked so turrible, I was sure you was hurted," the old woman was saying.

Helen gazed strangely at her bruised wrists, at the one stocking that hung down over her shoe top, at the rent that had bared her shoulder to the profane gaze of those grinning, beady-eyed Mexicans.

"My body's . . . not hurt," she whispered.

Roy had lost some of his white color, and, where his eyes had been fierce, they were now kindly.

"Wal, Miss Nell, it's lucky no harm's done. . . . Now if you'll only see this whole deal clear! Not let it spoil your sweet way of lookin' an' hopin'. If . . . you can only see what's raw in this West . . . an' love it jest the same!"

Helen only half divined his meaning, but

472

that was enough for a future reflection. The West was beautiful, but hard. In the faces of these friends she began to see the meaning of the keen sloping lines and shadows of pain, of a lean naked truth, cut as from marble.

"For the land's sake, tell us all about it," importuned Mrs. Cass.

Whereupon Helen shut her eyes and told the brief narrative of her expulsion from her home.

"Shore we all expected thet," said Roy. "An' it's jest as well you're here with a whole skin. . . . Beasley's in possession now, an' I reckon we'd all sooner hev you away from thet ranch."

"But, Roy, I won't let Beasley stay there!" cried Helen.

"Miss Nell, shore by the time this here Pine has growed big enough fer law you'll hev gray in that pretty hair. You can't put Beasley off with your honest an' rightful claim. . . . Al Auchincloss was a hard driver. He made enemies an' he made some he didn't kill. The evil men do lives after them. . . . An' you've got to suffer fer Al's sins, though Al was as good as any man who ever prospered in these parts."

"Oh, what can I do? I won't give up. I've been robbed. . . . Can't the people help me?

Must I meekly sit with my hands crossed while that half-breed thief. . . . Oh, it's unbelievable!"

"I reckon you'll jest hev to be patient fer a few days," said Roy calmly. "It'll all come right in the end."

"Roy! You've had this deal, as you call it, all worked out in mind for a long time!" exclaimed Helen.

"Shore, an' I ain't missed a reckonin' yet."

"Then what will happen . . . in a few days."

"Nell Rayner, are you goin' to hev some spunk an' not lose your nerve again or go wild out of your head?"

"I'll try to be brave but . . . but I must be prepared," she replied tremulously.

"Wal, there's Dorn an' Las Vegas an' me fer Beasley to reckon with. . . . An', Miss Nell, his chances fer long life are as pore as his chances fer heaven."

"But, Roy, I don't believe in deliberate taking of life," replied Helen, shuddering. "That's against my religion. I won't allow it. . . . And . . . then . . . think of Dorn, all of you . . . in danger!"

"Girl, how're you ever goin' to help yourself? Shore, you might hold Dorn back, if you love him, an' swear you won't give yourself to him. . . . An' I reckon I'd respect

474

your religion, if you was goin' to suffer through me. . . . But not Dorn nor you . . . nor Bo . . . nor love or heaven or hell can ever stop thet cowboy Las Vegas!"

"Oh, if Dorn brings Bo back to me . . . what will I care for my ranch?" murmured Helen.

"Reckon you'll only begin to care when thet happens. Your big hunter has got to be put to work," replied Roy with his keen smile.

Before noon that day the baggage Helen had packed at home was left on the porch of Widow Cass's cottage, and Helen's anxious need of the hour was satisfied. She was made comfortable in the old woman's one spare room and she set herself the task of fortitude and endurance.

To her surprise many of Mrs. Cass's neighbors came unobtrusively to the back door of the little cottage and made sympathetic inquiries. They appeared a subdued and apprehensive group, and whispered to one another as they left. Helen gathered from these visits a conviction that the wives of the men dominated by Beasley believed no good could come of this high-handed taking over of the ranch. Indeed, Helen found at the end of the day that a strength had been borne of her misfortune.

The next day Roy informed her that his brother John had come down late the preceding night with the news of Beasley's descent upon the ranch. Not a shot had been fired, and the only damage done was that of the burning of a hay-filled barn. This had been set on fire to attract Helen's men to one spot, where Beasley had ridden down upon them with three times their number. He had boldly ordered them off the land, unless they wanted to acknowledge him boss and remain there in his service. The three Beemans had stayed, having planned that in just this event they might be valuable to Helen's interests. Beasley had ridden down into Pine the same as upon any other day. Roy reported, also, news that had come in that morning, how Beasley's crowd had celebrated late the night before.

The second and third and fourth days endlessly wore away, and Helen believed they had made her old. At night she lay awake most of the time, thinking and praying, but during the afternoons she got some sleep. She could think of nothing and talk of nothing except her sister, and Dorn's chances of saving her.

"Nell, shore you pay Dorn a pore compliment," finally protested the patient Roy. "I tell you . . . Milt Dorn can do anythin' he wants to do in the woods. You can believe thet. . . . But I reckon he'll run chances after he comes back."

This significant speech thrilled Helen with its assurance of hope and made her blood curdle at the implied peril awaiting the hunter.

On the afternoon of the fifth day Helen was abruptly awakened from her sleep. The sun had almost set. She heard voices — the shrill cackling notes of old Mrs. Cass, high in excitement, a deep voice that made Helen tingle all over, a girl's laugh, broken but happy. There were footsteps and stamping of hoofs. Dorn had brought Bo back! Helen knew it. She grew very weak and had to fight herself to stand erect. Her heart began to pound in her very ears. A sweet and perfect joy suddenly flooded her soul. She thanked God her prayers had been answered. Then suddenly alive with sheer mad physical gladness she rushed out.

She was just in time to see Roy Beeman stalk out as if he had never been shot and with a yell greet a big gray-clad, gray-faced man — Dorn.

"Howdy, Roy. Glad to see you up," said Dorn. How the quiet voice steadied Helen! She beheld Bo, looking the same except a little pale and disheveled. Then Bo saw her and leaped at her, into her arms.

"Nell! I'm here! Safe . . . all right. Never was so happy in my life. . . . Oh-h, talk about your adventures! Nell, you dear old mother to me . . . I've had en-enough for-ever!"

Bo was wild with joy and by turns she laughed and cried. But Helen could not voice her feelings. Her eyes were so dim that she could scarcely see Dorn when he loomed over her as she held Bo. But he found the hand she put shakily out.

"Nell! Reckon it's been harder . . . on you." His voice was earnest and halting. She felt his searching gaze upon her face. "Missus Cass said you were here. . . . An' I know why."

Roy led them all indoors.

"Milt, one of the neighbor boys will take care of thet hoss," he said as Dorn had turned toward the dusty and weary Ranger. "Where'd you leave the cougar?"

"I sent him home," replied Dorn.

"Laws, now, Milt, if this ain't grand!" cackled Mrs. Cass. "We've worried some here. An' Miss Helen near starved a-hopin' fer you."

"Auntie, I reckon the girl an' I are nearer starved than anybody you know," replied

478

Dorn with a grim laugh.

"Fer the land's sake! I'll be fixin' supper this minnit."

"Nell, why are you here?" asked Bo suspiciously.

For answer Helen led her sister into the spare room and closed the door. Bo saw the baggage. Her expression changed. The old blaze leaped to the telltale eyes.

"He's done it!" she cried hotly.

"Dearest . . . thank God I've got you . . . back again," murmured Helen, finding her voice. "Nothing else matters! I've prayed only fer that!"

"Good old Nell," whispered Bo, and she kissed and embraced Helen. "You really mean that, I know. . . . But nix for yours truly! I'm back alive and kicking, you bet. . . . Where's my . . . where's Tom?"

"Bo, not a word has been heard of him for five days. He's searching for you, of course."

"And you've been . . . been put off the ranch?"

"Well, rather," replied Helen, and in few trembling words she told the story of her eviction.

Bo uttered a wild word that had more force than elegance, but it became her passionate resentment of this outrage done her sister.

"Oh! Does Tom Carmichael know this?" she added breathlessly.

"How could he?"

"When he finds out then . . . oh, won't there be hell? I'm glad I got here first. . . . Nell, my boots haven't been off the whole blessed time. Help me. . . . And, oh, for some soap and hot water, and some clean clothes! Nell, old girl, I wasn't raised right for these Western deals. Too luxurious!"

And then Helen had her ears filled with a rapid-fire account of running horses and Riggs and outlaws and Beasley called boldly to his teeth and a long ride and an outlaw who was a hero — a fight with Riggs — blood and death — another long ride — a wild camp in black woods — night — lonely ghostly sounds — and day again — plot — a great actress lost to the world — Ophelia — Snake Anson's hoodooed outlaws — mournful moans and terrible cries — cougar — stampede — fight and shots, more blood and death — Wilson a hero — another Tom Carmichael — fall in love with outlaw gunfighter if — black night and Dorn and horse and rides and starved and: "Oh . . . Nell, he *was* from Texas!"

Helen gathered what wonderful and

dreadful events had hung over the bright head of this beloved little sister, but the bewilderment occasioned by Bo's fluent and remarkable utterance left only that last sentence clear.

Presently Helen got a word in to inform Bo that Mrs. Cass had knocked twice for supper, and that welcome news checked Bo's flow of speech when nothing else seemed adequate.

It was obvious to Helen that Roy and Dorn had exchanged stories. Roy deliberated this reunion by sitting at table the first time since he had been shot, and, despite Helen's misfortune and the suspended waiting balance in the air, the occasion was joyous. Old Mrs. Cass was in the height of her glory. She sensed a romance here, and, true to her sex, she radiated to it.

Daylight was still lingering when Roy got up and went out on the porch. His keen ears had heard something. Helen fancied she herself had heard rapid hoof beats.

"Dorn, come out!" called Roy sharply.

The hunter moved with his swift noiseless agility. Helen and Bo followed, halting in the door.

"Thet's Las Vegas," whispered Dorn.

To Helen it seemed that the cowboy's name changed the very atmosphere.

Voices were heard at the gate; one that, harsh and quick, sounded like Carmichael's. And a spirited horse was pounding and scattering gravel. Then a lithe figure appeared striding up the path. It was Carmichael — yet not the Carmichael Helen knew. She heard Bo's strange little cry, a corroboration of her own impression.

Roy might never have been shot, judging from the way he stepped out, and Dorn was almost as quick. Carmichael reached them — grasped them with swift hard hands.

"Boys . . . I jest rode in. . . . An' they said you'd found her!"

"Shore Las Vegas. . . . Dorn fetched her home safe an' sound. . . . There she is."

The cowboy thrust aside the two men and with a long stride he faced the porch, his piercing eyes on the door. All that Helen could think of his look was that it seemed terrible. Bo stepped outside in front of Helen. Probably she would have run straight into Carmichael's arms if some strange instinct had not withheld her. Helen judged it to be fear; she found her heart lifting painfully.

"Bo!" he yelled like a savage, yet he did not in the least resemble one.

"Oh . . . Tom!" cried Bo falteringly. She half held out her arms.

"You girl?" That seemed to be his piercing query, like the quivering blade in his eyes. Two more long strides carried him close up to her and his look chased the red out of Bo's cheek. Then it was beautiful to see his face marvelously change until it was that of the well-remembered Las Vegas magnified in all his old spirit.

"*Aw!*" The exclamation was a tremendous sigh. "I shore am glad!"

That beautiful flash left his face as he wheeled to the men. He wrung Dorn's hand, long and hard, and his gaze confused the older man.

"Riggs?" he said, and in the jerk of his frame as he whipped out the word disappeared the strange fleeting signs of his kindlier emotion.

"Wilson killed him," replied Dorn.

"Jim Wilson . . . thet old Texas ranger! Reckon he lent you a hand?"

"My friend, he saved Bo," replied Dorn with emotion. "My old cougar an' me . . . we just hung around."

"You made Wilson help you?" cut in the hard voice.

"Yes. But he killed Riggs before I come up, an' I reckon he'd done well by Bo if I'd never got there."

"How aboot the gang?"

483

"All snuffed out, I reckon, except Wilson."

"Somebody told me Beasley did run Miss Helen off the ranch. . . . Thet so?"

"Yes. Four of his greasers packed her down the hill . . . 'most tore her clothes off, so Roy tells me."

"Four greasers! Shore it was Beasley's deal clean through?"

"Yes. Riggs was led. He had an itch for a bad name, you know. But Beasley made the plan. It was Nell they wanted instead of Bo."

Abruptly Carmichael stalked off down the darkening path, his silver heel plates ringing, his spurs *jingling.*

"Hold on, Carmichael!" called Dorn, taking a step.

"Oh, Tom!" cried Bo.

"Shore, folks, callin' won't be no use, if anythin' would be," said Roy. "Las Vegas has hed a look at red liquor."

"He's been drinking! Oh, thet accounts! Nell, he never . . . never even touched me!"

For once Helen was not ready to comfort Bo. A mighty tug at her heart had sent her with flying, uneven steps toward Dorn. He took another stride down the path and another.

"Dorn . . . oh . . . please stop!" she called, very low.

He halted as if he had run sharply into a

bar across the path. When he turned, Helen had come close. Twilight was deep there in the shade of the peach trees, but she could see his face, the hungry flaring eyes.

"I . . . I haven't thanked you . . . yet . . . for bringing Bo home," she whispered.

"Nell, never mind that," he said in surprise. "If you must . . . wait . . . I've got to catch up with that cowboy."

"No. Let me thank you now," she whispered, and, stepping closer, she put her arms up, meaning to put them around his neck. That action must be her self-punishment for the other time she had done it. Yet it might also serve to thank him. But strangely her hands got no farther than his breast and fluttered there to catch hold of the fringe of his buckskin jacket. She felt a great heave of his deep chest.

"I . . . I do thank you . . . with all my heart," she said softly. "I owe you now . . . for myself and her . . . more than I can ever . . . ever repay."

"Nell, I'm your friend," he replied hurriedly. "Don't talk of repayin' me. . . . Let me go now . . . after Las Vegas."

"What for?" she queried suddenly.

"I mean to line up beside him . . . at the bar . . . or wherever he goes," returned Dorn.

"Don't tell me that. *I* know. You're going straight to meet Beasley."

"Nell, if you hold me up any longer, I reckon I'll have to run . . . or never get to Beasley before that cowboy."

Helen locked her fingers in the fringe of his jacket, leaned closer to him, all her being responsive to a bursting gust of blood over her. "I'll not let you go," she said.

He laughed and put his great hands over hers. "What're you sayin', girl? You can't stop me."

"Yes I can. . . . Dorn, I don't want you to risk your life."

He stared at her and made as if to tear her hands from their hold.

"Listen . . . please . . . oh . . . please!" she implored. "If you go deliberately to kill Beasley . . . and do it . . . that will be murder. . . . It's against my religion. . . . I would be unhappy all my life."

"But, child, you'll be ruined all your life if Beasley is not dealt with . . . as men of his breed are always dealt with in the West," he remonstrated, and in one quick move he had freed himself from her clutching fingers.

Helen, with a move as swift, put her arms around his neck and clasped her hands tightly. "Milt, I'm finding myself," she said. "The other day when I did . . . this . . . you

486

made an excuse for me. . . . I'm not two-faced now."

She meant to keep him from killing Beasley if she sacrificed every last shred of her pride. And she stamped the look of his face on her heart of hearts to treasure always. The thrill, the beat of her pulses almost obstructed her thought of purpose.

"Nell, just now . . . when you're overcome . . . rash with feelin's . . . don't say to me . . . a word . . . a. . . ." He broke down huskily.

"My first friend . . . my . . . oh, Dorn, I *know* you love me," she whispered. And she hid her face on his breast, there to feel a tremendous tumult. "Oh, don't you?" she cried, in low smothered voice, as his silence drove her farther on this mad yet glorious purpose.

"If you need to be told . . . yes . . . I reckon I do love you, Nell Rayner," he replied.

It seemed to Helen that he spoke from far off. She lifted her face, her heart on her lips. "If you kill Beasley I'll never marry you," she said.

"Who's expectin' you to?" he asked with low coarse laugh. "Do you think you have to marry me to square accounts? This's the only time you ever hurt me, Nell Rayner. . . .

I'm shamed you could think I'd expect you . . . out of gratitude. . . ."

"Oh . . . you . . . you are as dense as the forest where you live," she cried. And then she shut her eyes again, the better to remember that transfiguration of his face, the better to betray herself. "Man . . . I love you!" Full and deep, yet tremulous, the words burst from her heart that had been burdened with them for many a day.

Then it seemed in the throbbing riot of her senses that she was lifted and swung into his arms, and handled with a great and terrible tenderness, and hugged and kissed with the hunger and awkwardness of a bear, and held with her feet off the ground, and rendered blind, dizzy, rapturous, and frightened, and utterly torn asunder from her old calm thinking self.

He put her down — released her. "Nothin' could have made me so happy as what you said." He finished with a strong sigh of unutterable wondering joy.

"Then you will not go to . . . to meet . . . ?" Helen's happy query froze on her lips.

"I've got to go," he rejoined with his old quiet voice. "Hurry in to Bo. . . . An' don't worry. Try to think of things as I taught you up in the woods."

Helen heard his soft padded footfalls

swiftly pass away. She was left there, alone in the darkening twilight, suddenly cold and stricken, as if turned to stone.

Thus she stood an age-long moment until the upflashing truth galvanized her into action. Then she flew in pursuit of Dorn. The truth was that, in spite of Dorn's early training in the East and the long years of solitude that had made him wonderful in thought and feeling, he had also become a part of this raw bold and violent West.

It was quite dark now and she had run quite some distance before she saw Dorn's tall dark form against the yellow light of Turner's saloon. Somehow in that poignant moment, when her flying feet kept pace with her heart, Helen felt in herself a force opposing itself against this raw primitive justice of the West. She was one of the first influences emanating from civilized life, from law and order. In that flash of truth she saw the West as it would be some future time when through women and children these wild frontier days would be gone forever. Also, just as clearly she saw the present need of men like Roy Beeman and Dorn and the fire-blooded Carmichael. Beasley and his kind must be killed. But Helen did not want her lover, her future husband, and the probable father of her children, to commit what she held to be murder.

At the door of the saloon she caught up with Dorn. "Milt . . . oh . . . wait . . . wait!" she panted.

She heard him curse under his breath, as he turned. They were alone in the yellow glare of light. Horses were champing bits and drooping before the rails.

"You go back!" ordered Dorn sternly. His face was pale, his eyes were gleaming.

"No! Not till . . . you take me . . . or carry me," she replied resolutely, with all a woman's positive and inevitable assurance.

Then he laid hold of her with ungentle hands. His violence, especially the look on his face, terrified Helen, rendered her weak. But nothing could have shaken her resolve. She felt victory. Her sex, her love, and her presence would be too much for Dorn.

As he swung Helen around, the low hum of voices inside the saloon suddenly rose to a sharp hoarse roar accompanied by a scuffling of feet and crashing of violently sliding chairs or tables. Dorn let go of Helen and leaped toward the doors. But a silence inside, quicker and stranger than the roar, halted him. Helen's heart contracted, then seemed to cease beating. There was absolutely not a perceptible sound. Even the horses appeared, like Dorn, to have turned to statues.

Two thundering shots annihilated this silence. Then quickly came a lighter shot — the smash of glass. Dorn ran into the saloon. The horses began to snort, to rear, to pound. A low muffled murmur terrified Helen even as it drew her. Dashing at the door, she swung it in and entered.

The place was dim, blue-hazed, smelling of smoke. Dorn stood just inside the door. On the floor lay two men. Chairs and tables were overturned. A motley, dark, shirt-sleeved, booted, and belted crowd of men appeared hunched against the opposite wall with pale set faces turned to the bar. Turner, the proprietor, stood at one end, his hands aloft and shaking. Carmichael leaned against the middle of the bar. He held a gun low down. It was smoking.

With a gasp Helen flashed her eyes back to Dorn. He had seen her — was reaching an arm toward her. Then she saw the man lying almost at her feet. Jeff Mulvey — her uncle's old foreman! His face was awful to behold. A smoking gun lay near his inert hand. The other man had fallen on his face. His garb proclaimed him a Mexican. He was not yet dead. Then Helen, as she felt Dorn's arm encircle her, looked further because she could not prevent it — looked on at that strange figure against the bar — this boy who had been such a friend in her hour of need — this naïve and frank sweetheart of her sister's.

She saw a man now — wild, white, intense as fire, with some terrible cool kind of deadliness in his mien. His left elbow rested upon the bar, and his hand held a glass of red liquor. The big gun, low down in his other hand, seemed as steady as if it were a fixture.

"Heah's to thet . . . half-breed Beasley an' his outfit!"

Carmichael drank while his flaming eyes held the crowd, then with savage action of terrible passion he flung the glass at the quivering form of the still living Mexican on the floor.

Helen felt herself slipping. All seemed to darken around her. She could not see Dorn, although she knew he held her. Then she fainted.

CHAPTER
TWENTY-TWO

Las Vegas Carmichael was a product of his day.

The Panhandle of Texas, the old Chisholm Trail along which were driven the great cattle herds northward, Fort Dodge where the cowboys conflicted with the cardsharps — these hard places had left their marks on Carmichael. To come from Texas was to come from fighting stock and a cowboy's life was strenuous, wild, violent, and generally brief. The exceptions were the fortunate and the swiftest men with guns, and they drifted from south to north and west, taking with them the reckless chivalrous vitriolic spirit peculiar to their breed.

The pioneers and ranchers of the frontier would never have made the West habitable had it not been for these wild cowboys, these hard-drinking, hard-riding, hard-living rangers of the barrens, these easy, cool, laconic, simple young men whose blood was tinged with fire and who possessed the strange power to transform into a magnificent and terrible effrontery toward danger and death.

Las Vegas ran his horse from Widow Cass's cottage to Turner's saloon, and the hoofs of the goaded steed crashed in the door. Las Vegas's entrance was a leap. Then he stood still with the door ajar and the horse pounding and snorting back. All the men in that saloon who saw the entrance of Las Vegas knew what it portended. No thunderbolt could have more quickly checked the drinking, gambling, talking crowd. They recognized with kindred senses the nature of the man and his arrival. For a second the blue-hazed room was perfectly quiet, then men breathed, moved, rose, and suddenly caused a quick sliding crash of chairs and tables.

The cowboy's glittering eyes flashed to and fro, and then fixed on Mulvey and his Mexican companion. That glance singled out these two, and the sudden rush of nervous men proved it. Mulvey and the sheepherders were left alone in the center of the floor.

"Howdy, Jeff. Where's your boss?" asked Las Vegas. His voice was cool, friendly; his manner was easy, natural, but the look of him was what made Mulvey pale and the Mexican livid.

"Reckon he's home," replied Mulvey.

"Home? What's he call home now?"

"He's hangin' out hyar at Auchincloss's," replied Mulvey. His voice was not strong, but his eyes were steady, watchful.

Las Vegas quivered all over as if stung. A flame that seemed white and red gave his face a singular hue.

"Jeff, you worked for old Al a long time, an' I've heard of your differences," said Las Vegas. "Thet ain't no mix of mine. . . . But you double-crossed Miss Helen!"

Mulvey made no attempt to deny this. He gulped slowly. His hands appeared less steady, and he grew paler. Again Las Vegas's words signified less than his look. And that look now included the Mexican.

"Pedro, you're one of Beasley's old hands," said Las Vegas accusingly. "An' . . . you was one of them four greasers thet. . . ."

Here the cowboy choked and bit over his words as if they were a material poison. The Mexican showed his guilt and his cowardice. He began to jabber.

"Shet up!" hissed Las Vegas with a savage and significant jerk of his arm, as if about to strike. But that action was read for its true meaning. Pell-mell the crowd split to rush each way and leave an open space behind the three.

Las Vegas waited. But Mulvey seemed obstructed. The Mexican looked dangerous through his fear. His fingers twitched as if the tendons running up into his arms were being pulled.

An instant of suspense — more than long enough for Mulvey to be tried and found wanting — and Las Vegas, with laugh and sneer, turned his back upon the pair and stepped to the bar. His call for a bottle made Turner jump and hold it out with shaking hands. Las Vegas poured out a drink while his gaze was intent on the scarred old mirror hanging behind the bar.

This turning his back upon men he had just dared to draw showed what kind of a school Las Vegas had been trained in. If those men had been worthy antagonists of his class, he would never have scorned them. As it was, when Mulvey and the Mexican jerked at their guns, Las Vegas swiftly wheeled and shot twice. Mulvey's gun went off as he fell, and the Mexican doubled up in a heap on the floor. Then Las Vegas reached around with his left hand for the drink he had poured out.

At this juncture Dorn burst into the saloon suddenly to check his impetus, to swerve aside toward the bar, and halt. The door had not ceased swinging when again it was propelled inward, this time to admit Helen Rayner, white and wide-eyed.

In another moment then Las Vegas had spoken his deadly toast to Beasley's gang and had fiercely flung the glass at the writhing Mexican on the floor. Also, Dorn had gravitated toward the reeling Helen to catch her when she fainted.

Las Vegas began to curse, and, striding to Dorn, he pushed him out of the saloon.

". . . What're you doin' heah?" he yelled stridently. "Hevn't you got thet girl to think of? Then do it, you . . . big Indian! Lettin' her run after you heah . . . riskin' herself thet way! You take care of her an' Bo, an' leave this deal to me!"

The cowboy, furious as he was at Dorn, yet had keen swift eyes for the horses at hand and the men out in the dim light. Dorn lifted the girl into his arms and, turning without a word, stalked away to disappear in the darkness. Las Vegas, holding his gun low, returned to the barroom. If there had been any change in the crowd, it was slight, but the tension had relaxed. Turner no longer stood with hands up.

"You-all go on with your fun!" called the cowboy with a sweep of his gun. "But it'd be risky fer anyone to start leavin'."

With that, he backed against the bar, near where the black bottle stood. Turner walked out to begin righting tables and chairs, and presently the crowd, with some caution and suspense, resumed their games and drinking. It was significant that a wide berth lay between them and the door. From time to time Turner served liquor to men who called for it.

Las Vegas leaned with back against the bar. After a while he sheathed his gun and reached around for the bottle. He drank with his piercing eyes upon the door. No one entered and no one went out. The games of chance there and the drinking were not enjoyed. It was a hard scene — that smoky, long, ill-smelling room with its dim yellow lights and dark evil faces, with the stealthy-stepping Turner staring in horrible fixity at the ceiling, and the Mexican quivering more and more until he shook violently, then lay still, and with the drinking somber waiting cowboy, more fiery and more flaming with every drink, listening for a step that did not come.

Time passed, and what little change they wrought was in the cowboy. Drink affected him, but he did not become drunk. It seemed that the liquor he drank was consumed by a mounting fire. It was fuel to a driving passion. He grew more sullen, somber, brooding, redder of eye and face, more crouching and restless. At last, when the hour was so late that there was no probability of Beasley's appearing, Las Vegas flung himself out of the saloon.

All lights of the village had now been extinguished. The tired horses drooped in the darkness. Las Vegas found his horse and led him away down the road and out a lane to a field where a barn stood, dim and dark, in the starlight. Morning was not far off. He unsaddled the horse and, turning him loose, went into the barn. Here he seemed familiar with his surroundings, for he found a ladder and climbed to a loft, where he threw himself on the hay.

He rested, but did not sleep. At daylight he went down and brought his horse into the barn. Sunrise found Las Vegas pacing to and fro the short length of the interior, and peering out through wide cracks between the boards. Then during the succeeding couple of hours he watched the occasional horseman and wagon and herder that passed on into the village.

About the breakfast hour Las Vegas saddled his horse and rode back the way he had come the night before. At Turner's he called for something to eat as well as for whiskey. After that he became a listening, watching machine. He drank freely for an hour, then he stopped. He seemed to be drunk, but with a different kind of drunkenness from that usual in drinking men. Savage, fierce, sullen, he was one to avoid. Turner waited on him in evident fear.

At length Las Vegas's condition became such that action was involuntary. He could not stand still or sit down. Stalking out, he passed the store, where men slouched back to avoid him, and he went down the road, wary and alert, as if he expected a rifle shot from some hidden enemy. Upon his return down that main thoroughfare of the village not a person was to be seen. He went back into Turner's. The proprietor was there at his post, nervous and pale. Las Vegas did not order any more liquor.

"Turner, I reckon I'll bore you next time I run in heah," he said, and stalked out.

He had the stores, the road, the village to himself, and he patrolled a beat like a sentry watching for an Indian attack.

Toward noon a single man ventured out into the road to accost the cowboy.

"Las Vegas, I'm tellin' you . . . all the greasers air leavin' the range," he said.

"Howdy, Abe," replied Las Vegas. "What'n

hell you talkin' aboot?"

The man repeated his information. And Las Vegas spat out frightful curses.

"Abe . . . you heah what Beasley's doin'?"

"Yes. He's with his men . . . up at the ranch. Reckon he can't put off ridin' down much longer."

That was where the West spoke. Beasley would be forced to meet the enemy who had come out single-handedly against him. Long before this hour a braver man would have come to face Las Vegas. Beasley could not hire any gang to bear the brunt of this situation. This was the test by which even his own men must judge him. All of which was to say that as the wildness of the West had made possible his crimes so it now held him responsible for them.

"Abe, if thet . . . greaser don't rustle down heah, I'm goin' after him."

"Sure. But don't be in no hurry," replied Abe.

"I'm waltzin' to slow music. . . . Gimme a smoke."

With fingers that slightly trembled Abe rolled a cigarette, lit it from his own, and handed it to the cowboy.

"Las Vegas, I reckon I hear hosses," he said suddenly.

"Me, too," replied Las Vegas with his head

held high like that of a listening deer. Apparently he forgot the cigarette and also his friend. Abe hurried back to the store, where he disappeared.

Las Vegas began his stalking up and down, and his action now was an exaggeration of all his former movements. A rational ordinary mortal from some Eastern community, happening to meet this red-faced cowboy, would have considered him drunk or crazy. Probably Las Vegas looked both. But all the same he was a marvelously keen and strung and efficient instrument to meet the portending issue. How many thousands of times, on the trails, and in the wide-streeted little towns all over the West had this stalk of the cowboy's been perpetrated! Violent, bloody, tragic as it was, it had an importance in that pioneer day equal to the use of a horse or the need of a plow.

At length Pine was apparently a deserted village, except for Las Vegas, who patrolled his long beat in many strange ways — he lounged while he watched; he stalked like a mountaineer; he stole along Indian fashion, stealthily, from tree to tree, from corner to corner; he disappeared in the saloon to reappear at the back; he went through the yards of the villagers and slipped around behind the barns to come out again in the main road; and time after time he approached his horse as if deciding to mount.

The last visit he made into Turner's saloon, he found no one there. Savagely he pounded on the bar with his gun. He got no response. Then the long pent-up rage burst. With wild whoops he pulled another gun and shot at the mirror, the lamps. He shot the neck off a bottle and drank till he choked, his neck corded, bulging and purple. His only slow and deliberate action was the reloading of his gun. Then he crashed through the doors, and with a wild yell leaped sheerly into the saddle, hauling his horse up high and goading him to plunge away.

Men running to the doors and windows of the store saw a streak of dust flying down the road. And then they trooped out to see it disappear. The hour of suspense ended for them. Las Vegas had lived up to the code of the West, had dared his man out, had waited far longer than needful to prove that man a coward. Whatever the issue now, Beasley was branded forever. That moment saw the decline of whatever power he had wielded. He and his men might kill the cowboy who had ridden out alone to face him, but that would not change the brand.

■ ■ ■ ■

The preceding night Beasley had been finishing a late supper at his newly acquired ranch when Buck Weaver, one of his men, burst in upon him with news of the deaths of Mulvey and Pedro.

"Who's in the outfit? How many?" he had questioned quickly.

"It's a one-man outfit, boss," replied Weaver.

Beasley appeared astounded. He and his men had prepared to meet the friends of the girl whose property he had taken over, and because of the superiority of his own force, he had anticipated no bloody or extended feud. This amazing circumstance put the case in very much more difficult form.

"One man!" he ejaculated.

"Yep. Thet cowboy Las Vegas. An', boss, he turns out to be a gunslinger from Texas. I was in Turner's. Hed jest happened to step in the other room when Las Vegas come bustin' in on his hoss an' jumped off. . . . First thing, he called Jeff an' Pedro. Then both showed yaller. . . . An' then, damn' if thet cowboy didn't turn his back on them an' went to the bar fer a drink. But he was lookin' in the mirror, an', when Jeff an' Pedro went for their guns, why he whirled quick as lightnin' an' bored them both. . . . I sneaked out an'. . . ."

"Why didn't you bore him?" roared Beasley.

Buck Weaver steadily eyed his boss before he replied.

"I ain't takin' shots at any fellar from behind doors. An' as fer meetin' Las Vegas . . . excoose me, boss! I've still a hankerin' fer sunshine an' red liquor. Besides, I ain't got nothin' ag'in' Las Vegas. If he'd rustled over here at the head of a crowd to put us off, I'd fight, jest as we'd all fight. But you see we figgered wrong. It's between you an' Las Vegas! You oughter have seen him throw thet hunter Dorn out of Turner's."

"Dorn? Did he come?" queried Beasley.

"He got there jest after the cowboy plugged Jeff. An' thet big-eyed girl, she came runnin' in, too, an' she keeled over in Dorn's arms. Las Vegas shoved him out . . . cussed him so hard we all heerd. . . . So Beasley there ain't no fight comin' off as we figgered on."

Beasley thus heard the West speak out of the mouth of his own man. And grim, sardonic, almost scornful indeed were the words of Buck Weaver. This rider had once worked for Al Auchincloss and had deserted to Beasley under Mulvey's leadership. Mulvey was dead and the situation was vastly changed.

Beasley gave Weaver a dark lowering glance and waved him away. From the door, Weaver sent back a doubtful scrutinizing gaze, then slouched out. That gaze Beasley had not encountered before.

It meant, as Weaver's cronies meant, as Beasley's long-faithful riders, and the people of the range, and as the spirit of the West meant, that Beasley was expected to march down into the village to face his single foe.

But Beasley did not go. Instead, he paced to and fro the length of Helen Rayner's long sitting room with the nervous energy of a man who could not rest. Many times he hesitated and at others he made sudden movements toward the door, only to halt. Not improbably he had not absolutely decided for or against this call for hours. Long after midnight he went to bed, but not to sleep. He tossed and rolled all night, and at dawn arose, gloomy and irritable.

He cursed the Mexican serving women who showed their displeasure at his authority. And to his amaze and rage not one of his men came to the house. He waited and waited. Then he stalked off to the corrals and stables, carrying a rifle with him. The men were there, in a group that dispersed somewhat at his advent. Not a Mexican was in sight.

Beasley ordered the horses to be saddled and all hands to go down into the village with him. That order was disobeyed. Beasley stormed and raged. His riders sat or lounged with lowered faces. An unspoken hostility seemed present. Those who had been longest with him were least distant and strange, but still they did not obey. At length Beasley roared for his Mexicans.

"Boss, we gotta tell you that every greaser on the ranch has sloped . . . gone these two hours . . . on the way to Magdalena," said Buck Weaver.

Of all these sudden uprising perplexities this latest was the most astonishing. Beasley cursed with his questioning wonder.

"Boss, they was sure scared of thet gun-slingin' cowboy from Texas," replied Weaver imperturbably.

Beasley's dark swarthy face changed its hue. What of the subtle reflection in Weaver's slow speech? One of the men came out of a corral leading Beasley's saddled and bridled horse. This fellow dropped the bridle and sat down among his comrades without a word. No one spoke. The presence of the horse was significant. With a snarling muttered curse Beasley took up his rifle and strode back to the ranch house.

In his rage and passion he did not realize what his men had known for hours — that, if he had stood any chance at all for their respect, as well as for his life, the hour was long past.

Beasley avoided the open paths to the house, and, when he got there, he nervously poured out a drink. Evidently something in the fiery liquor frightened him for he threw the bottle aside. It was as if that bottle contained a courage that was false.

Again he paced the long sitting room, growing more and more wrought up as evidently he grew familiar with the singular state of affairs. Twice, a pale serving woman called him to dinner.

The dining room was light and pleasant, and the meal, fragrant and steaming, was ready for him. But the women had disappeared. Beasley seated himself . . . spread out his big hands on the table.

Then a slight rustle — a *clink* of spur — startled him. He twisted his head.

"Howdy, Beasley," said Las Vegas, who had appeared as if by magic.

Beasley's frame seemed to swell as if a flood had been loosed in his veins. Sweat drops stood out on his pallid face.

"What . . . you . . . want?" he asked huskily.

"Wal, now, my boss, Miss Helen, says, seein' I am foreman heah, thet it'd be nice an' proper fer me to drop in an' eat with you . . . the *last time*," replied the cowboy. His drawl was slow and cool, his tone was friendly and pleasant. But his look was that of a falcon ready to drive deep its beak.

Beasley's reply was loud, incoherent, hoarse.

Las Vegas seated himself across from Beasley.

"Eat or not, it's shore all the same to me," said Las Vegas, and he began to load his plate with his left hand. His right hand rested very lightly, with just the tips of his vibrating fingers on the edge of the table, and he never for the slightest fraction of a second took his piercing eyes off Beasley.

"Wal, my half-breed greaser guest, it shore roils up my blood to see you sittin' there . . . thinkin' you've put my boss, Miss Helen, off this ranch," began Las Vegas softly. And then he helped himself leisurely to food and drink. "In my day I've shore stacked up against a lot of outlaws, thieves, rustlers, an' sich like, but fer an' out an' out dirty low-down skunk, you shore take the dough! I'm goin' to kill you in a minnit or so, jest as soon as you move one of them dirty paws of your'n. But I'll hope you'll be polite an' let me say a few words. I'll never be happy again if you don't. . . . Of all the . . . yaller greaser dogs I ever seen, you're the wurst! I was thinkin' last night, mebbe you'd come down an' meet me like a man, so's I could wash my hands ever afterward without gettin' sick to my stummick. . . . But you didn't come. . . . Beasley, I'm so ashamed of myself thet I gotta call you . . . when I ought to bore you, thet . . . I ain't even second cousin to my old self when I rode the Chisholm. It don't mean nuthin' to you to call you liar! Robber! Black-leg! A sneakin' coyote! An' a cheat that hires others to do his dirty work! By God!"

"Carmichael, gimme a word in," hoarsely broke out Beasley. "You're right, it won't do no good to call me. . . . But let's talk. . . . I'll buy you off. Ten thousand dollars. . . ."

"Haw! Haw! Haw!" roared Las Vegas. He was as tense as a strung cord and his face possessed singular pale radiance. His right hand began to quiver more and more.

"I'll . . . double . . . it!" panted Beasley. "I'll . . . make over . . . half the ranch . . .

510

all the stock. . . ."

"Swaller thet!" yelled Las Vegas with terrible strident ferocity.

"Listen . . . man! I take . . . it back! I'll give up . . . Auchincloss's ranch!" Beasley was now a shaking, whispering, frenzied man, ghastly white, with rolling eyes.

Las Vegas's left fist pounded hard on the table. "Greaser, come on!" he thundered.

Then Beasley, with desperate, frantic action, jerked for his gun.

CHAPTER TWENTY-THREE

For Helen Rayner that brief dark period of
her expulsion from her home had become a
thing of the past, almost forgotten.

Two months had flown by on the wings of
love and work, and the joy of finding her
place there in the West. All her old men had
been only too glad of the opportunity to
come back to her, and, under Dorn and Roy
Beeman, a different and prosperous order
marked the life of the ranch.

Helen had made changes in the house, by
altering the arrangement of rooms and add-
ing a new section. Only once had she
ventured into the old dining room where
Las Vegas Carmichael had sat down to that
tragic and fatal dinner for Beasley. She
made a storeroom of it, and a place she
would never again enter.

Helen was happy, almost too happy she
thought, and to that end made more than
needful of the several bitter drops in her

sweet cup of life. Carmichael had ridden out of Pine, ostensibly on the trail of the Mexicans who had executed Beasley's commands. The last seen of him had been reported from Show Down, where he had appeared, red-eyed and dangerous, like a hound on a scent. Then two months had flown by without a word.

Dorn had shaken his head doubtfully when interrogated about the cowboy's absence. It would be just like Las Vegas never to be heard of again. Also it would be more like him to remain away until all trace of his drunken savage spell had departed from him and had been forgotten by his friends. Bo took his disappearance apparently less to heart than Helen. But Bo grew more restless, wilder and more willful than ever. Helen thought she guessed Bo's secret, and, once, she ventured a hint concerning Carmichael's return.

"If Tom doesn't come back pretty soon, I'll marry Milt Dorn," retorted Bo tauntingly.

This fired Helen's cheeks with red. "But, child!" she protested, half angry, half grave. "Milt and I are engaged."

"Sure. Only you're so slow. There's many a slip . . . you know."

"Bo, I tell you Tom will come back,"

replied Helen earnestly. "I feel it. There was something fine in that cowboy. He understood me better than you or Milt, either . . . And he was perfectly wild in love with you."

"Oh! *Was* he?"

"Very much more than you deserved, Bo Rayner."

Then occurred one of Bo's sweet, bewildering, unexpected transformations. Her defiance, resentment, rebelliousness vanished from a softly agitated face.

"Oh, Nell. I know that. . . . You just watch me if I ever get another chance at him! Then . . . maybe he'd never drink again!"

"Bo, be happy . . . and be good. Don't ride off any more . . . don't tease the boys. . . . It'll all come right in the end."

Bo recovered her equanimity quickly enough.

"*Humph!* You can afford to be cheerful. You've got a man who can't live when you're out of his sight. He's like a fish on dry land. . . . And you . . . why, once you were an old pessimist!"

Bo was not to be consoled or changed. Helen could only sigh and pray that her convictions would be verified.

The first day of July brought an early thunderstorm, just at sunrise. It roared and flared and rolled away, leaving a gorgeous golden cloud pageant in the sky, and a fresh, sweetly smelling glistening green range that delighted Helen's eye.

Birds were *twittering* in the arbors and bees were *humming* in the flowers. From the fields down along the brook came a blended song of swamp blackbird and meadowlark. A clarion-voiced burro split the air with his coarse and homely bray. The sheep were bleating, and a soft *baa* of little lambs came sweetly to Helen's ears. She went her usual rounds with more than usual zest and thrill. Everywhere was color, activity, life. The wind swept warm and pine-scented down from the mountain heights, now black and bold, and the great green slopes seemed to call her.

At that very moment she came suddenly upon Dorn, in his shirt sleeves, dusty and hot, standing motionlessly, gazing at the distant mountains. Helen's greeting startled him.

"I . . . I was just looking away yonder," he said, smiling.

She thrilled at the clear wonderful light of his eyes. "So was I . . . a moment ago," she replied wistfully. "Do you miss the forest . . . very much?"

"Nell, I miss nothing. . . . But I'd like to

ride with you under the pines once more."

"We'll go!" she cried.

"When?" he asked eagerly.

"Oh . . . soon!" And then with flushed face and downcast eyes she passed on. For long Helen had cherished a fond hope that she might be married in Paradise Park where she had fallen in love with Dorn and had realized herself. But she had kept that hope secret. Dorn's eager tone, his flashing eyes had made her feel that her secret was there in her telltale face.

As she entered the lane leading to the house, she encountered one of the new stable boys driving a pack mule.

"Jim, whose pack is that?" she asked.

"Ma'am, I dunno, but I heered him tell Roy he reckoned his name was mud," replied the boy, smiling.

Helen's heart gave a quick throb. That sounded like Las Vegas. She hurried on, and, upon entering the courtyard, she espied Roy Beeman holding the halter of a beautiful wild-looking mustang. There was another horse with another man, who was in the act of dismounting on the far side. When he stepped into better view, Helen recognized Las Vegas. And he saw her at the same instant.

Helen did not look up again until she was

near the porch. She had dreaded this meeting, yet she was so glad that she could have cried aloud.

"Miss Helen, I shore am glad to see you," he said, standing bareheaded before her, the same young, frank-faced cowboy she had seen first from the train.

"Tom!" she exclaimed, and offered her hands.

He wrung them hard while he looked at her. The swift woman's glance Helen flashed in return seemed to shudder something dark and doubtful out of her heart. This was the same boy she had known — who she had liked so well — who had won her sister's love. Helen imagined facing him thus was like awakening from a vague nightmare of doubt. Carmichael's face was clean, fresh, young, with its healthy tan; it wore the old glad smile, cool, easy, and natural; his eyes were like Dorn's, penetrating, clear as crystal, without a shadow. What had evil, drink, blood to do with the real inherent nobility of this splendid specimen of Western hardihood? Wherever he had been, whatever he had done during that long absence, he had returned long separated from that wild and savage character she could now forget.

"How's my girl?" he asked, just as naturally as if he had been gone a few days on some errand of his employers.

"Bo? Oh, she's well . . . fine. I . . . I rather think she'll be glad to see you," replied Helen warmly.

"An' how's thet big Indian, Dorn?" he drawled.

"Well, too . . . I'm sure."

"Reckon I got back heah in time to see you-all married?"

"I . . . I assure you I . . . no one around here has been married yet," replied Helen with a blush.

"Thet shore is fine. Was some worried," he said lazily. "I've been chasin' wild horses over in New Mexico, an' I got after this heah blue roan. He kept me chasin' him fer a spell. I've fetched him back for Bo."

Helen looked at the mustang Roy was holding, to be instantly delighted. He was a roan almost blue in color, neither large nor heavy, but powerfully built, clean-limbed and racy, with a long mane and tail, black as coal, and a beautiful head that made Helen love him at once.

"Well, I'm jealous," declared Helen archly. "I never did see such a pony."

"I reckoned you'd never ride any hoss but Ranger," said Las Vegas.

"No, I never will. But I can be jealous

anyhow, can't I?"

"Shore, an' I reckon if you say you're goin' to have him . . . wal, Bo'd be funny," he drawled.

"I reckon she would be funny," retorted Helen. She was so happy that she imitated his speech. She wanted to hug him. It was too good to be true — the return of this cowboy. He understood her. He had come back with nothing that could alienate her. He had apparently forgotten the terrible rôle he had accepted and the doom he had meted out to her enemies. That moment was wonderful for Helen in its revelation of the strange significance of the West as embodied in this cowboy. He was great. But he did not know that.

Then the door of the living room opened and a sweet high voice pealed out: "Roy! Oh, what a mustang! Whose is he?"

"Wal, Bo, if all I hear is so, he belongs to you," replied Roy with a huge grin.

Bo appeared in the door. She stepped out upon the porch. She saw the cowboy. The excited flash of her pretty face vanished as she paled.

"Bo, I shore was glad to see you," drawled Las Vegas as he stepped forward, sombrero in hand. Helen could not see any sign of confusion in him. But indeed she saw gladness. Then she expected to behold Bo run right into the cowboy's arms. It appeared, however, that she was doomed to disappointment.

"Tom, I'm glad to see you," she replied.

They shook hands as old friends.

"You're lookin' right fine," he said.

"Oh, I'm well. . . . And how have you been these six months?" she queried.

"Reckon I thought it was longer," he drawled "Wal, I'm pretty tip-top now, but I was laid up with heart trouble for a spell."

"Heart trouble?" she echoed dubiously.

"Shore. . . . I ate too much over there in New Mexico."

"It's no news to me . . . where your heart's located." Bo laughed. Then she ran off the porch to see the blue mustang. She walked around and around him, clasping her hands in sheer delight.

"Bo, he's a plumb dandy," said Roy. "Never seen a prettier hoss. He'll run like a streak. An' he's got good eyes. He'll be a pet someday. But I reckon he'll always be spunky."

Bo ventured to step closer and at last got a hand on the mustang, and then another. She smoothed his quivering neck and called softly to him, until he submitted to her hold.

"What's his name?" she asked.

"Blue somethin' or other," replied Roy.

"Tom, has my new mustang a name?" asked Bo, turning to the cowboy.

"Shore."

"What then?"

"Wal, I named him Blue-Bo," answered Las Vegas, with a smile.

"Blue-Boy?"

"Nope. He's named after you . . . an' I chased him, roped him, broke him all myself."

"Very well. Blue-Bo he is then. . . . And he's a wonderful darling horse. . . . Oh, Nell, just look at him. . . . Tom, I can't thank you enough."

"Reckon I don't want any thanks," drawled the cowboy. "But see heah, Bo, you shore get to live up to conditions before you ride him."

"What!" exclaimed Bo, who was startled by his slow cool meaning tone of voice.

Helen delighted in looking at Las Vegas then. He had never appeared to better advantage. So cool, careless, and assured! He seemed master of a situation in which his terms must be accepted. Yet as well he might have been actuated by a cowboy motive, beyond the power of Helen to divine.

"Bo Rayner," drawled Las Vegas, "thet blue mustang will be yours an' you can ride him . . . when you're *Missus Tom Carmichael!"*

Never had he spoken a softer, more drawling speech, nor gazed at Bo more wildly. Roy seemed thunderstruck. Helen endeavored heroically to restrain her delicious bursting glee. Bo's wide eyes stared at her lover — darkened — dilated. Suddenly she left the mustang to confront the cowboy where he lounged on the porch steps.

"Do you mean that?" she cried.

"Shore do."

"Bah! It's only a magnificent bluff," she retorted. "You're only in fun. It's your . . . your darned nerve!"

"Why, Bo," began Las Vegas reproachfully, "you shore know I'm not the four-flusher kind. . . . Never got away with a bluff in my life! An' I'm jest in daid earnest aboot this heah."

All the same, signs were not wanting in his mobile face that he was almost unable to restrain his mirth.

Helen realized then that Bo saw through the cowboy — that the ultimatum was only one of his tricks.

"It *is* a bluff and I *call* you!" declared Bo ringingly.

Las Vegas suddenly awoke to direful and doubtful consequences. He assayed to speak, but she was so wonderful then, so white and blazing-eyed and charged with radiant fire, that he was stricken mute.

"I'll ride Blue-Bo this afternoon," deliberately stated the girl.

Las Vegas had wit enough to grasp her meaning and he seemed about to collapse.

"Very well, you can make me Missus Tom Carmichael today . . . this morning . . . just before dinner. . . . Go get a preacher to marry us . . . and make yourself look a more presentable bridegroom . . . *unless it was only a bluff!*"

Her imperiousness changed as the tremendous portent of her words seemed to make Las Vegas a blank stone image of a man. With a wild rose color suffusing her face she swiftly bent over him, kissed him, and flashed away into the house. Her laugh pealed back, and it thrilled Helen, so deep and strange was it for the willful sister, so wild and merry and full of joy.

It was then that Roy Beeman recovered from his paralysis to let out such a roar of mirth as to frighten the horses. Helen was laughing and crying, too, but laughing mostly. Las Vegas Carmichael was a sight for the gods to behold. Bo's kiss had unclamped what had bound him. The sudden truth, undeniable, insupportable, glorious, made him a madman.

"Bluff . . . she called me . . . ride Blue-Bo saf'ternoon!" he raved, reaching wildly for Helen. "Missus . . . Tom . . . Carmichael . . . before dinner . . . preacher . . . presentable bridegroom! *Aw!* I'm drunk again! I . . . who swore off . . . forever!"

"No, Tom, you're just happy," said Helen.

Between her and Roy the cowboy was at length persuaded to accept the situation and to see his wonderful opportunity.

"Now . . . now, Miss Helen . . . what'd Bo mean by pre-presentable bridegroom? Presents? Lord, I'm clean busted flat!"

"She meant you must dress up in your best, of course," replied Helen.

"Where on earth will I get a preacher? Show Down's forty miles. . . . Can't ride there in time. . . . Roy, I've gotta have a preacher. . . . Life or death deal fer me."

"Wal, old man, if you'll brace up, I'll marry you to Bo," said Roy with his glad grin.

"Aw!" gasped Las Vegas, as if at the fall of a sudden beautiful hope.

"Tom, I'm a preacher," replied Roy now earnestly. "You didn't know that, but I am. An' I can marry you an' Bo as good as anyone, an' tighter'n most."

Las Vegas reached for his friend as a

drowning man might have reached for solid rock.

"Roy, can you really marry them . . . with my Bible . . . and the service of my church?" asked Helen, a happy hope flushing her face.

"Wal, indeed I can. I've married more'n one couple whose religion wasn't mine."

"B-b-before . . . d-d-din-ner!" burst out Las Vegas, like a stuttering idiot.

"I reckon. Come on, now, an' make yourself pre-sent-tible," said Roy. "Miss Helen, you tell Bo thet it's all settled."

He picked up the halter on the blue mustang, and turned away toward the corrals. Las Vegas put the bridle of his horse over his arm, and seemed to be following in a trance, with his dazed rapt face held high.

"Bring Dorn!" called Helen softly after them.

So it came about as naturally as it was wonderful that Bo rode the blue mustang before the afternoon ended.

Las Vegas disobeyed his first orders from Mrs. Tom Carmichael and rode out after her toward the green rising range. Helen seemed impelled to follow. She did not need to ask Dorn the second time. They rode swiftly but never caught up with Bo and Las

Vegas, whose riding resembled their happiness.

Dorn read Helen's mind, or else his own thoughts were in harmony with hers, for he always seemed to speak what she was thinking. And as they rode homeward, he asked her in his quiet way if they could not spare a few days to visit his old camp.

"And take Bo . . . and Tom? Oh, of all things I'd like to," she replied.

"Yes . . . an' Roy, too," added Dorn significantly.

"Of course," said Helen lightly, as if she had not caught his meaning. But she turned her eyes away, while her heart thumped disgracefully, and all her body was aglow. "Will Tom and Bo go?"

"It was Tom who got me to ask you," replied Dorn. "John an' Hal can look after the men while we're gone."

"Oh . . . so Tom put it in your head? I guess . . . maybe . . . I won't go."

"It is always in my mind, Nell," he said with his slow seriousness. "I'm goin' to work all my life for you. But I'll want to an' need to go back to the woods often. . . . An' if you stoop to marry me . . . an' make me the richest of men . . . you'll have to marry me up there where I fell in love with you."

"*Ah!* Did Las Vegas Tom Carmichael say

526

that, too?" inquired Helen softly.

"Nell, do you want to know what Las Vegas said?"

"By all means."

"He said this . . . an' not an hour ago . . . 'Milt, old hoss, let me give you a hunch. I'm a man of family now . . . an' I've been a devil with the wimmin in my day. I can see through 'em. Don't you marry Nell Rayner in or near the house where I killed Beasley. She'd remember. An' don't let her remember thet day. Go off into the woods. Paradise Park! Bo an' me will go with you.' "

Helen gave him her hand while they walked the horses homeward in the long sunset shadows. In the fullness of that happy hour she had time for a grateful wonder at the keen penetration of the cowboy Carmichael. Dorn had saved her life, but it was Las Vegas who had saved her happiness.

Not many days later, when again the afternoon shadows were slanting low, Helen rode out upon the promontory where the dim trail zigzagged far above Paradise Park.

Roy was singing as he drove the pack burros down the slope. Bo and Las Vegas were trying to ride the trail two abreast so they could hold hands; Dorn had dismounted to stand beside Helen's horse, as she gazed down the shaggy black slopes to the beautiful wild park with its gray meadows and shining ribbons of brooks.

It was July and there were no golden red flames and blazes of color such as lingered in Helen's memory. Black spruce slopes and green pines and white streaks of aspens and lacy waterfall of foam and dark outcroppings of rock — these colors and forms greeted her gaze with all the old enchantment. Wildness, beauty, and loneliness were there, the same as ever, immutable like the spirit of those heights.

Helen would fain have lingered longer, but the others called, and Ranger impatiently snorted his sense of the grass and water far below. And she knew that, when she climbed there again to the wide outlook, she would be another woman.

"Nell, come on," said Dorn as he led on. "It's better to look up."

The sun had just sunk behind the ragged fringe of mountain rim when those three strong and efficient men of the open had pitched camp and had prepared a bountiful supper.

Then Roy Beeman took out the little worn Bible that Helen had given him to use when he married Bo, and, as he opened it, a light changed his dark face.

"Come, Helen an' Dorn," he said.

They arose to stand before him. And he married them there under the great stately pines, with the fragrant blue smoke curling upwards, and the wind singing through the branches, while the waterfall murmured its low soft dreamy music, and from the dark slope came the wild lonely cry of a wolf, full of the hunger for life and a mate.

"Let us pray," said Roy, as he closed the Bible, and knelt with them.

"There is only one God, an' Him I beseech in my humble office for the woman an' man I have just wedded in holy bonds. Bless them an' watch them an' keep them through all the comin' years. Bless the sons of this strong man of the woods an' make them like him, with love an' understandin' of the source from which life comes. Bless the daughters of this woman an' send with them more of her love an' soul, which must be the softenin' an' the salvation of the hard West. Oh, Lord, blaze the dim dark trail for them through the unknown forest of life! Oh, Lord, lead the way across the naked range of the future no mortal knows! We ask in Thy name! Amen."

When the preacher stood up again and

raised the couple from their kneeling posture, it seemed that a grave and solemn personage had left him. This young man was again the dark-faced, clear-eyed Roy, droll and dry, with the enigmatic smile on his lips.

"Missus Dorn," he said, taking her hands. "I wish you joy. . . . An' now after this here, my crownin' service in your behalf . . . I reckon I'll claim a reward."

Then he kissed her. Bo came next with her warm and loving felicitations, and the cowboy, with characteristic action, also made at Helen.

"Nell, shore it's the only chance I'll ever have to kiss you," he drawled. "Because when this heah big Indian once finds out what kissin' is . . . !"

Las Vegas then proved how swift and hearty he could be upon occasions. All this left Helen red and confused and unutterably happy. She appreciated Dorn's state. His eyes reflected the previous treasure that manifestly he saw, but realization of ownership had not yet become demonstrable.

Then with gay speech and happy laugh and silent look these five partook of the supper. When it was finished, Roy made known his intention to leave. They all protested and coaxed, but to no avail. He only laughed and went on saddling his horse.

"Roy, please stay," implored Helen. "The day's almost ended. You're tired."

"Nope. I'll never be no third party when there's only two!"

"But there are four of us."

"Didn't I just make you an' Dorn one? An', Missus Dorn, you forget I've been married often."

Helen found herself confronted by an unanswerable side of the argument. Las Vegas rolled in the grass in his mirth. Dorn looked strange.

"Roy, then that's why you're so nice," said Bo, with a little devil in her eyes. "Do you know I had my mind made up? If Tom hadn't come around, I was going to make up to you, Roy. . . . I sure was. . . . What number wife would I have been?"

It always took Bo to turn the tables on anybody. Roy looked mightily embarrassed. And the laugh was on him. He did not face them again until he had mounted.

"Las Vegas, I've done my best for you . . . hitched you to that blue-eyed girl the best I knowed how," he declared. "But I shore ain't guaranteein' nothin'! You'd better build a corral for her."

"Why, Roy, you shore don't savvy the way to break these wild ones," drawled Las

Vegas. "Bo will be eatin' out of my hand in aboot a week."

Bo's blue eyes expressed an eloquent doubt as to this extraordinary claim.

"Good bye, friends," said Roy, and rode away to disappear in the spruces.

Thereupon Bo and Las Vegas forgot Roy, and Dorn and Helen, the camp chores to be done, and everything else except themselves. Helen's first wifely duty was to insist that she should and could and would help her husband with the work of cleaning up after the sumptuous supper. Before they had finished, a sound startled them. It came from Roy, evidently high on the darkening slope, and was a long mellow pealing "halloo" that rang on the cool air, burst the dreamy silence, and rapped across from slope to slope and cliff to cliff to lose its power and die away hauntingly in the distant recesses.

Dorn shook his head as if he did not care to attempt a reply to that beautiful call. Silence once again enfolded the park and twilight seemed to be born of the air, drifting downward.

"Nell, do you miss anythin'?" asked Dorn.

"No. Nothing in all the world," she murmured. "I am happier than I ever dared pray to be."

"I don't mean people or things. I mean my pets."

"*Ah!* I had forgotten. . . . Milt, where are they?"

"Gone back to the wild," he said. "They had to live in my absence. An' I've been away long."

Just then the brooding silence, with its soft murmur of falling water and faint sigh of wind in the pines, was broken by a piercing scream, high, quivering, like that of a woman in exquisite agony.

"That's Tom!" exclaimed Dorn.

"Oh . . . I was so . . . so frightened," whispered Helen.

Bo came running, with Las Vegas at her heels.

"Milt, that was your tame cougar," cried Bo excitedly. "Oh, I'll never forget him! I'll hear those cries in my dreams!"

"Yes, it was Tom," said Dorn thoughtfully. "But I never heard him cry just like that."

"Oh, call him in!"

Dorn whistled and called, but Tom did not come. Then the hunter stalked off into the gloom to call from different points under the slope. After a while he returned without the cougar. And at that moment from far up in the dark ravine drifted down the same wild cry, only changed by distance, strange and tragic in its meaning.

"He scented us. He remembers. But he'll never come back," said Dorn.

Helen felt stirred anew with convictions of Dorn's deep knowledge of life and Nature. And her imagination seemed to have wings. How full and perfect her trust, her happiness in the realization that her love and her future, her children, and perhaps grandchildren, would come under the guidance of such a man! Only a little had she begun to comprehend the secrets of good and ill in their relation to the laws of Nature. Ages before men had lived on the earth, there had been the creatures of the wilderness, and the holes of the rocks and the nests of the trees, and rain, frost, heat, dew, sunlight, and night, storm and calm, the honey of the wild flower and the instinct of the bee — all the beautiful and multiple forms of life with their inscrutable design. To know something of them and to love them was to be close to the kingdom of earth — perhaps to the greater kingdom of heaven. For whatever breathed and moved was a part of that creation. The coo of the dove, the lichen on the mossy rock, the mourn of a hunting wolf, and the murmur of the waterfall, the ever-green and growing tips of the spruces and the thunderbolts along the battlements of the heights — these one and all must be actuated by the Great Spirit — that incalculable thing in the universe that had produced man and soul.

And there in the starlight, under the wide gnarled pines, sighing low with the wind, Helen sat with Dorn on the old stone that an avalanche of a million years past had flung from the rampart above to serve as camp table and bench for lovers in the wilderness. The sweet scent of spruce mingled with the fragrance of wood smoke, blown in their faces. How white the stars, and calm and true! How they blazed their single task! A coyote yelped off on the south slope, dark now as midnight. A bit of weathered rock rolled and tapped from shelf to shelf. And the wind moaned. Helen felt all the sadness and mystery and nobility of this lonely fastness, and full on her heart rested the supreme consciousness that all would someday be well with the troubled world beyond.

"Nell, I'll homestead this park," said Dorn. "Then it'll always be ours."

"Homestead! What's that?" murmured Helen dreamily. The word sounded sweet.

"The government will give land to men who locate an' build," replied Dorn. "We'll run up a log cabin."

"And come here often. . . . Paradise Park," whispered Helen.

Dorn's first kisses were on her lips then, hard and cool and clean, like the life of the man, singularly exalting to her, completing her woman's strange and unutterable joy of the hour, and rendering her mute.

Bo's melodious laugh, and her voice, with its old mockery of torment, drifted softly on the night breeze. And the cowboy's "*Aw, Bo!*" drawling his reproach and longing, was all that the tranquil waiting silence needed.

Paradise Park was living again one of its romances. Love was no stranger to that lonely vastness. Helen heard in the whisper of the wind through the pines the old earth story, beautiful, ever new and eternal. She thrilled to her depths. The spear-pointed spruces stood up, black and clear, against the noble stars. All that vast solitude breathed and waited, charged full with its secret, ready to reveal itself to her tremulous soul.

ABOUT THE AUTHOR

Zane Grey™ was born Pearl Zane Gray at Zanesville, Ohio in 1872. He was graduated from the University of Pennsylvania in 1896 with a degree in dentistry. He practiced in New York City while striving to make a living by writing. He married Lina Elise Roth in 1905 and with her financial assistance he published his first novel himself, *Betty Zane* (1903). Closing his dental office, the Greys moved into a cottage on the Delaware River, near Lackawaxen, Pennsylvania. Grey took his first trip to Arizona in 1907 and, following his return, wrote *The Heritage of the Desert* (1910). The profound effect that the desert had had on him was so vibrantly captured that it still comes alive for a reader. Grey couldn't have been more fortunate in his choice of a mate. Trained in English at Hunter College, Lina Grey proofread every manuscript Grey wrote, polished his prose, and later she managed their financial affairs.

Grey's early novels were serialized in pulp magazines, but by 1918 he had graduated to the slick magazine market. Motion picture rights brought in a fortune and, with 109 films based on his work, Grey set a record yet to be equaled by any other author. Zane Grey was not a realistic writer, but rather one who charted the interiors of the soul through encounters with the wilderness. He provided characters no less memorable than one finds in Balzac, Dickens, or Thomas Mann, and they have a vital story to tell. "There was so much unexpressed feeling that could not be entirely portrayed," Loren Grey, Grey's younger son and a noted psychologist, once recalled, "that, in later years, he would weep when re-reading one of his own books." Perhaps, too, closer to the mark, Zane Grey may have wept at how his attempts at being truthful to his muse had so often been essentially altered by his editors, so that no one might ever be able to read his stories as he had intended them. It may be said of Zane Grey that, more than mere adventure tales, he fashioned psycho-dramas about the odyssey of the human soul. If his stories seem not always to be of the stuff of the mundane world, without what his stories do touch, the human world has little meaning

— which may go a long way to explain the hold he has had on an enraptured reading public ever since his first Western novel in 1910.

The employees of Thorndike Press hope you have enjoyed this Large Print book. All our Thorndike and Wheeler Large Print titles are designed for easy reading, and all our books are made to last. Other Thorndike Press Large Print books are available at your library, through selected bookstores, or directly from us.

For information about titles, please call:
(800) 223-1244

or visit our Web site at:
http://gale.cengage.com/thorndike

To share your comments, please write:
Publisher
Thorndike Press
295 Kennedy Memorial Drive
Waterville, ME 04901